Praise for *MA*

"*Match* is a fantastic page-turner that will fill many nail-biting hours of suspense. Amy Peele has done it again! You are in for a medical mystery treat."
—Louann Brizendine, MD, *New York Times* best-selling author of *The Female Brain*

"*Match* is another fascinating thriller set in the complex world of organ transplant. Readers will delight to return to the crazy friendship between Sarah Golden and Jackie Larson and their attempts at amateur sleuthing. Peele cleverly manages to keep the tension high while expertly weaving in a touch of romance and a heavy dose of humor to deliver the perfect mystery. You won't be able to put it down!"
—Michelle Cox, author of the Henrietta and Inspector Howard series

"*Match* is a fun, adventurous romp that expertly weaves the reality of transplant medicine with a page-turning mystery! Amy Peele is the kind of writer we need more of in the world."
—Sara Connell, best-selling author of *Bringing In Finn*

"*Match* is a captivating story where Bay Area kidney transplant nurse Sarah Golden confronts a series of murderous crimes that lead her into a world of greed, corruption, fear, and terror where she must fight for her own survival. Amy Peele knows what makes a great medical thriller, and has created one of the best in *Match*. Highly recommended!"
—DP Lyle, author of the Jake Longly Thriller Series

"There is nothing better than a murder mystery that keeps you guessing right up until the very end, and *Match* does exactly that. I loved the way Peele accurately captured the complexity, and beauty, of paired-exchange transplantation while keeping the reader thoroughly entertained."

—Carolyn Light MPA, Executive Director of Transplant UCSF, altruistic paired exchange living-kidney-donor

"It is so refreshing, and entertaining, to read a mystery that accurately portrays kidney transplantation and the nuances of the paired-exchange process—a great read!"

—Garet Hil, Founder of National Kidney Registry

"When I first read *Cut* by Amy S. Peele, I was hooked. Now with her second book in this series, *Match*, I have renewed my Amy S. Peele Fanclub membership! *Match* will take you on a wild ride of friendship thrust into the world of donor transplants, politics, murder, and survival!"

—Jane Ubell-Meyer, Bedside Reading

"In *Match* we are plunged back into the unshakable friendship of the characters we met in *Cut* . . . Peele offers a story that is straight from the heart and still manages to inform us about the world of kidney transplantation. A warm and wonderful read."

—Betsy Graziani Fasbinder, Award winning author & Host of *The Morning Glory Podcast*

Hold

A Medical Murder Mystery

Amy S. Peele

SHE WRITES PRESS

Published 2022
Printed in the United States of America
Print ISBN: 978-1-64742-245-5
E-ISBN: 978-1-64742-246-2
Library of Congress Control Number: 2022909599

For information, address:
She Writes Press
1569 Solano Ave #546
Berkeley, CA 94707

Interior design by Tabitha Lahr

She Writes Press is a division of SparkPoint Studio, LLC.

This book is dedicated to:

All of the scientists and clinicians who are actively researching the potential of inducing tolerance so that transplant recipients will not suffer a lifetime of side effects and the financial strain of paying for the anti-rejection drugs. When this is achieved, it will open the door for increased utilization of all procured organs for transplantation. The dream is that rejection will become a thing of the past, making transplant much more affordable for all those on waitlists.

The work of the Transplant and Organ and Tissue recovery community is far from over.

22 people die daily while waiting
and **116,000** patients are currently waiting.
1 donor can save 8 lives.

Please be sure to make your decision about being an organ & tissue donor and share it with your loved ones.

Lastly, this book is dedicated to my dear friend Sandy Ginter, who battled stage 4 bone cancer for over 8 years—they gave her 2 years and she fought hard. She left the planet peacefully on March 13, 2022, her family by her side. I will miss her terribly.

Chapter 1

"You did it! Jack, we did it!" Sarah yelled as she followed Jackie, who was pushing her way through the sweaty tourists packed in like sardines at Floridita.

A small quartet jammed into a corner near the front door set the mood for celebrating in the Havana bar. A curvaceous young Cuban woman with prominent cheek bones, graceful on four-inch clear acrylic heels, moved her hips fluidly one way as her thick light brown hair flowed in the opposite direction. Her strong voice permeated the air in perfect rhythm with the bongo player, marinating the patrons with her rich version of Cuban classics. She made Sarah think of Jennifer Lopez—and of the fact that she would never even be able to stand up, let alone move like that, in those heels.

The infamous establishment, best known for having been Ernest Hemingway's favorite watering hole, was filled with clinking cocktail glasses and laughter from patrons standing shoulder to shoulder.

Jackie muscled her way to the far back corner of the bar and claimed the only two open seats in sight, which happened to be next to a life-sized statue of Hemingway. Photographs of him and his close friend Fidel Castro dotted the nearby walls.

"Two daiquiris, *por favor*." Jackie raised two fingers.

The waiter, dressed in a crisp white shirt and wearing a red apron tied around his waist, slipped away and returned moments later with two chilled glasses.

"*Salud!*" Sarah gently tapped Jackie's glass, then watched Jackie's face as she took a big gulp.

"This tastes like sugar water blessed with a hint of rum," Jackie said. She raised her drink again and finished it off in one long slug, then put the empty glass on the bar. "How's a gal supposed to get a buzz from this?" She waved at the bartender to bring another round.

Sarah finished her first drink. When the second one arrived, she lifted the fresh glass. "To my best friend in the whole wide world—and now a private investigator! You go, girl!"

Again she clinked Jackie's glass, and they both took a sip.

"So, what are you going to do with it?" Sarah looked at her best friend, her heart bursting with pride and love.

"With what?" Jackie feigned confusion.

Sarah elbowed her. "Your license!"

"Who the hell knows! All I know is that there's no stopping me now."

"Can you believe Handsome and Laura gave us this whole trip as a surprise?"

"I think we earned it." Jackie shrugged. "You have been stay-at-home mom extraordinaire since Wyatt was born, and last year was intense. Thankfully his new kidney is working and your household is peaceful. Now you get to start a new chapter of your life."

"This long-distance relationship with Handsome has been running me ragged," Sarah said. "Miami every other month for a three-day weekend, him coming out to San Francisco every other month . . . it's a miracle we're still together! Must be the great sex." She smirked.

"*Salud* to that!" Jackie lifted her glass.

After they tapped glasses once again, Sarah sipped her drink and gazed around at the crowd, then she glanced over at Jackie and noticed that her friend was also savoring the moment. She leaned over and hugged her friend, thinking, *How lucky am I?*

• • •

After enjoying a third daiquiri, Sarah and Jackie made their way through the dense crowd to the ladies' room, where of course there was a line.

When they finally emerged from the bathroom, Sarah noticed Benita, their guide, standing by the front door and motioning that it was time to leave.

Jackie danced her way toward Benita. Sarah followed her, laughing at how the other tourists smiled as Jackie waved her arms up in the air and twirled around to the music.

Once outside, they followed Benita to the 1953 Buick Roadmaster convertible she had booked for the day with a handsome driver, of course, because why not?

Before leaving for Cuba, Sarah had reached out to Dr. Lopez, the Chief of Transplant at the Havana medical center, and inquired if he could recommend a guide and also permission to tour his transplant center. Of course he'd been thrilled to oblige; like most people in the transplant world, he had great admiration and respect for Dr. Bower and his team at the San Francisco Global Organ Transplant Institute, recognized as the premier international program. Dr. Lopez had recommended Benita, a promising young medical student who could use the extra money.

As Sarah and Jackie hopped in the back seat, Benita turned and gave them each a brown bag. "I bought you each some snacks for the ride, as we won't have time to eat before the tour." She righted herself in her seat and nodded to their driver. "*Vámonos.*"

The driver steered the car onto the road as Jackie and Sarah munched on the nuts and chips in their snack bags. Benita pointed out various buildings of interest, including the National Building, made of local limestone dug from nearby San Lazaro quarries. Tall palm trees offered a soft contrast to the other brightly colored vintage cars driving slowly down the avenue; Sarah drank it all in.

They soon pulled up to the medical center, and after instructing the driver to pick them up in an hour, Benita ushered Sarah and Jackie out of the car.

"This way, ladies. Dr. Lopez is waiting for you in the conference room on the third floor."

• • •

Sarah couldn't help but notice how old and decrepit the interior of the hospital halls looked. She looked over at Jackie as they walked toward the elevator, and her friend grimaced and muttered, "We're definitely in a third-world country."

Benita turned her head. "We are indeed—however, everyone in Cuba does get free health care."

"More than we can say for the US," Jackie said.

Benita waved them into the elevator, then stepped back. "Third floor," she reminded them. "See you after!"

After the elevator creaked its way up to the third floor, they exited and found the conference room. When they entered, the transplant team, all wearing their white lab coats, stood up.

A man who Sarah assumed to be Dr. Lopez approached. "Ms. Golden, Ms. Larsen," he said warmly, "we are honored to have you visit. Please come in and have a seat. Before we provide you with an overview of our programs, however, I must extend our condolences for your loss."

"Loss?" Sarah sat down, her brow furrowed.

Dr. Lopez's eyes widened. "You haven't heard, then?"

"I don't know what you're referring to," Sarah said slowly. "I'm not checking my work emails and we're off social media, as this is a long-overdue vacation for us both." She scanned the faces around the table; everyone on the staff looked downward, refusing to meet her gaze.

"Sadly, our international transplant community lost four of its top immunologists last night in a fatal car crash. It seems they were having a meeting in advance of the upcoming immunology conference in Chicago to discuss their findings surrounding inducing tolerance for kidney transplant patients." He handed Sarah his phone and showed her the *New York Times* article.

As she skimmed it and read the names of the deceased, she gasped. "Oh my God! I knew all of them. Dr. McKee worked at our program; we have several coordinators assigned to his studies."

Jackie moved closer and wrapped an arm around her. "Isn't he the one you loved, Sarah? 'Nicest member of the team,' I remember you saying."

Sarah took a tissue from her purse and wiped her eyes, shaking her head. "He had four kids. His youngest just turned two, a month ago."

Dr. Lopez sat next to her. "I'm so sorry, Ms. Golden . . . I thought Dr. Bower would have contacted you, but I understand why he didn't want to bother you on vacation. It's a tragedy indeed; the entire transplant world had their hopes pinned on the research of this esteemed group of scientists."

“I don’t want to be insensitive,” Jackie said quietly, “but can someone explain to me what ‘tolerance’ means in the transplant world?”

Dr. Lopez perked up a bit. “Tolerance is the holy grail of transplant. If we can convince the body not to reject a kidney, or any organ for that matter, without using any drugs long term—that’s what we call ‘inducing tolerance’—that means our patients will be free of all the side effects of these drugs, which can be very unpleasant.”

Jackie nodded. “My son, Wyatt, received a living donor kidney transplant a year ago, which is working great, but the drugs he has to take are no fun for a nine-year-old boy’s body—or for his parents’ pocketbooks. Plus, he just suffered a rejection, which meant getting subjected to even more drugs.”

Sarah was barely registering the conversation taking place; she was still in shock. She cleared her throat. “I appreciate you sharing the news, Dr. Lopez,” was all she could manage.

Dr. Lopez nodded. “Of course. Are you . . . still interested in a tour? I understand completely if you need time to recover from this shock.”

Sarah shook her head. “No, no, please, I’d like to continue as planned.”

“Well then,” he said gently, “let me have the members of our team introduce themselves and then we’ll show you the facility.”

• • •

By the time everyone was done with introductions, Sarah was feeling more like herself. As the group prepared to head out for the tour, Jackie raised her hand like a kid in class.

“I do have one question about this tolerance deal,” she said. “If it’s so important, then why do the cells they’re targeting only get a lower-case ‘t’ and ‘b’—if they’re such a big deal they should at least be capitalized, don’t you think?”

The whole room cracked up.

"You can see why I love this gal," Sarah said, shaking her head. "Always thinking outside the box—*way* outside the box."

Dr. Lopez continued, "We perform about one hundred kidney transplants annually here in Havana, all the patients who need a kidney transplant in Cuba come to our program. We're just now ramping up our living donor program since our deceased donor numbers are consistently low. In fact, I sent your lead living donor coordinator, Kayla Newman, an email a while ago to ask for her support but never heard back . . ."

Sarah's stomach clenched. Another loss. "Unfortunately, Kayla was killed last year; it was a huge loss to our program. I can certainly have her replacement reach out to you and share our protocols with you. We were really able to ramp up our living donor kidney numbers with some new donor screening technology, and revamping the intake process helped as well."

"I'm so sorry to hear about Ms. Newman," Dr. Lopez said. "And I would be most grateful for any information you can share."

As everyone else got in the elevator to go up to the transplant floor, Dr. Lopez put a hand on Sarah's arm and drew her aside. As the doors to the elevator closed without her friend inside it, Jackie put her arms up in the air, her eyes signaling, *What the hell!?*

A bit taken aback, Sarah looked up at Dr. Lopez, who looked directly into her eyes, his expression grave.

"I need your help, Ms. Golden. I was in close contact with all the doctors that died in the car crash; they had shared the protocol they were using for the tolerance study—off the record, of course—and I used it with one hundred patients here, none of whom did particularly well. A number of them died, in fact. I was about to send the data to Dr. McKee when I heard about the accident. If you know anything about the study, would you please tell me? I can't put any more patients in it now—especially because I wasn't officially part of it to begin with. If you have any information that might help my patients, I beg you, please share it."

Sarah sighed. "I'm afraid I don't have much to do with the research studies except managing the coordinators who work for the researchers. I wish I could help you, but this simply isn't my area of expertise. You may want to give Dr. Bower a call, he can probably help you."

Dr. Lopez leaned toward her. "Dr. Bower doesn't know anything about this—he would have never approved."

She stared back at him in disbelief; the silence between them was profound.

"Would you meet me tomorrow for lunch? I'd like to share the protocol and my results with you, and get your input. Please."

Sarah shook her head. "I'm not sure if there is anything I can do."

"Please, Ms. Golden—I have to talk to someone. I was hoping my research would open the doors to some possible academic appointments in the states. This study had the possibility of getting me and my family out of Cuba."

At this, Sarah softened. Cuba was forbidden to participate in any study or exchange with the US because of the economic embargo put into place after the 1959 revolution. She felt for this man; she had to at least try to help him.

"Okay, then, I'll meet you for lunch . . . but please don't have any expectations," she pleaded. "I really don't know if there's anything I can do."

"Thank you, Ms. Golden!" He took her hand and kissed it. "It means the world to me and my family—it would be our dream and privilege to live in the United States of America."

No pressure there, Sarah thought, shaking her head, as her host pressed the call button for the elevator.

• • •

After the tour, Dr. Lopez escorted Sarah and Jackie outside, where Benita was leaning against their vintage ride. Benita's face lit up when she saw Dr. Lopez.

"How is my star student doing?" he asked jovially.

"I'm excited to be escorting these wonderful women around and hearing all about the transplant program where Ms. Golden works," she said, her eyes sparkling. "What an exciting place to live and breathe all that is transplant!"

"Yes, Ms. Golden is indeed lucky enough to work at the Mecca of the transplant world—and she has been kind enough to agree to meet me for lunch tomorrow to discuss our tolerance protocol. Would you make a twelve o'clock reservation for us at the Hotel Saratoga?"

"Happy to take care of that, Dr. Lopez. Okay, ladies, it's off to the cigar factory, as requested by Ms. Larsen. I was able to arrange a private tour!" Benita opened the door and pulled the front seat forward so Jackie and Sarah could slide in.

Once they were on the road, Jackie elbowed Sarah. "Lunch tomorrow? That's not on our vacation agenda! You pinky swore that there would be no work on this trip. I already gave you the transplant tour."

Sarah sighed. With a glance toward Benita in the front seat, she whispered, "Dr. Lopez literally begged me. I don't think I can help him, but I felt so bad for him . . . and I am so freaked out about Dr. McKee and those other three doctors getting killed. I didn't have the heart to say no."

"How about we lift your spirits with some delicious local rum before we go taste some cigars? I'm really sorry about those doctors, but let's try to enjoy ourselves . . . our time in Havana is almost over." Jackie wrapped her arms around Sarah.

Sarah leaned into her friend, grateful for the comfort. "I know you're right," she said quietly, "but this whole thing feels really off: four of the most prominent immunologists in the world all killed in the same car, and now Dr. Lopez tells me he was unofficially part of the study they created?"

"You may have something there," Jackie said. "The timing of this is definitely suspect. Tell ya what, when I get home, I'll use my new PI connections to see what I can find out about the cause of the crash, no charge."

Sarah chuckled. "You're on."

"Hey Benita," Jackie said in a louder voice, "can we stop at a bar before we head out to the cigar factory? My friend here needs a little libation."

Benita checked her watch. "We're early for the tour, so yes, absolutely!" She directed the driver in rapid Spanish.

Jackie settled back in her seat with a satisfied smile, but Sarah's mind was still swirling with questions.

Chapter 2

The driver stopped the car in front of what looked like an apartment building.

Jackie felt skeptical. "Is this a bar?" she asked, eyeballing the run-down beige building. "They could be taking us in there to kill us. Nobody would even know how to find us."

"Earth to Jackie—we're in Cuba. I'm sure Benita knows what she's doing." Sarah shook her head and chuckled.

Benita's eyebrows rose at Jackie. "You sure have a wild imagination."

"Very wild." Sarah grinned.

They followed Benita through the front door and into a large but sparsely appointed room: one round table to the right, a pool table in the middle, and a long bar to the left. Cuban music was playing softly in the background and four men were slouched over the round table, conversing and drinking beers.

Not exactly "ambience central," but it'll do the trick, Jackie thought.

"What would you like?" Benita asked. "We can stay for thirty minutes, we don't want to be late for our tour."

"I think I can get a reasonable buzz going with a double-shot rum and coke," Sarah said.

"Works for me," Jackie said. "If they sell rum by the bottle here, can you get one of those too?" She noticed the four fellas at the round table gawking at her as she moved toward the pool table.

"*Hola*." She took the rack from the pool table, racked up the balls, and found a pool stick.

"*Hola*," the men responded with smiles.

Jackie nodded her head sideways toward the pool table and raised her eyebrows; she didn't know how to ask them in Spanish if they wanted to play. They all shook their heads back and forth. Jackie shrugged as Benita approached with two tall glasses filled with rum, coke, and a few ice cubes.

Jackie took her drink from their guide and held it up. "*Salud* . . . let's show these fellas our game!"

Sarah half-emptied her glass in one go, then set it down and broke the triangle of balls, sending them in all directions. "Looks like I have solids and you have stripes, Jack."

"Bring it on, Golden," Jackie taunted her. "I will kick your ass—just like in nursing school when we conned those dumb college boys at Butch McGuire's on Rush Street." She took down her rum and coke in one fell swoop.

"We never paid for a drink back in the day." Sarah finished her cocktail and motioned to Benita to get another round. "We are on vay-*cay*-tion, Jackie!"

Jackie was relieved to see that Sarah was starting to relax. She hit the next three balls cleanly into the pocket and then missed one. She passed the pool cue back to Sarah as Benita came back with their second round.

"You're damn straight—only two more days in Cuba, let's make this one a good one." Jackie drank half of her second drink and then let out one of her classic loud burps. She looked over at the men, who were laughing. "It's the coke," she called out, completely unabashed. "*Lo siento.*"

Sarah made two more shots, then Jackie cleared the pool table with five minutes to spare.

They set their empty glasses down on the bar and followed Benita out. As they exited, Jackie looked over her shoulder and yelled, "*Muchas gracias!*" The men and bartender smiled back.

Outside, Sarah slung an arm over Jackie's shoulders. "The beverage break was a great idea, Jack. Thank you."

Jackie reached up and gave her friend's hand a squeeze. "Any time, pal."

• • •

When the trio entered the cigar factory, Benita approached the woman at the counter and conversed with her in Spanish as Jackie and Sarah perused the array of cheaply framed black-and-white photos hanging on the small lobby's walls. There was one big one of Fidel Castro with his arm around Ernest Hemingway, big cigars hanging out the sides of their mouths. Another depicted the three sizes of cigars: *Fina*, *Mediano*, and *Grueso*.

"Look at this one," Sarah said, pointing to a long one with a pretzel-like shape. "It looks like a lady crossing her legs tightly because she has to pee—like, *now*."

As they both laughed, Jackie felt a light tap on her shoulder.

She swiveled around to find a thin, distinguished-looking gentleman standing before her. "Are you Jackie Larsen?" he asked.

"Did anyone ever tell you, you look like that guy on that Dos Equis beer commercial—you know, the one with the most interesting man in the world?" Jackie smiled up at him.

"Looks like the rum has worked its magic, eh Jack?" Sarah giggled.

"Yes, I have been told that by some Americans who visit our factory, though we don't get those commercials here in Cuba," the man said. "Forgive me, introductions first—I'm Duardo Mirabal, a manager here, and Benita's uncle. Benita apologizes for not joining us for the tour; she was called back to the hospital. Your driver will be outside for you when we are finished."

"Works for me," Jackie said cheerfully. "I am indeed Jackie Larsen, and this is Sarah Golden."

"Lovely to meet you both. Tell me, young ladies, what brings you to our cigar factory? We usually get mostly male visitors." Duardo motioned with his arm for them to follow him.

"I've been smoking cigars off and on since I was fifteen . . . so seventeen years, if my math is right."

Duardo's eyebrows raised. "Was it part of your family custom?"

"Actually, my father always wanted a son," Jackie explained. "On Sundays he would sit in our backyard, enjoy a cigar and a beer, and listen to the Cubs play baseball. It was the only time I could see him, since he worked six days a week on the railroad, so I'd sit outside and watch him relish his cigar. One day, I asked if I could have one." Jackie inhaled deeply—the stale, pungent aroma of dried tobacco hung in the air—and continued on the exhale, "He was the best dad he could be. He taught me that good cigars are made from one tobacco leaf, carefully rolled and then trimmed. He also showed me how to trim the end of a cigar, light it, and how to keep it lit." Jackie shared.

"It's certainly a skill that we believe everyone should know," Duardo said. "Your father taught you well."

He led the two women through a door and onto the floor of the cigar factory, from which they proceeded into a smaller room where a handful of women were bent over a long table, a huge stack of tobacco leaves on one side and the completed cigars on the other.

As they watched the women work, Duardo described why their cigars were so highly sought after. It was due, he said, to their high quality control process and use of only the finest tobacco leaves. The women never looked up at their observers as they carefully inspected each leaf, throwing the imperfect ones into a basket on the floor and then rolling the rest into perfectly tight cigars.

Jackie noted the precision with which they worked.

"Is it true that these ladies can make more money than a doctor can here in Cuba?" Sarah asked.

"That is correct," Duardo said somberly. "I'm guessing my niece told you that; she worked here to save money for medical school. We are very serious about our cigars—it is an art and our patrons depend on our consistency." He pointed over to the front of the room, where a man was using some type of machine to test a rolled cigar. "The last step of whether the cigar makes it to the finish line is over there. He's checking for the evenness of the roll."

Jackie watched as the man quickly checked each cigar and discarded those that didn't pass muster into a basket. "This is some operation you have here," she said, impressed. "I'm ready for a good cigar and another drink!"

Chuckling, Duardo led them to a tidy office just off the factory floor. "If you'll wait for me here, I'll be right back with those cigars."

Jackie plopped down into a chair as Duardo shut the door behind him. "What a production, eh? It's nice to see the women making some good money."

"I was thinking the same thing," Sarah said, sitting down next to her.

"I'm hungry, thirsty, and ready to go back to our hotel—but first I want to order a couple boxes of their best cigars. I'm sure we can figure out how to get them out of the country. Maybe we can tell them we have some tissue and blood samples—get a label declaring HUMAN TISSUE to put on the container from Dr. Lopez when we have lunch with him tomorrow?"

Sarah glared at Jackie. "I'm not asking him for that, you wack job. You can hide them somewhere in your suitcase or backpack—I'm sure you'll be creative, just don't tell me what you decide on. I'm not going to jail with you; I love you, but not that much."

Duardo returned with two boxes. "Our finest cigars, courtesy of Dr. Lopez," he said, handing them to Jackie.

Sarah's eyes widened. "Oh no, we can't—"

"He will not take no for an answer," Duardo insisted. "He looks forward to seeing you both for lunch tomorrow."

"Really, please thank Dr. Lopez, but we can't accept this gift," Sarah objected.

"You'll have to take that up with him," Duardo said with a shrug. "Orders are orders."

Jackie had no such hesitation. "Thank you so much, Duardo; you've made my day, and I can't wait to enjoy one of these Montecristo Petit Tubos."

Duardo escorted them outside—their driver was there waiting for them, as promised—and bid them farewell. "Ms. Larsen, Ms. Golden, it's been a pleasure."

"Oh please, call me Sarah," Sarah said quickly.

"As you wish . . . Sarah," he said smoothly.

Sarah flushed pink.

"One last question," Jackie said before he could walk away. "If I wanted to order more of these, how would I go about that?"

Duardo handed her his card. "We'll see what we can work out when the time comes."

Jackie flashed Sarah a mischievous sideways grin. "Thanks, Duardo, I'd appreciate that." She shook his hand, and he strode back toward the factory.

They slid into the backseat. Sarah looked over at Jackie.

"I just love the way he said my name with that soft *s* . . . it's soft and sexy. Maybe I can teach Handsome to say it that way."

Jackie shook her head, "I know he loves you, but don't push it, Golden."

• • •

When their driver let them out at the hotel, he handed Jackie the bottle of rum Benita had procured for them at the bar.

"*Muchas gracias, señor*," Jackie said.

They both waved as he pulled away, then headed inside and took the old, rickety elevator up to their floor.

"How about I pour us a rum to sip and we can sit on our balcony?" Sarah offered as Jackie unlocked their room door.

"Perfect," Jackie said, pushing the door open. "I'd like to keep this nice buzz going." She kicked off her sandals and went straight out to the balcony, where she sat in the one of the black wrought iron chairs. Sarah came out with two glasses of rum, handed one to Jackie, and sat next to her. They both put their feet up on the balcony rails at the same time, and they broke into laughter.

"*Salud*," Jackie said for the twentieth time that day.

They clinked, sipped in silence, and stared out on the plaza below, where several musicians were playing melodic Cuban music. After a while, Jackie looked over at Sarah, whose forehead was creased with worry.

"I can see your mind going a mile a minute," Jackie said. "What's up?"

"I can't stop thinking about why and how those doctors died," Sarah said. "It's so sad."

"We'll tackle that when we get home," Jackie said. "For tonight, try to enjoy yourself. Let's call home and check in, and then we can get ready to go see the Buena Vista Social Club tonight—Benita got us front-row seats, remember? It's going to be incredible."

"You're right," Sarah said. "Maybe talking to Handsome will make me feel better." She rose. "I'll make the call inside, spare you the gooey romantic talk."

"Appreciate it," Jackie said with an exaggerated grimace.

Sarah went inside; Jackie, still savoring her rum, remained sitting on the balcony. Cuba was three hours ahead of the Bay Area, but it was Laura's work-from-home day; she could probably take a moment to chat right now. She fished her phone out of her pocket and dialed.

"Hey sweets," Laura answered on the second ring.

"Hi honey," Jackie said, "how's my family?"

"Everyone is healthy and happy here," Laura said. "Wyatt's annual check-up was exceptional; his kidney is working perfectly, they even lowered a few of his immuno-suppressive drugs."

"That's the best news!" Jackie cried. "And how are you doing? Taking care of yourself, I hope."

"You know, I am! Since my mom is here I've stayed in the city a couple nights, and it's made a world of difference. The housing allowance they gave me with this new promotion is a game-changer. I'm getting a shit-ton of work done 'cause I can get to work by five in the morning, rested and ready."

"Amazing," Jackie said. "Plans for the weekend?"

"I'm taking Wyatt and a couple of his buddies to the Exploratorium Saturday, then out for pizza and ice cream," Laura said. "He's beside-himself excited."

Jackie's heart squeezed at the thought of her son's beaming face. "Is he home? I miss his mug."

"He's kind of a busy guy—he's at Ryan's house right now for an after-school hang. It's such a relief to let him spend time at friends' and not have to worry about what he eats or drinks anymore; he just gets to be a kid."

"It's truly the gift of life, if I can be corny."

"Be corny all you want, honey, it's so true. Oh, by the way, we got a call on the home phone from Maria in Miami, do you remember her?"

"How could I forget that sweet young woman? I'm so glad that asshole Sergio in is prison where he belongs, after what he did to her. Is everything alright with her?" Jackie took a sip of rum; the smooth, sweet liquid warmed her throat and melted downwards.

"She said her parents and her son are well but wanted you to call her when you get a chance. You want her number?"

"Sure, I'll call her when I get to Miami. I cannot thank you enough for sending me and Sarah on this trip of our dreams. We are having the best time. I miss you, of course, but this is just what we needed after last year's fiasco in Florida."

"We had us one hell of year, but we got through it. Thank you for staying with your crazy wife. And besides, Handsome and I both agreed you were long overdue for some best friend time away, so I can't take total credit. How's Cuba? Tell me everything."

"It's been amazing—communism is alive and well but we are seeing all the sights and I had the best time at the cigar factory today. The rum is off the charts too."

"You sound relaxed," Laura said. "I'm glad. Not to ruin your good feeling, but . . . did you hear about the four immunologists who were killed in a car accident? It's all over the national and local news, and apparently one of them worked at Sarah's transplant center."

"We just heard today from Dr. Lopez, the guy who runs Havana's transplant center. Sarah is freaking out a little, but

I've been able to temper her reaction with extra rum . . . for now, anyway. I may have to start an investigation now that I have my PI license; pro bono for her of course."

"No, no, no—you're *not* investigating a case in Chicago. Do the words 'car accident' and 'broken leg' ring a bell? Don't even think about it, Jackie!"

"I can at least make a few calls just to see if there were any cut brake lines," Jackie protested. "Some people in my PI class were from Chicago—it would just be a quick call."

"That's not the deal we made, honey!" Laura said firmly. "You said you were going to find a firm that investigates cheating spouses; benign work, no guns needed. You have a family. Do you remember the conversation we had when *we* agreed on your new career? You promised it would be something you can do when Wyatt is at school and summer camp."

Jackie finished her rum and took a breath.

"Hello? Jackie, are you there? You don't need to be a female Columbo, my love."

Jackie flashed on the disheveled TV detective. "I'm here, I'm here, and yeah, I know. I know. It's just so weird, don't you think?"

"I do—and I also think there are excellent detectives in Chicago who can handle this. The FBI is also on board, as the doctors were all from different states. I think you can pass on this one. Do you hear me?"

"Yes, yes, I hear you. Anyway, Sarah and I are heading out soon to enjoy our last night in Havana. I'll keep you posted on our arrival in Miami. Thank you again for this! Can't wait to give you a huge hug when I get home."

"I can't wait either, and you are so welcome, honey," Laura said. "Now go on, live it up—but not too much! Please behave yourself; no arrests, no monkey business, you got it? Get your ass home in one piece."

"No monkey business," Jackie promised. "Love you too."

Chapter 3

Three CEOs from the top pharmaceutical companies were seated around the polished, dark walnut table of the Ritz-Carlton's ninth-floor royal suite. The assistant manager quietly stood off to the side, ready to provide these high rollers anything they desired.

Victor Botsworth, CEO of Lago, sat at the head of the table, his impeccable posture and tailored dark blue suit accentuating his athletic physique. He gracefully clasped his hands together, a habit that always brought him calm when things were tense. "Thank you both for joining me on such short notice."

"Perfect timing since I was planning on flying to our Switzerland office tonight," Otto Penton, thin and gray-haired, said in his thick German accent. "Given the recent news, I'm pleased we could all meet."

Victor motioned toward the assistant manager. "Does anyone need any more coffee or something to eat before I ask staff to leave?"

"Please refresh my coffee and bring me a glass bottle of Pellegrino with a wedge of lemon, light on the ice," Erika Mason—elegant, brunette, and wearing a Chanel suit—requested.

When the task was complete, Victor dismissed the man with a nod. "We all have things to do and places to go, so let's proceed." He double-checked to make sure they were alone, then said, "I know we were all saddened to hear the news of four such accomplished immunologists getting killed in a car crash. It's a huge loss to the transplant community, not least because of what it means right now: an immediate halt to what was supposed to be a landmark research study on inducing tolerance."

"Dr. McKee was on our advisory board," Erika chimed in. "It is indeed a huge loss. I spoke to him before he got in the car and he was so excited about finishing the first phase of the study and preparing for next steps. I understand the NIH has stepped in and asked that all the study results be sealed and sent to them immediately; as you both know, they were partially funding this joint effort."

"My concern is that the public and transplant community may point the finger at our companies since we have the most to lose if and when inducing tolerance is successful," Victor jumped in. "I would like to believe that none of us had anything to do with this catastrophic accident; however, I think it would be prudent for us to pool some resources to hire our own private investigator to find out exactly what happened. Thoughts?"

Otto looked back and forth at his two colleagues. "If any reporter digs deep enough they'll find out that our industry is valued at almost five billion dollars and growing. I support this investigation; however, I do feel the need to be assured by you, Victor, that the utmost discretion will be utilized."

"Agreed." Erika frowned.

"Of course," Victor said. "If you are both amenable to it, I will find the right person to discreetly conduct the investigation, leaving no paper or money trail behind."

"That sounds reasonable." Otto tapped the table in front of him with his index finger. "Do you have an amount in mind?"

"I think if we each contribute fifty thousand cash that should be more than enough. I will update you via a phone call once the investigation is underway—and, of course, once I have the results."

Otto stood up. "Sounds fair. I'll have my assistant get you the money. I must be on my way, I have a flight to catch. Lovely to see you both." He walked over to shake both their hands.

"Cash flow shouldn't be a problem for the foreseeable future since all patients will need our drugs once they are transplanted," Erika said, standing to follow Otto out. "Since Canada and Europe have socialized medicine, we should enjoy our US gravy train as long as we can. I'm in. Nice to collaborate on something instead of competing for a change." She leaned over to shake Victor's hand as well, then made her way to the door, which Otto was holding open for her.

"I will be staying here at the Ritz tonight; I have an early plane to San Francisco tomorrow morning. If you could be sure to get me the cash no later than eleven tonight, that would be preferable."

"Of course, not a problem," Otto said.

"You will hear from my assistant shortly," Erika said.

Victor couldn't resist staring as Erika moved her sleek body through the door. His usual type was younger and blonder, but she was a stunner. "Always nice to see you, Erika," he called after her. "Do you have plans for dinner tonight? I'd love to catch up."

"I'm sorry, I'm needed back home; maybe some other time." Erika slipped on a pair of dark gloves and joined Otto in the elevator.

Only slightly deflated by Erika's rejection, Victor stood in front of the large window and enjoyed the splash of fall colors in Central Park. They had all avoided asking each other if they had any hand in the car accident, he observed. He texted Angelo, a contact from New Jersey, to call him ASAP. After he sent it, he made a call.

"Dr. Bower's office," answered a young woman.

"Hi, this Victor Botsworth; may I speak with Dr. Bower?"

"Dr. Bower is in the operating room but will return your call when he's free."

"I wanted to confirm our meeting and dinner for tomorrow."

"Yes, it's on his calendar. What restaurant will he be meeting you at?"

"My assistant, Valerie, will get back to you on that. Thank you." Victor ended that call and immediately called his assistant's cell.

"Hello Valerie, I need you to do a few things."

"Absolutely."

"I need you to get the current net worth of the pharmaceutical companies Penton and Mason run—text them to me as soon as you get them. I also need to know what fiscal year they work within and what, if any, dividends Mason's stockholders received in the last year. Penton's company is privately held, so you'll need to do some digging and be persistent. Valerie—these numbers are very important. Also get the total number of transplants performed in 2016, that will give us a good idea what the drug utilization was."

"I understand; I'll get right on that. Anything else?"

"Confirm my flight to San Francisco tomorrow, and my dinner reservations with Dr. Bower—be sure we have a private table as far away from other tables as possible. Make sure the restaurant is within walking distance of the Fairmont and confirm my suite there as well. Once everything's settled, call his assistant and get her all the details."

"No problem," she said briskly. "Oh, and Mr. Botsworth . . . I took the liberty of sending flowers to the families of the four immunologists who were killed in that tragic car accident. I remember when you had them all out to visit our headquarters; they were so kind. I feel so awful for their poor families."

"It is a tragedy. Thanks for taking care of that. You know where I am if you need me."

"Yes sir, I do. I'll take care of everything. One more thing: your hair salon called with a reminder that you have an appointment next week. Do you want me to confirm that or reschedule?"

"Keep it on the books; the black is starting to come back in, and I prefer people thinking I'm older than I am. This salt-and-pepper look was a great idea, Valerie."

"Thanks, boss. You do look very distinguished."

• • •

Victor was relaxing on his room's leather couch in a silk robe a couple of hours later, enjoying a Pappy Van Winkle bourbon, when he checked his phone and noticed that Angelo had texted him back.

He immediately called back.

"Yeah?" a gruff voice answered.

"Hello Angelo, it's your old pal Victor—it's been a long time, how the hell are you?"

"It can't be good if you're calling me—what do you want?"

"I need you to find me a top-notch PI—keeps their mouth shut no matter what—and I need them yesterday. What do you have?"

"I got shit, that's what I got—whaddaya think, these people are growing on trees around here? Jesus Christ. When do you need them? This is gonna to cost you."

"You find the right guy, and of course you'll be paid well. Have I ever stiffed you?"

"No, and it wouldn't be wise to start. Okay, I'll go shopping. What kind of price tag are we talking for the PI?"

"Let's start with a hundred thousand, they need to be able to get intel from the FBI and local cops in Chicago immediately. You heard about those doctors who died in the car crash?"

"Yeah, read about it in the paper, it was all over the news. I don't even know what an immunologist is, though—and frankly, unless they can help me bet on the right horse at the track, I don't care."

"Still playing the ponies?" Victor snorted. "Some things never change. Well look, I want to know how that crash came about, and I want to know before anyone else, I don't want to read about it in the paper. You got it?"

"Got it. But I can tell you right now it's gonna cost more than a hundred K."

"Get me the right guy and we'll go from there. I need someone discreet and with smarts; this could blow up fast if not done right."

"Yeah, yeah, yeah, like I've never done anything like this before. I'll let you know when I find the dude." Angelo ended the call.

Victor took another sip of his bourbon and took in the New York skyline, all lit up by the setting sun.

Chapter 4

While Jackie talked to Laura on the balcony, Sarah called Handsome.

He picked up right away. "Hello, my Cuban vixen. I hope you're getting into some good trouble."

"You know I am, wise guy. You and Campos catching all the bad guys?"

"Yes," he said, his voice suddenly serious, "and some bad news on that front."

Sarah's stomach tightened; she sat up in bed. "Are you okay?"

"I'm fine, honey, but Campos is not. We went to bust a bunch of known drug dealers this morning, and the second we rang the doorbell they started shooting from inside. She was hit."

"Oh my god!" Sarah's eyes filled with tears. "Is she going to make it?"

"We think so," he said, his voice trembling, "but it's still touch and go. She took two bullets from a sawed-off shotgun that went right through her leg, shattered her femur, and just missed her femoral artery. She was in surgery for over three hours; now she's in surgical intensive care. I'm worried. We got help right away—you know how fast the EMTs respond when they hear 'officer down'—and I was able to tie off above the bleeding to slow it down, but she lost a lot of blood. Bishop hasn't left her side."

"Bishop must be going insane, they just moved in together a month ago." Sarah was pacing the room now. "Shit! Is there anything I can do?"

"No, honey, and I don't want you to let this ruin the end of your trip. You just have as much fun as you can so you can tell her all your insane stories when you get back."

"You must be a wreck. I wish I was there to take care of you."

"There's nothing you can do, just promise you'll come home in one piece. I miss you."

"I really miss you too. You have to promise to text me as soon as you have an update, okay?" Sarah took a healthy sip of rum and reminded herself that Handsome needed her to be the strong one right now. Forcing calm into her voice, she said, "Campos is strong and fit as fiddle—she'll pull through. Let Bishop know he can call me anytime if he has medical questions; this has to be freaking him out since he almost faints at the sight of any kind of blood—typical CPA. And how are you holding up? You had a front-row seat to the shooting."

"I'll be honest, I'm kinda freaked out too, but once they took Campos away in the ambulance and back-up arrived, we tore through that house and caught those motherfuckers," he said, fire in his voice. "It'll be a long time before they get out, especially since they shot a cop."

"It had to be so scary for you, honey. Please take it easy for now, okay?"

"I will," he promised. "I'm taking my nephews out for pizza tonight and those knuckleheads always make me laugh—teenage humor, you know?"

"Perfect," she said, "you all have the sense of humor of a thirteen-year-old."

"Give me some credit . . . maybe fourteen?"

"How many times have you all watched *Ferris Bueller's Day Off*?"

"You know that's our monthly ritual." Handsome chuckled. "Okay, you win. Just for the record, though, you have to admit that when people get older they lose their sense of humor."

Sarah was relieved to hear his voice lightening up. "Almost everyone does—except Jackie."

"That one is in a league of her own, I'll give you that," Handsome said.

"Tonight is our last big Cuban hurrah—we're going out in style, Buena Vista Social Club."

He let out a big sigh. "Yeah . . . your last big nights anywhere have usually gotten you both in trouble, so remember you're in Cuba, not the US, and there's not much I can do to save your ass there. You got it, Golden?"

"I got it," Sarah said. "Tomorrow we're having lunch with Dr. Lopez, the head transplant surgeon I told you about. We toured his hospital today—totally different vibe than our transplant center. Lovely man but likely stuck in Cuba for the rest of his life. He shared the bad news about the four immunologists who were killed in Chicago."

"Oh, you heard," Handsome said, sounding disappointed. "I didn't want to ruin your trip—you knew them, didn't you?"

"Oh yeah—Dr. McKee was on our team, and the three other docs visited our center several times as visiting professors, gave grand rounds. Huge loss to the transplant community, they were real-deal scientists."

For a second time during their call, tears threatened. But before Sarah or Handsome could say anything else, Jackie yelled from the balcony, "You'll see Prince Charming soon—how about refreshing my beverage?"

"Just a minute," Sarah said into the phone, "my services are requested." She set the phone down and took the bottle of rum to Jackie, "Here you go. Save some for me, you lush!"

"Better get back here soon," Jackie said with a smirk. "Lots of activity happening down on the street."

The aroma of barbecue meat wafted up.

"That smells like heaven," Sarah said. She glanced down and saw tourists checking out a line of vintage cars and three guitar players and a young woman singing. "Looks like we're missing the party. Let me just finish up with Handsome."

As Jackie took a long draw on her cigar and gently blew the smoke out, Sarah reentered the hotel room and picked up her phone. "The rum is working its magic on me. How about I check in with you tomorrow? Cuba is calling." She walked to the patio door and took in another whiff of barbecue.

"Sounds like a plan," Handsome said. "But hey, real quick—how's the wild woman from Borneo doing?"

Sarah caught Jackie's eye. "Hey Larsen, Handsome wants to know how you're doing."

"I'm in heaven! Cuban rum, a good cigar, and my best friend—what else does a gal need?"

"Don't forget to stay out of trouble, if at all possible," Handsome reminded Sarah. "We'll talk soon. I love you, Sarah Golden."

Sarah grinned. "Love you back. And take care of yourself—I need you in tip-top shape when I get home! I hope you took a few days off."

"You know I did. We'll go to dinner, watch some good movies, and do whatever else you want to do."

"I have a few ideas," Sarah said, smiling wickedly. "I've been learning some new dance moves here."

"Tease!" Handsome laughed. "Okay, go have fun. Bye, honey."

• • •

That evening surpassed everything else Sarah and Jackie had experienced on their trip. The actual Buena Vista Social Club band played, and Cuban dancers graced the stage with their perfect form and rhythm.

"All these dancers are professional ballerinas—ballet is a big deal here," Sarah shared as they cheered the performers on. "I remember my aunt was invited to Cuba to consult on their costumes a couple years ago."

"I remember—the year we *almost* went to Cuba," Jackie said. "Their bodies are so beautiful, they dance with such precision. I could watch this all night."

The announcer entered the stage after the song ended and the dancers retreated. "We'd love to invite one of our guests up to sing the next song, 'Bésame Mucho,'" he said, scanning the crowd with a smile. "Anyone out there know the words?"

Sarah's jaw dropped open as Jackie leapt up from her seat and hopped on the stage, practically knocking the announcer over.

"It's one of my favorite songs in world!" she cried.

"Tell us your name and where you're from," the announcer said after recovering his equilibrium.

"I'm Jackie." Jackie beamed at the audience. "I've been enjoying your rum, so I'm a bit tipsy, and I'm from California."

Sarah felt her face flush on Jackie's behalf. She couldn't imagine being onstage like that. But then again, Jackie did love the spotlight.

"Welcome, Jackie," the announcer boomed. "We are so delighted that you're enjoying your time here in Havana." He waved to the band. "Shall we?"

The band started to play "Bésame Mucho," and the announcer handed Jackie the microphone. To Sarah's shock, she didn't miss a beat or a word, swaying her hips to the music while the audience clapped and laughed. When the song finished, she got a standing ovation.

"Thank you!" she shouted over the applause. "And I want to introduce my best friend in the world—Sarah Golden." She pointed over to their table.

Blushing but beaming, Sarah stood up, nodded, and waved. Jackie handed the microphone back to the band leader and hopped off the stage.

Sarah threw her arms around her friend when she got back to the table. "You killed it, Jack—you were amazing! Having you been practicing in Spanish?"

"Thanks, buddy." Jackie dropped into her seat with a satisfied grin on her face. "Since my mother-in-law is living with us we've been watching telenovelas, so my Spanish has improved, and I've been practicing 'Bésame Mucho' in the car—it really is my favorite song!" She lifted her glass to Sarah. "*Salud!*"

"*Salud*," Sarah echoed with a giggle.

• • •

Jackie and Sarah didn't get back to their hotel until the early hours of the morning. After their driver delivered them safely home, they floated up to their room and flopped down in their side-by-side beds.

Jackie looked over at Sarah. "Are we the luckiest best friends in the world or what? I love you."

"I love you too, Jack," Sarah said sleepily.

"We need to go away and celebrate our friendship every year from now on, no excuses. Okay?"

Before Sarah could answer, Jackie was snoring.

Chapter 5

Jackie cracked her eyes open when she felt tapping on her shoulder, and Sarah's face appeared above her.

"Good morning, Bésame," Sarah said cheerfully. "I have a latte and pastries waiting for you on the balcony; time to get up and clear the fog before we get picked up for lunch!"

Jackie closed her eyes again and smiled. "We're still in Cuba and I'm not feeling any signs of a hangover, even after all that rum."

"We were sipping the good stuff all night," Sarah pointed out. "And now that we've finally learned to drink lots of water in between our alcoholic bevvies, our hangover quota is a lot lower. Come on, party girl, it's our last night to go big." She headed outside.

Jackie rolled out of bed, shuffled out to the balcony, picked up the cup of coffee, and took a long sip. "Putting that sprinkle of cinnamon on top is a nice touch." She sat down next to Sarah and took a bite of the cherry pastry she'd picked up for her. "Yumm." After savoring the flavor for a moment, she looked at her friend. "I forgot to tell you last night . . . when I spoke to Laura, she told me Maria called and wants us to call her when we get back to Miami."

"Sergio's Maria?"

"That's the one! Laura said it didn't sound like an emergency, she just wanted to speak with us. Her son would be two now, right?"

Sarah thought for a moment, then nodded. "Yep, that sounds right. Thank God Sergio's still behind bars—right where he belongs for what he did to her entire family. It was so satisfying to see him and Amanda get what they deserved."

"That was one hell of a chase pursuing those two—Miami, Chicago, Rodeo Drive! Just think, if you hadn't been working at that Miami transplant center and taken care of Amanda, you would never have met Handsome and I would never have met Biker Bob. At least some good came out of that mess."

Jackie turned to Sarah with a big smile—but her smile turned to a frown when she saw Sarah's face.

"I had some really bad news about Campos last night," Sarah said, tearing up. "I figured it could wait until today . . . we were having such a good time last night."

"Shit, what happened to Campos?" Jackie's volume escalated.

"She and Handsome got shot at right as they were about to bust a bunch of drug dealers. Handsome wasn't hit, but Campos took two shots that went straight through her leg. They're not sure if they can save the leg. She's in surgical intensive care, Bishop hasn't left her side."

Jackie's shoulders sagged. "That's some scary shit. How's Handsome doing?"

"He said he was 'a little' freaked out, which means he's *really* freaked out."

A loud car horn interrupted them. Jackie got up and looked down over the railing to see that their driver was waving at them.

"Shit, he's here! I better throw on some clothes. You go downstairs and I'll be there in a few."

Sarah managed a smile. "Sure thing."

• • •

"*Hola*," Jackie called to the driver as she exited the hotel.

He was waiting with the passenger door open; Jackie hurried over and slipped into the back next to Sarah, and off they went.

Jackie looked over her shoulder; there was that black sedan again, following them. She'd seen the same car last night, both on the way to the club and back. *My PI training is already paying off*, she thought. *But who would be following us here? We haven't done anything wrong for a change.* She pulled out her small pocket mirror so she could see if they were still following without craning her neck around.

They were.

"Pocket mirror? When did you start carrying that?" Sarah laughed, "You don't wear lipstick."

"Mind your business, just practicing some skills," Jackie said lightly. She didn't want to worry Sarah unnecessarily; she had enough on her mind at the moment.

• • •

The maître d' was standing right outside the opaque glass double doors when they arrived at the Hotel Saratoga.

"Ms. Golden?" he asked as they approached.

"Yes," Sarah responded.

"Please follow me, Dr. Lopez is waiting for you ladies."

"Kinda a big deal, eh Golden?" Jackie teased.

"You know it, sister."

As they entered the formally appointed dining room, Dr. Lopez—dapper in a beige linen jacket—stood up and pulled out a chair for Sarah. The maître d' did the same for Jackie, then placed a white linen napkin on each woman's lap and said, "*Buen provecho*," before returning to his post.

"I took the liberty of ordering your lunch, as I have to get back to the hospital for a case in an hour," Dr. Lopez said.

"Perfect timing—we're taking a car tour to look at all the fancy mansions Castro took over after this," Sarah said.

"Forgive me if I get right to the business at hand, then." Dr. Lopez took out a thick eight-by-eleven envelope and handed it to Sarah, "This is the modified protocol I used—almost exactly what your team was using, but I wasn't able to adhere precisely to the protocol."

Sarah put the envelope on the table without opening it, a concerned look on her face. "Dr. Lopez, I don't think I can help; if Dr. Bower had no knowledge that you were conducting the study and now Dr. McKee is dead, I can't be the messenger. I hope you understand."

Dr. Lopez leaned close to her and whispered, loud enough for Jackie to hear, "You don't understand. I beg you to at least look at our results; I jotted a few notes down on our numbers. I had communicated with all four immunologists running this study, and they had all agreed I could unofficially be part of it if Victor Botsworth from Lago Pharmaceuticals would send me the drugs—and he did. I've been working with Victor under the table for over five years now. He was willing to share protocols and experimental drugs as long as I kept things to myself—which I've always been able to do. Up until now, everything has been off the record on both our parts."

"I don't think you should be telling me any of this," Sarah said, shaking her head. "Doesn't Cuba have a federal agency that oversees clinical trials, like our NIH?"

"Our system is nowhere as sophisticated and there's no money for research here," Dr. Lopez said. "Our government wants to train as many doctors as possible to take care of all our citizens and export the Cuban-trained MDs."

"I've never heard of exporting doctors," Jackie piped up. "What exactly does that mean?"

"It has been a long-standing effort to increase our global reputation, and it's been a huge success," Dr. Lopez explained. "We've sent over four thousand Cuban trained doctors to underserved areas in Brazil, and in return Cuba receives two-hundred-seventy million dollars annually from their government. This has been done in many other countries as well; in fact, our government brings in over eight billion dollars annually exporting doctors and nurses."

"I guess it's one way to get out of the country," Jackie said with a shrug. "Who knew?"

"Yes," Dr. Lopez said, "though clearly it's not totally a voluntary effort. And not everyone wants to leave Cuba, contrary to popular American belief. We have exceptional primary care here and believe in preventive medicine; a doctor is based in the neighborhood they serve and is trusted, so our citizens see them often; and thus our life expectancies rival those of much richer countries."

"I understand the local doctors don't get paid well and usually have a second job," Sarah volunteered.

"That's true, Ms. Golden; however, they seem to enjoy serving their local communities." He frowned. "That said, we have limited access to second and third-tier antibiotics and you need a prescription for medical supplies as basic as aspirin and Band-Aids, so you can understand why research is frowned upon here—we just don't have the resources. If my government gets wind of what I've been doing, it will not end well. But ethically, I need Dr. Bower to know our outcomes. I ended the study due to the high incidence of severe complications and deaths."

Jackie heard Sarah let out a sigh. She watched as her friend opened the envelope, removed the contents, and intently study them as lunch was delivered.

"This looks delicious," Jackie said, clapping her hands together. "I'm starving. We had a late evening last night—I made my Cuban debut with the Buena Vista Social Club." Jackie puffed out her chest, waiting for a laugh or some reaction, but when Dr. Lopez kept his attention focused on Sarah, she pulled her notebook out of her backpack and started writing madly.

Sarah glanced over at her, lifting one eyebrow.

"This is my first international case," Jackie mouthed to her.

Sarah shook her head slightly and continued to read.

Dr. Lopez held up his menu—to block anyone who might be listening or reading his lips, Jackie assumed—and said, "I told Victor about the complications and deaths. Ever since, I haven't been able to get a hold of him, he's disappeared on me. I'm sure he had no idea you would be in Cuba. My government could make my life miserable if Victor reported me: I could lose the position at the university that I have worked so hard to secure, or worse." He placed the menu back on the table.

Sarah put the papers down. "It must be so hard to be under a microscope all the time, when all you're trying to do is advance the science of transplant."

"This particular study is *not* advancing our science," Dr. Lopez said, "and I was planning on sharing my data with the other four immunologists. If there's anything I can do to protect our transplant patients from harm's way by sharing my outcomes, I feel it is my professional responsibility to do so. Would you at least tell Dr. Bower about the complications and deaths?" He pointed to the papers on the table. "It's all documented. I did get accepted to present the preliminary results of one of our other studies at the international meeting in Prague later this year, but the Cuban government denied my visa." He sighed.

"I was supposed to meet with several universities who were interested in recruiting me. I was hoping to get an educational visa; it would have been my family's ticket out."

"I'm sorry to hear your visa was denied; Dr. Bower will be attending that meeting, he has several abstracts to present." Sarah put most of the papers back into the envelope and handed it back to Dr. Lopez. Jackie watched her quickly fold several pages in half and put them in her purse discreetly. "I'll do what I can, no promises. I'm just glad you stopped the study before more patients died."

"Thank you so much, Ms. Golden. If there is any way you can let Dr. Bower know of my dilemma, I'd be so grateful." Dr. Lopez looked at his watch. "I've got a case; I must be on my way. I hope you both enjoy your last day in Havana—safe travels home tomorrow." Dr. Lopez stood and shook Sarah's hand, then Jackie's. Nice to meet you too, Ms. Larsen."

Jackie watched him leave, and then looked back at Sarah and glanced where Dr. Lopez had been sitting. "I think he left his envelope."

"Shit, I really didn't want this entire study. I'll see if we can leave it at the desk for Benita to pick up." Sarah grabbed it.

Jackie scanned the restaurant and noticed there was only one other seated table in the room, occupied by a man and woman in black suits. The man had a prominent scar over his right eye; the woman sported aviator sunglasses.

They looked a little too interested in what was going on at our table, Jackie thought, and as she and Sarah walked by their table, she reached out her hand. "Hello, my name is Jackie Larsen, I'm a private investigator from the United States of America. You sure were interested in what we were doing just now—can I help you?"

They both remained seated and casually looked up at Jackie and then over at Sarah.

After a beat, the aviator sunglasses gal responded, "*No entiendo el inglés.*"

"Oh—I've heard that one before." Jackie chuckled. "I bet you understand English just fine. You didn't by chance see me perform last night, did you? Or did you have to stay outside because your government wouldn't spring for the cover charge? If that's the case, you missed a great show." Jackie smirked and proceeded toward the door, where Sarah was waiting for her, shaking her head.

"We're going home tomorrow, Jackie, don't make any trouble. Seriously." Sarah gave her a pained look.

• • •

As their driver delivered them back to their hotel after a two-hour drive around the Vededo neighborhood—the area where the grand houses the wealthy lived in before Castro took over—Jackie noticed the pair from the restaurant parked outside.

"Looks like our friends Scar Face and Aviators are back," she said. "Maybe we should invite them up for a drink, have a little chat."

"Don't even think about it, Larsen." Sarah tugged her forward, toward the hotel entrance. "We're going upstairs to pack, smoke cigars, and finish our rum. The end."

"Where's your sense of adventure, Golden? Don't go soft on me now, we've only got a few good years of mischief left in us. It can't be against the law to talk to these thugs."

Sarah dragged her to the elevator, maintaining a firm grip on her arm. "Simmer down, Nancy Drew. We have an early flight tomorrow."

Chapter 6

Sarah let out a gasp as she entered their room; their belongings were scattered all over the floor, suitcases emptied out, dresser drawers open. "What the hell!"

The hotel phone rang. Jackie picked it up. "This is Jackie Larsen."

"Ms. Larsen, you and Ms. Golden have two visitors in the bar who are most anxious to see you. Can I tell them you'll both be down?"

"First of all, I want you to call the police—someone broke into our room and went through all our personal belongings. Second, we don't know anyone who lives here, so *no*, we are not meeting anyone downstairs."

Jackie hung up.

The phone rang again.

"What!" Jackie demanded.

"I'm very sorry, but these guests are with the Cuban authorities and they are insisting you meet with them—either here or at the police station."

"We are American citizens! We have rights!" Jackie hung up again. She grabbed a cigar and snipped off the end as she told Sarah, "Some authorities are downstairs and we have to go down and meet with them or else they're going to throw us in the slammer. This is really bullshit."

Sarah heaved a sigh. "Fine. Let's get this over with so we can clean up this mess and pack."

Jackie lit her cigar, took a long drag, and poured a little rum for both of them. "They can wait a minute. This should take the edge off of whatever crappy news is coming our way."

• • •

Scar Face and Aviators were sitting at a table in the bar, casually drinking short glass bottles of Coke, when Jackie and Sarah entered the room.

"Please join us," Aviators said.

Feeling more nervous by the second, Sarah sat in one of the empty seats at their table. With obvious reluctance, Jackie followed suit.

Scar Face motioned the bartender over and ordered a bottle of rum and four glasses.

Jackie looked at Aviators. "The sun's going down, don't think you need those sunglasses anymore. Plus, I never trust anyone I can't look in the eye."

The woman took off her glasses and looked straight at Sarah. "Are you Sarah Golden?"

The waiter brought the bottle of rum just then. Sarah waited until he filled each glass and left before nodding and saying, "That's me."

"Why don't we toast before we begin." Scar Face lifted his glass.

Sarah and Jackie didn't move.

"What do you want?" Jackie demanded, halfway rising from her seat.

Aviators put her hand on Jackie's arm. "Best you just sit still, my friend."

Sarah tensed as Jackie's eyes locked with Aviator's, but Jackie cooperated; she sat back down and said, "We'll give you five minutes; you can't keep us here."

"Actually, we can," Aviators said. "In our country you are considered guilty until proven innocent."

"Well we have no idea what you want with us," Jackie said, "so how 'bout you tell us what can we help you with so we can get this thing over with?"

"We're going to need the envelope Dr. Lopez gave you—any medical protocols developed here in Cuba stay here in Cuba," Scar Face said.

"Who are you, the police?" Jackie asked.

Aviators smiled grimly. "We are . . . private detectives who work very closely with the authorities."

"I'm a PI too, just passed all my tests—glad to meet a member of the club." Jackie put out her hand but the woman didn't reciprocate. Jackie let her hand drop to her lap. "Who's your client?"

"We're not at liberty to say—and we're not 'PIs,'" Scar Face responded.

Sarah looked in her bag for the envelope—and it wasn't there. She proceeded to empty the bag's entire contents on the table, and then she looked over at the two detectives. "I must have left it in the car . . . unless you have it, Jack?"

Jackie pulled her backpack up into her lap. "I don't see it," she said, and went on to pull out cigars, snacks, a small rum glass she'd borrowed from the Hotel Saratoga, a half-filled bottle of Havana Club 7 Años . . . Sarah watched the detectives' eyes widen; it was as if Jackie had a Mary Poppins bag, with all the things she kept removing.

After tossing the last item on the table, Jackie looked up. "Not in here. Maybe you can call our driver, it's likely in the car—so sorry."

The detectives stood up.

"If we don't find it, you two will be staying in Cuba until we do. Dr. Lopez should have known better than to share any documents with you. He will be taken into custody and will not be released until we get it back." Aviators laid her business card on the table. "Call if you happen to find it."

Jackie's nostrils flared. "We're leaving here tomorrow, one way or another—we've done nothing wrong. And by the way, do you happen to know who ransacked our room?"

"Do I need to remind you, Ms. Larsen, that you are not in the US and you must abide by *our* laws while in Cuba?" Scar Face said. "Taking a medical document out of the country is against the law. And no, I don't know who ransacked your room. Maybe you should be more careful about who you associate with."

He and Aviators stood up to leave.

"Call us if you happen to find the protocol," he added before they walked out of the bar.

Sarah and Jackie polished off their rum and looked at each other.

It was Sarah who broke the silence: "I can't stay here any longer, Jack," she said. "I have to get back to Handsome and back to work, and you need to get home to Laura and Wyatt. More importantly, we don't want to end up in a *Cuban prison*."

"For once we behave, and somehow we *still* get in trouble with the law." Jackie slapped the table. "What's the big deal with this protocol? Did you actually read it?"

"I read the findings—which were alarming—but not the entire document. There wasn't time at lunch, and I didn't want to take those papers with me. Now I'm wondering what else was inside. When we get upstairs you call Benita right away and tell her to warn Dr. Lopez."

"Poor guy." Jackie shook her head. "Sounds like he's in for a world of trouble."

• • •

They entered their room to find a sealed envelope on the floor with Sarah's name on it.

Jackie tried to hand it to her but Sarah shook her head.

"You open it," she directed.

Jackie tore it open and started reading the typed contents out loud: "Sarah Golden—you need to turn in that protocol to the authorities. Forget everything you read and heard from Dr. Lopez and never mention it to anyone, especially Dr. Bower! If you decide to disobey this message we can't be responsible for what may happen to your grandmother in Chicago or your friend Jackie's family. Safe trip home."

"How dare they threaten us and our families!" Jackie fumed as she handed Sarah the letter.

Sarah reread it. "Whoever sent this is scared that I'll tell Dr. Bower and he'll share the information with his international research network. But I can't just pretend I didn't see that protocol—there are too many lives at stake here." Sarah started pacing. "This is important information that has to be shared; I'll just have to figure out how to do that without jeopardizing the safety of our families. And I'll need some proof to show Dr. Bower, too; I can't just waltz into his office and declare that Cuban patients are dying without data to back it up."

"To think we were almost at the finish line of our vacation without incident." Jackie snorted. "Maybe take a photo with your phone once we find the file, before we return it?"

Sarah shook her head. "If they take my phone and see the photos, that's hard evidence that I'm taking the protocol out of the country—straight shot to the slammer for sure." She put the letter in her purse. "I'll figure something out. But I'll tell you one thing: no one is going to hurt our families. These people don't know who they're dealing with."

Jackie grinned. "Damn straight, Golden."

Chapter 7

"I don't have time for this shit!" Victor complained out loud as he paced back and forth in his penthouse suite at the Fairmont, dialing Valerie.

"Hey boss, how's Frisco?" she answered brightly.

"Beautiful city, but we've got a situation in Cuba."

"Cuba?"

"Cuba," he said firmly. "Remember our old friend Dr. Lopez, begging us for free drugs for all his studies? Well, no good deed goes unpunished."

"What's going on and what can I do to help?"

"I got these two broads in Cuba nosing around . . . they met with Dr. Lopez and he gave them his research protocol. From what my source there tells me, they'll be heading back home to share the results with Dr. Bower."

"Shit," Valerie said. "Dr. Bower doesn't know anything about that, we were working with Dr. McKee confidentially. Who are these women?"

"Sarah Golden and Jackie Larsen."

"*The* Sarah Golden—Bower's right-hand woman?"

"That's the one. And her friend Jackie apparently thinks she's some kind of super-sleuth. Anyway, I've got a full plate here in San Francisco, so I'll need you to handle this. I'll give you the name of my contact in Cuba. Those women cannot leave Cuba with that protocol—no paper trail. Do what you have to do, just be sure you confirm that our contact has the protocol and all of Lopez's results before those women get on a plane. And Lopez will never get out of Cuba if I have anything to do with it."

"I'm on it," Valerie said. "Seems like Golden has a penchant for trouble, doesn't it?"

"You can say that again," Victor growled. "Bower shared all the gory details of her near-death experience in Miami at dinner last night. She's lucky she survived." He pinched the bridge of his nose in frustration. "This woman could be trouble for *us*, too. Bower really trusts her to run his operations, including all their studies—told me he couldn't run his program without her."

The hotel phone rang.

"I've got to take this. Keep me posted."

"Will do, boss."

• • •

A bellhop rang the bell to Victor's suite just a few minutes later. Victor opened the door, took the large, heavy envelope from the young man's hand, and slipped him a ten.

"Thanks," the bellhop said. "Can I get you anything else sir?"

"No thanks."

Victor closed the door and opened the envelope; inside was a burner cell phone and a note from Angelo: *Call me from this phone as soon as you get this, I've got what you need.*

Victor turned on the burner phone and punched in the number Angelo had scribbled on the note.

"Angelo here."

"It's Victor. Thanks for taking care of the phone. You ready to get to work?"

"As soon as you pay half up front, in cash. It's going to cost at least 250K."

"Fine," Victor said, tamping down his annoyance. "I need this handled—I'm not going to argue with you. I'll have someone make the drop. Usual place in Jersey?"

"You're lucky it's not more; I did a little digging, and they're keeping this case on lockdown. I found someone on the inside but they're risking their career to talk, so you have to make it worth their trouble."

"I get it, I get it. Did you find anything out yet?" Victor was pacing back and forth in the living room.

"The NIH have hired their own investigator, a woman by the name of Nixie Klein. She is a serious badass, they brought her in a couple years ago when there was a huge data breach. Word is she does not suffer fools and always gets results—one way or another."

"Too bad you didn't get to her first."

"You couldn't afford her. We have someone inside that will be working with us, though. We can get this done, but it will likely get complicated with Klein on the case. I may have to increase the price, depending on how things go."

"Just get me the information as soon as you can," Victor said. "I need to know if the car was tampered with, if so by whom, every move those docs made before they got in the car, who they met with, all of it. And I need to know it ahead of this Klein woman. Last thing I want is to find out that one of the Big Pharma companies was behind this."

"Got it. I'll pick up the cash and get this party started. Keep this burner phone nearby, I'll call you with updates."

"Fine, fine," Victor said. "Just get it done, now. This is a ticking time bomb; if it goes the wrong way there will definitely be a federal investigation, and we can't let that happen. The faster you close this out, the bigger the bonus."

"I hear you. I'll be in touch."

• • •

As Victor approached the table at the restaurant downstairs, he could tell the two nurses were checking him out head to toe. He was used to it; he was a handsome man.

He pasted on a smile. "Good afternoon, ladies, I'm so glad you could meet me on such short notice."

The two women returned his smile. "Not like we're busy, since they closed down our studies and made us send everything to the NIH," Debbie, a short, dimpled woman, replied.

"It's always nice to see you, Victor." Chris winked at him and tossed her hair. "We don't usually get to leave the hospital for lunch."

The waiter appeared to take their orders and refresh their waters. When he left, Victor donned his most sincere expression.

"First, my condolences for your loss—I know that you were both close to Dr. McKee. His family must be devastated. How you both holding up?"

Chris leaned in. "It's very sad, surreal. One day our study is breaking news in the transplant community, then everything comes to a screeching halt."

"This morning we were briefed by the university attorney not to discuss the study or anything about Dr. McKee since there is an FBI investigation underway," Debbie said. "The FBI is at our facility right now, meeting with Dr. Bower. I thought they died in a car accident, not sure why the FBI is involved! I can't believe Sarah's in Cuba while all this is going down . . . I wonder if she even knows what happened?"

"Even if she's not still in Cuba, she probably hasn't heard

. . . too busy having her way with Handsome," Chris said slyly. "I sure would be if he was my boyfriend."

"Who's Handsome?" Victor asked. "That's an interesting name."

"Let's be honest," Chris said, "that could be *your* name too, if you don't mind me saying."

Debbie let out a laugh. "It's what she calls her detective boyfriend who lives in Miami; they're quite the couple. His real name is Rodney something. Strong, I think."

Victor nodded, storing that information away for future use. "So, what are you two going to do with all this newfound time? We have several openings for nurse researchers, if you'd like me to put in a good word for you."

"That's generous of you," Debbie said, "but we're swamped right now, actually. The study got cut short but we're stuck dealing with the aftermath. You wouldn't believe all the paperwork."

"I understand from Dr. Bower that your living kidney donor program is the biggest in the country," Victor said. "Congratulations on that."

Chris paused from buttering a roll to say, "We didn't have anything to do with that; our job was to enroll as many pre-transplant patients as possible in the tolerance research study . . . and we were cranking. Do you know what's going to happen to all those patients now?"

"Hopefully we'll get to start over again soon," Victor said. "I'm sure once the dust settles on this investigation, we will."

"That's good to hear." Debbie patted her mouth with the linen napkin. "Do you think someone murdered those poor doctors?"

Victor shook his head. "I can't imagine who would want them dead, they were so close to the holy grail . . . but stranger things have happened."

"Seems to me your industry stands to lose lots of money if we crack this one," Chris offered. "No more drugs, and maybe even being able to transplant more patients who can't afford the drugs, would be a huge gift to our patients, but it wouldn't exactly be good for business in pharma land."

"The goal is to get everyone that wants a transplant transplanted," Victor said firmly. "Let me put your mind at ease: the pharma industry would never, ever get mixed up in any foul play."

He heard the burner phone, which he'd stashed in his briefcase, start to buzz.

"I need to take this," he said, rising from his seat. "Please feel free to order dessert. I'll be right back."

Chapter 8

Jackie studied Sarah's face. "I can tell you're using your noggin to figure out how we do this without us getting locked up."

She grabbed the bottle of rum and two glasses, stepped over all the clothes on the floor, and went out to the balcony. "Come out here," she called. "I don't want to talk about that letter until you and I have a full, delicious glass of this rum. We have to drink it anyway, can't take an open bottle on the plane."

Sarah followed her onto the balcony and sat down. "For the record, we were having a fabulous time until we had lunch with Dr. Lopez and the shit hit the fan."

"Ain't that the truth," Jackie said. She took a sip of rum and closed her eyes. "This has to be the smoothest rum I've ever had, even when Biker Bob and I went to the Rum Wreck bar in Florida—and that's saying something, their collection was amazing." Jackie looked over at her friend and knew exactly what she was thinking. "We're not letting this ruin our last night here. Benita said she'll get a hold of the driver, and if there is anything in the car they'll bring it to those thugs. Everything's being taken care of."

They finished their rum in companionable silence, then Sarah looked over at Jackie.

"Let's get the hell out of here and walk around," she said. "We can throw everything in our suitcases when we get back."

"You got it." Jackie leaned over the balcony railing. "Hey," she shouted, "if anyone wants to go through our stuff again we're going out, so come on up and have at it."

Several folks in the park looked up at her, puzzled looks on their faces.

Sarah rolled her eyes, but she couldn't help but laugh. "You're ridiculous, Larsen."

• • •

Brightly colored vintage cars lined the perimeter of the park and locals were strolling about and enjoying the music filling the air like they didn't have a care in the world. As Sarah and Jackie wandered, the rum worked its magic on Jackie. It seemed to have done the same for Sarah; she could see that her friend's shoulders had moved away from her ears and were back down where they were supposed to be.

Various street vendors invited them to buy their trinkets. Jackie bartered one for a sweet puppet for Wyatt and Sarah bought two bags of chips and handed one to Jackie. They ducked into a local bar to grab some Cuba libres, then continued their stroll.

They came to a halt as they looked up and saw a pizza box tied to a rope being lowered down to a boy on the street. He took the box and waved at the woman on the roof.

Jackie waved at her and in her broken Spanish yelled up at the lady, "*Por favor, pizza para mi and mi amiga!*"

The lady smiled and rubbed her thumb and fingers together.

Jackie nudged Sarah. "You have any pesos left, Golden?"

Sarah pulled out a bunch of paper bills out of her purse and held them up toward the pizza lady. "*Cuanto cuesto?*" Her Spanish was even worse than Jackie's.

When the lady put all five fingers up, Sarah placed the bills in the small cup attached to the rope and up it went.

While they waited, they people-watched.

"These people sure don't have much but they all seem so content and relaxed," Jackie said. "This music could put anyone in a good mood."

A few minutes later, the pizza headed down toward them.

Sarah untied the box and brought it over to Jackie, and they both devoured it.

"I have no idea what we're eating, but it's delicious," Sarah said, the tomato sauce dripping down both sides of her mouth. She used the wax paper like a napkin to dab at the sauce.

"It's not Chicago pizza but it is damn good—and I'm a little backed up, so if this loosens things up before we get on the plane I'm good with that." Jackie popped her last bite into her mouth.

Sarah laughed.

Bellies full, the best friends strolled down the street, constant music playing in the background. Beautiful young women were swaying their hips, shoulders exposed, large hoop earrings and brightly colored lips tantalizing the gentleman observers. But the best part for Jackie was that Sarah actually seemed to be enjoying herself, despite the uncertainty surrounding their return home.

After an hour of wandering, Jackie sighed, knowing fun time was over. "Well, Golden, I think it's time. Ready to go up, pack, and get ready to bid *adiós* to Cuba?"

"*Sí, sí*," Sarah said. "This was just what I needed—great idea, Jack."

As they entered the lobby, the front clerk motioned for them to approach the desk. "Excuse me, ladies, this arrived when you were out." She slid it toward them. "The man who left it said he found it in his backseat."

"Gracias." Sarah opened the thick envelope, pulled out a sheaf of papers, and began studying them.

"Are you going to use your photographic memory and memorize all the details?" Jackie asked, leaning over her shoulder.

Sarah shook her head. "You know I don't have a photographic memory; I can hardly remember my social security number some days. And with all that rum on board, it's a nonstarter. I just want to see if anything jumps out—and then I'm going to have this lovely lady call the authorities so they can pick up the folder."

Jackie watched closely as Sarah scanned the documents, but her friend's face gave nothing away. After flipping through all the dense paperwork, Sarah put the stack back into the envelope and handed it to the desk clerk. "Please call our friends and let them know it's all theirs."

The clerk nodded and retrieved the card Scar Face and Aviators had left for her.

"Well?" Jackie whispered as they headed to the elevator.

Sarah shook her head. "We'll talk about it later."

• • •

Back in their room, Jackie poured the remainder of the rum in their glasses, and she and Sarah sipped as they gathered their clothes and packed in silence, the music below serenading them.

Within minutes of laying their heads on their pillows, Jackie heard a light snore coming from Sarah's bed. Seconds later, she was out too.

Chapter 9

Benita accompanied them to the airport in the morning.

"Your driver found the envelope in the backseat of his car and dropped it off at our front desk last night," Sarah shared.

"Great," Benita said. "I know Dr. Lopez was concerned. Hopefully they'll stop hounding him now. And he sends his sincere apologies for any trouble he may have caused you both. I hope it didn't ruin your last night."

"We're all good," Sarah said. "The fact that we can leave the country without any problems is all that matters."

"And in fact, we had a wonderful time last night!" Jackie raved. "Even sampled some of your rooftop pizza. Let's just say it took care of my constipation."

Benita let out a loud laugh.

Sarah winced. "Jackie, do you need to share *everything*? Really!"

"That's okay, Sarah," Benita said, still chuckling. "Our pizza seems to have that effect on almost everyone."

"Thank you, Benita," Jackie said. "Sarah is such a prude sometimes. On a different note, do you know how many cigars they let you take out of the country? I've got those two boxes, less a few, that Dr. Lopez was kind enough to gift me."

"You should be okay with the two boxes—just be sure to declare them." Benita pulled her car up to the departure area, got out, opened the trunk, and helped them get their bags out.

"Benita," Sarah said quietly as they stood behind the car, "is Dr. Lopez going to be okay? Are they going to put him in jail? I feel so bad. . . ."

Benita gave her a wan smile. "I don't know," she said quietly. "But whatever happens, it's not your fault. He made his own choices." Speaking more loudly, she said, "Have a safe journey, and thank you for coming to visit. Maybe someday we will be able to come visit your transplant program." She gave them each a warm embrace.

"I sure hope so," Sarah said, and she meant it. "Please do stay in touch."

Benita got back in the car and waved good-bye. Jackie and Sarah pulled their bulging suitcases into the customs area.

"Just for the record, know we weren't followed to the airport," Jackie whispered to Sarah as they stepped into line. "The coast is clear and we're almost home."

"I saw you using your 'secret mirror' the entire time on the drive here," Sarah said, shaking her head. "You're going to have to figure out a different way to track the enemy when you hit the mainland. And don't show that trick to anyone you're interviewing with for your perfect PI job—they'll think you're a mental patient."

Jackie was still rolling her eyes at this feedback when Sarah felt a tap on her shoulder.

"Excuse me, ladies, will you follow me?" A man in a police uniform motioned for them to follow him.

"Shiiiiiit," Sarah said.

"Who are you and why are you pulling us aside?" Jackie demanded.

The man said nothing.

"Helloooo—we're American citizens!" Jackie persisted.

The man continued without reaction, leading them past the long line to a closed room immediately past the customs booth. He opened the beaten door, guided them inside, and left.

Two large women in tight-fitted inspectors' suits, all holstered up, stood before them. The only difference between them seemed to be that one had bangs and one didn't.

"Please put your bags on the table and take everything out of your pockets," the one with bangs commanded. "Remove everything but your blouse and pants, and take off your shoes . . . *por favor*."

Jackie folded her arms over her chest. "Have we done something wrong, Officer?"

"We received a call that you may be moving contraband out of the country," No Bangs said.

Jackie reached into her backpack, pulled out the two boxes of cigars, and slid them over the table. "Just take them! I was told that we could take two boxes of cigars, but apparently I was misinformed. Sure glad I smoked a few before they were confiscated. Your country really needs to make friends with the US—we are suffering over there for lack of your excellent cigars."

"You can keep the cigars, *señora*, you can bring two boxes with you." No Bangs waved a hand at the boxes. "Now please empty your bags, purses, and backpacks."

Jackie frowned. "But—"

"We're going to miss our flight, Jackie, stop talking, and do what they tell us." Sarah bit her lower lip as she emptied out her purse, trying to contain her anxiety.

The customs officers' eyes widened as Jackie turned her backpack upside down and out poured an avalanche of stuff. Several blouses, underwear, and socks that wouldn't fit in her suitcase, plus all her souvenirs, and a variety of other items. They then sorted through her clothes, treasures, coasters, matches, old cookies wrapped in a napkin, Wyatt's carefully wrapped puppet, and more until everything had been examined.

Sarah's small purse didn't have much in it—lipstick, small mirror, passport, tissue, a laminated photo of her and Handsome, antacids, and a pill container. As the officers went through the tiny pile, a rancid smell filled the room and everyone's nose puckered.

Sarah held back a laugh. "Jack, you didn't."

"It's the pizza," Jackie protested, "I couldn't hold it any longer!"

Bangs pinched her nose shut. "Do you need to use the *baño*?"

"Nope," Jackie said cheerfully, "it's just gas right now. But the sooner you get us through here the happier everyone's noses will be."

Besides seeming disgusted by the smell, the officers looked disappointed. Sarah didn't need PI training to understand that the officers had something specific in mind they were looking for, and they hadn't found it yet.

"Are we done here?" Jackie asked.

"We just need to pat you both down," No Bangs said. "If you would both lean against the wall, we can finish this up and then let you go."

Please don't touch my chest, Sarah thought. She had taken great care to make sure there were no weird bumps in her bra where she had hidden the papers. She restrained herself from looking down at her blouse.

"Do we have to stand in that long line again or can you at least escort us to the other side?" Jackie asked as she approached the wall. "Seems like getting us through fast is the least you can do after all this."

Bangs snapped on a pair of gloves. "We can get you right through if you pass inspection in here—which, given your stomach problem, may be the best course to follow for everyone." She wrinkled her nose.

Sarah took her position next to Jackie, and the customs inspectors commenced with patting them both down thoroughly.

Sarah felt her pulse quickening and beads of sweat forming on her forehead. She caught her breath when she glanced at No Bangs's face and noticed her glaring at her, but then the woman said, "Must be that pizza."

Sarah nodded her agreement, trying to hide her relief.

"That's the best airport massage I've gotten in a long time," Jackie quipped as her search ended. "You gals know your business."

Both officers stepped back.

"I need to ask you both," No Bangs said, "are you carrying any documents out of our country? Did you get anything from our medical center?" She directed her question and gaze at Sarah.

"Nope," Sarah said quickly.

"No," Jackie answered.

"Please collect your belongings and we can get you on your way, then."

Jackie stuffed everything back in her suitcase and backpack. Once they were ready to go, Bangs led them past the customs booth and to the other side, where passengers were scurrying for their flights.

"Thank you for visiting our country," the officer said. "I hope your visit was enjoyable."

"I had so much fun—and thanks for letting me keep my cigars. If I wasn't married, you'd be in trouble, young lady." Jackie winked.

Bangs flushed bright red, then turned on her heel and darted away.

• • •

After the seatbelt sign went off in the air, Sarah made a beeline to the bathroom and then back to her seat.

Jackie looked over at her as she sat down. "I ordered us each a double rum and Coke—Golden! You didn't!" She stared at the papers in Sarah's hand.

Sarah put her hand on her chest to intentionally slow down her breathing, which was so fast her chest was heaving up and down. "I just took the pages with the results—there's no way those idiots would know what to look for."

The flight attendant came by with their drinks; Sarah snatched hers from her and took a big gulp.

Jackie was still staring at her.

"I thought you were going to stay out of this, Golden," she said. "You could have gotten us arrested—in *Cuba*, no less. I don't want to know anything; I don't want to be an accomplice when you're charged with international espionage. That way I can honestly say I had no knowledge of any of this when they make me take the witness stand." Jackie finished her drink in one go, then turned her back to Sarah and proceeded to fall asleep.

Sarah finished her drink as she studied the complicated results from Dr. Lopez's study. She gasped as the flight attendant was walking by.

"Are you alright, ma'am?"

Sarah hadn't even realized she had made a sound. "I-I'm fine," she stammered. "Just reading an interesting article."

The attendant left and Sarah took a deep breath.

Now she understood why the Cuban officials wouldn't want this information getting out of the country. Twenty of the one hundred patients had died two weeks into the study, and another fifteen had lost their kidney and had to go back on dialysis. From her various conversations with Dr. Lopez and his team during the tour she knew the Cuban government didn't like spending too much money on any one person's healthcare, so the cost of a failed kidney transplant and then their return to dialysis would of course be seriously frowned upon.

Sarah closed her eyes and mulled over what to do with this information. Should she ignore the study results? What could she do, anyway? Dr. Lopez could be in a Cuban jail by now—who knew what they would do to his family, she'd heard stories. Would they make him tell them what was missing from the protocol? If he did, she could be in trouble. And what about pharma sending their drugs to Cuba? Did this have anything to do with Dr. McKee and his colleagues getting killed?

"Sarah, everyone's getting off the plane—we're home!" Jackie nudged her friend. "I sure hope we get through customs without another frisking, although if I get a good-looking TSA gal I wouldn't object."

"You're ridiculous," Sarah said. "We're on US soil now; the Cubans can't exactly do anything to us now."

"Where did you put those papers?"

Sarah pointed to her breasts. "They add a little lift, don't you think?"

Jackie looked closely. "The girls do look a little bigger than usual."

They were still laughing as they deplaned.

• • •

Handsome was waiting right outside the arrival doors with a vibrant bouquet of flowers, wearing the biggest grin Sarah had seen in a long time. Suddenly warm all over, she dropped her bag and gave him a long hug as they enjoyed a soft, delicious kiss.

"I missed you so much," she whispered in his ear.

"I missed you too, my love." He eased out of their embrace, handed her the flowers, and turned to Jackie. "Welcome home, Jack—thanks for getting my gal back here safe. Can I take your bag?"

"Help yourself, and you are welcome. I was on my best behavior most of the time; your girlfriend, not so much."

Handsome lifted both big bags, and they began walking toward the airport parking garage.

"Jackie brought down the house at the Buena Vista Social Club singing on stage," Sarah told him. "It was a moment I'm sure everyone who was there will never forget, including me. When I hear 'Bésame Mucho' from now on, I will only see the looks on all those tourists' faces."

She and Jackie traded off sharing the rest of the details about that fun night as they followed Handsome out to his truck. Once all the luggage was secured in the back, Handsome assisted both of them up and into the cab.

"Damn this is high off the ground—what the hell, Handsome, do you really need this big-ass truck?" Jackie said. "What do you use it for, carting around criminals?"

"You never know," he said, "I may have to tie you two up and throw *you* in the back if you don't start behaving."

"He watched too many Ford commercials during all the sports events on TV," Sarah explained. "They plant their 'buy this truck and you're a stud' seed, and next thing you know all the big boys are buying their trucks."

Handsome gave Sarah a smile, gently touched her hand, and started the car.

Sarah closed her eyes for a moment, her skin tingling from his touch, and then her eyes opened wide. "Wait, first things first—how's Campos? Give us the update."

"She's going to be fine," Handsome said. "She's in for a long-haul recovery process; she'll be off work for a good four to six months, depending on her rehab. But she's determined to get back sooner, of course. And Bishop is going to be by her side every step of the way."

Jackie leaned forward and patted Handsome's shoulder. "That had to be one scary-ass scene. You okay, buddy?"

Handsome's facial muscles tightened as he answered, "It was pretty fucking scary, I'd be lying if I told you otherwise. Those assholes had a sawed-off shotgun."

"Are you going to get a temporary partner?" Sarah asked as she massaged his neck.

"We'll see," he said. "I still have a shit ton of paperwork to do after the mini-vacation I'm taking while you're here, and then I'm taking a couple weeks off to come out to stay with you, honey." He looked over at Sarah with a grin. "Maybe longer. Who knows?"

"Won't break my heart." Sarah gave him a peck on the cheek.

"I need to call Maria really quick," Jackie said from the backseat. "We've been texting back and forth about dinner tonight. She'd like us around six, sound good?"

"Sounds good to me." Sarah said, and Handsome nodded his assent. "Be sure to ask her what we can bring."

"On it," Jackie said.

• • •

Handsome pulled his giant truck up in front of a corner dive neighborhood grocery ten minutes later.

"They should have plenty of ridiculous piñata options for you in there," he told Jackie. "And don't forget the candy fillers! Let's make Marco's second birthday celebration one he'll never forget."

"Be right back!" Jackie hopped out of the truck and went inside.

Sarah took her seat belt off, slid over to Handsome's side of the front seat, and planted a long kiss on his soft lips. Then she hugged him tight. "I'm so glad you're okay," she said softly. "You both could have gotten killed . . . I couldn't take that."

"Believe me, I hear you," Handsome said. "That was the closest call I've ever had in my fifteen years on the force. I'm not sure if Campos will be coming back; I know she wants to, but I need some time off and I wasn't even hit." He pulled Sarah close to him again.

They'd been sitting like that for a few minutes when a loud knock sounded on Jackie's window. They both looked over, startled—and burst out laughing.

Jackie was carrying a Pokémon piñata the size of one of Handsome's truck tires. She opened the back door. "A little help would be nice," she teased. "You two are in there locking lips and I'm doing all the heavy lifting here!" She threw two big bags of candy into the far side of the backseat. "How am I supposed climb into this monster truck with this monster piñata?"

Sarah hopped out of the cab to help. "Nice work, Larsen," she said, grabbing the piñata. "This kid will never forget his Aunt Jackie. Talk about a lasting impression—it's probably bigger than him!"

Once Jackie was settled Handsome hopped back on the freeway. "We'll drop everything off at my place, freshen up and then head out for dinner," he said. "We still have a couple hours."

"Sounds good to me," Jackie said. "I could use a nice long shower, some American bath products, and a thick towel. You two can do whatever suits your fancy—like I don't know what that is." Jackie chuckled. "Cuddle."

"What time is your flight tomorrow?" Sarah asked.

"Nine," Jackie said. "Any chance of a ride there?"

"No problem, at your service," Handsome said. "We'll be heading in that direction anyway."

Sarah twisted toward him. "Where are we going?"

"You'll see, it's a surprise." He shot her a mischievous grin.

They arrived at Handsome's condo, he brought the luggage up and Jackie made a beeline to the bathroom, shouting, "Don't disturb me!" over her shoulder.

Handsome took Sarah by the hand, led her to his bedroom, shut the door, turned on some soft music, and whispered in her ear, "I love you, Sarah Golden—welcome home," as he wrapped his arms around her. It was the tightest hug Sarah had ever gotten from him.

• • •

They arrived at Maria's house promptly at six. Sarah saw a Harley motorcycle parked in the driveway and perked up. "How exciting, Biker Bob is here! I haven't seen him in such a long time; he's always on a cross-country motorcycle trip with his senior Hells Angels friends when I come to town."

Sarah and Handsome preceded Jackie, who was attempting to keep the piñata behind her back, on the walk up the drive.

Jackie whistled as she took in the new digs. "This place is way nicer than the old one," she said.

"They're moving up in the world," Handsome said. "Glad to see that the money she got from that dickwad Sergio went to some good."

He knocked and the door opened immediately. A small boy looked up at them, his wide, soft brown eyes framed by long eye lashes and dark brown hair.

"Hi," he said shyly.

Sarah let out an audible gasp; Marco was the spitting image of Sergio.

The boy peeked around Sarah and Handsome and saw the enormous piñata in Jackie's arms; his big eyes grew saucer-size. "Mamá!" he called. "Pikachu!"

They heard Maria's voice before she arrived at the door. "Marco, is that anyway to greet our guests?" She opened the door wide. "Welcome! Please come inside."

Sarah gave her a huge hug. "You look wonderful, and your son is gorgeous. What a treat it is to see you."

Handsome gave Maria a hug. "Looks like they'll let anyone in here," he said, gesturing toward Biker Bob and Zuzu in the living room.

Chuckling, the duo strode over to shake hands, which Zuzu followed up with a hug.

"Just got here, bro," she said. "Nice to see you too . . . sorry to hear about your partner, hope she's okay."

"Thanks," Handsome said. "Happy to say she's on the mend."

Jackie slapped hands with Zuzu and Biker Bob. "Good to have our crackerjack unofficial detective team back together again!" she said. "We never would have caught Sergio or Kayla's killer without the two of you. Nice to see you, Zuzu."

Watching the exchange, Sarah thought of Kayla. It had been only about a year since her death; she wondered how Zuzu was dealing with that tragedy after all these months.

Jackie turned toward Marco and squatted down so she was eye-level with him. "I thought you might like a piñata, little guy." She reached over and moved his thick, curly hair away from his face. "What do you think, you up for the challenge?"

Marco looked over at his mom. "Mamá?"

"Yes, Marco, we'll play after dinner . . . if your new friend Jackie can wait until then." Maria grinned. "Speaking of which, dinner is almost ready! I'll be right back."

As Maria went into the kitchen, Luisa and José Chavez, her parents, walked in using the back door.

Jackie rushed over and gave Luisa a hug. “You look great!” she said. “It’s so nice to see you both. Your grandson is *muy guapo*.”

“We are so blessed,” Luisa said, beaming. “He is the joy of our life.”

Maria called everyone outside to a screened-in gazebo, where a festive table was set and a variety of delicious dishes awaited.

“Everything looks and smells amazing,” Sarah declared, her mouth watering, as she surveyed the table’s offerings: grilled shrimp on skewers drizzled with a garlic butter, steaming bowls of beans and rice, fried plantains, fresh avocado, limes, and tostones.

“Please, everyone sit,” Maria said as she placed a large pitcher of freshly made limeade in the middle of the table.

After everyone was seated, José stood, glass in hand.

“Welcome to our new home,” he said. “We are so grateful for all you did to help us and that we are here celebrating together tonight.”

Everyone lifted their glasses and toasted.

“I’ll see you all later, I’m diving in to this feast!” Jackie announced before shoveling in her first mouthful.

Silence took over as the sounds of forks hitting plates and sighs of satisfaction filled the space. Sarah could not help but stare at Marco, nestled between his grandmother and Jackie. She also noticed that Jackie was watching Zuzu closely, and remembered what Jackie had shared with her the previous year: that she’d developed a little crush on Zuzu when they’d gone to the gay disco in Miami together.

“Piñata, Abuela?” Marco asked hopefully as people’s plates began to empty.

“Soon, *mijo*, soon,” Luisa said. “Go play if you’re done.”

Marco jumped down from his seat, left the gazebo, and ran to the play structure in the backyard.

"I must share that we are in touch with Sergio," Maria announced. "He is Marco's father, and we will not deny Marco that knowledge when the time is right."

Sarah stopped chewing. After what they'd gone through to get Sergio arrested? After how horrible he'd been to Maria and her family? She could hardly believe her ears. Looking around, she saw that Jackie, Handsome, Zuzu, and Biker Bob were all staring at Maria, probably thinking the same thing.

Handsome broke the silence. "I'm not sure that's such a good idea," he said carefully. "I respect your decision, but . . . Sergio is serving prison time for a reason. He had your brother killed."

"Yes he did," José interrupted, "But our son was no saint, as you know; he was a violent gang member. He was still our son and we must all forgive, hold on to the good memories we had of him, and move forward. But he was no innocent."

Sarah watched Maria, who kept her eyes locked on her father.

"We should not let the worst mistake we make in our lives define us," José continued. "Sergio has been writing to Maria and has expressed his deepest regrets for what he did."

Everyone around the table was visibly fidgeting now.

"Of course it's your decision," Sarah jumped in, "and we know you will always keep the best interests of Marco a top priority. Just know we want you all to be safe after all you've been through."

"I loved him," Maria offered, "and I know at some level he loved me too. I did not respond to his letters for a long time, but he kept sending them, so I finally read them, and in every one he apologized and begged me to send some photos. We're the only family he has."

Handsome was sitting next to Maria. He put his hand on her shoulder. "Family is the most important thing in the world. I understand, I truly do."

With that, he stood up and walked around the table to Sarah, got on one knee, and pulled a ring box out of his pocket.

Sarah's cheeks were burning, and she was holding her breath.

"I was going to wait until we were alone tomorrow, but then I thought, all the people at this table played a part of how Sarah and I met and fell in love—so yes, sometimes bad things create good things." He looked into Sarah's eyes. "Sarah Golden, will you marry me?"

"Holy shit, this is really happening," Jackie blurted out. "It's about damn time!"

Handsome opened the blue velvet box. Sarah looked at a large, pear-shaped diamond ring and then into Handsome's loving brown eyes.

"Yes—I'll marry you," she said, tears streaming down her cheeks.

As everyone around the table clapped, Handsome placed the ring on her finger, stood up, pulling her up along with him, and took her in his arms for a passionate kiss. Sarah gave herself over to the kiss for a long moment, then pulled away and surveyed the table.

"You are all a part of my family and I am so happy you were present for this unexpected announcement," Sarah declared.

Jackie made her way over to where Sarah and Handsome stood and embraced her best friend.

"Especially you, Jack," Sarah whispered, squeezing her tight.

"I am so happy for both of you," Jackie said. "We finally have lift-off; I could just bust my buttons! I would not have missed this for the world." She grabbed a teaspoon from the table and, using it as a pretend microphone, and started to sing “Chapel of Love.”

Marco came running to see what all the laughter was about and then turned to Jackie.

“Piñata?”

Jackie glanced at Maria, who nodded in the affirmative. Jackie sprinted out of the gazebo and into the yard. Marco clapped his hands and ran after her.

The remainder of the table looked on in amusement as candy spilled all over the back lawn.

Chapter 10

Everyone was in a jovial mood on the way to the airport the next morning, especially after they stopped for coffee.

Sarah turned around from the front seat after they got on the freeway. "I'm going to miss you, Jack."

"I'm going to miss you too," Jackie said, "but I think I'm leaving you in good hands with your fiancé. How's that sounding?"

A goofy smile took over Sarah's face. "I can get used to that."

"I sure hope so," Handsome said. "And I know you two are attached at the hip and all, but you'll see each other again in a few days. Plus, Jackie, you have so much to look forward to—I know you've been missing Wyatt, Laura, and, dare I say, even your mother-in-law. Then there's your new PI career!"

"Yeah, the job thing is exciting for sure—and I can't wait to get my hands on my boy and hug my wife and, yes, even my mother-in-law." Jackie bounced in her seat, almost spilling her coffee. "She's the reason I got to go to Cuba, after all."

Handsome briefly glanced over his shoulder at her. "Speaking of your new PI job . . . I noticed you and Maria having what looked like a serious discussion last night. Anything we should know about?"

"Actually she did share some information with me when you two were dancing in the backyard last night," Jackie said. "I didn't want to kill the wedding bell buzz last night, but it's about the deaths of those immunologists in Chicago."

"I'm not interested in anything Sergio has to say," Sarah declared. "I was done with him when he tried to have my best friend killed."

"From what Maria said, he's in a part of prison where they're treated like VIPs—get the local papers delivered, have access to television and liberal visiting privileges . . . I guess money can buy things anywhere." Jackie shook her head. "Anyway, he asked Maria to come see him in a couple weeks, sent her a ticket and everything. And she's going, no talking her out of it. I told her to keep her distance but she didn't listen to a word I said; she's still in love with him."

"That can't be good," Sarah said. "What did Sergio tell her about our dead immunologists? I can't imagine what he would know about that world; he was too busy banging women and living the high life."

"Maria told me he was very remorseful about almost getting me killed last year, and he's trying to find a way to make amends to both of us for all the shit he caused. He's been learning everything he can about the accident since it hit the news." Jackie took a sip of her coffee. "He's supposedly making this his full-time project; he says he still has lots of connections in the outside world—especially in Chicago, since he went to University of Chicago for his MBA."

"If Maria can get any information on this, I'm sure we can send it to the Chicago PD, right honey?" Sarah tapped Handsome's shoulder. "I mean, Jackie and I have solved two murder mysteries—we should have some street cred by now."

Handsome shook his head. "I thought we agreed after what happened to you last year that you and Sherlock back there were going to get out of the detective business." He signaled for the airport exit.

"Well technically I'm a private investigator now, so it would be in my job scope to entertain this type of case," Jackie said. "However, I believe Sarah has committed to avoiding any involvement with this case—right, Golden? We have a wedding to plan, jobs to get back to, life goes on."

Jackie knew exactly what Sarah was thinking as she looked forward, not responding.

"Did you tell your fiancé about the souvenir you brought back from the Havana transplant center?" Jackie poked Sarah's shoulder.

Handsome looked over at Sarah and then back at the road as he eased into Terminal 2.

"Looks like we're here, Jack," Sarah said. "I'll give him the lowdown after we get you on your way."

Handsome pulled the truck up to the curb; Sarah quickly hopped out and opened Jackie's door.

"You had to bring that up?" she hissed. "There's really nothing to tell."

"I think you need to tell Handsome everything." Jackie shrugged. "You're going to marry the guy, and if I learned anything in marriage counseling last year it's that you've gotta be open and honest with your partner—avoids blow-ups down the road."

As Handsome came around from the back of the truck with Jackie's luggage, Jackie reached over and gave her friend a long hug. "See you soon back in the Bay. I'm so happy for you!" She hugged Handsome and made her way to the sliding glass doors.

Before she stepped through, she turned around and yelled, "How about we go to Hawaii next time?"

"I'm there," Sarah yelled back.

Chapter 11

Victor paced back and forth in SF Transplant's lobby, waiting to be escorted to the Chair of the Immunology Department.

A tall, slender man approached, "Excuse me, I'm Dennis. Are you Victor Botsworth?"

Victor stuck his hand out. "That's me. Thanks for coming to retrieve me; security has sure gotten tight around here. Dr. McKee always had me meet him up in the research office on the fourth floor."

The two men walked down a long hall and entered the elevator. "Security is intense since FBI got involved," Dennis explained. "When we get to Dr. Sethna's office we'll need your driver's license, a local number you can be reached at, and a business card; they're making us keep a thorough log of everyone who enters our labs, even the guys who deliver our research mice."

The doors opened and Victor followed Dennis down the familiar hall. There was actual yellow crime tape closing off Dr. McKee's office and a few other doors.

"Wow, this is crazy," he said. "Overkill, if you ask me."

"I know." Dennis shrugged. "I don't make the rules—but I must say, it's nice to have some fresh faces around. It livens things up. And I love true crime stuff, so this is right up my alley." He tapped on Dr. Sethna's door.

"Come in!" a voice from inside called.

Dennis let Victor in, then poked his head through the threshold. "I'll be at my desk if you need anything else, Dr. Sethna." With that, he closed the door and left them to their meeting.

"Please be seated, Mr. Botsworth." Dr. Sethna leaned back in her leather chair, a beautiful view of Golden Gate Park visible through the window behind her. "Dr. McKee spoke of you often and how much he enjoyed working with you and your company."

"It was a professional privilege; he was such a gifted scientist." Victor studied Dr. Sethna's face; her gaze was focused downward. "I am so sorry for your loss, and I can't even imagine what his wife and kids must be going through."

"It's a huge loss for them, our department, and science," Dr. Sethna said. "He was very close to a major breakthrough that would have opened up the floodgates for so many more patients to get a transplant; to lose him now . . ." She sighed heavily. "So what can I do for you today, Mr. Botsworth?"

Time to turn on the charm, he thought.

"First, please call me Victor," he said warmly. "I believe you and I met several years ago—in Rome, at the International Immunology meeting. You presented your paper on bioelectric stimulation for specific kidney proteins, if I remember it correctly."

"Good memory, Victor, thank you."

"It was an excellent study. And your New Kids on the Block number at the karaoke welcome party that first night—you could have a career as a singer, if I may say. I also follow you on Twitter; @newkidneysontheblock—very clever."

He hoped this was enough softening up to get her to give him what he'd come for. He reached into his briefcase and retrieved the protocol file.

"As I'm sure you know, we were completing a tolerance study with all four doctors' medical centers when the accident happened. We were supposed to discuss their findings that very afternoon." He handed Dr. Sethna the summary document with all the center names, numbers of enrollees, and preliminary findings. "As you can see, all the centers maxed out their enrollment."

Victor watched Dr. Sethna's eyes taking in the outcomes as she quickly flipped the pages. She sat straight up and leaned forward. "I appreciate your dedication to this project, Victor. Regrettably, I'm not able to discuss anything else with you at this time due to the fact that it's part of an active FBI investigation."

Dr. Sethna handed Victor back the protocol summary, stood up, and walked toward her closed office door. "We do appreciate the close relationship we continue to have with your company, and hope to participate in more studies once authorities get to the bottom of this sad event."

Victor placed the protocols back in his briefcase and followed Dr. Sethna out. Several doctors in white lab coats, in addition to several formally dressed corporate-looking people, were seated in the waiting area just outside her door. Dennis handed her a pile of phone messages and said, "The FBI is here. I told them you were booked for the day but they insisted on waiting."

Victor put his hand out. "Thanks for your time Dr. Sethna."

She shook his hand. "Thank you, Victor. Let's hope we get to the bottom of this soon."

• • •

Just as he pushed the elevator's down button, he heard someone calling his name. He turned around to find one of the business suits he'd seen in Dr. Sethna's waiting room—a short woman with mousy brown hair—speed-walking toward him.

She held out her hand. "Hi Mr. Botsworth, Allison Wesley from the FBI. You were on our list to contact today, how lucky are we to run into you here. Do you have a few minutes to chat with me and my associate?"

Victor's briefcase started buzzing. "Nice to meet you, Allison. Unfortunately I am running to another meeting, so now's not a good time." The phone kept buzzing. "I really need to take this call." He dug the burner phone out of the briefcase and answered, "This is Victor."

Allison didn't move; Victor saw her stare at the phone in his hand and then back at him.

"I'll call you right back, Dr. Black." Victor ended the call and got in the elevator.

Unsurprisingly, Allison followed him inside.

"I am so sorry," he said, "I am just jammed today." He held out his card. "Call my assistant, she does my schedule."

Allison took the card. "I've already spoken to Valerie. She said you're unavailable until next week. This can't wait till next week, I'm afraid."

The elevator doors opened on the first floor and they exited. Victor walked briskly toward the lobby.

"We are on a short timeframe to investigate this case," Allison said, keeping pace with him. "We need to speak with you today."

"I'm late for my next appointment," Victor said. "But how about we meet later—say five tonight? I'm staying at the Fairmont."

"My partner and I will be in the lobby of your hotel at five. We just have a few questions. Thanks for fitting us in." Allison turned around and headed back into the medical center.

As soon as she was out of hearing range, Victor dialed Angelo back, who picked up right away.

"Who da hell is Dr. Black?"

"Listen," Victor snapped, "you better have something for me. Things are heating up and I have the FBI on my ass. They were standing there when you called and saw me answer the burner cell—not good."

"How the fuck was I supposed to know where you were? I'm not a fucking mind reader." Angelo coughed. "Anyway, I got some good news and some other news."

"I need good news—and make it fast." Victor was ready for a stiff drink and it wasn't even noon.

"The brakes on the car were tampered with, so whoever goes down on this it's first-degree murder—four counts. They found prints and they're running them through the system, should hear as soon as they find something. Turns out our friend on the inside of Chicago PD knows the detective the NIH hired, Klein, and she's sharing her updates. Not only is the FBI involved but now DOD has skin in the game, they hired their own investigator."

Victor heard the click of a lighter, and then the unmistakable sound of a smoker's exhale. *What I wouldn't do for a cigarette*, he thought. He'd quit a year earlier, but right now it was hard to remember why.

"Refresh my memory—DOD?" he asked, peering down at his watch. "I'm going to be late for my next meeting so make this fast." Dr. Bower was a stickler for promptness; he didn't want to keep him waiting. He needed him on his side in all this.

"Department of Defense. Seems they've been studying

whatever the fuck those dead doctors were studying. I'm working on the name of their guy, but clearly they will have access to more sophisticated systems—satellite footage from before the accident, and more. Word is that the White House wants this story buried, out of the news, so the spotlight goes back on them."

"Keep me posted; as soon as you have something, call. And send me a new burner phone; the FBI could be listening to us right now, for all we know."

"Doubt it—but fine, take out the chip and throw that phone away as soon as we hang up. I'll send you another."

Angelo ended the call.

• • •

Victor arrived at Dr. Bower's office with seconds to spare. Bower's assistant greeted him with her warm smile. "He's inside. So you know, he has a hard stop in twenty minutes."

"Understood." Victor nodded at her and then walked into Bower's office and closed the door behind him. "Thanks for seeing me, I know you're jammed." He sat down across from Bower and waited for him to finish whatever it was that he was doing on his computer.

After a long pause, Bower looked up from his screen. "There seem to be a lot of investigations going on around Dr. McKee and his colleagues' deaths, so if you can shed any light on what you know, that would be helpful. We don't have time for investigations, as you can appreciate."

"I know how busy everyone is, of course," Victor said. "Unfortunately, I don't know much about the various investigations underway. I did meet with Dr. Sethna just now and was able to show her the same results I shared with you over dinner the other night, however. Even though the NIH has put everything on hold, we could officially close the study with what we had before the car accident; between the four programs, we have more than enough patients enrolled."

Doing things this way would eliminate some of the deaths and adverse side effects so the study results would look better—eliminate those patients who hadn't completed the study.

"Dr. Sethna was . . . reluctant to share any information with me, given the circumstances, but is there any way you can make that decision since technically they're your patients?" Victor knew it was extremely unethical to even bring this up; there was a strict protocol on how research studies were approved and completed by all academic centers. "I know it's a big ask, but if we wait until all these investigations are over, we'll lose valuable time."

Dr. Bower glared at Victor. "That would be political suicide! You know as well as I do that our Institutional Review Board prohibits us from interfering with any ongoing studies unless the primary investigator petitions them for an emergency review. Since Dr. McKee is dead and Dr. Sethna is not interested, that's a firm no from me. Frankly, I'm a little alarmed you're asking; you know the rules."

"Believe me," Victor said hastily, "this was the last thing I wanted to ask you. I'm just getting a lot of pressure from our board. I agreed to bring up the issue with you, but I knew what the answer would be and I totally accept where you're coming from." Victor stood up to leave. "Thanks for your time."

Dr. Bower seemed appeased by the apology. "Crazy times with all these investigations," he said in a friendlier tone. "And I thought CMS and UNOS site inspections were bad." He stood and shook Victor's hand. "Do let me know if you hear anything."

"Will do."

Victor opened the door to find Allison Wesley and her partner sitting in the waiting area. With a curt nod in the agents' direction, he quickly left the office and hailed a cab outside.

Once he was in the cab, he took a roll of antacids out of his brief case. He unpeeled them and popped the whole lot in his mouth.

Chapter 12

"Where are we going? Come on, give me a hint. Please?" Sarah looked at Handsome who was grinning from ear to ear. "Must be really good with that smile." She kissed his cheek, then assessed the landscape as they drove. "We're heading south, toward Miami. We usually go the opposite direction to your place."

Handsome shook his head and chuckled. "Not telling." He cocked his head and shot her a sideways glance. "What was Jackie talking about when we dropped her off at the airport? I have good hearing, you know. Something about how you should tell me something? Tell me what's going on and maybe I'll give you the first letter of where we staying."

"Deal. I did take a few pages from Dr. Lopez's research study; his data is clear that patients are dying from this tolerance protocol, and I really need to understand it before I decide if—and that's a big if—I'll show Bower. Lopez got the protocol and drugs under the radar and now all doctors he worked with are dead and this Botsworth guy from Lago pharmaceuticals has threatened him to keep his mouth shut or he'll tell the Cuban government what he was doing."

Sarah lowered her window and took in the crystal blue ocean, the sound of the waves gently touching the sandy beach, the salty sea air.

"I know you're aware that taking those papers out of Cuba put you and Jackie in harm's way. You're lucky you weren't discovered." Handsome shook his head slowly. "Sarah, you promised me your days of sleuthing were over. We have so much to look forward to, and I don't want anything to get in our way—God knows it took us long enough to get here."

Sarah kept her gaze on the water. "Dr. Lopez was desperate; he just wants Bower to know his outcomes so more patients don't die unnecessarily."

Handsome's tone got serious. "Sarah—I almost lost you last year. We are never going there again. I want us to create a calm, wonderful life together."

Sarah sighed. "And I want the same thing, you have to know that. I just feel so bad for Dr. Lopez—and, honestly, I'm concerned for our patients too."

"Dr. Bower is smart enough to know where Dr. McKee was in his research before he died. You told me the research teams updated faculty every month. Didn't you attend those meetings?"

"I missed every one of those meetings; they were at seven in the morning on Fridays, and they all coincided with my trips out here to see you. So I have no idea what the status of the study was before Dr. McKee's death." The more Sarah took in the ocean air, the calmer she felt. "But of course you're right. I'll let it go." Suddenly, she felt a wave of excitement. "Okay, I told you what was going on—now spill! Where are you taking me so I can have my way with you?"

"It starts with an 'A,'" Handsome said. "I'd never heard of it, but Campos and Bishop raved about it." Handsome took the next exit.

"I don't have a clue what it could be, but if they loved it I know it will be amazing." Sarah held her left hand out the truck window so the sun would cause her new engagement diamond to sparkle. "Never in a million years did I imagine wearing an engagement ring and getting married."

Handsome glanced over at her and grinned. "I've never been happier, Sarah." He reached over and rested his right hand on her thigh. Her body tingled—and as they drove through gilded wrought-iron gates onto a cobblestone street that curved to reveal a domed cupola with robust fountains bookending a Greek statue. Her eyes widened.

Handsome turned off the engine as two gentlemen dressed in beige suits with cranberry-colored A's embroidered over their right jacket pockets approached each of their truck doors and opened them in unison.

"Welcome to the Acqualina Resort," the one on Handsome's side said. "You must be Mr. and Mrs. Golden."

Handsome handed him his car keys.

Sarah chuckled and glanced over at Handsome. "Nice touch using my last name instead of yours." She nudged him. "This is seriously a place for the rich and famous."

They walked into the elegantly appointed lobby and approached the beautiful brunette receptionist behind the grand walnut desk.

"Welcome to the Acqualina, Mr. and Mrs. Golden," she said brightly. "We have you down for two nights in the honeymoon suite with an ocean view."

This must be costing him a year's salary, Sarah thought.

They took the elevator up to the fifteenth floor and Handsome opened the door to their suite. They were greeted with a bouquet of yellow roses lightly accented with baby's breath, a bottle of Domaine Carneros Brut Rose, two Waterford crystal glasses already filled with bubbles, and an assortment of fresh fruit, cheeses, and crackers.

"My favorite sparkling wine, all the way from Napa?" Sarah threw herself into Handsome's arms and passionately kissed him.

He scooped her off her feet and carried her into the bedroom. *Never in my wildest dreams*, she thought, barely noticing the gorgeous ocean view, as his light touch sent shivers through her.

Handsome slowly disrobed her and then they made their way on to the bed, soft sheets brushing against her skin as if someone was lightly touching her with a feather.

The next two hours were bliss the likes of which Sarah had never known.

• • •

Sarah looked up. Handsome was gazing at her as she lay on her back with a smile her face could barely accommodate.

"I love you, Sarah Golden," he said. "I have never loved anyone more." He gave her a long, sweet kiss. "You ready for a glass of champagne, my fiancée?"

"Yes please, my love." She put her left hand up and looked at the only thing she was wearing—her sparkling diamond. "We're engaged!"

Handsome handed her a glass and rejoined her in bed. "To us, forever and ever," he said, then kissed her.

Bubbles tickled her lips and mouth as she enjoyed her first sip. "I've never been this happy in my whole life," she said. "I want to freeze this moment—make it go really slow so we can savor each morsel of each other."

“That’s the plan, my love.” He reached for the bottle beside the bed and refilled their glasses, then gazed into her eyes. “How would you feel about getting married soon?”

“I already said yes, didn’t I?” Sarah laughed.

“I mean *soon* soon,” Handsome said. “Like . . . next month soon.”

Sarah gaped at him. “Plan a wedding in one month? Are you crazy?”

“Just about you,” Handsome said. “I know we’ll have to do some planning, but I don’t want to spend any more days not married to you than I have to now that I’ve put a ring on your finger, Sarah Golden. What do you say?”

“I say . . . yes, of course,” Sarah said, smiling. “It’s always yes with you.”

• • •

Over the next two days they mostly stayed in their suite. They did make it out for one oceanside candlelight dinner, but aside from that one experience, the only person they saw was the man who delivered their room service.

On their last day they enjoyed a poolside private cabana. Handsome went for a run on the beach while Sarah swam laps. As she toweled off in their cabana, she overheard a man’s voice from a nearby cabana talking tersely to someone on his cell. What got her attention was when he said, “Victor, you have to get this handled or the investors will not be happy and you may be looking for a new job.”

It can’t be that *Victor, can it?* Sarah dismissed the thought, but she still peeked outside to see if she could see who was talking. Just as she poked her head outside, a tall blond man walking past the cabana, his crystal blue eyes pierced through her. *Attractive but scary-looking*, she thought. This was the first time she had thought about Cuba since arriving at the resort, but now she recalled the intensity of Dr. Lopez's plea, and it sent her mind churning.

Several minutes later Handsome entered the cabana soaking wet. "I took a swim in the ocean after my run—so refreshing!" he sighed. "How's my gal?"

"I've never been so relaxed in my life," Sarah said, deciding on the spot not to mention the blond man or Cuba. "I wish I could bottle it up and take a sip every day."

"It's amazing what can happen when we shut out the whole world," Handsome remarked.

"So true," Sarah murmured.

• • •

On their way to the airport, Sarah stared at Handsome as he concentrated on his driving.

"I don't want to go back; can we just live in our suite forever?" She rubbed his neck and watched him grin.

"That's the dream," he said. "Maybe we can at least go back for our honeymoon!"

"Actually," Sarah said, "Jackie and Laura never had a honeymoon, so I was thinking maybe they could join us after we're in Maui for a week. It's always been a dream of Jackie's to go to Hawaii . . ."

"A joint honeymoon? That's a new twist, but I'll consider it."

"We don't have to decide right now," Sarah said, "but you know we'd have a blast with them."

Handsome shot a look at her. "If you promise me that you'll completely drop the Dr. Lopez thing, then maybe."

Sarah sighed. "It was nice to get away from all that, but full disclosure I'm still concerned about Dr. Lopez and his family. I need to figure out a way to get Dr. Bower the results somehow, without exposing the connection to me."

"I'm guessing he'll figure out they came from you, regardless," Handsome said. "Just give them to him and be done with the whole thing."

"Fair enough." Sarah picked at the seat cushion next to her. "I did hear a man on his cell in the one of the cabanas speaking curtly to a guy named Victor," she said, trying to sound casual. "But that's probably a coincidence."

Handsome went rigid. "Sarah—you have to turn that shit off. You can't save everyone, okay?"

"Easy for you to say," Sarah burst out. "You didn't watch Dr. Lopez begging me. He risked his life giving me that information. Those fucking pharma people sent him those trial drugs under the table—that's big-time illegal in the US. They should be held accountable." She sat back with her arms crossed over her chest.

A few minutes passed with neither of them willing to talk. Finally, Handsome broke the silence.

"I agree this all sucks, a lot," he said carefully, "but we have a wedding to plan and a new life to start together. I know you don't want to hear this, babe, but sometimes the bad guys win; believe me, I have a front-row seat to that." He rested his hand on Sarah's. "I love you, Sarah. I just want you to be safe."

Sarah felt her entire body relax under his touch. "I know you do."

Handsome waited a moment, then changed the subject. "I booked my flight out for next weekend," he said, his tone lighter. "I have two days of interviews with the SFPD and Oakland PD, and the Chief from San José called and invited me down there. One way or another, I'll be getting a job in the Bay Area and we'll be looking for a house." He grinned. "Having you sleeping next to me every night, wherever we land, will be wonderful. I'm excited to plan a small wedding, too—maybe at one of the wineries in Sonoma or Napa?"

They talked about possible venues and guests as they made their way to the airport. After Handsome pulled up to curb at the departures area, he grabbed Sarah's bags from the back and moved them on the sidewalk. "You call me as soon as you land—promise?"

"Promise." She held his face with both hands and planted one long, luxurious kiss on his lips. "There's plenty more where that came from."

Warmth flooded her whole body as she took her bags through the airport doors; she knew Handsome was watching her, so she looked over her shoulder and blew him a kiss before the doors shut behind her.

Once she was settled on the plane, she pulled up the movie *Bridesmaids*, ordered a double rum and coke, and laughed her way across country.

I'm the luckiest woman in the world, she thought.

• • •

Sarah arrived at the transplant center at five the next morning; she was still on East Coast time. The office was nice and quiet, since the rest of the transplant staff wouldn't wander in until eight. She unlocked her office door and was welcomed by a thick stack of phone messages and mail. Her voicemail light was blinking away; she set everything down and went to a café on the third floor for a latte and scone.

While she was waiting for her coffee, she felt a light tap on her shoulder.

"Welcome back, Sarah, we missed you." Dr. Bower was in his scrubs, ready for a day in the OR. "How was Cuba?"

"Latte!" the barista called out.

Sarah reached for her coffee as she considered what to say—and what not to say. "It was a blast," she told him. "Jackie and I had so much fun; it's amazing how people can stay so positive amidst the stark poverty. It was everything I hoped for and more. We did go to the Fusterlandia neighborhood you recommended—the tile work and colors were amazing, so thanks for the suggestion!"

"You should thank Dr. Lopez," Dr. Bower said. "He's the one who told me about it. Were you able to see him?"

"We had a nice lunch and tour of his transplant service. What a wonderful man." Sarah gazed downward, thinking, *Not the right time.*

"I wish there was a way we could bring him here to join our team," Dr. Bower said thoughtfully. "He's extremely talented in transplant immunology, he'd be a perfect fit." His eyes clouded. "I'm not sure if you got the news in Cuba, but I assume by now you've heard the horrible news about Dr. McKee?"

"Actually, Dr. Lopez shared that with me when I saw him," Sarah said. "He seemed quite devastated. You may want to give him a call, he has such high regard for you."

"Maybe I will." Dr. Bower nodded. "I'm hearing that it could have been foul play; at this point everyone and their brother is involved, from the Chicago PD to the FBI." He gestured toward the elevator, and Sarah fell into stride beside him. "It's been stressful for our staff," he continued, "and now we have the FBI demanding we meet with them, like we know anything."

They stepped onto the elevator.

"How's Dr. McKee's family doing?" Sarah asked. "I know you socialized with them."

"The kids are still in shock and Betsy, his wife, has been emotionally paralyzed. Who plans for this kind of thing?" Bower's voice was gruff with sadness. "You need to meet with his research nurses first thing, by the way; they are drowning in the paperwork required to tie up all the loose ends of the study."

The elevator doors opened on the sixth floor, where the

ORs were, and Dr. Bower exited, and then put his hand on the doors to keep them open. "Oh, and I need you to call Lago, the drug company. The CEO, Victor Botsworth, is in town and I need you to meet with him as soon as possible."

Victor Botsworth? Sarah did her best not to react visibly to the name.

"Pull up the email from me, it's got the information you need, including his contact information. I'll be in the OR all day—we're doing a living related liver transplant and then two kidney transplants—but come find me if you need me. And Sarah . . . no more trips to Miami for a while. I need you to get this place buzzing."

"Roger that, Dr. Bower," Sarah said.

The elevator doors closed, leaving her alone, and she shook her head. "Jumping right back into the chaos," she said out loud.

• • •

Back in her office, Sarah closed the door and started to sort through all the emails in her inbox—there were only *five hundred*. She was confident every one of them needed an immediate answer. Her cell phone rang and she looked down. Handsome.

"Hi love," she answered, smiling goofily.

"Hello you," he said, "I miss you something bad. How's reentry?"

"Usual chaos du jour," she said. "Already saw Bower and he was clear that there can be no more travel for me for a while, so it's good you'll be coming my way—my fiancé." She held her left hand out and admired her engagement ring. "Send me your flight information so I have something to look forward to."

A knock at Sarah's door made her jump a little in her seat. "I need to go, they know I'm here," she whispered. "Call me tonight!"

"Will do," Handsome said. "Take it easy today; everyone will want a piece of you now that you're back, and I want some of you left when I get there. I love you."

"I love you too."

• • •

When Sarah opened her office door, a distinguished-looking man in an expensive suit was standing there.

"Hello, I'm Victor Botsworth from Lago—Sarah Golden, yes?"

Sarah nodded.

"Dr. Bower texted me that you're back and encouraged me to see you before all hell breaks loose for you," he said. "Okay if I come in?"

Sarah stood and stared at him for a moment, thinking, *So this is the asshole who sent Dr. Lopez the drugs*. She faked a smile. "Come on in, Mr. Botsworth, have a seat," she said. "I don't have much time, as I need to catch up on all my emails and then start back-to-back meetings at eight . . . so what can I do for you?" Sarah intentionally gave her visitor half her attention as she resumed her seat at her desk and watched as the number of emails in her inbox escalated.

"First, it's nice to finally meet you—and please, call me Victor," he said warmly. "Dr. Bower speaks so highly of you and your work. I understand you just returned from Cuba; I hope the trip was enjoyable." He leaned back in his chair. "I understand from Dr. Bower you and I will be working together with your research nurses on closing out Dr. McKee's studies."

Sarah ignored his question about Cuba. "Dr. Bower did mention I needed to contact you but I can see you are right here, so that's one thing I can take off my plate. I'm not sure how much help I can be; the research coordinators reported directly to Dr. McKee. I do their performance reviews but that's it." She turned to her computer screen; the email numbers had leveled off at nine hundred. "Looks like I have a few emails to answer. Why don't I speak with Dr. Bower when he's out of surgery later today and then I'll give you a call?" She stood up and walked toward her office door.

Victor stood and followed her. "Here's my business card," he said, pressing it into her hand. "I'll be staying at the Fairmont all week; please don't hesitate to reach out. I had a wonderful lunch with your colleagues Debbie and Chris earlier this week. Seems they're a bit overwhelmed right now, but they're very loyal—I tried to steal them away to our company and they weren't even remotely interested. Great gals."

"You could never match the salary and benefits package they get here, but nice try," Sarah said, jaw clenched. "Say . . . do you know a Dr. Lopez, a transplant doctor who works in Cuba?"

Sarah watched Victor's jawline tighten and lips purse. Just then, her desk phone started to ring. "Sorry," she said lightly, "I need to get this." She waved Victor out, closed her office door, and picked up the phone. "This is Sarah Golden."

"Hi Sarah," a brisk female voice said. "My name is Nixie Klein, I'm working with the NIH to investigate the tragic car accident that took place in Chicago last week. Can I have a few minutes of your time? It's regarding Dr. McKee's research. Dr. Bower directed me your way."

Chapter 13

After a long cross-country flight from Miami to San Francisco, Jackie got home, walked through the front door, threw her suitcase on the couch, and threw her arms around Wyatt.

"Missed you so much, Mama," he said. "Did you have a great time in Cuba?"

A small dog ran up to Jackie and started to bark.

"Who's this?" she asked. "Are we dog sitting?"

Wyatt grinned. "He's our new dog, Mama! We wanted to surprise you; he's a rescue dog." He stuck out his lower lip. "They were going to kill him if somebody didn't adopt him."

Jackie bent down and the pup came right up to her and licked her face. Even though she wasn't much of a dog person, she couldn't resist his charm. "He is cute," she said, laughing. "What kind is he?"

Jackie looked up and saw Laura standing behind Wyatt. "He's a mutt," she said. "Part terrier, part dachshund, and who knows what else."

"He's a good dog, Mama, goes to the bathroom outside and everything." Wyatt's big brown eyes studied Jackie's face.

"My transplant doctor said it was okay to get a dog since I'm doing so good."

Laura had always wanted a dog. Jackie looked at her. "Did we name him already?"

"His name is Dusty, Mama, and he is real smart!" Wyatt proceeded to have him sit, give him his paw, and fetch a small ball.

"Very impressive!" Jackie said. "And are you going to help walk him and clean up after him, Wyatt?"

"Yes I am!" he exclaimed. "I promise! Mom made me sign something at the shelter before she'd let me bring him home; he's going to be one of my Boy Scout projects."

Jackie stood up, shaking her head. "Wow, I'm gone ten days and I come home to a new dog. Welcome to our family, Dusty. I better stay close to home or next time there will be an elephant in the front yard!"

They all laughed. Jackie hugged Wyatt.

"I sure missed you, buddy. You look terrific; I think you got taller."

"I got a 100 percent on my check-up with my transplant doctor—she said if she could she would give me an A+, *and* she said maybe if I keep doing this good, maybe someday I won't have to take any drugs anymore."

"That's amazing!" Jackie gave him another hug and a kiss on his forehead as Laura stood behind him, waiting her turn. Wyatt hugged her back then ran back to his video game.

As Dusty followed him, tail wagging, Jackie and Laura embraced and enjoyed a long kiss.

"I missed you, honey," Laura said. "But I'm glad you got some girlfriend time with Sarah."

"I missed you too, but Cuba was amazing—so many stories to tell." Jackie lowered her voice. "So is Wyatt becoming tolerant of his kidney?"

"Aren't we up on immunology, Miss Smarty Pants!" Laura nudged her. "Is our Sarah teaching you all about tolerance?"

"You know it!" Jackie said.

Laura laughed. "Well we're not quite to tolerance yet, but things are looking great. They were actually able to lower his anti-rejection drugs based on this last visit—so exciting. By the way," she added, "I made reservations at our favorite steak place for tonight, Mom's going to feed Wyatt. I don't know if you remember this, but I'm leaving tomorrow for a conference, so tonight's our only chance to get some alone time till I get back from that."

Jackie smacked her forehead. "The conference! I had totally forgotten. Well, we'll have to make the most of tonight, won't we?" She winked at her wife.

Grandma popped her head out of the kitchen. "Welcome home, Jackie! Looks like you got some sun, and you look rested too. Nice to see you home safe and sound."

"I did!" Jackie strode over to give her a quick hug. "It was quite a trip. Thanks for helping Laura hold down the fort."

"My pleasure. I can't wait to hear about your trip, but it looks like you have a hot date, so we'll catch up later." Grandma threw her own wink Jackie's way, then went back into the kitchen.

Jackie and Laura grinned at each other.

"I'll run upstairs to take a quick shower and change," Jackie said. "Then I'll be ready for that hot date!"

• • •

While getting dressed, Jackie reflected on all she and Laura had been through in their time together. Over a year had passed now since Laura had cheated on her and Jackie thought their marriage was over—but they had both rolled up their sleeves, and it was incredible where they were now. They'd gone to therapy and committed to making time for their relationship; Laura had negotiated for more support at work, so that even after being promoted again she was still doing a thousand times better at balancing her job with their home life. Jackie felt like they were closer than they had ever been—so much so that they were considering having another kid or possibly taking in a foster child.

She was still thinking about all this as they got in the car to head to the restaurant—until, suddenly, she remembered all the excitement in Miami.

Jackie looked over at her wife. "Can you believe Handsome proposed at Maria's house? They're getting married! I'm so excited I can't stand it."

"It's about damn time those two got over themselves and made a commitment," Laura said. "I'm so happy for Sarah, it's been a long time."

"Damn right," Jackie said.

• • •

Over a nice long dinner, Jackie shared all the news about the trip.

"You should see the rock he gave her," she crowed, "it's a huge, pear-shaped diamond ring. Golden is finally letting her guard down . . . I am *so* happy for her!"

"That's amazing! I can see the bachelorette party now . . . oh Lord help us all." Laura rolled her eyes.

After telling the story of her getting on stage and singing "Bésame Mucho" ("and bringing down the house, thank you very much!"), Jackie recapped the crazy scene with Dr. Lopez and then, after reassuring Laura that it was nothing to worry about, said, "I'm curious now—what do you know about inducing tolerance?"

"Well!" Laura said, rubbing her hands together. She went on to explain that there was an old study back in the early eighties where they'd determined that one should avoid giving dialysis patients any blood for fear of sensitizing them against a kidney. Then Sarah's program turned that idea on its head when they started donor-specific transfusions and discovered that giving patients blood from their living donor actually made the kidney last longer.

"It was a big deal back in the day but I don't know what the latest updates are," Laura admitted. "But I'm going to do some homework, especially since Wyatt may be developing tolerance."

Jackie beamed. "Our little overachiever."

"Meanwhile, we've gotten several calls from some law firms and medical private investigating firms interested in interviewing you, my undercover agent!" Laura leaned across the table and gave Jackie a kiss. "You're already in demand—proud of you, honey."

Jackie flushed pink with satisfaction "Thanks babe. I'm excited to find the right firm. Those Cuban PIs were not very respectful when I told them I was a PI."

Laura frowned. "Why would you be talking to Cuban PIs? Please don't tell me you and Sarah got into some kind of trouble. We're not going there again, are we?"

"Nope!" Jackie threw her hands up in surrender. "Done with all that stuff—I promise!"

• • •

Jackie saw Laura off early Monday morning, then got Wyatt ready for school. As she drove him there, she caught a glimpse of him and Dusty nestled together in the backseat.

"You look like you found your best friend there," she said.

"I love him so much, Mama." Wyatt put his arms around Dusty, who reciprocated with several big licks on Wyatt's face. "Can I bring some friends over after school? Grandma said she'd make us Rice Krispies Treats."

"If Grandma said it's okay, it's okay with me." Jackie fake wagged her finger at him. "Promise you'll walk Dusty, not Grandma, though."

"Promise, Mama."

• • •

With Laura and Sarah both out of town, Jackie had a couple of low-key days at home, hanging out with Wyatt when he was around, and doing some research on the firms she was set to have interviews with later in the week when he wasn't.

Sarah called Wednesday morning, just after Jackie dropped Wyatt at school.

"Hey girlfriend," Jackie answered, "how's the first day back at the plant? Missing me already?"

Dusty started barking.

"Is that a dog I hear?" Sarah asked.

"Yup, that's Dusty—they went and got a rescue dog while I was gone."

"A dog? You hate dogs!"

"Well, Golden, the deed is done. At least he's cute and well-behaved." Jackie shook her head. "Anyway, we have bigger fish to fry—have you heard anything from Dr. Lopez?" Dusty jumped in her lap and licked her nose. "And did you give Bower the study results you stole?"

"No and no, but the head of the pharma who sicced those Cuban detectives on us came by my office early this morning," Sarah said. "He's slimy as hell . . . and of course I have to work with him on closing out the study. I'm going to need my private investigator on the case."

"I'm here for you," Jackie said. "But first . . . tell me about your secret getaway! Where did he take you!?"

"Just check out the Acqualina resort in Miami," Sarah said. "I'll share the details when I see you. It was the most luxurious place I have ever been to. Handsome outdid himself."

"I can't wait to hear everything. I'm heading into the city for a few informational job interviews after I drop this pooch at home, so I can meet you somewhere afterwards to talk about all this. I do have one quick question for you now, though: Who are the possible suspects for our dead doctors? I'm thinking pharma and NIH, and then I always have a third, 'unknown' category. What are you thinking?"

"It could absolutely be either of the above, but it could also be someone we're not even thinking about," Sarah said slowly. "Most, if not all of the transplant folks want tolerance—it's the dream—so I'm guessing no one inside the clinical programs. Believe me, I've been racking my brain since I got back." She heaved a sigh. "Hey, I have to run to my fifth meeting today—text me when you're done with your interviews and I'll see if I can meet you for a drink. A day without Jackie and a Cuba libre is a day without fun. In the meantime, can you do me a favor and try to get a hold of Benita? I'm worried about Dr. Lopez and his family. I want to know if they're okay."

"You got it. Take it easy; I'll talk to you later."

"Good luck at your interviews—can't wait to hear about them!" Sarah said quickly before ending the call.

• • •

Jackie's first interview was scheduled at the Hyatt Regency off the Embarcadero. As she approached the lobby bar, a tall, slender woman in a tight skirt and blazer stood up. Jackie immediately recognized her from her photo on the company's website. She made straight for her.

"I'm Mindy Press," the woman said as Jackie approached. "You must be Jackie Larsen." She towered over Jackie.

Jackie looked up and made eye contact. "That's me."

Mindy directed Jackie to sit down next to her and pulled out a leather portfolio. "Thanks for sending your resume—though to be honest, it seems you have no experience of note here." She skimmed the one-page document. "Our law firm deals with very exclusive clientele in the sports world—sometimes athletes and trainers themselves, sometimes their spouses. Privacy and confidentiality are imperative. Let's just say that some marriages should never have happened and we need someone who can fade into the background and follow a cheating spouse so that we can get our client the best settlement possible."

Sports figures sound good, that would be fun, Jackie thought. "I do have some experience," she said, "but it's in solving murder cases—though of course I did that with help from a few of my friends. However, I would hope that you and your firm could train me in your ways. I'm a quick learner, I can tell you that."

Mindy closed her portfolio. "We have six PIs working for us now but we just got an influx of divorce cases, so we need someone who is ready to hit the ground immediately. You make a good point about training; we do have specific protocols regarding how we acquire evidence, so we can ensure everything we learn will hold up in court if the case goes that far. Although ours are usually settled in our conference room—amicably, for the most part."

"Well, Mindy, your firm does sound interesting," Jackie said. "I have several other informational interviews today. My family life is my highest priority, so if that's not something you and your firm value, we may not be a good fit. That said, I am a very hardworking woman and I would give you a hundred percent during my working hours." *But I'm not wearing any of the fancy clothes or high heels, that's for damn sure.* "Is there, um . . . a dress code?"

Mindy laughed. "Whatever helps you blend in."

"Excellent," Jackie said.

Mindy stood up, put her hand out, and shook Jackie's. "I appreciate your candor today. I'll update my staff about our visit here, and we'll discuss your candidacy further. Nice to meet you, Jackie."

• • •

Jackie met with a variety of firms that day. One was a medical firm that wanted her to take photos of people who were suing for fake disability, a job that would require her to sit in the back of a van for hours on end. Several workers' compensation firms that required a great deal of paperwork and computer time. None of them appealed.

It was after six when she got back to the parking lot and texted Sarah: *I know you're still at the plant, I'll be by in fifteen.*

Sarah responded with a thumbs up.

Jackie quickly checked her email and saw that Benita had responded to her message from earlier in the day.

"Dr. Lopez and his family are nowhere to be found," she'd written. "I won't be able to communicate with you or Sarah any longer. Our emails are being monitored."

Chapter 14

Victor paced back and forth in his penthouse suite. "I hear you, Leland. I know this is a delicate situation. I'll take care of things. There will be no loose ends, I promise."

Victor remembered when he and Leland were in their MBA program at University of Chicago and they went on a field trip to listen to an esteemed group of venture capitalists. They both walked away with their mouths watering, thinking about all the money they could make and what they'd do with it. Leland had finished his medical training and passed his boards, only to decide not to practice medicine, before going to business school. With his stellar credentials, he was hired by SEA—Science Enterprise Associates, the top bio-tech and pharma venture capitalist firm in the world, worth over ten billion dollars—as soon as he finished the program. As would be the case at any venture capital firm, it was Leland's job to ensure that his investors made huge profits—and when they made money, so did he, which provided him with every imaginable luxury.

"Are you listening to me, buddy?" Leland's tone was concerned. "The investors have risked a lot of money on this new drug your company is researching. If it's not going to happen, they need to know sooner rather than later so they can sell their Lago stock while it's still high. I can buy you some time, but you have to get this cleaned up, and fast. I'm here for you—anything you need, just call."

"Thanks," Victor said. "I may need your help with encouraging a few people to mind their own business—keep you posted there." He checked his watch. "Look, man, I've gotta go. I have a meeting downstairs." He was not about to mention that the meeting was with the FBI; Leland wouldn't like that one bit.

"Have some fun," Leland said. "I hope you get lucky tonight. That always cheers you up."

Victor allowed himself a smug smile. "You got that right."

"Keep me posted," Leland said. "The more communication the better until this all disappears."

• • •

Before heading downstairs, Victor had just enough time to take a quick shower, during which he reviewed the last two days he had spent at the transplant center. He'd known he disliked Sarah Golden from the moment he'd set eyes on her—not bad-looking, but when she'd mentioned Dr. Lopez her glare had pierced right through him. He was almost positive that she knew what had happened in Cuba and maybe even had evidence to prove it, even though his Cuban spies said it was all cleaned up.

He dried off, wrapped his towel around his trim waist, and sized himself up in the full-length mirror before him. Keeping up with his early-morning fitness regimen had really paid off. *Not bad for a forty-five-year-old*, he thought.

His cell phone started ringing. He glanced at the caller ID. Valerie.

"Hi boss, how you doing?"

Victor grunted.

"I know that grunt. I can only imagine. I've been fielding lots of phone calls from the FBI and the NIH. Did Leland get in touch with you?"

"He sure did, just hung up."

"He was really pushing me for information about exactly what you were doing in San Francisco. I told him to get all the details from you. Did you see I got your FBI meeting moved till six tonight, and then you're meeting that research nurse from the transplant center in the bar just afterward? I think she may be reconsidering your job offer. She was asking me all these questions about Lago and if I liked working here."

"Do me a favor," Victor said, smelling blood in the water. "Keep in close touch with her, like you're becoming best friends. I may need you to get some inside information from her about the study. So far I've been hitting a brick wall when I ask anyone for an update on the outcomes. I'll work my magic on her tonight too; between the two of us, we'll get her to talk."

"Absolutely," Valerie said. "FYI, I did get a call from Legal today and they said to direct all inquiries from anyone around our tolerance study to them. I did tell them that you were meeting with the FBI this evening and they seemed fine with that. You know the drill: Don't answer any direct questions, be friendly, and always wave the confidentiality flag."

"Got it," Victor said. "Well, since we all have to sign confidentiality agreements with all the research institutions, that won't be hard to deflect. Worst-case scenario we'll just lawyer up and smother them with paper. That will slow them down. The show must go on, and we have lots of patients depending on us to get them transplanted safely."

"They should pay you to do a commercial." Valerie giggled. "I'll text you if I hear from anyone else. Oh, I almost forgot—our regional manager in Chicago wants to update you on their tolerance study data. Seems his Chicago programs had better outcomes than most, so we may be able to make that our lead when we go out with our press release."

"Great idea. Set up a call with her for tomorrow so I can hear firsthand."

"Done and done. Take care, and try to enjoy yourself."

"I will. You're the best." Victor hung up.

• • •

The two FBI agents were sitting in cozy chairs in the lobby when Victor came down. Before they could suggest moving, he sat down across from them. He wanted this over with.

"I appreciate your both being so flexible. What can I do for you? I have another meeting in thirty minutes." He made a show of checking his watch.

Allison, the female agent who had chased him down at the transplant center, began.

"As I'm sure you are well aware, it has been confirmed that the car accident that took the lives of four immunologists in Chicago last week was intentional."

"I don't believe I had heard that it was confirmed—but then, you would know better than I," Victor said. "And I must tell you how deeply saddened the transplant community, myself included, is about this huge loss."

"What can you share about the studies your name—or, rather, Lago's name—is attached to?" Allison asked. "We have spoken to Dr. Bower and all the other transplant chiefs at the four medical centers, and all of them have pointed to you as a resource they trust and who would be able to explain what these scientists were doing before they were murdered."

"Murdered!" Victor gaped at her. "That's a strong term. I can assure you that I had absolutely no knowledge about specifically what they were doing before this horrible event occurred."

Allison sat back in her chair and crossed her long, slender legs, which Victor scanned while she gave him the silent treatment.

"As CEO of Lago, my name is on every study we do—but that doesn't necessarily mean I know each one intimately. Though I wish I could, believe me." He widened his eyes, trying for a sincere look. "We are so fortunate to be involved in so many groundbreaking studies that change lives every day."

Allison continued to push. "Tell us what you know about the scientists. We know you and your research team met with them on a regular basis."

"They were hardworking, dedicated, passionate people who were on a path to making transplants available to all those waiting for new organs—without being subjected to the side effects of the anti-rejection drugs our current transplant patients have to take."

"Wouldn't your company and several others stand to lose billions of dollars if that were to happen?" Allison's male FBI partner jumped in.

"We are a team dedicated to getting more patients transplanted, regardless of what drugs they do or do not use," Victor said smoothly.

"Have you met with the other drug companies who have a huge stake in this game?" the male agent pressed.

Victor glanced again at his watch. "I really must go. Please feel free to contact our legal department with any other questions. I hope you and your team find out who's behind this horrible incident and put them behind bars."

He stood up, as did the agents.

"We will be contacting you again, Mr. Botsworth," Allison declared. "We're meeting with Sarah Golden tomorrow.

Something tells me we may have more questions for you after that."

Victor's stomach tightened. "Ms. Golden certainly seems to have her finger on the pulse of her team. Good evening." He gave a curt nod before walking away.

I can't imagine she would have the nerve to tell them about Dr. Lopez, he thought as he pressed the button to the elevator. *Time to charm my research nurse—I need someone close to Golden to monitor her moves.*

• • •

When Victor entered the bar, he saw Chris sitting at a window table looking out at the San Francisco Bay and illuminated Ferry Building. Walking up beside her, he remarked, "I never get tired of looking at this view; what a beautiful place to live."

Chris turned her head toward him and smiled. Her long brown hair and sweet dimples caught his eye, as did her low-cut blouse, which revealed inviting cleavage. "I agree. I love living here, although it is expensive."

Victor sat down and a server approached their table to take their drink order.

"I'll have a Manhattan with Maker's Mark, please, extra cherries," Chris said.

"I'll have your best bourbon—neat, please," Victor said.

Once they had ordered, Chris launched in.

"Thanks for meeting with me, Victor. I've been giving your kind offer of a possible job with Lago some serious thought. I even spoke to your amazing assistant, Valerie, who FedExed me your annual report. She included several articles recently published in the *New York Times* and the *Atlantic* about the groundbreaking research Lago's doing. I had no idea you were so diversified."

"Yes, our company is on the cutting edge of many life-saving drug studies," Victor said, spreading his hands wide.

"It's a very exciting place to work. I'm very happy to hear that you've given my offer more thought. We can always use research nurses of your caliber at Lago. Can you tell me a little more about your clinical background?"

Over the course of several drinks, Chris shared much about her ten years in clinical research at SF Transplant. After one year of floor nursing on the transplant service, she knew that wasn't for her. When Dr. Bower suggested research, she joined Dr. McKee's team.

She was still talking when their server approached for the fourth time and asked, "Would you like another drink?"

"I'm good." Victor waved her away, then leaned in toward Chris. "If you don't have to get home to your family, I'd love to take you to dinner."

"I'm a single gal, living alone," she said, cheeks flushing. "I'd be delighted to have dinner with you."

"When I had dinner with Dr. Bower he said Mastro's Steakhouse was great," Victor said. "I'll give them a quick call and we can cab over—sound good?"

"Sounds great!" she said. "I love a good ribeye with all the fixings, and with all the hustle bustle about the studies and Sarah just back from her vacation, I forgot to eat lunch today. Things are moving fast with her driving the bus."

"Dr. Bower really does depend on her, doesn't he?" Victor said, keeping his tone casual. "He's probably relieved she can handle all these investigators so he can operate."

"Sarah is his golden girl for sure." Chris laughed. "Golden, get it? Honestly, the rest of us rarely get to speak with him; we have to deal with her first, and she gets to decide if we get to meet with him at all. It makes me crazy, and the other coordinators hate it too. Let's just say she never gets invited to any of our birthday celebrations outside of work."

"That sounds very frustrating," Victor said. "I wouldn't do well with that setup at all." He handed the waitress his card and stood. "Let me just call Mastro's to reserve us a table, and we'll continue this conversation."

• • •

After he and Chris had ordered their meals and a bottle of Italian red, Victor lifted his glass.

"Here's to you closing out that study and hopping on to a new one." He tilted his head. "I know your program always has multiple studies going on."

"Yes," she said slowly. "But I definitely want to speak to you further about a position with Lago. As you can tell, I don't particularly care for working for Sarah—and I'm already vested, so I'm not tied to the job."

"I did have the opportunity to meet Sarah, and she was rather curt with me," Victor said. "Probably too much on her plate."

"No," Chris said quickly. "That's Sarah—all business, no play, at work."

"I know working in the transplant world doesn't really allow folks to have much of a private life," he said. "I've seen it at so many programs—staff burn out."

"Oh Sarah has plenty of private life," Chris said, her face dour. "The past year she's traveled constantly to see her boyfriend in Miami—whenever he's not here visiting her, that is. It's quite the bi-coastal romance. And she just returned from a trip to Cuba, on top of it all." Chris took a sip of wine.

"With her boyfriend?" Victor asked.

"Her best friend from nursing school, Jackie. They're pretty inseparable."

"Cuba—that's certainly an interesting destination." Victor lifted an eyebrow.

Chris shrugged. "I guess they'd been planning it for a while but this time it really happened."

"Where did they go to nursing school?" Victor asked.

"Somewhere in Chicago, I think?" Chris pursed her lips. "I think I remember something about Sarah's grandmother living there? Apparently she helped raise her or something, and they're super close."

Chris dug into her baked potato and ribeye, and Victor allowed the silence for a while as they both enjoyed their meal. Eventually, after ordering a grappa for each of them to close out the meal, he resumed conversation, careful to make it about the potential job.

"Tell me more of what you're looking for at Lago, Chris," he said. "Would you be willing to relocate to New Jersey, where our research hub is located?"

"I would consider relocating if the offer was good enough," she said with a sly smile. "It would be hard to leave the Bay Area, but let's just say I could be bought." Her hand flew to her mouth. "But please don't mention our conversation to anyone at my program! I'm just window shopping at this point."

"Not to worry," he assured her, "this conversation is confidential. The only other person who knows we're talking is Valerie, and she is extremely trustworthy."

Chris relaxed again. "Good to know. I'm truly excited to learn more, and we can go from there. I'll be so relieved when all this FBI and NIH stuff is put to bed. Sarah just got back today, and she's already got me and Debbie on a tight schedule; we have to send her and several other department heads a *daily report* on our progress. Talk about micro-managing."

"Maybe you could give Dr. Bower and the others the updates directly, take something off Sarah's plate," Victor offered. "Do you think she'd be open to that?"

"Not a bad idea," Chris mused. "I'll run the idea by her. She is a bit of a control freak, but I also know her boyfriend is coming into town soon, so she may welcome the offer."

"You sure seem to know a lot about her coming and goings," he said lightly.

"Her assistant is a good friend of mine, so I get all the intel. If Sarah really tries to boss me around, I want to make sure I have some dirt to share with Dr. Bower. She's not perfect, take it from me." She rose from her seat, wobbling a little as she did. "Can you excuse me? I need to use the restroom." She bent over, exposing her ample breasts, and put her hand on Victor's shoulder. "Don't you run away; I'll be right back."

"I'll be waiting for you." He stood up as she walked away. *This is working out better than I would have hoped*, he thought.

• • •

Victor had already paid the bill and was finishing his grappa when Chris returned from the bathroom.

"I must say, Victor, you are such a good listener—and not bad to look at, either," Chris slurred. She kissed his cheek.

"Thanks, Chris," he said. "I've had such a wonderful evening with you; I hope while I'm in town we can do this again."

"I would love that—it'll give me something to look forward to," she said.

He flashed her his most charming smile. "Me too. Now let's get you a cab home, shall we?"

• • •

Back at his suite, Victor got ready for bed. He glanced at his phone as he was about to plug it in to charge, and there was a text from Valerie: *Top three drug companies producing anti-rejection drugs estimated net worth—over 4 billion dollars.*

No wonder Leland is stressed out, he thought. *Those vulture capitalists are making a killing. Time for me to get a bigger piece of that pie.*

His thoughts were interrupted by the ringing of his burner cell.

"It's me," he answered. "Must be late for you . . . What's up?"

"I do my best work in the middle of the night while everyone else is getting their beauty rest," Angelo said. "I'll make this quick. Not good news. Klein, the NIH's investigator, has the FBI focused on you and your drug company buddies. You better be prepared for them to be up your ass. I'm still digging around for other suspects; if it wasn't you and your pals, whoever cut those brake lines left no evidence. The prints they found on the car didn't match any known criminals."

Victor heard Angelo take a long inhale of his cigarette, once again setting off his old nicotine cravings. "Keep digging," he said, "and make it fast, Angelo—there's another ten thousand in this for you if you wrap it up by next week!"

Victor ended the call only to have another phone ring—this time the suite's land line. "Hello," he snapped.

"Mr. Botsworth, your friend Leland sent you a nightcap and it's on the way up."

He felt his eyebrows shoot up in surprise. "Sounds good. Thanks."

Seconds later, there was a quiet knock at his door; he opened it and there before him stood a stunning blonde with legs for days in a short dress and four-inch heels.

"I'm Gina," she purred. "Leland sent me; he said you'd know what to do."

Chapter 15

"Nana, it's so good to hear your voice! I missed speaking with you when I was in Cuba. Did you get my postcard? I sent it from Miami." It was after seven in the evening and Sarah was standing outside of the hospital, waiting for Jackie to pick her up.

"I missed you too, sweetheart. And yes, I got the postcard—so sweet of you to send me something."

"And I'm engaged, Nana!" Sarah bounced a little where she was standing. "I'm so happy."

"Did Handsome tell you he called me before he proposed?" Nana sounded almost breathless with excitement. "He's a keeper, that one."

"Yes, he is." Sarah grinned. "We're planning a fall wedding in wine country, and you better be there."

"I wouldn't miss it for the world. And I can have my plus one, too?"

"Nana, you wild woman." Sarah laughed. "Who are you leading on this time—Frank from your card club, or Dennis from your bowling team?"

"Ha!" Nana scoffed. "They're both too old. It's your Mo. He had me on his comedy radio show last week and we laughed for hours. What a sweet boy he is."

Sarah thought about the last time she'd seen her old boyfriend, just before she went to Florida to try to become Wyatt's living kidney donor. Mo had called Handsome's house many times after Sarah was discharged from the hospital following her near-death incident in Miami.

"Your Mo was not excited to hear about your engagement." Nana clucked her tongue. "I think he still has eyes for you—but it's too late for him, clearly. Still, he's been so sweet; he comes by my house once a week, like the old times when you two were dating. We have tea and I make him mandel bread and give him a tin to take to the radio station for all those hardworking folks there."

"I love that you two are hanging out," Sarah said sincerely. "And sure, he can be your plus one—you cradle robber!" She spotted Jackie pulling up. "Gotta go. Jackie is here. Love you, Bubbe."

"Love you back, my little Sarala. Give Jackie a big hug from me, and you two stay out of trouble!"

"Trouble? Us?" Sarah chuckled. "Love you." She put her cell in her work bag and hopped into Jackie's SUV.

"I was just talking to Nana," she said, leaning in for a quick hug. "She sends her love. Excited about the wedding—and she's been hanging out with Mo."

"Love me some Nana." Jackie's forehead creased. "Mo, huh? How's Handsome feel about that?"

Sarah shrugged. "Hey, Handsome knows I'm all his . . . every part of me. We had the most romantic time ever at the Acqualina resort—you have got to take Laura there, by the way. Best sex in my whole life." Sarah put her hand on her heart.

"That's saying something. I'll look into it when I get my first paycheck," Jackie said as she pulled away from the hospital.

"And we made a big decision while we were there," Sarah said. "We're going to do the wedding next month!"

Jackie's mouth dropped open. "Wait, seriously?"

"He said he can't stand not being married to me a minute longer than is absolutely necessary," Sarah explained, blushing.

"Well, hard to argue with that," Jackie said. "Guess we'd better get planning!"

"No kidding," Sarah said. "But enough about me—how did your interviews go today?" Sarah asked. "Did you knock their socks off? Multiple offers?"

"I do have some fun options to consider."

"Can't wait to hear about them—but the quicker we get to a drink, the better. It's been a hell of day."

"You got it." Jackie picked up the speed a little. "Bad news on the Cuba front: I heard back from Benita. Dr. Lopez and his family are missing and she said she can't email us anymore, as they're monitoring her account."

"Oh shit!" Sarah tensed. "Do you think the Cuban government killed them? I can't imagine they would go that far over a stupid protocol, would they? Maybe I can get Dr. Bower to try to get in touch with him. I'll bet that evil dude Botsworth has something to do with this. He was at my office door at dawn's crack, and when I mentioned Dr. Lopez his face tightened."

"What did he say?" Jackie asked as she maneuvered into a spot in front of the bar.

"He didn't have a chance to answer me; my office phone rang and I closed my door in his face."

"Okay, I need to know everything," Jackie said, throwing the car into park. "But first, drinks and snacks!"

• • •

When their salads and onion rings arrived at the table they both dove into the rings, dipping them in ranch dressing.

"I think he could tell that I knew something," Sarah said around her mouthful of fried onions. "I gave him my most evil glare, he may well have a burn mark in the back of his head. The plant is crazy busy—what else is new. I had back-to-back meetings today. Since the study was officially put on clinical hold by the NIH, Bower just wants it closed out as quickly as possible, but at the rate my research nurses are working . . ." She threw up her hands. "Who knows? I'm going to spend some hands-on time helping them. Maybe I can see if our patients' outcomes are the same as the ones Dr. Lopez shared with me." She rolled her eyes. "Chris and Debbie are not happy about me teaming up with them; I guess they'll have to shorten their two-hour lunches." She took a big sip of her rum and coke.

"Whatever you gotta do, girl, just get it done and behind you," Jackie said. "We have a wedding to plan—and, more importantly, a bachelorette party in the making."

"I can't wait. Only requirement: Handsome made me agree that we'll stay in the United States, just in case there are any arrests. He has lots of friends Stateside, but anywhere else it gets tougher for him to help out."

"I can work with that." Jackie popped another onion ring in her mouth.

"I'm tired of being a manager." Sarah sighed. "Clearly the coordinators are a nine-to-five crowd, so I'm going with that—plus, Dr. Bower was very clear: no more traveling for me. He wants me at work, period. I've been thinking I may want to transition to working a regular staff job—three twelve-hour shifts one week, four the other. No management, it's just a glorified babysitting job."

"That's big," Jackie said, eyes wide. "Would you leave transplant altogether?"

"If I can't get a job on the transplant floor, then yes." Sarah threw up her hands. "I want a normal life. I don't want to feel guilty that I'm not working hard enough or long enough."

"I can't imagine you not working in transplant, it's been your passion for so long . . . but it is a park-your-life-at-the-door job."

"You got that right," Sarah said, looking down at her plate of food. "I want to have time to enjoy planning my wedding and becoming a wife; who knows, I may even have a few rug rats." She looked up and noticed Jackie studying her face. "What are you staring at?"

"*You*," Jackie said. "I've never heard you talk like this before—marriage, kids, the whole shebang. That must have been some getaway; good for you! I can show you the ropes, obviously, but I'm going to tell you now that you're not gonna like some of those soccer parents."

"Who said our children will play sports? I was thinking ballet and classical music lessons."

They both laughed.

"Anyway, spill it—how were the interviews? Who will be the lucky firm to make use of your fine sleuthing skills?"

"Some of those firms were seriously boring." Jackie shook her head. "They wanted me to investigate workers' comp fraud—sit in a white van all day and take photos. No thanks. I really like the first firm I met with, though. They represent very wealthy athletes whose spouses are cheating on them. We're talking NBA and WNBA superstars, tennis pros, baseball players. And I figure if I'm going undercover in the fancy locker rooms, I get to wear a sweat suit, tennis shoes, and a baseball cap. I may not work out, but I can fake it."

"I love it!" Sarah clapped her hands together. "This is perfect for you. When do you start?"

"I don't officially have the job yet, but the office manager called me right before I picked you up, and I could tell she liked me. They want me to shadow their key PI tomorrow, see how I do. Meanwhile, they'll be doing a background check and reference check. I gave them your name, Handsome's, Biker Bob's, and Zuzu's." She glanced at her watch. "Whoops, it's getting late! I need to drop you and head home to see my boy."

• • •

As Jackie pulled her SUV up in front of Sarah's apartment, she said, "I'm excited for you, my friend. Big things are happening for you! But my advice: hold on to the job until the wedding, and then we'll see what's next. Hell, maybe you could get your PI license and join me?"

Sarah laughed and shook her head. "Not going to happen. But I may need you to swing by the Fairmont soon and hang out in the lobby to see what Botsworth's up to—he's staying there, he said. Maybe follow him, see what you can find out regarding Dr. Lopez and his family? He's never seen you unless the Cuban investigators sent him a photo, which I doubt." Sarah opened the car door.

"On it," Jackie said. "Do you have a photo of him you can text me?"

"Just go to the Lago website, you'll see his mug." Sarah wrinkled her nose. "He's a looker and a charmer—at least, he seems to think so. If you do follow him, keep your distance; you're my undercover gal. Meanwhile, I won't be able to escape him; he'll be coming to the plant every morning for our briefings, Bower invited him. I don't think he should be there but there's no changing Bower's mind once he's made it up."

"Happy to do my part," Jackie said.

Sarah gave her a thumbs-up and Jackie drove off.

• • •

Sarah took a long, hot bath when she got home. She was in the kitchen in her pajamas, making herself a cup of calming tea, when her cell rang. "Hello, this is Sarah."

"Oh hey, Sarah, it's Chris from work. So sorry to bother you at home. Do you have a few minutes?"

"Sure." *If I had a nickel every time someone asked me that, I'd be a millionaire*, she thought. *It's never a few minutes.*

"I know we're meeting in the morning for an update but I had a thought I wanted to run by you. Would you like me to lead the morning briefings and communicate them out? I'm very knowledgeable about all the moving parts of the study. I can see how busy you are, so I'm happy to pitch in."

Sarah blinked. This was not what she expected.

"I really appreciate that, Chris," she said. "Why don't you plan on running tomorrow's meeting? I was planning to call in for this one anyway. If it goes well and none of the other team members object, then I'll pass the baton to you completely. Sound good?"

"Sounds great," Chris said, sounding a little surprised.

"You know how to use the database and generate a report, right?"

"With my eyes closed."

"Great, I'll talk to you in the morning then." Sarah felt some of the weight lifting from her shoulders. "You should really think about becoming a manager; you've got the skills, Chris."

"No thanks, that job has no appeal at all." Chris snickered. "I'm glad you're in the driver's seat, I'd kill some of those whiny coordinators in a minute. Say—are you going to Dr. McKee's memorial tomorrow afternoon?"

"Absolutely; actually, I sent out an email a few minutes ago to let everyone know they can leave work for it . . . though of course they'll need to make up the hours."

"Oh, I don't ever check my email after five—I don't think any of the coordinators do—so thanks for the heads-up."

"Of course." Sarah stifled a yawn. "Well you have a good evening, Chris. See you tomorrow."

Sarah ended the call, poured her tea, and called Handsome.

"Hi Mr. Golden," she flirted. "How is my love tonight?"

"Insanely busy and ready to see you, that's for sure. I'm still at work closing out cases before I fly out to you. I'd be even more under water if it weren't for Campos; she's at home recovering now, and she offered to help with paperwork."

"How's she feeling?" Sarah asked.

"Physically she's hurting, but she's off all the pain meds and going to physical therapy. I have a suspicion she may ask for a desk job after this—she's definitely struggling mentally after all this. I don't really think she should be doing any work yet, but she begged me to give her something to take her mind off things, and the chief said okay."

"I can't imagine going back in the line of duty after getting my leg almost blown off by a shotgun." Sarah shivered at the thought. "Give her my best."

"Will do. And I'll see you very soon!"

"I cannot *wait* to see you," Sarah said with a sigh.

"What's on tap for you tomorrow?" Handsome asked.

"I'll be working from home in the morning, then heading to the office for a bit . . . then Dr. McKee's memorial is tomorrow afternoon. It's going to be tough to see his poor wife and kids."

"So sad," Handsome said somberly. "Any news about a possible suspect? Nothing in the newspapers; they really shut that story down faster than usual."

"No clue about suspects," Sarah said, "but we are up to our eyeballs in investigators from the FBI and NIH . . . and of course that jerk CEO from Lago is here on site, making a pest of himself. I've got more work than three people can handle. I may be ready to throw in the towel on this job, babe, it's too much. I want a calm, regular life."

"Well *that's* news," Handsome said. "I know how much you love transplant; I guess I never thought I could get you out of there, even with a crowbar. But I support you no matter what you want to do—you know that, right?"

"I do," Sarah said, butterflies swirling in her stomach. "It means a lot to me to have someone like you to depend on; it's a first time for me. I'm not making any impulsive moves, don't worry; I just wanted to let you know what I was thinking. Jackie thinks I should wait until after our wedding and honeymoon. Be nice to use my vacation time, our Cuba trip barely made a dent in all the days I've accrued."

"Let's talk about it when I get there and can love you up," Handsome said. "Nothing we can't figure out together. For now, you get some rest—you sound exhausted. Love you."

"Love you too." Sarah hung up.

How lucky am I to have such a wonderful man in my life? she reflected, not for the first time, as she shuffled off to bed.

• • •

Sarah joined the early-morning briefing from home. After kicking things off, she informed everyone that Chris was going to lead it going forward. She was pleased to see that Chris did a great job with it.

Sarah went into the office at ten, just in time to run the all-staff meeting. The mood was somber as she called the meeting to order.

"I know many of you will be attending Dr. McKee's memorial today," she began. "I'll be there too, of course. Let's please be sure that there'll be enough staff onsite to care for our patients, however. And I know many of you have noticed we have some visitors from the FBI investigating this tragic event; if you are approached by anyone, please redirect them to me." Sarah noticed a hand up in the back. "Yes, Chris, do you have a question?"

Chris stood up and everyone turned their head in her direction. "Are we safe?" she asked. "If they killed Dr. McKee, how do we know they aren't coming after his research team next?" As she went to sit down, she added, "Whoever 'they' are."

As all heads turned back to the front of the room, Sarah said, "We have no evidence that anyone on our transplant team is in danger—if we did, we would of course let you know immediately. Dr. Bower and I are simply working with our legal department and law enforcement to expedite this investigation. In the meantime, we need you all to keep providing the excellent care you always do; and as always, if you have any concerns, please contact me directly. I'd also like to give a shout-out to our living donor kidney team: they had their best month ever, fifteen transplants!" Sarah initiated applause and the staff followed.

After sharing a few more program updates, Sarah ended the meeting and motioned for her assistant to come forward.

"Would you clear my calendar after the memorial service?" she murmured to her. "I know I was supposed to meet with the FBI and have that call with the NIH investigator, but I'd love to push those out. I've just got too much on my plate right now."

Her assistant nodded and then left the auditorium. Sarah watched as the staff leisurely walked out. *Last year I was up here telling them about a dead coordinator; now we have a dead doctor*, she thought. *What the hell? I just want to take care of transplant patients, not solve murders.*

• • •

Sarah was late leaving the office; she barely made it through the church doors before Mrs. McKee delivered her eulogy.

She grabbed a seat in the last pew as folks shuffled to make room for her. Sniffles could be heard, and she saw folks dabbing at their eyes as the eulogy continued. She was digging for a tissue in her purse when the man next to her handed her one.

"Thank you," she whispered, only look up into Victor Botsworth's eyes.

He gave her a creepy smirk as he lightly touched her hand with the tissue, then leaned over and whispered, "So sorry for your loss. I'd like to have a quick chat with you after the funeral."

Sarah's stomach tightened, and a bitter taste filled her mouth. She left the church before the service ended.

Chapter 16

Jackie got an early start Thursday morning, hoping to avoid city traffic. She had to look hard at all her worn sweatpants before finding one black pair without holes. She paired those with her comfy Women's March T-shirt, then threw on a gray sweatshirt and tennis shoes.

She took a quick glance in their full-length bathroom mirror before heading out. *If this isn't blending in, nothing is.*

She listened to public radio news during her drive. When she heard, "Today San Francisco Global Transplant Institute will mourn the loss of one of their prominent scientists, Dr. Thomas McKee, in a tragic car accident in Chicago. Three other prominent scientists died in the accident, and the FBI has confirmed their deaths were officially a homicide. There are no suspects at this time. Allegedly these four physicians were about to announce the preliminary results of their study on a new drug that could potentially eliminate the need for all other anti-rejection drugs, which experts say could be a game-changer for thousands of potential transplant patients. The NIH is also cooperating with the FBI. This is the second death of a staff member at this prestigious transplant program due to murder, as one of their coordinators was killed last year. The killer was arrested and tried and tried for first degree murder in that case, and is now serving time in prison. Next up, the weather and traffic."

Jackie turned the volume down and called Sarah.

"What the hell, Jack?" she said groggily. "It's five thirty in the morning."

"I'm on the road already, beating the traffic," Jackie said. "Your program is all over the news. They're talking about Dr. McKee's death, and they even referenced Kayla's murder last year. I wanted to check in with you before I turn my phone off, since I'm going to be shadowing PIs all morning. Any updates on the case?"

"Nope, nothing. But ugh, after all this radio coverage I'm sure my email box will be blowing up."

"I can't even imagine—never dull for you, Golden. Guess where I get to do my shadowing?"

"Jack," Sarah whined, "my eyes are hardly open; I haven't had my coffee yet. No quiz show questions."

"Fair enough, I'll just tell you: I'm going to a 7:00 a.m. yoga class at the Bay Club. And no, it's not chair—it's something called 'Vinyasa flow' yoga, whatever that is."

"Jackie, you can't do that class, you won't be able to walk afterwards!" Sarah sounded alarmed. "You may have to think of a different way to observe your suspect; just wet one of those small towels and put it on your forehead like you just finished a cardio class, sit at the juice bar, and wait. I know how you groan when you exert yourself. You're supposed to keep a low profile, remember?"

"Yeah, yeah," Jackie said.

"Can you tell me who the suspect is?" Sarah asked.

"No can do. Highly confidential. I have to go now. I'll call you later."

Sarah yawned. "Okeydoke. Go get 'em."

• • •

When Jackie walked into the lobby of the Bay Club—twenty minutes ahead of schedule—she had a bounce in her step. She'd collected some good intel already, and class hadn't even started yet.

She immediately saw the PI she was assigned to sitting near the entrance, reading a yoga journal. Jackie sauntered past and gave her a slight nod, and then continued toward the registration desk and signed in as a guest of one of the law firm partners.

The chirpy desk clerk had clearly had her share of coffee. "I'll need you to sign this waiver. You're registered for the Vinyasa flow yoga. Have you done yoga before?"

Jackie took in the ninety-pound clerk. "Not *this* type of yoga. Would it be possible to observe first?"

"How about since you're here super early I introduce you to our fabulous yoga instructor, Zen, and you can decide together how you should approach this class."

"That sounds great." Jackie followed her back to the yoga studio, where a svelte woman was preparing the room.

"Good morning, Zen!" the clerk said. "This is Jackie Larsen; she's a guest today, and new to Vinyasa; she wanted to speak with you about your class. I'll leave you two to talk things over."

Chirpy departed and Jackie watched as Zen laid down two yoga mats.

"Why don't you sit down and let me know what type of yoga you have practiced before?" she suggested.

I sure hope I can get back up, Jackie thought as she lowered herself onto one of the mats. "I've mostly tried chair yoga," she volunteered. "I have some videos from the Chopra Center and I just love them."

"The Chopra Center—good for you, Jackie." Zen's voice was gentle, soothing. "However, this is a very active flow class; we do a warm-up and then a lot of sun salutations and other flows. Do you think you're up for something like that?"

"I know how to do those in a chair," Jackie said. "Would that be possible?"

"Why not, since you already know them that way." Zen nodded. "I'll set you up in the back of the room. Just do what you're comfortable with."

More students were coming in now, so Zen quickly got Jackie a chair and directed her to the back of the room, then began greeting her regulars. Jackie saw the other PI take a spot up front and unroll her yoga mat. *All these people must not eat*, she thought as she surveyed the room.

The class began slowly, but things quickly picked up. Jackie stayed in her chair for most of it, though she did try a few downward dogs on the mat, doing her best not to groan. The cheating spouse in question was extremely limber and fit—it was no surprise that most of the men in the room were watching her perfect form and flexibility.

At the end of class, the last pose was savasana, better known as corpse pose; it was Jackie's favorite pose, as it only required her to lie down, relax, and close her eyes. Though not all the way, of course. She kept at least one eye on her target the whole time.

• • •

Thirty minutes after class ended, she met the PI at the designated café.

Martha was sitting in the corner with a steaming cup of tea, checking her cell, when Jackie walked in. Jackie grabbed a cup of black coffee, then joined her.

"Nice to meet you in person, Martha," she said. "Thanks so much for letting me shadow you this morning; not sure if I was much help, but I enjoyed it!"

"Thank you, Jackie, for being so flexible," Martha said warmly. "This certainly was a last-minute request. I appreciate your jumping right in." She cocked her head, eyes focused on Jackie. "Tell me what you observed during your time at the club."

"I noticed our suspect was in her car, parked as far away as you can from the gym, thirty minutes or so before class. Mr. Basketball hopped inside her car for a long good-morning kiss and embrace. Then he got out alone and sauntered inside. She followed about ten minutes later. I gave her a good lead, then followed her into the lobby."

Martha nodded her head in the affirmative. "Notice anything else?"

Jackie paused. "I think they know someone is watching them; it seems like they're being super careful. He kept glancing over his shoulder as he walked through the parking lot, and they made no contact once they each got inside. In fact, I never saw him again after he went inside the club. During class, there were several male yoga students staring at her for sure. Perfect body, face—she's got it all going on. She and the yoga teacher seem to know each other; they chatted after class. She left straight from class, got in her car, and left."

"Anything else?" Martha pushed.

Jackie narrowed her eyes in thought. "This is a long shot, but from what you emailed me about yoga girl, she's not well off, so how is it that she's driving a new BMW? Maybe a gift from him? Also, she was wearing a wedding band. Is she married? You didn't mention that in your email."

Martha smiled. "She is not married; some women just wear a wedding band to deter anyone from asking them out, which seems to be the case here. We are about to close this case out, actually; we're meeting with his attorney today. He did buy her the car, and it looks like he'll be leaving his wife for her shortly. But he will be paying a hefty sum as he exits. We've been following both of them for a couple months—tracking where they go, what they eat, where they sleep—and we've got plenty of photos that he won't want the newspapers to see. Let's just say his goose is cooked."

Jackie finished her coffee. "Are these early-morning classes a routine part of the job?"

Martha shrugged. "You have to go wherever the suspects go, whether that's an early class or meeting or a late-night party. You have to be able to fade into the background in a gym or a hotel lobby or a bar. You've clearly got the gym look down, but you'll need dress clothes for some jobs too."

Jackie thought about Martha's comments. "When I met with Mindy I did tell her my family was my top priority. These early and late stakeouts will mean me not seeing my son or wife at all in either the mornings or evenings some days . . . how often does this job require this level of surveillance?"

Martha shrugged once again. "Honestly, it varies—but when we need you, we need you. There are days and nights when nothing happens but we still need you there. It can get boring waiting for something to happen, but you never know when you're going to get something crucial." She handed Jackie her card. "Give me a call and we'll go from there. I think you do have some solid PI skills and instincts, but we'd need to train you our way, and that would mean we'd want you to sign at least a two-year contract. We've trained too many folks that have left after a year, and that doesn't work for our firm."

Jackie studied the card. "I want you to know that I'm really interested in working with you and your firm. I did my own research and your firm is highly respected and professional. You've dealt with some really high-profile cases that never hit the media. I like that you don't smear people's reputation just because they needed a dish on the side. I'll discuss the crazy schedule with my wife, and see how she feels about it."

Martha put her hand out, and Jackie responded with a firm shake.

"That's a strong grip you have there." Martha sized her up and down. "You're a smart, solid gal; I think you'll be a good fit for us if your family is on board. And that *does* matter to us. Last thing we want to do is break up a healthy family."

"I appreciate that—and your time," Jackie said. "I'll get back to you as soon as possible. If it's a go, when would I start?"

"Tomorrow too soon?" Martha chuckled. "We have more cases than we can handle at the moment. Apparently, marriage is a dying tradition and folks don't know how to end it without drama."

Martha and Jackie walked out of the café together.

"Do you ever work overseas—say, Cuba?" Jackie asked.

"All the time." Martha nodded. "Our clients travel extensively, and where they go, we go. We make it our business to get real-time evidence, and during travel is usually when people let down their guard—they tend not to think anyone is watching when they're not at home. We close a lot of cases that way. We're not cheap, but we are very good at what we do."

As Jackie watched Martha drive away in her Mercedes, she thought, *That Martha's a straight shooter; I can definitely work with someone like her.*

• • •

When Jackie checked her phone back in her SUV, she had several texts and voicemails: one from Laura, one from Sarah, and one from a number she didn't recognize. She read Sarah's text first: *Do you have time to go to Victor's hotel today? I have a bad feeling about him. Call me.*

Laura's voicemail was sweet: "Hi honey, miss you and Wyatt! The conference is great—dinner tonight at a fancy restaurant, wish you were here to go with me. Hope your shadowing went well. Love you."

The last voicemail was weird—a woman's voice, not one Jackie recognized: "If this is Jackie Larsen, your friend Sarah Golden is heading for trouble."

What the hell? Jackie frowned. She definitely didn't like the sound of that.

She rang Sarah right away.

"Hello?" Sarah answered, her voice low.

"This is Jackie Larsen, PI," Jackie said, trying out her new title.

"Hold on, I'm just walking out of a meeting . . ."

Jackie could hear movement on the other end of the line as she waited.

"Okay, I can talk now," Sarah said. "Are you still in the city? Sounds like it went well!"

"Yup! Just finished shadowing, and they're interested in hiring me. But first things first: I got a weird voicemail from a stranger; I have no idea who she is, but she said you're heading for trouble—what's up with that?"

"Hmm, that's weird . . . Who the hell knows, when have I even had time to get in trouble since we got back from our trip?"

"I called the number and the message said it was disconnected, like those stupid spam calls. I'm worried, though; we can't have anything happen to you after last year's close call."

Sarah exhaled sharply. "I don't even want to think about that nightmare. I mean, Jack, there's nothing we can really do with that information besides stay sharp and try to be careful, right?"

"Right," Jackie said. "Will do."

"Good. So, your shadowing went well? You like the work?"

"I really do," Jackie said.

"I'm so happy for you. I can't talk long, but hey, can you to go over to the Fairmont and see what Botsworth is up to? I'm doing everything in my power to avoid him, but I need your help. He makes me want to puke."

"Sure, I can go right now. He's not at your office today?"

"No, I haven't seen him lurking."

"Okay, I'm on it. I'll text you when I get there and let you know what's happening."

"Thanks, Jack."

• • •

Jackie called Laura as she steered toward Victor's hotel.

"Hey babe!" Laura answered brightly.

Jackie smiled at the sound of her voice. "Hi honey! What's this fancy place you're going to tonight?"

"I've never heard of it before, but everyone says it's the best in LA. Honestly, I can't even remember the name." Laura laughed. "How did your morning go?"

"It was fun!" Jackie said. "I took a yoga class, of all things, and afterward I met with Martha, the lead PI at the firm. She said she thinks that with some training, I'll make a good PI. I'm excited . . . but there is one big drawback."

"What?" Laura asked

"I will need to work some early mornings and some late nights sometimes," Jackie said. "I told her I'd need to discuss that with you first." She held her breath, waiting for Laura's reaction.

"Do you want the job?"

"I do. I know it will be a big learning curve, but this is one of the best firms in town . . . and it's so fun!"

"You sound so happy," Laura said. "I want this for you. My mom can hold down the fort when we're both working . . . why don't you go for it and we'll figure out the logistics as things unfold?"

"They want a two-year commitment since they will be spending a lot of resources training me," Jackie said. "You okay with that?"

"Between you, me, and Mom, I think we can handle it," Laura said confidently.

Jackie could hardly contain her smile. "Thanks, honey. I'll let them know and we can go from there. I'll have to go to Target and get some nice clothes; sounds like I'll have to dress up for some of these jobs."

"Target?" Laura laughed. "I think maybe you want to go to Nordstrom; they have much classier clothes. There's a woman at the one I go to who's super helpful and stylish; I'll send you to her."

"Okay, okay, I'll go to your fancy lady—why not?" Jackie said as she pulled over just down the block from the Fairmont. "Gotta run, babe. Love you."

"Love you too, working girl."

Working girl, Jackie thought. *I like the sound of that!*

• • •

After calling Martha to let her know she was officially interested in the job, Jackie walked into the ornate lobby of the Fairmont, still wearing her gym clothes and a Cubs baseball cap, and sat in a chair that gave her a great view of the front door. She took that day's *San Francisco Chronicle* off the table next to her and started reading the sports section, keeping it high enough to hide her face but low enough to see all the comings and goings. She had checked Lago's website, so she knew what Botsworth looked like now; he could have been

Idris Elba's twin. *What a hottie*, she thought. *Too bad he's a first-class dick.*

About a half-hour later, Botsworth walked in, a tall blonde on his arm. He motioned for her to take a seat in the lobby, then walked alone toward the front desk.

Still holding her paper up, Jackie casually glanced over at the blonde, who was now on her cell. She was close enough that Jackie could hear her side of the conversation.

"Don't worry, Leland, I plan to stay here as long as you want me to," she said, keeping an eye on Botsworth. "He has no real idea who I am, just knows that you sent me and he trusts you. Just so you know, I'll be shopping with your credit cards." She giggled.

Botsworth turned away from the front desk and headed back toward the blonde.

"Got to go, talk soon." She slipped her phone into her purse as Botsworth sat next to her.

"Who were you talking to?" he asked.

"A friend in New York," she said casually. "Were you able to get us dinner reservations at the French Laundry?"

"Not looking promising, but the front desk said they will do their best. I need to run upstairs and make a few calls, then I have to go the transplant center. I hate to leave you, but duty calls." His eyes roamed over her body.

"Don't you worry about me," she said. "I'm meeting up with a friend, and I have some serious shopping to do. You have my cell number; if you'd like to get together later, give me a ring."

She kissed him on the cheek, then rose and sashayed her way out of the hotel.

Jackie got out of her seat and trailed after Botsworth as he moved toward the elevators. Several shoppers with multiple bags happened to cram into his elevator at the last minute, so she was able to squeeze in with them. Botsworth swiped his key card and punched the button for the penthouse. As the shoppers gabbed away about their purchases, he stared at his phone.

The shoppers exited one floor before the penthouse. Jackie had no choice but to get off the elevator with them.

Guess I'll go back down to the lobby and wait for him to show up again, she thought, disappointed.

• • •

Jackie was back in her chair in the lobby, pretending to read the *Chronicle*, when Botsworth finally emerged again. He was talking on his cell, and he looked pissed.

Right as he passed by Jackie, he hissed, "I was pretty clear, Angelo—I need you to get eyes on her."

Jackie shot up from her seat and followed after him, confident that he was too distracted by his conversation to notice her.

"Don't put her in the hospital unless you have to, but give her a good scare—and do it pronto," Victor said before shoving his way through the hotel's front doors.

Jackie stopped short and let him go. She'd heard enough. Now that he was gone, it was time to return to his room and see if she could figure out a way in.

Chapter 17

As Victor approached Dr. Bower's office, right on time for their scheduled meeting, Sarah Golden came out.

"He's not in there—complications in surgery," she said curtly, then briskly walked past him.

Victor turned and followed her down the hall. "Ms. Golden—Ms. Golden, do you have a minute?" he called after her.

She kept walking.

He quickened his pace. "Ms. Golden, please—just a minute."

She turned around. "What can I do for you, Mr. Botsworth? I'm late for a meeting."

"I'll walk with you," he said as he caught up to her. "And please, call me Victor. And perhaps I can call you Sarah?"

No response. She started walking again. He kept pace with her.

"You're in really good shape," he said. "You must be a runner."

Once again, no answer.

"I wanted to invite you and your research team for dinner at the Tonga Room tomorrow night," he said. "Everyone has been working tirelessly; I feel it's the least I can do. I was going to ask you earlier, after Dr. McKee's funeral, but you ran out before I got the chance."

"Thank you for your kind offer, *Victor*, but I'm busy tomorrow night," Sarah said coldly. "But I'm sure Debbie and Chris would welcome a break; they've been working twelve hours a day. Feel free to ask them directly."

She opened the door to the stairwell and started ascending. Victor followed; he'd cracked harder nuts than her before.

"I'm sorry if I've offended you in any way, Sarah," he said. "I just want to help you and your team get through this crazy time."

She stopped on the landing. "I appreciate that, and it's clear to me that Dr. Bower has the utmost confidence in you and your company. But I'm trying to keep our program running, and this research issue is just one of many fires I'm putting out right now. Nothing personal, I just don't have any time to spare. Now, please excuse me."

She continued up the stairs; this time, Victor let her go.

• • •

When Victor knocked on Chris and Debbie's office door a few minutes later, Chris opened the door and smiled. "Victor! What a pleasant surprise. Please come in—so sorry everything is a mess."

Victor surveyed the piles of charts and files that covered every counter, as well as their desks. "Hi Debbie, how are you today?" He injected sympathy into his tone. "I imagine the memorial yesterday was emotional for both of you."

Debbie turned her head, revealing bloodshot eyes and pale complexion. "It was." She gestured to the mountain of paperwork surrounding her. "And this is not what I signed up for, I can tell you that. Thanks for asking. How are you, Victor?"

"I'm good—here to help, if I can!" Victor walked over to the long counter and surveyed the stacks of charts. "How many more cases do you have left to follow up on?"

Chris maneuvered herself between him and the charts. "You're not really supposed to be in here, Victor."

"Like anyone cared before," Debbie snapped. "Two weeks ago, we could've died in here and they wouldn't have found our bodies for days. Now every Tom, Dick, and Harry is stopping by like they're interested."

"She's a little cranky," Chris volunteered. "Sarah just made her cancel the two-week vacation she was supposed to leave for next week."

"That's horrible." Victor gave her a sympathetic look. "I'm so sorry to hear that, Debbie."

"Sarah can run off to Cuba and Miami to see Mister Wonderful but we have to stay here and do all the grunt work," Debbie muttered. "I hope she softens up a little once he comes to town. Now that she's engaged, maybe she'll quit and leave us all alone."

"We can only wish, Deb." Chris shrugged. "Let's do four more charts and then go to lunch. By the way, I can't find those pathology reports anywhere—I checked online and they're not in the system. Did you get the file with the paper reports?"

"There's a small box over there." Debbie pointed at the end of the long counter. "Check there. It's so weird that they didn't do the prescribed weekly biopsies the protocol called for, I've only been able to find a couple per patient."

Victor listened quietly, knowing that the less hard data—say, weekly kidney biopsy results—existed, the better, since the data could pick up rejection more quickly from a biopsy than from bloodwork. Fewer biopsies meant his company's new anti-rejection drug would show more promise.

"How about I take you two for a coffee and a pastry across the street?" he suggested. "You both need a break, and it's beautiful outside."

"How would we know? We don't have any windows down here in the dungeon. They always give the research staff shitty offices," Debbie complained.

"We can't leave, but you're welcome to bring us coffees, if it's not too much trouble," Chris offered.

"Sounds perfect! What would you like? I'll run and get it and bring it back." Victor fashioned one of his winning smiles, and they both beamed back at him.

• • •

When Victor returned with coffee and croissants, Chris and Debbie cleared some space and sat down with him.

"Thanks so much, Victor," Debbie said, her sour demeanor gone. "That was very kind of you."

Just then, the door to the office opened and Sarah walked in. When she saw Victor, her neutral expression turned into a glare.

"Victor, you need to leave. You know better than to be in here with all this data. Really! Sarah held the door open and extended her arm. "Please."

Victor nodded toward Debbie and Chris, unfazed. "I've made reservations at the Tonga Room for dinner tomorrow night and hope you two can join me. Feel free to bring a date. Let me know if that would work for your schedules. Sarah, we'd love it if you could join us too."

When Sarah didn't respond, he left the office and Sarah stepped inside and closed the door. He paused outside the closed door and heard Sarah raise her voice inside.

"That guy has some balls coming down here and bothering you," she said. "You both know we can't have anyone—I mean *anyone*—outside our team involved in closing this study out. What were you thinking?"

"He just brought us coffee, Sarah, don't get your panties in a bundle," Chris retorted. "It was a kind gesture, and he didn't see or touch anything. God forbid anyone would be nice to us for a change," she added with sarcasm.

Victor's burner cell started buzzing and he quickly moved away from the door.

"Making any progress on our Chicago project?" he asked, striding down the hall.

"I have someone in Chicago who's watching the house," Angelo said. "She's very busy for an old lady—lots of company."

"You need to get this taken care of. I don't care what you do, I just need her frightened enough to call her granddaughter. Text me as soon as it's done."

"Got it, Chief—but just so you know, this is extra. We didn't talk about anything like this when you first called me."

"Fuck, Angelo—just tell me how much and then get it done."

• • •

When Victor made it back to Bower's office, his assistant was at her desk. "He'll be right with you," she said. "He's just talking to a possible living kidney donor."

Victor smiled, sat down, and checked his emails. Several emails from the Chicago research team updating him on their progress, and a request for him to call his sales rep there at his earliest convenience. He looked over at Bower's assistant. "Any idea how long he'll be? I need to make a quick call."

"At least another ten minutes. I'll let him know you're here when he comes out."

"Thanks so much." Victor walked down the hall and called his Chicago rep. "I've got a meeting with Dr. Bower in ten minutes; what can you tell me?"

"I'll be quick," the rep said. "We've closed the study here, as there were no life-threatening complications. It seems they did only monthly, not weekly, biopsies, so the reports were not conclusive. The study patients are still receiving their drugs and getting routine follow-up appointments but the attending wants to know what's next. Is there any way we can initiate a modified study and keep this cohort of patients in the new study?"

"Great question," Victor said. "I'll run that up the flagpole. It looks highly likely that we can; I think this is just a small speed bump. Tell your attendings that I'll be in touch in a couple of days. Meanwhile, I want you to wine and dine the hell out of the research staff; I need clinical details, and fast. You know the drill."

"You know I do. I'll keep you posted."

"I'm counting on you. I'd love nothing better than to give you a big end-of-the-year bonus." Victor ended the call and walked back to Bower's office just in time to see him walking a family out the door. He looked tired.

"Hey Victor," he greeted him. "I need to take a quick bathroom break; go ahead in and take a seat. I'll be right back."

Victor went in to the office and casually surveyed the various files piled high on every available surface. He stopped when he saw a note on top of one stack from Sarah: *Dr. Bower: you need to see these study results from Dr. Lopez, he's very concerned.*

Victor glanced out the door. Seeing no one, he took the file and quickly looked inside. He was not happy to see that the file contained several pages of the study results that his Cuban spies had assured him were in Cuba. *Damn it. I'll deal with this later.* He slipped the folder in his briefcase just before Bower rounded the corner with a cup of hot coffee in hand.

"I've been up since four a.m.," he explained. "Tough liver case. And then there was the memorial . . ." He closed his eyes briefly. "I've got to go back to the OR in about fifteen minutes, but I was hoping you could fill me in on how the other programs are doing closing out their studies." He sat down and took a big slurp of his coffee.

"I just spoke with my Chicago team and they already closed the study," Victor said. "They want to transition their patients into a modified study, though, which I think we can do. I have a few loose ends to tie up around that, but I think we'll be good to go. Would you want us to include you in that when it happens?" Victor realized he was gripping his briefcase close to his chest. He forced himself to relax.

"Absolutely. Keep me posted. I have to return a few calls . . . anything else?" Bower was already looking at his phone messages.

"I hate to throw anyone under the bus, but Sarah Golden has been less than friendly toward me and I was wondering if you could put in a good word," Victor said. "I'm just here to help, not disrupt anyone's work. It's just that all the other programs have finished closing their studies and I wanted make sure yours wasn't too far behind."

"Sarah's great at her job, but she can be a tough one to deal with." Bower sighed. "I'll speak with her. There's no reason she should have an attitude—frankly, none of us have time for that bullshit. I'll call her before I scrub in."

"Your research nurses, on the other hand, have been angels," Victor said warmly. "I'm taking them to dinner tomorrow night to keep their spirits up; I invited Sarah, but she's busy."

Bower stood up and extended his hand to Victor. "I'll talk to her. She really can be very kind and charming when she wants to be. We're all under a lot of stress right now."

"I understand completely, Dr. Bower, and thank you. I'll keep you posted on the next study; if you need anything from me in the meantime, just call. I'll be in town for a while longer."

• • •

Victor waited until he was safely outside the transplant center's walls before taking Sarah's folder out of his briefcase and flipping through its contents. Dr. Lopez's notes warning Dr. Bower about the adverse effects of the Lago's study drugs and asking him to call him immediately were meticulously thorough. Victor caught himself gritting his teeth. *That motherfucker Lopez—he's dead!*

He called Valerie and started walking.

"Hi Boss, how you doing?"

"Not good. What's the update on Cuba? Where's Lopez? I need *him* gone, I need his *family* gone. He is a huge liability. I just found a file full of shit he gave Sarah Golden when she was in Cuba. I was told that nothing left that country. You need to find whoever screwed up, and let them know I am not happy and they are not getting paid. They'll be lucky if I don't have someone take them out. Then find a new person to locate the Lopez family and take care of it."

"I've been trying to locate Dr. Lopez and his family and they are nowhere to be found," Valerie said. "Maybe your Cuban team already took care of them?"

"I wouldn't trust that for a minute. I need you to figure out what the fuck is going on; I need this nipped in the bud."

"I have a little good news," Valerie said hopefully. "We got the green light to modify the study, which means our teams can start working with all the research teams to get the new studies through their investigative research boards right away. We used the excuse that the old protocol put undue burden on the patients, and it worked; they approved reducing biopsies from weekly to monthly."

"That is great news." Victor's jaw unclenched itself. "Send me the emails so I can study them and then I'll get things rolling here. Let's keep this train on the track. As soon as you have the facts about Cuba, call me."

"Will do. Oh, I got a call from Angelo, he says he needs me to drop off some cash—regular place. Something about Chicago work?"

"That guy," Victor muttered. "Yeah, give him another ten thousand."

"You take care," Valerie said. "You sound really stressed out."

"I am," he admitted. "I'm going back to my hotel, then I'm going for a run along the Embarcadero. A little exercise will do me good."

"Good for you. Talk later."

Victor hailed a cab just as he hung up the phone. He slid inside and exhaled slowly. "Fairmont, please."

Chapter 18

Sarah was furious when she found Victor with Chris and Debbie, but she had no time to dwell on that: she had back-to-back meetings for the rest of the afternoon. She was just about to head home to finish cleaning her apartment for Handsome when she got a text from Dr. Bower: *I need to see you now, scrubbing in for a case.*

Maybe he saw Lopez's study file on his desk and wants more details, she thought. She took the stairs and arrived a little breathless at the OR. After putting on a white jumpsuit, shoe coverings, a hair net, and a mask, she found Dr. Bower in the OR, gowned and gloved.

"Sarah." He acknowledged her with a nod. "I had a brief visit with Victor Botsworth from Lago today and he informed me that you have been less than kind to him while he's been trying to help us clean up this mess. Is that right?"

Sarah's furrowed her eyebrows and felt her mouth go dry. "I don't trust the man, it's that simple."

"Well I don't need you to trust him. I had a relationship with him long before you joined our team and his company has been very generous with us over the years—providing access to needed resources, sponsoring our annual conference in Carmel, and more. So I need you to roll out the red carpet for him. Go to dinner with him tomorrow night with our research team. Just go along to get along. Once this study is closed out and the new one is rolled out, you won't have to deal with him anymore."

She blanched. "New study?"

"I don't have time to discuss that right now—just play nice, okay? And I need you to drop everything to work with Chris and Debbie to get this study closed; we're the last program to finish, and I don't like hearing that." Dr. Bower looked over at the anesthesiologist. "Is our patient under and comfortable?"

"All good here," the doctor said.

"Scalpel," Dr. Bower requested.

Sarah bit the side of her mouth. "Did you see the file I left on your desk earlier?"

"I haven't had time to look at anything," Dr. Bower said, not looking up from his patient.

Sarah left the OR suite fuming. *Just suck it up*, she told herself. *For now, anyway.*

• • •

After Sarah had removed all her OR coverings and was walking toward the patient waiting area, she saw that she had a text from Handsome: *Chief needs me home another week . . . so sorry, honey. I'll call tonight. He knows I have one foot out the door.*

Sarah's heart sank; all she wanted to do was to be in his arms. *What else can go wrong today?*

• • •

Jackie called right as Sarah slumped into her chair at her desk.

"Yo, Golden," she said cheerfully. "On my way home, been a busy day for this almost-hired PI! I'm having some fun with this gig. How you doing?"

"Horrible and horrible," Sarah moaned. "Just had a lovely encounter with Bower in the OR where he ordered me to make Victor Botsworth my best friend, and to stop everything and help the research team close out the study. Oh yeah, and Handsome had to delay his trip for another week."

"That all sucks," Jackie agreed. "I do have a little good news for you, though!"

Sarah logged on to her email and stifled a groan when she saw how many new messages she had in her inbox. "I would love some good news, please."

"I did some undercover work at Botsworth's hotel this morning. Overheard some stuff in the lobby while he was there with this model-looking blonde, and I even got into his room after he left."

Sarah's mouth opened. That was a lot more than she'd expected Jackie to accomplish. "Wow, Jack, nice job!"

"It was a breeze." Jackie sounded very satisfied with herself.

"Not surprised about the blonde." Sarah rolled her eyes. "Did you find anything in his room?" Sarah started to scroll through the mountain of emails before her to see if anything was marked urgent.

"His room was meticulously tidy—he's a total neat freak. There was a lace thong hanging on a towel bar in the bathroom, could barely fit over my left thigh. No loose papers anywhere; his laptop was there, but I don't know how to crack the passwords yet so I couldn't get in. I did find a pad of paper next to the phone and he'd clearly ripped off some pages, so I used the pencil-rub-over-the-top-blank-page trick and made out a couple of names: Leland, Valerie, Lopez, and Golden."

Sarah stopped scrolling through her email. "Valerie is his assistant; I have no idea who Leland is; not happy my name is on his list. I had a few run-ins with him today. That guy thinks he's god's gift to women and can charm the pants off anyone."

"He's a player, no doubt about that. I did some fun digging about his company and where they get their funding and found the name Leland Ackerley; he's associated with a venture capitalist firm that invests a bundle in Lago. Not sure if the connection between him and Botsworth runs any deeper than that, but after Wyatt's in bed tonight I plan to do a major search on both of them to see what I can find."

"Thanks for all your help," Sarah said, tearing her gaze from her screen. "So, tell me more about this morning. You said you enjoyed it?"

"I had a blast—I think I found my dream job," Jackie gushed. "I even spoke with Laura and she's cool with the fact that some of the hours will be a little crazy . . . in fact, she couldn't be more supportive. They're doing a background check, and if all goes through I need to be back in the city tomorrow for my first official day of work!"

"You sound jazzed—I haven't heard you talk like this for a long time." Sarah's bad mood lifted in the face of her friend's excitement. "I'm so happy for you. Do you think our temporary arrest in Mexico will show on the background check? I'm guessing no." Sarah smiled when she thought about their experience in Puerto Vallarta five years earlier.

"Technically they didn't book us, we just had to stay with that Mexican policeman until we sobered up and paid for the glasses we broke when we were dancing on the bar." Jackie laughed. "No paper trail there. And we sure did have fun, didn't we?"

"The best. Need one of those nights sooner than later now that Handsome's not coming out any time soon." Sarah's mood dipped again at that thought.

"When Laura gets home from her conference let's start brainstorming our next adventure," Jackie suggested.

"Once this research study is put to bed we're going to celebrate for sure," Sarah agreed. "Okay, I'm going to work late tonight—clean up my email before heading home. Kiss Wyatt for me."

"Will do. Assuming I pass that background check, I'll be in the city tomorrow, so let's plan on seeing each other. I'll text once I hear from my new firm!"

"Sounds good."

A knock came at Sarah's door.

"Gotta go, Jack, duty calls. See you tomorrow." Sarah put her cell on her desk and opened the door.

Debbie was standing there crying; Chris was just behind her, a comforting hand on her shoulder.

"I can't take the pressure," Debbie blurted out between sobs. "I need a break or leave of absence."

Sarah's stomach sank. "Come in, please." She ushered both women inside and pulled out a chair for each of them. She circled her desk, sat down herself, and asked gently, "What's going on?"

"There's lots of missing biopsy reports and it may be my fault," Debbie wailed. "I may have only put the orders in for monthly when it should have been weekly. We could get disqualified from the study. Dr. Bower is going to fire me, I just know it!" She put her hands over her face and let out guttural sounds as she sobbed.

Sarah looked over at Chris and then back at Debbie. "I'm not sure what we can do, but let's figure this out together. I was already planning to drop everything else on my plate and help you both full-time starting tomorrow, so you just tell me what you want me to do. I'm not as experienced with research protocols as you are, but let's see . . ." She drummed her fingers on her desk, thinking. "Did you call radiology to see what order they had?"

"I did call them," Chris said, "but they'd already left for the day. If you could follow up with them tomorrow, that would be great; you have more pull with them than we do." She handed Debbie a tissue. "I'll forward you the email."

Sarah looked at each of them in turn; they were clearly exhausted. "You both need to go home and get a good night's rest," she said. She left her chair, walked around her desk to Debbie, and gave her shoulder a squeeze. "We'll figure this out together. And I guess we're having dinner with Victor tomorrow night—that'll be fun, right?" She hoped her feigned excitement was believable.

"Thanks, Sarah." Debbie stood up and gave her a hug. "It's been so chaotic since Dr. McKee died, with the NIH pushing us to get them everything. It's just too much pressure."

"I agree," Sarah said. "I'll make some calls and see if I can get us an assistant to document everything—one less thing for you to worry about—and I'll get a hold of radiology to track down the biopsy hiccup first thing tomorrow."

"Thanks Sarah," Chris said. "We both really appreciate your help and understanding, it means a lot. Do you know what time we're supposed to meet Victor for dinner tomorrow?"

Sarah went back to her computer and scrolled through her email until she got to one from Botsworth. "He said seven o'clock," she said. "And apparently, not only is he taking us to the Tonga Room at the Fairmont but he's reserved a hotel room for each of us for the night so we don't have to drive home!"

"That's amazing," Chris said. "And it's a Friday night, so we can really live it up! Count me in. Deb, are you game?"

Debbie smiled for what Sarah imagined was the first time all day. "This is a gift from heaven. I can't remember the last time I stayed in a fancy hotel. Yes, of course I'm game!"

Sarah chuckled. "Why the hell not. I'm in too. I'll email him back and let him know we'll be there." She quickly responded to his email, then looked at her haggard coordinators. "Now you both go home and get some rest. I'll see you tomorrow evening."

After Chris and Debbie left, Sarah sighed and rested her head in her hands. *I'm sure Botsworth is pure evil, but I need to take care of my team. A dinner and an overnight won't hurt anyone.*

• • •

After pouring herself a glass of wine at home, Sarah called her fiancé. She was sure he was asleep, but she needed to hear his voice, even if just on voicemail.

To her surprise, he picked up, "Hello my love."

She slapped her forehead. "I woke you up, didn't I?"

"You did," he admitted, "but it's always good to hear your voice. How's my future wife? I'm so sorry I had to delay my trip."

"Tired and happy to hear your sleepy voice." Sarah took a sip of her wine. "And don't worry about me; I want you to take care of the home front and come when it feels comfortable. Truth is, that until I close out this NIH paperwork, I'll be super preoccupied anyway—so you do what you need to do at the precinct and I'll get this thing done, and when you do get out here, we'll take a drive up to wine country to select our wedding venue."

"And that's why I'm marrying you—great plan." She could hear the smile in his voice. "And now I'm going back to sleep, because it's almost one in the morning here and I have to be back at work in six hours. Love you."

"Love you more."

• • •

After hanging up with Handsome, Sarah soaked in her tub, sipped her wine, and thought about her day, recalling her interactions with Botsworth and Dr. Bower. *I need to stop being mad at them—it takes too much energy*, she decided. *I'll do what Dr. Bower asks and let this Lopez thing go—I can't do anything about it anyway.*

Making the decision lifted a weight from her shoulders. She relaxed into the warm water and let her mind drift to more pleasant things.

• • •

Sarah waited until after her first cup of coffee to check her email the next morning. Of course Botsworth had responded in the middle of the night, saying how happy he was that she and the research coordinators had accepted his offer and providing all the details they would need. Sarah forwarded his email to Chris and Debbie, packed an overnight bag, and headed to the transplant center.

After she dropped her stuff in her office, she headed over to radiology and popped into her manager friend's office.

"Hey Colette," she said cheerfully. "It's Friday—ready for a fun weekend?"

"You bet your sweet ass I am." Colette chuckled. "Say, I got your email this morning and I looked into the biopsy orders right away. It's really weird. Dr. McKee overrode the order that Debbie put in for weekly biopsies—changed it to monthly about halfway through the study. That shouldn't have happened, since studies like that are all protocol driven. Any idea why he would do that?"

"That *is* weird." Sarah frowned. "Let me check with the research team. I appreciate you looking into it. You do know that Dr. McKee was killed in a car accident?"

Colette nodded. "I did see that on the news—I'm so sorry. I didn't know him but I heard he was brilliant." She glanced at her computer screen. "Yikes, I have to run to a meeting. Let me know if you need anything else!"

• • •

Sarah stood before the coffee cart in front of the transplant center, deep in thought. *Why would Dr. McKee change an order?* It just didn't make sense.

She ordered her double espresso and continued ruminating while it was being prepared.

"Sarah."

She barely heard her name the first time.

"Sarah." It came a little louder this time, and she looked over—it was Dr. Bower.

"Oh, good morning Dr. Bower! Good to see you. I thought about what you said and I decided to lighten up, hunker down, and get this NIH study put to bed. Sooner we do it, the sooner we can get on with making this program soar, right?"

Dr. Bower's smile lit up his entire face. "That's the Sarah I know. Keep me posted; see you at selection."

Sarah collected her espresso and smiled back. "You got it."

• • •

Just as Sarah finished her desk work, Jackie called.

"Just the woman I wanted to talk to!" Sarah said. "Are you still home?"

"I am. Why?"

"Have I got a deal for you. I'm having dinner with my research team and Botsworth, and then he popped for an overnight at the Fairmont for each of us. I thought maybe you'd want to meet up after dinner and spend the night with me there? I know Laura's out of town, but maybe Grandma can watch Wyatt—what do you think?"

"Good timing, Golden, 'cause I just got a call that my background check cleared and they want me to come to the office and finish my onboarding paperwork today. They want to bring me up to speed on the cases I'll be following, and then I have a very early surveillance assignment in the city tomorrow morning—so it'll be great to be there already, rather than commuting from San Rafael. And as always, I'll be happy to be your roommate."

"Congrats on clearing the background check! Call me when you're done with your work in the city and I'll let you know my room number at the Fairmont."

"I'll text you. See you tonight."

• • •

The rest of Sarah's day flew by with more work than she could have ever hoped to complete. When she finally managed to escape the office, she checked into her room at the Fairmont and changed into her outfit for the evening: a sexy dark blue silk blouse, a black skirt with a slit up the side, high heels, and pearl drop earrings. As she sized herself up in the full-length bathroom mirror, she told herself, *Have fun tonight, Golden! You're taking life way too seriously—and after all, how often do you get to go to the Tonga Room?*

She headed downstairs to the Tonga Room's entrance, where a fresh-faced hostess greeted her.

"I'm here as a guest of Victor Botsworth," Sarah said.

"Mr. Botsworth is expecting you. His other two guests have already arrived."

The hostess escorted Sarah to a red leather banquette, where Botsworth stood up as soon as he laid eyes on her.

"Sarah! I'm so glad you decided to join us."

As he blatantly checked her out from head to toe, she sized him up as well. He was wearing a crisply ironed, open-collared white shirt, a pair of dark brown corduroy pants, and a black jacket with a handkerchief neatly tucked into the breast pocket.

What a looker, Sarah thought. *Too bad he doesn't have the personality to go with it.*

She slid into the booth next to Chris and glanced over at what Debbie was drinking. "Is that the Tonga Room's world-famous Mai Tai?"

"I'm on my second one, it's delicious," Debbie responded with a silly grin.

The waitress was waiting for Sarah's order.

"I'd love a Mai Tai as well," Sarah said quickly.

"We'll have a round for the table," Victor declared.

The two hours that followed were filled with stories from Botsworth about the Tonga Room's history. It was transformed in the 1940s by a fancy Metro Goldwyn Mayer's set director, he told them, and the floating lagoon stage across from them was built from the remains of a schooner that once traveled between San Francisco and the South Sea Islands. Delicious dishes graced the table as everyone enjoyed the live music, food, ambience, and drinks. To Sarah's surprise, she had fun.

"I need to head up to my room," Chris finally said as Botsworth paid the bill. "Unless anyone wants to go dancing?" She looked at their host hopefully.

"I haven't gone dancing in years," Debbie said. "I'd love to go."

"I'm afraid I can't tonight, ladies," Botsworth said. "But you two have a great time!"

After thanking him for the lovely evening, the two nurses wobbled off to find a dancing spot.

"I guess I should head out too," Sarah said. "I had a wonderful evening, Victor, thank you. I'd like to apologize for being so rude to you these last couple days."

"No need to apologize," he said. "We are all under a lot of stress and needed to let off a little steam—that's why I suggested this dinner. But do you really have to go so soon? Would you like a nightcap before you head out?"

"That would be lovely." Sarah nodded. "Please excuse me, I need to use the ladies' room. I'll be right back." She stood up and noticed that she was really feeling the rum. She checked her phone on the way to her room and saw a text from Jackie: *Running really late, I'll meet you in your room.*

Okay, Sarah wrote back. *I gave the front desk your name, you can pick up a key on your way in just in case I'm not there to let you in when you arrive.*

• • •

Over a nightcap of 151 rum, Sarah and Victor discussed their shared love of transplant and hopes for the future.

He's really not so bad, Sarah thought. *Maybe I misjudged him.*

As she finished her rum, she started to feel really light-headed, which she normally never felt, no matter how much alcohol she drank. She kept blinking her eyes to gain focus.

"I may need you to escort me to my room," she said, a bit embarrassed. "I think I may have had too much to drink."

"No problem," he said smoothly. "What's your room number?"

Sarah gave him her key and room number, her mind swirling. Victor held her arm and helped her to her room. Once inside, she had to sit down.

"I don't know what I drank," she slurred, "but I need to lie down."

The last thing she saw was Victor's face as he helped her into bed.

Chapter 19

After Jackie dropped Wyatt off at school Friday morning, she drove into San Francisco for her first official day of work at Malecki and Blanche. She'd packed an overnight bag with her gym clothes and was wearing her best pair of jeans and a red cardigan sweater that Laura had gotten her years earlier. She'd even put in her gold post earrings—*Best foot forward*, she thought.

She cleared her throat as she approached the grand front desk, where the receptionist gave her a warm welcome and then directed her to Martha's office.

The first half of her day was filled with lots of paperwork and various training modules the firm required. Once she had completed all that, she was invited into her first staff briefing meeting.

"I'd like to introduce our newest PI, Jackie Larsen," Martha said to kick off the meeting. "She's fresh out of school, so she doesn't have any bad habits like the rest of you." She winked at her colleagues.

Jackie scanned the room: there were four women and three men, all casually dressed, sitting around the conference room's oak table.

"Nice to meet you," she said. "I'm very excited to be part of your team."

"It's about time we got some more help," a burly guy said. "There's only so much surveillance any one person can do." He put up his hand and gave her a wave. "Hank here—say, Jackie, do you like sitting in vans for hours?"

"It's all part of the job, and I'm a team player," she said cheerfully, "so sure, why not? And if I'm doing something wrong, let me know."

"Believe me, they will." Martha looked around the table. "I'm sure you all remember when you first started, so go easy on her."

After a few chuckles and grunts, she continued, "Let's do a rundown. We just got three big new divorce cases—and I mean *big*—that I'll be assigning today, but let's start with the ones we already know." Martha began to read out client names and the PI assigned to each one gave a brief update.

Jackie noticed her hand was shaking a little as she took copious notes about the details that were expected at the briefings. *These're some really big names*, she thought.

Thirty minutes in, Martha looked over at her. "How you doing over there?"

"All good here, I'm a quick learner," Jackie said. "Clearly I'm working with the 'A' team, and I wouldn't want it any other way." Jackie took a sip of water as the other PIs gazed at her and nodded.

"Hank, I want you to show Jackie how to fill out and submit the surveillance reports online," Martha said. "Then hand off your three existing cases to her; I need you front and center on these new cases."

Hank looked over at Jackie. "It'll cost you a cheeseburger and fries."

"A man after my own heart—you got it," Jackie said. "Red's Java House okay?"

Hank laughed. "Excellent taste—it's my favorite place."

"I think we're going to get along just fine," Jackie said, grinning.

• • •

Jackie was feeling pretty overwhelmed by the time Hank finished showing her the ropes of the reporting system, but he was patient with her, and they had a good time chatting at lunch afterward. As they finished up their burgers, she said, "I feel much better now that I have some food in my system. I think I'm ready to continue my lessons." She tossed some money on the table for their bill, and they walked outside together.

"You've got to make sure to eat, Jackie, especially when you're on stakeouts," Hank said. "I always have a bag with snacks in the van in case I can't leave. And the most important thing to remember is to never drink too much water or coffee; what goes in must come out, and if the action starts there's no way you can leave the van."

"No worries on that front, I've got the bladder of a truck driver," Jackie said.

"Good to know." Hank chuckled.

As they stepped off the elevator to their office, Martha was waiting for them. "Welcome back. Jackie, let me show you your cubicle."

Jackie smiled. "My first real office!" She tossed Hank a wave. "Thanks again, man. See you soon."

Martha led her past the partners' fancy offices—all the doors were closed—and around a corner. Jackie stopped in her tracks; there were several brightly colored balloons attached to her new space, along with a handmade sign that read, "WELCOME JACKIE!" All the PIs who had been at the morning briefing were gathered together—including Hank, who had somehow managed to get there before her and Martha—and they clapped when they saw her.

She put her arms out wide. "Wow, what a welcome. Thank you."

One by one, they all gave her a quick pat on the back.

Hank was last. "We put together an array of fun items to make you feel at home while you're here." He handed her a large gift bag. "Once you've unpacked and gotten settled let me know; I'll come back over here and we can have you log in and try filling out those forms online."

Jackie took the bag. "Gee, thanks!" *The PTA moms at Wyatt's school have never been this nice to me*, she thought, smiling to herself. As her coworkers dispersed back to their stations, she sat at her L-shaped desk and ran her hand over it—it was clean and smooth—and she noted the corkboard border above the desk with stick pins in it. Then she proceeded to unpack her gift bag.

There were several bags of nuts, gum, lip balm, a roll of toilet paper, handy-wipes, a large magnifying glass, black sunglasses, a black baseball hat, and a picture frame she could tack up on the corkboard above her desk after she brought a photo from home to put inside. The last item was an empty, gallon-size plastic container with a Post-it on it that read, *In case you have to pee in the van*. She shook her head and laughed. *All I need now is a Foley catheter with a bag in case I ever have to stay in there extra-extra long.*

She peeked over her cubicle and said, "Thanks everyone. I think you covered everything."

She sat back down, squirming happily. *It's happening; I'm going to become the best PI ever!*

• • •

When Jackie looked up again it was already six in the evening. Shocked that the day had gone by so fast, she called home.

Grandma picked up right away. "Jackie! How was your first day? I'm dying to hear."

"It was amazingly hard—and so much fun," Jackie said. "Lot to learn, and I'm excited for it all. Is Wyatt around?"

"You bet—we were just about to have dinner, but I haven't dished it up yet. Wyatt, your mama is on the phone."

Jackie heard him running toward the phone.

"Hi Mama—how was work?"

That was the first time he had ever asked her that question. Jackie's chest warmed with a flush of pride.

"Oh, buddy, it's a blast. Learning so many things—can't wait to tell you all about it. How was school?"

"Same stuff," he said. "Spelling, math . . . but oh, we got to go to the library for a really cool story time with a real reptile guy, he even brought snakes and lizards. I invited Grandma but she said no, she doesn't do reptiles."

Jackie laughed. "That sounds fun. Maybe we can invite him to your next birthday party."

"That would be way cool! Um, Mama? I gotta go. Dinner's ready."

"Go ahead, buddy. Love you. And hey, did Grandma tell you the plan? I'm staying with Aunt Sarah in the city tonight since I have to work early here tomorrow."

"Yeah, she told me. You'll be home tomorrow though, right?"

"Sure will. Till then, you be good for Grandma, okay?"

"I will, Mama. Bye."

So this is what it's like to be the one working and calling home, Jackie thought. *Up until now, Laura's always been the one to play that part*. She couldn't have wiped the shit-eating grin off her face if she'd tried.

She kept working on her computer and filling out forms until she was bleary-eyed. Eventually, Hank walked by her desk and said, "Hey Larsen, it's almost nine—way past quitting time. You don't want to make the rest of us look like slackers. Go home, get some rest. You need to meet me here tomorrow morning at eight sharp."

"Roger that." Jackie carefully closed out her computer and walked to her car, texting Sarah that she was on her way as she went.

• • •

Jackie nearly had a heart attack when she walked into Sarah's room and found Victor Botsworth furiously sifting through the contents of her friend's briefcase. She scanned the room and spotted Sarah sprawled out on the bed.

"What the hell are you doing?" Jackie charged at Botsworth.

He backed away, holding up his hands. "I'm not doing anything! My friend Sarah was drunk and I helped her up to her room. I was hoping she had some Advil or something I could leave by her bed when she wakes up—she's going to have one hell of a hangover, she and the other nurses enjoyed multiple Mai Tais at dinner. Anyway, who the hell are you?"

Jackie ignored him and sat next to Sarah, gently shaking her friend's arm in an attempt to rouse her. "You're no friend of Sarah's," she hissed. "And you need to leave—*now*."

"Okay, okay, I'm going," he said, but instead of walking away he moved closer to Jackie. "Tell Sarah I hope she feels better; I never pegged her as a big drinker." He cocked his head. "I don't think we've been formally introduced; I'm Victor Botsworth, CEO of Lago Pharmaceuticals. Not the ideal circumstances to meet a new person, but . . ."

He put his hand out; Jackie just stared at him. "I'm Jackie Larsen, Sarah's best friend. I'm not sure what really happened here, but I'm going to figure it out—you can count on that. Now please get the fuck out of here." Jackie rose, walked over to the door, and flung it open.

As soon as Botsworth was gone, Jackie returned to Sarah. "Hey, Sarah—wake up, honey. Jackie gently shook her again and, receiving no response, went into the bathroom, rinsed a washcloth with cold water and placed it on Sarah's forehead. "Sarah, wake up."

When Sarah only moaned, Jackie slammed her fist on the bedside table. "I bet that motherfucker drugged you!" She grabbed some ice cubes out of the small fridge, wrapped them in the washcloth, pulled Sarah up to a seated position, and leaned her against the headboard. "Hey, girlfriend, wake up." She placed the washcloth over Sarah's forehead and lightly slapped her cheeks. "Wake up."

Sarah moaned again. "Jaaaaackieeeeee?" she slurred. "Where am I? I feel like I'm floating."

Jackie moved the icy cloth all over her face and Sarah started to slowly open her eyes.

"That's it." Jackie kept moving the cloth, from her face to behind her neck. "Girl, I think that asshole put something in your drink." She helped Sarah move to the side of the bed and shift her legs over the edge. "I'm going to take you into the bathroom for a cold shower, okay? Put your arms around my neck."

Sarah complied, and Jackie half-dragged her to the bathroom, where she sat her on the toilet and started the shower.

"This is a really great high, Jack," Sarah murmured. "Those Mai Tais must have something really special in them." She looked around her, suddenly confused. "What are we doing in the bathroom?"

"I'm going to help you take a cold shower so you can wake up. I'm going to take your party clothes off now, okay?" Jackie kicked her own shoes off, then stripped Sarah down.

"Here we go, get ready." She maneuvered Sarah into the shower and of course got herself wet too. "Put your head under the water now."

"What the hell!" Sarah groaned. "Get me out of here, it's too cold. Didn't you pay your heating bill?"

Jackie laughed. "Sarah, we're at the Fairmont—in your room, remember? You need to open your eyes and look at me."

Sarah opened her eyes wide and gazed at Jackie with a perplexed look. Then she closed them.

"Open your eyes again," Jackie insisted. "I need you to wake up."

"I will if you get me out of this freezing water," Sarah said, sounding more like herself. "What the hell!"

"There's my friend." Relief coursed through Jackie. "Come on, now, let's get you a robe and some hot coffee."

• • •

Fifteen minutes later, Jackie had Sarah dried off, robed, and sitting upright in bed, drinking a cup of hotel room coffee.

"You okay, Golden?" she asked as she took a seat on the edge of the bed.

"You're ruining a really great buzz, Jack, but I'm good." Sarah looked down at her cup of coffee, which she was grasping with both hands. "Wait, it's late . . . why am I drinking coffee? I'll never sleep."

"Just drink it; I think that asshole Victor drugged you." Jackie narrowed her eyes. "What do you remember about tonight?"

Sarah gingerly sipped the coffee, then slowly moved her head from side to side. "I decided to go with the program. Bower said I need to play nice with everyone, including Victor, so I did." She took another sip of the coffee. "I think I just drank too much."

"I've seen you hammered, my friend, and this isn't booze," Jackie said. "I think he slipped you a mickey. Drink some more coffee. What's the last thing you remember?"

Sarah looked at Jackie. "Well, first we had a great meal and many beverages . . ."

"Were Chris and Debbie with you and Victor at dinner?"

"Yes, but they left before the after-dinner drink. They went dancing. It's Friday right? They're were going to live it up."

"It *is* Friday night, good remembering." Jackie mimed drinking. "Finish your coffee. I'm starving—I'll order room service, then we can piece this night together."

Jackie picked up the phone and ordered herself a rib-eye steak with all the fixings, wine and dessert.

"If that asshole is picking up the bill," she said as she set the phone back down in its cradle, "I'm going big."

Sarah smiled. "Go for it." She pulled the comforter up around her and finished the coffee. "I'm so glad to see you. Last thing I remember is feeling really dizzy after we finished our after-dinner drink and asking Victor to help me to my room. Next thing I knew, you were putting a freezing cold washcloth on my face. That's all I got."

"I walked in your room and Victor was rifling through your stuff; looked like he'd dumped your entire briefcase and purse out on the table." Jackie's lip curled up in disgust. "He was clearly looking for something. My guess is that he thinks you still have something from Lopez's study. What else could he be looking for?" Jackie refilled Sarah's coffee mug and brought it back to her. "So . . . do you? Have anything else from Lopez, that is."

Sarah sipped the coffee. "I kept copies of everything I put on Bower's desk and put them in my car for safekeeping. But now I think we should just drop this whole Lopez thing." She looked down into her mug. "What's the point, anyway?

We have our lives to think about, and I can't play detective anymore."

As much as she wanted to figure this mystery out, Jackie knew Sarah was right. "I agree," she said. "You're getting married, I have a new job, and life is good and uncomplicated. Let's enjoy that."

There was a soft knock on the door. "Room service," a muffled voice called.

"Coming." Jackie opened the door and let the man roll the cart draped with a white linen tablecloth and bearing several silver domes inside.

"Frank zinfandel," the man said. "Lovely choice. Would you like me to open that for you?"

"Absolutely," Jackie responded.

He poured her a small sip to taste, a white napkin draped over his arm. Jackie could see that he was studying her as she swirled the wine around the glass and then took a sip.

"Delicious," she said with a contented sigh.

"Would you both like a glass?"

"No, thank you." Jackie quickly responded. "Just one for me."

The waiter smiled graciously and filled her glass. "Anything else I can get for you?"

"I think we're all good."

He handed her a black leather holder containing the bill. She signed it and added a hundred-dollar tip. He nodded and quietly departed.

As Jackie tucked into her steak, she realized just how hungry she was. "I haven't eaten since lunch," she said through a mouthful of food. "I'm *starving*." She looked over at Sarah, and was relieved to see that she had some color back in her face.

A cell phone started to ring.

"That's not mine," Jackie said, still busy chewing. "Must be yours, wherever it is."

The ringing kept going, to the tune of "My Boyfriend's Back."

"Isn't that Mo's ring tone?" Jackie asked as she looked through the jumble of stuff Botsworth had dumped on the table. "You're going to have to change that now that you're engaged." She found the phone and answered. "Sarah Golden's secretary, how may I direct your call?"

"Hey Jackie," Mo said. "Good to hear your voice."

"Everything okay? You sound a bit groggy." Jackie had had many conversations with Mo over the years, and he always had a lilt to his voice. But not tonight.

"There's been an accident," he said. "Nana and I were driving in my car and someone ran us off the road. They just gave me something for the pain—seems I have a broken arm and a couple of broken ribs."

Jackie's heart sank. "Is Nana alright?" She hit the speaker button and handed Sarah the phone.

"Nana is not great," Mo said. "She's getting a CAT scan of her head and then she's going to the neurology floor for observation. I'll text you her room number as soon as I get it. I'm so sorry—I didn't see the car until it was next to us and pushing us off the road. Maybe it was a drunk driver, I have no idea, they sped off so fast."

There was some shuffling on his end of the line. Sarah was just staring at the phone, apparently speechless from shock.

"I have to go, the doctor is heading my way. I'll send you the update." Mo ended the call.

Sarah began to sob. "My poor Nana—what have I done, putting her life in danger?" She grabbed a tissue; snot was already running down her nose, and the tears would not stop. "My life is too stressful right now. I can't take it."

Jackie put her arms around her friend. "We'll get to the bottom of this. I promise."

Chapter 20

Back in his suite, Victor re-read all the Lopez study documents and realized some of the data pages were missing. *Maybe Lopez only gave her part of the study,* he thought.

His burner cell buzzed and he picked up. "Angelo."

"Happy to talk to you too. I'm letting you know we took care of the grandma. Some young guy was with her in the car too, they're both in the hospital."

"Good job. Time to up the pressure for these ladies. Why don't you send another message to Larsen?"

"No prob," Angelo said. "What's the message?"

"That her family is next if she doesn't butt the hell out of this."

"Got it."

"Those bitches will be sorry they ever messed with us," Victor snarled. "I don't know why they can't just mind their own fucking business."

"Done." Angelo ended the call.

Victor donned his robe, poured himself a bourbon, and put on ESPN—he needed a break.

The sports announcer was sharing highlights from the Warriors' game that night. They'd killed the Chicago Bulls;

Steph Curry was out of control with his three-point shots. *That guy is insanely talented.* Victor shook his head with appreciation.

He started to scroll through the emails on his phone to see if there was anything urgent. He stopped when he saw a brief note from Leland: *Flying to SF tonight—need to see you first thing in the morning. Staying at Fairmont. I'll come up to your suite. Order breakfast for seven.*

Victor sighed. "Fuck!" He finished his bourbon and showered, then called down to room service and ordered breakfast to be delivered promptly at six forty-five, all the while thinking, *Enough of this insanity.*

• • •

As usual, Leland arrived fifteen minutes early the next morning. Victor was ready for him.

"Leland, you son of a bitch—how the hell are you? Haven't seen you in a long time." Victor shook his hand and then gave him a bear hug.

"You look great, Vic," Leland said.

"You look very fit and dapper yourself." Victor admired his friend's dark blue suit, which fit his slender, six-foot-four frame like a glove. "That suit from Bergdorf Goodman in New York? No one makes them better."

"Remember when we couldn't even afford to buy a pair of socks there?" Leland responded. "Now I have them make me four new suits a year, one for each season."

"You're living the dream; next you'll be on the cover of *GQ*," Victor said.

Both chuckling, they walked into the dining area, where a full breakfast was laid out, silver domes still covering the food. Victor handed Leland a cup of black coffee and they both took in the view of the city as they drank in silence.

"We're going to have a few more visitors this morning," Leland informed him. "I took the liberty of inviting several mutual friends who happen to be out this way too. They should be here any minute."

Victor ran his hands through his hair and glared at Leland. "What's this about, exactly?"

Before Leland could answer, there was a knock at the door. When Victor opened it, he found two men and a short woman, all dressed in sharp suits, standing in the hall.

Leland approached and greeted the guests. "Thanks for meeting us on such short notice; please, come in." He waved them in. "Victor, this is Nixie Klein, Brad Carlson, and Frank Cohen."

"Nixie Klein as in NIH investigator Nixie Klein?" Victor asked.

"I own a private investigation firm that specializes in working with your industry," Klein said with a curt nod. "Have we met?"

"We haven't had the pleasure but I've heard of your work through a colleague," Victor explained. "Nice to meet you." He shook her petite, soft hand, noticing the rather large diamond ring on her left hand as he did. "Nice to meet you as well, Brad and Frank." He shook their hands.

"I'd like to make this meeting as short as possible," Leland said. "Don't want to waste anyone's time Please, have a seat and help yourself to coffee or water."

What the fuck is happening? Victor thought, but he maintained his composure.

"Victor, I'm going to cut to the chase here," Leland said. "We all know there has been a series of unfortunate events in the last couple of weeks, and those events are putting investors in a bit of a quandary about their current holdings with your company. As your friend, I think it's best if we sideline you for a couple weeks; we'll clean up this mess, and then we'll bring you back with a nice bonus. I spoke with your board, and they agree. We think you're too close to the situation, and with the close relationships you've developed with all the major players in the transplant business, you're too valuable of an asset to lose."

Victor tapped his finger on the table, jaw clenched. "I am handling things just fine. I do so appreciate your concern and generous offer, however, Leland."

"It's not an offer, Victor," Leland retorted.

"My firm has been doing a thorough investigation into how—and more importantly, why—these four immunologists were killed, and it's complicated," Klein piped in. "I'm not able to divulge any information, as this is a highly confidential case, but I *can* say that your name has come up in several different places. Let's just say I don't think anything or anyone can be traced to you directly, but it's time to take you off the field. It's in everybody's best interest."

"And who the hell are you, Brad and Frank? Since everyone here seems to know so much about me, I'd like to know." Victor's tone was getting terser by the moment.

"We work with several investors managing their portfolios," Brad said. "We're not at liberty to share their names, but they were concerned enough to deploy us to the West Coast to be present for this conversation."

Victor shook his head and looked over at Leland in disbelief; then he looked down at the table.

"We are ready and able to clean up this situation," Klein said, "and then everyone can get back to their lives. I just need a few pieces of information before you head out for your retreat, Victor."

"*Retreat?* You're going to tell everyone I'm going on a *retreat* right in the middle of this chaos? No one at any of the transplant programs will trust any of you!" Victor's heart was racing.

"We're not having any direct contact with the transplant centers," Leland said, "that just wouldn't be prudent. However, I understand that two women, one of whom one works closely with Dr. Bower here in San Francisco, recently met with Dr. Lopez in Cuba—I believe their names are Sarah Golden and Jackie Larsen?"

Victor nodded with a scowl.

"We just need you to give us an update on their whereabouts and what they actually know, if anything."

"They have nothing to do with anything," Victor snapped. "They're just two nosy broads who I'm handling just fine."

"That's not what I'm hearing," Klein said.

Victor watched her look over at Leland.

"Listen, Victor," he said in a conciliatory tone, "I can see how this kind of change in plans can be upsetting—but the sooner we get all the details from you, the faster this can all go away and we can get you back on deck. It's important that you share what you know with Nixie." Leland pulled an airplane ticket from the inside pocket of his suit coat. "Here's a first-class ticket to Maui." He slid it across the table to Victor. "After you brief her, I've got a car waiting downstairs to take you to the airport."

Victor clenched his fists. "This is just bullshit, pure and simple, Leland, and you know it."

"I'm going to have to disagree with you on this one, buddy." Leland looked over at Brad and Frank. "I know you have a tee time; after Nixie and Victor talk things over, I'll send you a quick update you can share with your bosses."

The two gentlemen nodded and stood up.

"It looks like you and Nixie have things well in hand here," Frank said.

With that, they excused themselves and left.

Victor stood up and paced around the suite, trying to piece together how he got to this place.

"I need to use the powder room," Klein said. "I'll be right back."

When she disappeared into the bathroom, Leland approached Victor. "You're taking this all way too personally, man. It's not your fault we've found ourselves in this predicament; we just have more sophisticated ways of going about things. Trust me, you will come out of this smelling like a rose. I've never let you down yet, have I?"

Victor was still too mad to look at him, but he had to admit to himself that no, Leland never had let him down before.

"Please, just tell Nixie what you know and then let's get you the hell out of here. You've been under a lot of undue stress. Wait till you see the place I got you on Maui—five stars."

Victor shook his head. "I can't leave now; we're starting a new, modified study at all the transplant centers that participated in the original one. There are lots of moving parts, and I'm the only one who can orchestrate this at a national level. I know the results will show what you and your vulture capitalist colleagues were counting on—another huge profit. I just need some time."

Leland shook his head. "There is no time left to give, Victor."

Klein walked back in the room.

"Why don't you give Nixie all the details about Jackie and Sarah," Leland said. "I need to make a few calls."

Victor cleared his throat. "Fine. You tell me what you know, Nixie, and I'll fill in the blanks."

"That's not how this is going to work, Victor," she said firmly. "I told you I can't share any, and I mean *any*, details about the case. If you can just tell me how involved these two women are in this case, best you can, that would be great." Klein took out a leather-bound notepad and opened it.

Victor shrugged. "Jackie Larsen is Sarah Golden's best friend. As far as I know, she has little or no involvement in the case at this time."

"I have to stop you there," Klein said. "I know that she is a new PI and has been emailing some of her PI friends in Chicago, trying to dig up as much as she can about the car accident. I am very well-connected to the entire PI community. Are you aware that she has been trailing you while you've been staying here?"

Victor's eyes opened wide. "Not sure about that—I just met her in person last night."

"Believe me, Victor. We've been checking on her entire family: we know where they live, we know where her wife is at this very moment. I'm nothing if not thorough. Now, what can you tell me about Sarah Golden?"

Victor gazed past Klein as he answered. "She's Dr. Bower's right hand—knows the ins and outs of his entire operation. She's a tough nut to crack, but I got that done last night. She's engaged to a Miami detective who's moving out here to set up house with her. She's close to her grandmother, who is in the hospital as we speak; my team took care of that way before you were on the scene, by the way." He straightened his shoulders. "Sarah and Jackie seem to have little or no involvement in this case, but just to be sure we've taken a few measures. Sarah did get some fake research data from a Dr. Lopez in Cuba, who was unofficially involved in the clinical trial, but I got my hands on all the paperwork he gave her—it's now in the fireplace behind you, in ashes." Victor took a break and watched as Klein took notes.

"Good to know." She tapped her pen against her notebook. "I'm less concerned about Lopez. I *do* need to know what the initial outcomes of the primary study showed at SF Transplant." Victor watched as she kept writing. "Unfortunately, I haven't been able to get any information out of Sarah's team yet. The studies at the other three programs were inconclusive, best I can tell, so I'm not sure we need to be making such a big deal of all this. The new, modified study is already starting at these programs, and SF Transplant will be starting it this week if all goes well."

She closed her notebook and stood up. "Thanks, Victor. I know this whole situation is unsettling for you; just know we will use discretion to wrap it up without a trace to you." She looked over at Leland, who was on the phone in the other room, and waved. "Let Leland know I'll meet him downstairs when he's done. Nice to meet you; sorry it's under these circumstances. But hey, enjoy Maui! I wish someone would hand me a first-class ticket there."

Victor snorted. "How about I give you mine?"

• • •

Ten minutes after Klein left, Leland finally got off the phone.

"Out of sight or not, I'll need to track this new round of studies," Victor said, planting himself in front of him. "I will do that from Maui; I don't need your permission."

Leland put up his hands in surrender. "I have no problem with that; just don't meddle in anything else. Put your out-of-office message on and do not under any circumstances talk to the press or anyone else that wants an update. Now, go pack. I've got this."

Victor reluctantly went into his bedroom, where he called Valerie—only to get an out-of-office message stating she was on vacation and would be back in two weeks. *Leland must have gotten to her as well. Damn it! This means now I'll have to clean up the Cuba-Lopez situation myself.*

He threw his suits into his garment bag and the rest of his clothes and toiletries into suitcase. He wasn't exactly packed for a tropical vacation. He'd have to buy a whole new vacation wardrobe in Hawaii.

"I did suggest that your assistant take some time off too,"

Leland said, popping his head into the room. "If she's not there she can't answer any inquiries from anyone, right?"

Victor scowled. "Right."

"I'll walk out with you . . . sure you have everything?" Leland asked.

"Like you care."

"You'll get over this, believe me." Leland opened the door to the suite, and he and Victor rode the elevator down without a word.

• • •

Leland waited by the side of the desk as Victor checked out.

"Checking out Mr. Botsworth?" the cheerful desk clerk asked. "We hope you enjoyed your stay with us—was everything satisfactory?"

"It was, thank you." Victor pulled out his company credit card and handed it to her; as she took it, he felt a tap on his shoulder.

He turned around, and there was Sarah Golden; he could see Leland standing a couple feet behind her. Sarah put her arm up to slap him and Leland quickly stepped forward and caught her hand before she could land the blow. She whirled around to see who had grabbed her arm.

"Take your hands off of me!" she screamed. "Who the fuck are you?"

"Just a friend," Leland said mildly. "I don't think you want to do that."

Sarah squinted at him for a moment, as if trying to place him, but then she shook her head. "How would you know?" She pulled away from him. "That asshole"—she turned back toward Victor—"*drugged me* last night, and Dr. Bower is going to hear about it." She stepped closer to Victor, her face red. "If I find out you had anything to do with my grandmother's accident in Chicago, I will ruin you and your company. That's a promise."

Victor felt a trickle of sweat dripping down from his forehead and could feel everyone's eyes on him. He knew Nixie Klein was watching the entire scene.

"Excuse me, ma'am, you need to keep it down," the receptionist interjected.

Victor looked directly into Sarah's eyes. "I have no idea what you're talking about." He turned his back to her, finished paying his bill, and proceeded out front, where a limo driver was holding the door open for him.

Chapter 21

Sarah charged out of the Fairmont and watched Victor's limo leave. Then she called Jackie's cell.

"You are not going to believe what just happened," she blurted the second Jackie answered.

"I'm on a stakeout with Hank, I can't talk," Jackie whispered. "I'll call you on my lunch break, if I get one."

The valet brought Sarah's car and she drove toward her apartment, her hands visibly shaking as she grasped the steering wheel. She pulled over to the side of the street, put the car in park, and started to sob; guttural sounds emerged as she held her head in her hands.

A car honked behind her. "Lady," the driver yelled, "are you going or coming?"

"I have no fucking idea!" she screamed back.

Sarah closed her eyes and took a few deep breaths. Then she blew her nose, wiped her eyes, and merged back onto the street.

• • •

As soon as she was back in her apartment, Sarah threw her stuff on the couch and called Handsome.

"Hello my love, how's your Saturday going?"

Just the sound of his voice sent her careening into tears again. "It's horrible," she wailed. "Everything is crashing down!" She grabbed a box of tissues. "They hurt Nana. I was drugged last night . . ."

"Sarah, Sarah, slow down, take a breath," Handsome said. "What the fuck are you talking about, you were drugged? Who did that? And what happened to Nana?"

Sarah took a deep breath, exhaled, and let the tears flow. "Victor Botsworth drugged me last night when I was out with him and two nurses from the research team at the Tonga Room. Jackie found him digging through all my stuff in my room and me passed out on the bed."

"I'm going to hurt this guy, big time," Handsome growled. "I'm booking the first flight I can get and coming out there—things are way out of control."

Sarah stared at her kitchen wall as if in a trance, unable to respond.

"Sarah—Sarah, are you there?"

"I'm here."

"Did he hurt you?"

"No, just drugged the fuck out of me. But thank God Jackie was already planning on spending the night at the Fairmont or who knows what would have happened." She stood up, put him on speaker, and went into her bathroom, where she found the bottle of Xanax she kept on hand for emergencies. She popped one of the small pills into her mouth. "I have to chill the fuck out. I'm jumping out of my skin right now." She walked into the kitchen, grabbed a bottle of sparkling water, poured herself a big glass, and took a long drink.

"Is Nana okay?" Handsome asked. "What happened? When I talked to you yesterday afternoon, everything seemed fine."

"It *was* fine." Sarah sat back down on the couch. "After Jackie kicked Victor out of my room and got me sobered up, Mo called from Chicago—had to be after midnight there."

"Mo?"

"Yeah, he was with Nana when they got run off the road and hit a tree. His arm is broken, and Nana hit her head on the windshield. She was unconscious when they brought her to the ER, but she's awake now. I spoke to her this morning. She's still in the hospital, they want to watch her for another day, but she's insisting that she's fine. She's mostly mad because she's missing her card game tonight." Sarah had to smile a little at that part.

"She's a tough old broad, just like her granddaughter," Handsome said proudly. "Why was she with Mo?"

"Apparently he takes her out to dinner on Fridays, she looks forward to it every week." Sarah grabbed her softest, most fuzzy comforter and covered herself with it. "He really loves Nana. It's actually very sweet."

"He does know that we're engaged—right?" Handsome sounded a bit miffed.

"He wasn't the first person I called today, if you're asking that," Sarah said, stiffening, "and there's nothing between us anymore. I've told you that more than once. And just so you know, I cannot deal with a jealous boyfriend right now."

"Honey, I'm sorry, but is it so crazy for me to be a little on guard with Mo? You were sleeping with him when we were broken up, you used to be engaged to him, and now he has a standing Friday date with your grandmother. Maybe you can cut me a little slack."

"Fair enough," Sarah admitted.

"Anyway, I'm coming out there ASAP, and we'll figure this whole thing out when I get there. But I need to know—did you drop the whole Lopez thing, for real?"

"I did drop the entire thing," Sarah said. "I put the folder with all his study papers on Bower's desk, and that was it. Case closed. Don't care if doctors were murdered, patients got sick and died, what have you . . . I can't save everyone, I washed my hands of it."

"I just needed to hear you say that," Handsome said, sounding relieved. "And Jackie's not snooping around with her new PI license, right?"

"She did a little snooping a couple days ago, but she's got a new job now and we both agreed case closed, even if it's not. Not our job, and no one else seems to care so, why should we, right?" Sarah sighed.

"I've seen you two in action; I'll believe it when I see it with my own two eyes." Sarah could practically see him rolling his eyes. "I'm going to make my plane reservations right now. Why don't you take a long, hot bath and try to relax, and I'll call you back in a bit with my flight info, okay? I need to tell the Chief I'm heading out. Hey, you want some good news?"

"Please."

"Campos is back at the precinct. She's sporting a leg cast and using crutches and she's doing desk work for now, but she's so glad to be working. She can pick up some of my workload. And she said to tell you congratulations, you got yourself a real catch." He cleared his throat. "Her words, not mine."

"Tell her she's right," Sarah said playfully, "and that she better lose those crutches, because she's got a wedding to attend and we'll be doing some serious dancing there!"

"I'll let Campos know. Hey, maybe we can entice Nana to come out for the wedding a few days early, spoil her a little."

Sarah brightened. "Nana would love that. She loves San Francisco—cable cars, Irish coffee, she'll want to do all the tourist things. That's a great idea." Her mind swiveled back to the problem at hand. "For now, though, I need you to help figure out who ran her and Mo off the road and if it had anything to do with this stupid Lopez thing. I know you have friends at the Chicago PD . . . Pretty please?"

"I'll see what I can find out," Handsome said doubtfully. "Those types of things are hard to trace unless Mo got a make on the car or a license plate."

"You do remember that note I found in my hotel room in Cuba, threatening my family."

"I do—but Sarah, we need to be done with this. It's a pretty far stretch from Cuba to Chicago. There are such things as accidents not related to anything." His tone grew more gentle. "You try to relax. I need to make some arrangements. Love you."

"Love you too. Thank you for being here for me. I can't even imagine having to go through this alone."

"I'm here for you *always*—not going anywhere. Let you know when I've booked my flight."

Sarah ended the call, then sat back and snuggled under her comforter. The pill was starting to work its magic on her; she felt much better already.

She sat up, opened her laptop, and checked her work email. After learning that Dr. McKee had changed the biopsy protocol order from weekly to monthly, she had sent the other three transplant programs that had participated in the recent study a quick note the previous day, asking if they'd done weekly or monthly biopsies. She was just curious. All three programs had responded saying that indeed their docs had changed the frequency from weekly to monthly midway through the study.

Sarah shook her head; fewer biopsies would make it look like the drug was working better than it really was. *Nope—not even going there*, she thought. She shut her laptop, curled up under her blanket, and closed her eyes.

Chapter 22

Jackie got home right before Wyatt was going to bed. She had had a long day with Hank. Their stakeout had lasted well into the evening, and she'd had to keep her cell phone turned off. Once she'd turned it on, she'd seen multiple texts and voicemails from Sarah, but she hadn't called her back yet; she wanted a few minutes with her son first.

She walked inside their beautiful bungalow to a fresh floral bouquet sitting on the dining room table with a card addressed to her; the room was softly lit by lamps and she could hear Grandma's voice upstairs, reading to Wyatt.

"I'm home," she announced.

Wyatt came running downstairs, Dusty right on his heels. "Mama! I missed you today." He wrapped his small arms around her.

"I missed you something awful too, buddy." She dropped her backpack and black bag and picked up his thin nine-year-old body. She kissed his cheeks and they rubbed noses.

"What's in the black bag, Mama?" Wyatt asked as Jackie put him down and petted Dusty.

"You are not going to believe what I got to take home." Jackie carried the bag over to the living room coach and sat down. "I can't wait to show you everything."

Wyatt sat next to her and watched as Jackie removed a surveillance camera with different lenses, a video recorder, collapsible tripod, and a small silver case that contained a variety of small- to medium-size microphones attached to wires and clips. His eyes widened as he surveyed all the gadgets. "Can I try the video cam?" he asked.

"Not tonight, but we will absolutely play with these later," Jackie promised. "However, they're very expensive, so you can't touch anything unless I'm with you or I'll get in trouble with my boss, okay?"

"Okay, Mama," Wyatt agreed. "Can I at least touch the camera?"

Jackie glanced upstairs and saw Grandma tapping her watch. "Okay, you can hold it for a second, but then it's time for bed. Maybe tomorrow I'll give you the whole rundown on how they work. We can pretend Grandma is the criminal and we'll follow her. How does that sound?"

"Yes, and let's bug her room too!" Wyatt skipped up the stairs and Jackie followed him.

"What kind of criminal will I be, Wyatt?" Grandma asked in jest.

"A bank robber on the run!" Wyatt responded.

"Okay," she said, "but I can't really run too fast, so be nice . . . and no handcuffs. Deal?"

"Deal."

After Wyatt said good night to his grandmother, Jackie and he took turns reading one of his favorite kid detective books, *Top Secret Adventures*.

"I want to be a detective just like Aunt Sarah's boyfriend," Wyatt said after they finished the story.

"You'd make a great detective," Jackie said, "and Aunt Sarah's boyfriend is coming out this week, so let's talk to him about it." She tucked him in and kissed his forehead. "Love you, junior detective."

"Love you too, Mama," he said sleepily, "and I'll hire you to be my own private investigator when I grow up."

Jackie's heart just melted. "I'll be ready. Good night, buddy."

• • •

"You want some dinner, Jack?" Grandma asked from the kitchen when Jackie came downstairs. "I made some chicken nuggets and a salad, there's a lot left over."

"I'm good—my trainer Hank and I got some burgers and fries when we finally finished things up tonight." Jackie put her black bag by the door and then headed into the kitchen. "I think I will have a drink and a cigar on the back deck to celebrate my first full day of work, however—would you care to join me?" Jackie poured herself a rum and coconut water with lime.

"I'm going to head upstairs and read before I hit the hay," Grandma said, "but thanks for offering. Oh, I forgot to tell you: Laura called and said she's coming home early, she misses all of us too much. She's taking a late-morning flight from LA tomorrow and was hoping you'd pick her up at the airport."

"I would love to pick her up!" Jackie said. "I miss her, we hardly had any time together after I got home from Cuba. I'll text her and let her know." She wrapped her mother-in-law in a hug. "I'm so glad you're here, and thanks for taking care of Wyatt. I really do appreciate it."

"I know you do." Grandma squeezed her back. "It's my privilege to be part of my grandson's life, and yours and Laura's too. You're both doing a great job being moms. That little boy adores you."

"I think he loves his grandma a lot too."

• • •

After Grandma headed upstairs, Jackie took her drink and one of her Cuban cigars outside. She cut off the tip, sucked on the end to ensure it was moist, lit it with one of her long cigar matches, and took a long draw. "That's what I'm talking about," she said as she slowly blew out the smoke. When she went to close the cigar box, she noticed there was a piece of paper tucked under the cigars and pulled it out. It read, *If you're reading this note and haven't heard from me, you need to call Duardo Mirabal at the cigar factory. Don't contact Benita, you'll put her in harm's way*. Dr. Lopez had written Duardo's number and ended the message with, *Please help my family get out.*

This thing is not going to go away, Jackie thought.

She took another long draw of her cigar, followed by a sip of her drink, and then called Sarah and left her a voicemail—"Call me as soon as you can, Golden, we've got a situation here"—and then proceeded to read all of the text messages and listen to all of the voicemails Sarah had sent her throughout the day, including a story about a stand-off with Botsworth in the lobby of the Fairmont. The last message was that she was on her way to pick up Handsome at the airport.

Jackie took a few minutes to herself, smoking her cigar and sipping her drink. *I wonder if I should tell her about this note. We did promise Laura and Handsome that we were done with all of this crazy sleuthing.* She swirled her drink, considering. *I'll call her tomorrow*, she finally decided. She should enjoy her time with Handsome tonight.

• • •

Done with her cigar and back inside the house, Jackie was about to go upstairs to go to sleep when she once again noticed the beautiful flower arrangement that had greeted her when she first got home and realized she hadn't opened the card.

"It was so thoughtful of Laura to send these," she whispered to herself, taking in the colorful array of flowers as she opened the card: *Good luck with your new job*, it read. *Keep your nose out of the transplant world or else you and your family will pay.*

Jackie's heart stopped. It was too late to call the florist to find out who had sent them, although she had her suspicion: Victor. She picked up the arrangement and dumped it outside in the garden, then poured herself another drink and went upstairs to watch *Queer Eye* on Netflix. If that couldn't take her mind off everything, nothing could.

• • •

Laura was waiting for Jackie at the curb when she pulled up at Arrivals at SFO the next day. Jackie jumped out, hugged Laura, grabbed her bag, and jumped back into the SUV.

Laura gave her a questioning look as she slid into the passenger's seat.

"I don't want those airport-cop assholes blowing their whistles and waving their stupid arms at me like I'm the Unabomber," Jackie told her.

"Good strategy. Anyway . . ." Laura leaned over and gave her a nice long hello kiss. "I missed you."

"I guess you did!" Jackie smiled as she pulled the car away from the curb. "I missed you too. How was your conference? Didn't you present an abstract?"

"I did indeed—and it went better than I expected!" Laura said. "Someone from the NIH approached me about a possible grant. I'm so excited. I'd be collaborating with several other medical examiners in Chicago, Boston, and Miami."

Laura started rubbing the back of Jackie's neck, and Jackie relaxed into her touch; it always calmed her down.

"Hey, how's our boy doing?" Laura asked. "I called him every day, but you know little boys are always too busy to stay on the phone. I'm so glad my mom is here; it makes everything run smoothly."

Jackie stroked Laura's arm as she looked at the road. "Our boy is *so* happy. He's been taking great care of Dusty. And he has a birthday party all day today—won't be home till after dinner—and your mom has plans this afternoon, so we'll have the house to ourselves for a few hours. It's so good to see you and touch you; I'm so glad we'll both be home together tonight, sleeping in the same bed."

Jackie looked over and saw a twinkle in Laura's eyes.

"I can't even remember the last night we got the whole house to ourselves—sounds great," she said. "I hope it involves food. I'm starving; my flight was so early that I didn't get a chance to eat."

"Actually, I made us an early lunch reservation at Cavallo Point."

"Ooh!" Laura gave the back of Jackie's neck a squeeze. "You can't beat that view of city and the Golden Gate bridge—I'm excited. Anyway, tell me all about your first day of work."

Jackie shared everything with Laura—well, almost everything. She decided to leave out all the crazy stuff about Sarah and Cuba, at least until after lunch.

• • •

During a long, leisurely lunch, Jackie and Laura shared more about their time apart, then went out to the porch, sat in the rocking chairs, and took in the view holding hands.

Laura looked over at Jackie. "Let's make some fun plans for the holidays. I'm thinking we could rent a cabin up in Lake Tahoe—get Wyatt some ski lessons, drink hot cocoa by the fireside, have a real winter Christmas!"

"You're sure planning ahead." Jackie chuckled. "It's only August, and we have Sarah's wedding before that. But yes, I'd love to head up to Tahoe . . . I just have to check with my boss to see if I can get the time off." Jackie glanced over at Laura and saw her grinning. "What?"

"Look who has a boss now! My working girl." She nudged Jackie. "On a different note: I'm a little afraid to ask, but what are you thinking about for Sarah's bachelorette party?"

"This last week has been such a whirlwind, with me starting my new job and Sarah having a horrible time at work—honestly, I really haven't given it much thought. I do have some fun ideas, but I have to make some calls and wait till Sarah's world slows down a bit before I make any decisions. Handsome came in from Miami yesterday, so I'm sure she'll be in a better mood this week."

"What's going on with Sarah?" Laura frowned. "I thought things were calming down."

"Let's get the car and head home while it's quiet and we can have some alone time," Jackie said. "I'll update you while we drive."

• • •

As they drove north on 101, Jackie shared everything about the research study, Victor Botsworth, Nana's accident, and Sarah being drugged.

"Holy shit!" Laura's mouth dropped wide open. "I can't believe you're just telling me this now. Did Sarah call the police and have him arrested?"

"It's complicated," Jackie said. "Botsworth and Dr. Bower are tight and Bower *just* gave Sarah a serious talking-to about being nice to Botsworth, being a team player, blah blah blah."

"Who the fuck cares?" Laura demanded. "What would have happened if you hadn't interrupted that asshole?"

Even with her eyes on the road, Jackie could see Laura staring at her.

"Does this have anything to do with that whole Lopez issue in Cuba? And what else aren't you telling me? I can tell when you leave some things out."

Jackie felt a flush creeping up her neck. "SF Transplant gets a lot of financial support and benefits from Botsworth's company; it would have been Botsworth's word against Sarah's, and at this point Sarah thinks Bower would believe Botsworth, which sucks but is probably true." Jackie turned the car off at their exit.

"And? Have you been keeping your nose clean like you promised?"

Jackie glanced over and saw Laura glaring at her. "Full disclosure," she said, "I did do a little surveillance in the lobby of the Fairmont a few days ago—but Botsworth had no idea who I was until I walked in on him in Sarah's room. I was not in harm's way *at all*... honestly!" Jackie pulled into their driveway and turned off the ignition. "Let's finish this conversation in the house."

She got out, grabbed Laura's bag from the trunk and went inside. She waited for Laura to come through the front door, but she didn't.

She peeked outside; Laura was still sitting in the passenger's seat.

Jackie walked back outside and tapped on the car window. "Please come inside. Please?"

Laura shook her head.

And we were off to such a good start at lunch, Jackie thought, opening the passenger door. "Babe, c'mon," she pleaded.

Laura slid out past her and stomped toward the house just as her mom came out, all dressed up.

"Welcome home, honey," she said, "how was your tri—uh-oh, you're wearing your angry face." She darted an amused look in Jackie's direction. "I'd know that one anywhere."

"Hi Mom," Laura muttered. "Not a good time right now. Have fun. We'll talk when you get home."

A car horn interrupted them.

"That would be Hal, he's taking me for an afternoon drive since it's such a beautiful day. Take a deep breath, sweetheart, everything will turn out just fine—it always does."

"Ever the optimist, Mom. Have fun." Laura gave her a kiss on the cheek, then paused. "Who's Hal?"

"Just a friend—a nice older gentleman who moved here from New Jersey recently. I met him last time I was at bingo. Bye."

Laura watched her mom dance off to Hal's car and drive off, a bemused look on her face. Then she swiveled back to Jackie, confusion replaced by a scowl. "Inside. Now."

• • •

After watching Laura pour herself a glass of wine and go out to the backyard, Jackie made herself a drink and joined her.

"Honey, I am so sorry," she said, head hung low. "I didn't think our conversation would go south so fast."

Laura shook her head. "What did you expect, Jack? That I would hear the news about Sarah, who is family, and then you breaking a promise to stop this insane sleuthing, and I would want to go upstairs and make love to you after all that? Seriously. Where is your head?"

Jackie walked over to her. "I love you so much, Laura. I wouldn't do anything to jeopardize our family, *ever*."

She went to kiss Laura; Laura pulled back.

"But that's exactly what you *did* do. We've worked so hard to get to this place in our relationship, and now I feel like I can't trust you." Laura suddenly noticed the flowers Jackie had dumped outside the night before. "What's with the flowers?"

Jackie briefly turned away from Laura. *Here it goes.*

When she turned back again, Laura had taken a seat. She sat down in a chair facing her.

"I came home last night and they were here. I thought they were from you until I read the card after Wyatt went to bed."

"I didn't send you flowers, Jack . . . I was going to take you away for an overnight in the city for a proper celebration next weekend. Who are they from?"

Jackie took a big gulp of her drink, then pulled the card out of her jacket and handed it to Laura.

"Good luck with your new job," Laura read out loud. "Keep your nose out of the transplant world, or else you and your family will . . . *pay?*" Laura dropped the card on the ground. "So now you've dragged your family into your irresponsible behavior too? Un-fucking-believable!"

"Please don't go there," Jackie pleaded. "I did nothing to earn those flowers! I just started my new job; I haven't had time to do anything related to this Lopez thing. I just came home last night and the flowers were here. I don't know who they came from, I didn't even have a chance to contact the florist."

"But you were going to get to that tonight, right? Don't bullshit me, Jackie. Now our family is in harm's way because of you." Laura shook her head in disgust. "I think I need to go upstairs and take a bath and you need to stay away from me so I can calm down. I feel I have been more than patient with you over the past couple years, but I'm at the end of my rope right now." Laura started up the stairs.

Jackie bent down to retrieve the card Laura had just dropped. When she straightened back up, she shouted after her wife, "And you *cheated* on me, so don't act like you're Miss Perfect, Laura!" Jackie was past contrition now; she was fuming. "I'm going for a ride; you soak in the bath and let me know when I can come home so we can move past this."

She stormed out, slamming the front door behind her.

Chapter 23

Victor was in the Ambassadors' Club at SFO, drinking a double bourbon and checking his email to see if Valerie had responded to him from her private email. Nothing. He tried her cell phone again and it went straight to voicemail.

Frustrated, he gave up on Valerie and placed a call to Arthur Butler, the president of Lago, on his home phone line.

"Butler residence," a young woman's voice answered.

"Is Mr. Butler available? This is Victor Bosworth."

"Mr. Butler is out at the moment. May I take a message?"

"Would you please be so kind as to ask him to call me on my cell phone at his earliest convenience?"

"Mr. Butler is out of town and won't be back for several weeks," she said. "But I'll be sure to let him know you called upon his return."

"Thank you so much," Victor said, putting on the charm. "Would you be able to tell me where he is?"

"I can't give out that type of information, but if you'd like to call his office assistant, she may be able to help you. Have a good evening."

Victor barely took a breath before calling Arthur's assistant's cell. She picked up, but she didn't sound happy.

"It's the weekend and I'm out with my family," she said quietly. "What do you need, Victor?"

"I really need to talk to Arthur. Do you know where he is?"

"I don't," she said. "He and his wife planned a trip to celebrate their fortieth anniversary overseas. I think they were going on a cruise, but I'm not sure."

"That sounds lovely," Victor said acidly. "When you do hear from him—I know he always keeps in touch, even on his vacations—would you let him know I called and I really need to speak with him?"

"His wife was adamant that he turn off his work email and cell for this one, but yes, I'll let him know if he does call or email. What shall I tell him this is regarding?"

"It's about our tolerance clinical trials; there's been a rather big problem, and it's best he hears from me and no one else."

"I believe he was already briefed on this before he left for vacation," she said. "But yes, of course, I'll give him your message."

Leland didn't miss a thing, that bastard, he thought, but he kept his tone even as he said, "Thanks, I really appreciate that."

Victor motioned for another bourbon and checked the monitor in the club. His flight to Maui was delayed three hours. *Fuck Leland, I'm not going to Maui.* He slammed back the bourbon, left the bartender a generous tip, grabbed his bags, and called an Uber back to the city.

• • •

Once he was safely checked back into the Fairmont—he'd explained to the receptionist that it was important for his privacy to use a different name this time—Victor placed a call to Chris.

"Hi Victor," she said. "So nice to hear from you. What's up?"

"If you don't have plans for dinner tonight, I'd love to take you out," he said.

"Two nights in a row? What a treat—I'd love that! Where shall I meet you?"

"Why don't you meet me in the lobby of the Fairmont and we'll catch a cab from there. How's seven sound?"

"Perfect!" she said. "See you soon!"

• • •

Victor was down in the lobby when Chris entered wearing a short dress and high heels.

"You look smashing, Chris." He kissed her cheek. "I hope you like Greek food; I made us a reservation at Kokkari."

"Love that place!" Chris smiled. "I haven't had Greek food in years."

They made small talk in the cab on the way there. Once they were seated, Victor took charge of ordering, including a bottle of wine.

"So tell me, Victor, why this dinner out?" Chris asked coyly. "You just took us to the Tonga Room last night, if you recall. Thank you for that, by the way. Debbie and I had such a wonderful time."

"I'm glad you enjoyed it," Victor said. "I certainly had a lovely evening with you and Debbie too. Sadly, I think Sarah had too much to drink; I had to help her to her room after you two left, she could hardly walk."

"Yikes, that must have been embarrassing."

"I was glad I was able to help her up to her room," Victor said gallantly. He leaned forward and lowered his voice. "I hate to tell tales out of school, but she didn't have very nice things to say about the work you and Debbie were doing wrapping up the study."

"Are you fucking kidding me?" Chris exploded. "We've been working our asses off, getting home after nine at night. We got everything off to the NIH right before we met you at the Tonga Room. I even ran Bower down in the OR to sign off on paperwork. Dr. Sethna, Dr. McKee's boss, stayed late and signed off on her part as well. She said we did such a thorough job that she wants us to take lead on a new study she's running."

"I met with her last week," Victor said, nodding. "She's amazing—so talented."

"Well as far as I'm concerned, Sarah can go fuck herself—pardon my language." Chris tossed her head. "I've already decided I'm leaving transplant and either joining Dr. Sethna's team or maybe your company, if that's still on the table."

Their food arrived and the waiter refreshed their wine. "That's why I wanted to see you tonight," Victor pounced. "I have an offer for you as head of our nurse research team. It starts at one hundred and fifty thousand a year, plus a sign-on bonus of five thousand and four weeks paid vacation. I wanted to give it to you in person."

Chris stopped eating and looked over at Victor. "That's an amazing offer, I'm flattered. Can you tell me more about the team I'd be managing? And a bit about the kind of benefits the position would offer?"

Once Victor shared all the details, he could tell Chris was all but in. "When do you think you could start, Chris?"

"I'd need to give three weeks' notice," she said, "but now that we've wrapped up things on the old study, I could leave earlier as long as Dr. Bower is cool with it. Debbie could run this new study with her eyes closed." Her eyes opened wide. "Speaking of . . . What about Debbie? Do you have anything for her?"

"Not at this time, I'm sorry to say—but once you're on board you may find something for her. Is she interested in leaving?"

"I don't think so, I just wanted to ask. She has lots of family in the Bay Area. I think she's a lifer at SF Transplant."

Victor raised his glass. "Well, their loss is our gain. Here's to you joining Team Lago, Chris."

Chris clinked her glass against his. "Of course I'll need to see everything in writing before we finalize the deal. I'm looking forward to meeting Valerie in person." She smiled. "It feels like we could be fast friends."

"Valerie is on vacation," Victor said, biting back his annoyance at her disappearance. "But as soon as she's back she'll send you the offer letter with all the details. I think you'll be glad you joined our team; we have so many growth opportunities at our company. We pay for you to attend the international transplant meetings, as well as the big ones here in the States."

They finished their meal and ordered an after-dinner drink. Victor glanced over at Chris, who was leaning back in her chair, wearing a sweet, slightly fuzzy smile.

"Just between friends . . . would you be willing to share the findings of the study now that that all the paperwork has been closed out?" Victor sat back and watched Chris carefully.

She shrugged. "Why not, they're going to be public soon. We got a call from an intense woman who works for the NIH . . . Nixie something. She was insistent we not speak to anyone, but she's not my boss."

Victor nodded and sipped his Greek liqueur. *Now we're getting somewhere.*

Chris took a sip of hers too. "That's some strong stuff there." She set her glass down and looked directly into Victor's eyes. "The short story is that it looks like the study results were very questionable, but there were enough small, positive outcomes that they'll spin those and declare that the study demonstrated an important step to achieving tolerance—which is true, as long as no one digs deep into all the clinical indicators."

Victor leaned forward, frowning. "Chris, you know that's not going to fly. The scientific community is quite rigid regarding declaring victory. If the original study hypothesis does not achieve all the promised outcomes, then it's a failure. Seems we have a long way to go; we'll likely figure out how to transplant a pig kidney successfully before we're able to reach that golden ticket of tolerance." He shook his head. "But you must admit it is an exciting journey—one I expect we'll be chasing for some time."

"It *is* exciting," Chris agreed. "That's what makes me want to stay at SF Transplant: it's where the real work happens. I love patient contact and working with our team."

"I'm curious, did this Nixie person say why you had to keep everything under wraps?"

"Oh yeah, you'll love this one." Chris rolled her eyes. "She said the NIH is going to announce the preliminary results at the immunology conference next week in Chicago. The NIH spokesperson will share the data, such as it is, during the conference on Saturday; and the society is going to honor all four immunologists who died at a cocktail party Saturday evening."

"That's news to me." Victor's eyes widened. "We're the sponsors of that cocktail party; I just signed off on it. Not cheap, by the way." He narrowed his eyes. "Well, I'll be there to hear firsthand what they have to say." *No wonder Leland wants me out of town.* "How's the enrollment going for the modified study?"

"We're almost full since we basically transferred most of the primary study patients over," Chris said. "The modified protocol requires weekly kidney biopsies; actually, the first one did too, but for some reason Dr. McKee changed that to monthly and never told Debbie or me. Sarah was going to check with the other three programs to see if they changed their protocol too. Technically the results of the first study are null since they went off protocol but no one seems to care, including that Nixie person."

Victor cocked an eyebrow. "Did Sarah share what the other programs did?"

"Nope, not her style to share that kind of thing." Chris flapped a hand in the air dismissively. "I'm sure she'll tell Bower and Sethna. I'm so done with the politics of this whole thing. Sarah's such a control freak."

"That must be tough to be around day in and day out," Victor said sympathetically.

The waiter placed the bill down and Victor gave him his credit card.

Chris shrugged. "Anyway, I'm guessing that we'll be able to close the new study and report the results at next year's meeting in Rome."

"Hopefully you'll be attending that meeting as our employee." Victor winked at her. "With a generous expense account, of course."

"Sounds like a dream." Chris glanced at her watch. "Yikes, it's late—time just flew by tonight! I need to head out. Sarah called a meeting for 7:00 a.m. sharp tomorrow to finalize the timeline for the modified study; Debbie, Dr. Bower, and Dr. Sethna will all be there. Bower's got a case at eight."

They both stood and walked outside.

"I think it would be best if you don't mention our dinner tonight to Sarah or anyone on the team," Victor suggested as he stepped into the street to flag down a cab for Chris.

"Hey, it's Sunday night; what I do on my personal time is none of their business," Chris said. "And I'd appreciate it if you kept my interest in Lago quiet until the ink is dry too."

A taxi pulled over in front of them.

"This one's for you! We'll get an offer letter out to you in the next couple weeks; until then, I know nothing." Victor grinned and put his hand out. "Deal?"

"Deal." Chris shook his hand, then hopped in a cab.

• • •

Only once Victor was back in his suite did he realize he had left his burner cell in his briefcase. When he took it out, he saw three missed calls from Angelo. He called him back.

Angelo picked up on the fourth ring.

"It's after midnight," Angelo groused, his voice groggy. "Just a minute."

After some scuffling around on the other end, Victor heard the click of a lighter.

"I saw you called three times," he said. "Thought it was important enough to call you back."

"It *is* important. I am totally fucking confused here. I'm working for you—right?"

"That's the way it's always been," Victor said, frowning. "Why?"

"This arrogant guy called me, tried to pressure me about what I was doing for you. When I refused to tell him, he threatened me. I'm not really sure how he found me, I work in a small network. Seems someone blabbed."

"Was his name Leland?" Victor clenched his teeth.

"It sure was. He said if I do one more thing you ask, or touch those two women, or do any more snooping around the car crash, I'm dead." Victor heard him take a long drag of his cigarette. "Who the fuck is this guy?"

"Fuck!" Victor slammed his fist down on the desk in front of him. "Believe it or not, he's a good friend of mine. *Was* a good friend of mine."

"Some fucking friend. Well he sounded pretty serious, so I'm going take a powder for a while."

"That's probably a good thing, I think you've done what you can do. Do I owe you any more money?"

"Nope. Valerie has already dropped off the cash for the Chicago work. We're good."

"Thanks. I'll throw the burner phone in the garbage after I take the chip out."

"Good. One more thing. Before I heard from your asshole friend, I did some more digging around the car crash. My guy in Chicago said the FBI has no suspects and no prints. Case is cold. They're closing it out and moving on to other things."

"Thanks for letting me know. Were you able to find out if anyone was digging into the pharmaceutical companies as suspects?"

"Never heard a hint of that, so seems your pals are free and clear if they did anything. No big news there; cover-ups are getting better and better these days. No trace of anything."

An idea occurred to Victor. "Hey, how would you like a free ticket to Maui and a place to stay? Call it a bonus."

"Why the hell not? Be nice to get away."

"You'll have to transfer the ticket to your name, but that shouldn't be a problem with your connections. I'll send you the details."

"Thanks Victor."

"Sure."

After leaving identical voicemails for the other CEOs of big pharma, Erika Mason, and Otto Penton—"Coast is clear; enjoy your Sunday"—Victor paced back and forth in his suite, unable to stop thinking about his next moves.

It was after one in the morning. He'd call Bower tomorrow to schedule a dinner.

Chapter 24

While Sarah waited at the San Francisco airport cell phone lot for Handsome's flight to land, she called her grandmother.

"Hi Nana, how are you feeling?"

"I'm fine," her grandmother insisted. "Just some bruises—and a concussion, which just means I have a great excuse for forgetting things now."

"Oh Nana." Sarah felt entirely helpless. "I'm so sorry this happened to you. Really, how are you?"

"It's not your fault, honey. Some drunk drove us off the road. Luckily your Mo is a good driver; it could have been worse."

"He's not *my* Mo anymore," Sarah said gently. "He's more your Mo than mine now. And I'm so grateful he was with you and that you're home safe and sound."

"He has been so sweet," Nana said, "checking on me every day. And his aunt Mabel comes by the house every day to play a few rounds of poker, too—she's not very good, by the way, but it's a nice way to pass the time." She chuckled. "Anyway, how are you, my Sarala?"

"I'm good," Sarah lied. She wasn't about to worry Nana; she would focus on the positive. "I'm waiting for my fiancé to land—he's flying in from Miami right now. He's got lots of job interviews this week, and we're going house hunting. I'm so excited!"

"You should be, sweetie." Nana sounded proud. "Getting married, settling down . . . If only your parents were alive to see this."

"I think they'd approve, don't you?"

"Oh yes," Nana said warmly. "And don't forget I have a little something set aside to help you pay for your wedding and new home. They left you a nice nest egg that has been doing well in the market over the last ten years."

"I'd almost forgotten about that," Sarah said. "Out of sight, out of mind! I'm glad it wasn't sitting in my bank account, though—you know me, I'm a spender. It'll be helpful when we start house hunting; the prices here are ridiculous, as always. Who knows—maybe we'll just move to Chicago and buy a house right next to you!"

"Like that movie *My Big Fat Greek Wedding*," Nana said gleefully. "We'd have such fun."

"We sure would." Sarah suddenly remembered Handsome's suggestion from the previous day. "Guess what? I have a surprise for you."

"I love surprises! Do tell."

"Handsome and I were talking, and we decided we'd like to fly you out early for the wedding. We can visit Fisherman's Wharf, take a streetcar ride, and sip a yummy Irish coffee at the Buena Vista. How's that sound?"

"That sounds wonderful," Nana said, "but I'll have to let you know about dates. I have a big poker tournament at the American Legion coming up, and if I win that we go to Madison, Wisconsin, for the next round—all expenses paid. I wouldn't miss your wedding for the world, of course," she added hastily. "But I may just be able to do both."

Sarah shook her head in wonder. "Nana, you are something else. I miss you."

"Miss you too but I need to go—time to watch the *Golden Girls*. You know I never miss it."

"I know it," Sarah said. "Okay, I'll call you tomorrow. Sleep tight."

"Give your fella a big hug for me."

"I'll give him ten, at least. Bye, Nana. Love you."

After Sarah hung up, she checked Handsome's arrival time: delayed one hour.

Good thing I brought the paperwork from the tolerance study with me. She spent the next hour reading all the details and taking copious notes. It was clear that the change in the frequency of the biopsies had seriously skewed the data. *None of this is right.*

She had an appointment with Dr. Sethna Monday afternoon; she'd bring her notes and go over them with her. She was sure she'd see what she was seeing.

• • •

When she finally got Handsome's text announcing his arrival, Sarah's stomach fluttered. She drove to the terminal and spotted her handsome fiancé on the curb, looking fit as fiddle in his tight jeans and black leather jacket. *Man that guy is buff—and he's mine!* she thought as she pulled up. She got out of the car, walked around to him, and planted a long kiss on his full lips.

Handsome picked her up and twirled her around. "Hello, my love."

She looked into his rich, deep brown eyes. "I'm so glad you're here." She hugged him tight—only to be interrupted by the loud whistleblower moving everyone along.

Laughing, they both hopped in the car. Sarah looked at Handsome. "You hungry?"

"Starving," he responded.

"Chinese? Burmese? Indian?"

"Fast food will do me just fine," he said, "the sooner the better. Happy to eat in the car on the way home." He kissed her cheek.

"I've got just the place," Sarah said with a smile as she pulled away from the curb.

• • •

Fifteen minutes later, Handsome broke the silence in between bites of his In-N-Out burger.

"How are you really doing, honey? I'm so sorry about what happened at the Fairmont. Thank God Jackie was there; you couldn't ask for a more committed friend. I'll be having words with that Botsworth asshole, just so you know." His tone grew dark. "I'm not asking for permission; I'm just letting you know."

Sarah nodded. "Honestly? It's been really tough. I was already questioning if I wanted to stay in this job, or even in transplant; now I'm wondering if I can tough it out till after our wedding. It's just too much."

"I know you, and things must be really bad for you to be talking like this," he said. "I'm here for you, honey. Whatever you need." He reached over and rubbed her shoulders.

Sarah sighed. "I just wish I knew what that was."

• • •

When Sarah and Handsome arrived at her apartment, she had several candles ready to light and a bottle of champagne waiting on ice.

After they were inside, she put her arms around him and held him against her, feeling the energy between their two bodies pulsating.

He took her face in his hands. “You’re safe, Sarah Golden. I will take care of you the rest of your life, no matter what, no matter where you go.”

Sarah tucked her head deep inside his shoulder and started to sob. She hadn’t realized how stressed out she was until now.

They stayed in each other’s arms for a good long while. Once Sarah was finally able to take a deep breath, she moved away. “I think I need something stronger than champagne. Would you like a bourbon?”

“Yes, but let me get it,” Handsome insisted. “You go sit on the couch and I’ll bring us both some.”

Sarah let out the longest sigh. “I guess I just hold on to all the emotions and hope they will go away,” she said as he ducked into the kitchen. “I know it’s not healthy, but until I met you that’s all I could do.”

Handsome came back with two snifters and handed her one. “You don’t have to do that any longer. I’m here for you. Can you accept that?”

Sarah held up her bourbon. “I can, I’m ready to trust you, love you, and let my guard down.”

She took a sip and felt the bourbon warm her throat. Handsome sat down next to her, and she snuggled up to him. He tipped her face toward his and gently kissed her. Her shoulders immediately relaxed; she set her drink down, wrapped her arms around his neck, and kissed him back, everything in her body tingling.

As if he could sense that, Handsome scooped her up and brought her into her bedroom. They slowly undressed each other between kisses and disappeared into passionate lovemaking.

• • •

The next morning, they lay on their sides, facing each other. Sarah stroked Handsome's face. She could see that he was studying her closely.

He kissed her nose. "Now that we've taken care of the important stuff . . . are you ready to tell me everything about this insanity so I can put on my detective hat and put an end to this nonsense with Botsworth?"

"I am."

"Everything, Sarah; don't leave out one thing."

"I won't."

"Okay, then," Handsome said. "From the beginning."

• • •

Sarah had finally finished telling Handsome everything about Cuba and Dr. Lopez, leaving nothing out this time—including how she'd smuggled those papers back in her bra. Now he was grilling her about what had happened since her return to San Francisco.

"So you got out with the papers and then you put them in a folder on Bower's desk," Handsome said, stretching out full-length in Sarah's bed. "What did he say about them?"

Sarah wrinkled her nose. "He never said anything. I'm not sure he's even seen them, he's been so busy. I did make a copy of everything I gave him, though, just in case I needed them for something."

"Where are the copies now?"

"In my purse, I re-read them while I was waiting for you at the airport."

"Lopez was unofficially conducting this study with drugs Botsworth sent him," Handsome mused, drumming his fingers on his stomach. "On the surface, it doesn't seem like such a big deal. If Botsworth were to get caught he'd likely just get a slap on the wrist, I'd imagine."

"Unless his actions were made public and the press got a hold of it." Sarah propped herself up on her elbow. "Lago has a pristine reputation; if he tarnished it like that, he would lose his job and all that went with it."

"So it's in his best interest to make Lopez and any evidence of his study disappear," Handsome surmised. "No trail, no problem."

"Correct. But I'm sure there are other players, assuming that all this is connected with the car crash in Chicago. Who else? Who would want all those brilliant scientists dead, and why?" Sarah flopped back down on her back next to Handsome.

"Does anyone know the outcomes of their studies, and could they be linked to Lopez's findings? Or would that even matter, since he wasn't formally part of the study?" Handsome grabbed a piece of paper and a pen from Sarah's nightstand and started jotting down notes.

"That's a great question," Sarah said. "I found out this week that Dr. McKee had changed an important clinical test to happen monthly when it was supposed to be weekly, according to protocol. And the other three doctors who died had done the same."

"That doesn't sound like such a big deal—not enough to kill them." Handsome rubbed his forehead.

"Maybe not, but it means all their studies were scientifically flawed," Sarah said thoughtfully. "The less you biopsy a kidney, the less you see rejection at the cellular level. My guess is that they could have claimed an early victory inducing tolerance with the new drug they were testing and that would have been a big deal."

Handsome yawned and stretched. "I think moving around will make me think better. You up for a walk?"

Sarah smiled and nodded. "A stroll through Golden Gate Park sounds like just what I need." She pulled Handsome up to sitting and kissed him. "Coffee and food first, though. I'll get a pot going, you raid the fridge."

• • •

"Okay," Handsome said as they passed a stand of eucalyptus trees, "who stood to lose if these doctors' studies were successful?" He looked down at the piece of paper in his hand, scrutinizing the notes he'd written down so far. They'd been walking for over an hour, going over and over everything they knew.

"There are three big pharmaceutical companies that produce most of the drugs that prevent rejection—Lago and two others," Sarah said, taking his free hand in hers. "If patients didn't have to take all those drugs, they could lose millions, if not billions in drugs sales. I'm guessing Lago would stand to lose the most."

"Any other players involved?"

"NIH partially funded this study, so they have skin in the game. They are very strict about everything science, and if a major medical center was caught messing with a protocol, the entire center could be in jeopardy of losing all their funding. That would be very bad for SF Transplant; we get the most funding from the NIH in the country, and have for years."

Instead of responding to this, Handsome grabbed her and spontaneously kissed her.

"What was that about?" she asked. "I'm not complaining, but . . ."

Handsome wrapped his strong arms around her and whispered in her ear, "Someone's been following us since we left your place. I wanted to see how far back they are."

She stiffened. "What do we do?"

"Just keep walking for now," Handsome murmured.

They continued down the path until they came across a bench. Handsome guided Sarah toward it, and they sat down.

He took his cell phone from his pocket. "I forgot to turn my phone on this morning."

"That's nice," Sarah said, trying to act normal. "It's good to let those phones rest so we can just be together without any interruptions. I left mine at home."

"Even better," Handsome said, smiling. "Mind if I check mine quickly, though? I told Campos to call or text if she needed any more information on a couple cases—and did I tell you my nephew broke his leg playing football yesterday? My sister was going to call to let me know how he's feeling."

"Oh no, poor guy!" Sarah said. "Of course, please, check away." She laid her head on his shoulder and they both watched his phone as the dings announced voicemails and texts.

"Looks like Jackie called *and* texted—we better give her a call." Handsome hit her number and put it on speaker.

She picked up on the first ring. "You two done having wild sex? I've got a situation here."

They both laughed.

"I'm fine, how are you, Jackie?" Handsome ribbed her.

"I think we need to meet in person today," Jackie said. "Can you meet me halfway—say, at the Starbucks in Tiburon—in about twenty minutes?"

Sarah could hear the tension in her friend's voice. "Is everyone okay Jack?"

"Not really," Jackie said, her voice cracking. "I think my family is in danger—and that's all I'm saying until we're in person. Can you meet?"

"Sure," Sarah said hastily. "We're out for a walk, but we'll go get my car and see you soon."

"Great." Jackie ended the call.

Handsome and Sarah briskly walked back to her place.

As they hurried along, Sarah couldn't help but glance over her shoulder a few times.

"What about the person you saw following us?" she whispered.

"Bigger fish to fry right now," Handsome said. "If they keep following us, we'll deal with it."

• • •

Jackie was waiting for them outside the Starbucks. When she saw Handsome, she gave him a big hug.

"Your timing couldn't be better, we have big problems," she said. "I need to hand off everything I know and then go home and save my marriage—again."

"What is it, Jackie?" Sarah said, near frantic with worry. "Is Wyatt okay?"

"He is right now," Jackie said darkly. "But someone sent a flower arrangement to our house yesterday; the card was addressed to me, I thought it was from Laura." She handed the card to Handsome and he and Sarah read it at the same time.

Handsome was quiet, but blinking so rapidly that Sarah could tell he was thinking at warp speed.

"You haven't touched this case since you kicked Botsworth out of my hotel room, right?" she asked Jackie.

"Not a thing," Jackie said. "But someone must have noticed I was snooping around the FBI investigation of the car crash. I just can't figure out how! I didn't leave a trail—no texts or emails, just calls to a friend who has been keeping me in the loop. And the only other thing I did was trail Botsworth at the Fairmont and break into his room. But that was before I started working full time—and I'm pretty sure no one saw me at the hotel."

"You broke into Botsworth's room?" Handsome shook his head and walked away from them.

"Sarah—Laura is beyond pissed." Jackie scuffed the toe of her shoe against the sidewalk. "And I can't blame her. Once I've download everything I know about this case to you two, I need to step far away from it. I wonder if we're going to have to leave our house for a while?"

Sarah put a hand on her arm. "I'm sorry, Jack, this is some scary shit."

Handsome walked back, planted himself in front of them, and looked directly at both of them. "Enough is enough," he said. "It's time for professional law enforcement now. Whoever sent you the flowers also has someone following us, and they clearly mean business. They could be the same people who had the doctors killed. So is there anything, and I mean *anything*, else you know that I should know?"

Jackie pulled a note out of her pocket. "I found this in my cigar box yesterday."

Sarah and Handsome read it. Sarah gasped. "Oh no, poor Dr. Lopez!" She looked at Handsome. "We have to help him."

"Stop," Handsome said. "There is no 'WE' here! *We* can't save Dr. Lopez or his family—end of story. *I*"—he pointed at his own chest—"will be investigating this case going forward, and I do not need or want your help. Are we clear here?"

Sarah and Jackie nodded.

"Good. Now, is there anything else you haven't shared yet?"

Sarah looked at Jackie. "What about that Leland guy—the name you got from the pad of paper in Botsworth's hotel room?"

"Leland Ackerley." Jackie nodded. "I did some digging and he's a big-time venture capitalist, works for Science Enterprise Associates. SEA does some heavy investing in Big Pharma. Lago is one of the companies they've invested in."

"If a venture capitalist firm has anything remotely to do with this case, we need to run, not walk, the other way," Handsome said. "They have more money than God and can afford to pay to make things—including people—go away at the snap of a finger. This is way out of our league. I'll need to call in a few favors to see if I can get you off their radar, if that's even possible at this point. I don't mean to scare you, Jackie, but people like this wouldn't think twice about killing you and your family. I'm guessing they were behind what happened to Mo and Nana."

Sarah's heart beat faster and faster the more Handsome said. "You're freaking me out here," she said. "Seriously. Can we bring this down a notch or two?"

"You *should* be freaked out, Sarah." Handsome looked over at Jackie. "And you should be too, Jackie."

"Oh, believe me—when I read that card, I started to shake. Do you think I should move my family somewhere else until it's safe?"

Handsome shook his head. "No point, they'd find you in a minute anyway. Just stay where you are, keep close tabs on Wyatt, and go about your life like it's business as usual. If anything out of the ordinary happens going forward, you are to do nothing about it—nothing but call me. Understood?"

"Understood." Jackie gave Handsome a quick hug, then threw her arms tight around Sarah. "Now I need to go home and hope Laura will talk to me. I'll keep you posted; there may be three of us sharing a bed at your place tonight, Sarah."

"The couch is always yours, my friend." Sarah chuckled, then her face grew serious and she grabbed Jackie's hand. "Be careful, okay?"

Jackie nodded. "You too, pal." With that, she hightailed it for her car.

"I'm going to take us to Ocean Beach so we can take a nice long walk along the water," Sarah said as they walked away. "Sound good?"

"Perfect," Handsome replied. He lowered his voice. "And by the way, we're still being followed."

Chapter 25

Jackie clenched her teeth as she thought about how to break all the news Handsome had just shared to Laura. She felt nervous—and conflicted. *I'm not sure I can back completely out of this investigation if my family is in danger.*

When she got home, Laura was reading the Sunday *New York Times* on the couch and her mom was in the kitchen making something that smelled delicious.

"Hi family," Jackie called out.

Dusty trotted over to Jackie and nudged her leg with his nose.

"Hey, little guy." Jackie bent down and petted him.

"Hey Jackie," Grandma hollered from the kitchen. "Hope you're hungry. Dinner in an hour."

"Always!" Jackie called back, then sat next to Laura on the couch. "Anything good in the news?"

Laura ignored her and kept reading.

"How about we go for a little walk?" Jackie suggested. "It's such a beautiful day."

"Not in the mood." Laura retorted.

"How about I make you a cup of tea?" Jackie tried again. "Or maybe a stiff drink?"

Laura put her paper down. "How about you tell me everything that's going on—and let's bring my mother in on the whole story, too, since some insane person has our home address and she's the one who's always here with our son?"

Jackie studied Laura's face. "Do you really think we should tell your mother? I don't want her to be freaked out."

"Do you have a better idea, Jackie?"

"I do have a bit of good news," she volunteered. "Handsome is in town! And he's going to take charge of all this so that Sarah and I can step away completely—in fact, he's insisting upon it."

"Well, that means at least two of us have our heads screwed on straight," Laura acknowledged, softening slightly.

Jackie sat back and pondered how to explain everything that was going on. Should she lay out the whole story? Or just the parts of it that were most relevant for her mother-in-law to know?

"Mom," Laura sang out, "can you come in the living room? Jackie needs to talk to you."

Shit, Jackie thought. *Well, here goes nothing.*

• • •

Even after she'd explained much of what had transpired in the last couple of weeks, Jackie could tell her mother-in-law was still not quite grasping the seriousness of their situation. She paced back and forth in the living room while Jackie thought through her strategy.

"What all this means is that we're going to need you to keep a close eye on Wyatt going forward," she said, pacing the room. "Instead of him going to a friend's house to play, have him invite them over here. I'll even buy a second handset for his PlayStation—that'll keep them busy for hours."

Jackie wrote down Handsome's cell number in large print and handed it to her mother-in-law. "If anything happens—if you think there's someone following you when you take Wyatt to school, or you see a suspicious car hanging around the house—text Handsome right away, he's on duty."

Grandma raised her eyebrows. "I can do that."

"If Handsome doesn't respond right away, call me, Laura, or Sarah—and if for some reason we don't respond, dial 911."

"I'm getting scared," Grandma said. She was now rubbing her hands on her apron, over and over. "Are we going to be okay? Is someone really going to try to kill us? Should we just go stay somewhere else till this blows over? Maybe I could ask Hal if we can stay with him. He lives within walking distance of Wyatt's school . . ."

"No," Laura hopped in. "We want to keep things as normal as possible for Wyatt."

Grandma nodded. "I was going to have Hal come over for a drink some evening this week . . . should I tell him not to come?"

"Not at all," Jackie said. "Feel free to invite him over any time. Everything as normal as possible, remember? And this is your home too."

"Thank you. I do feel very at home here." The oven timer went off in the kitchen. "Pot roast is done!" Grandma retreated to the kitchen to tend to it. "Dinner in fifteen!" she called over her shoulder.

"Let's go upstairs and hash out the rest of our game plan," Jackie said. "I need to talk to you in private."

Laura frowned. "Fine."

Jackie led the way upstairs.

• • •

When they were alone, Jackie broke down.

"Laura, I am so sorry about all of this—I really am. I

need you to forgive me, please. You have to know I would never have gotten involved in any of this if I thought it would endanger our family." She buried her face in her hands. "I'll do whatever you want me to do—I can quit my job and stay home, if you think that's best. Our family is the single most important thing to me in the world."

Laura stepped toward her and wrapped her arms around her. "You don't need to quit your job," she said. "But I do need you to be prepared to stop whatever you're doing and leave work right away if my mom calls. Can you promise that?"

"Yes, absolutely." Jackie sat on the edge of the bed and patted the space next to her.

Laura sat down and let out a deep sigh.

Jackie rubbed her back. "We'll get through this, honey. Now that Handsome's on deck and knows everything, I think we'll be okay."

"I hope you're right, Jack."

"Dinner's ready!" Grandma called from downstairs.

Laura and Jackie enjoyed a tender kiss.

"That feels good," Laura said. "It's been a while."

"It has," Jackie agreed. "From now on there'll be a lot more of that—I guarantee it."

• • •

After dinner, Laura helped her mom clear the dishes and Jackie went up to their room to call Sarah.

"Everything okay?" Sarah answered breathlessly.

"Some good news for once!" Jackie announced. "Did some brainstorming over dinner tonight with Laura and her mom, and I need you to block Friday, Saturday, and Sunday of next weekend—we're going to Chicago for your bachelorette party."

"Chicago?" Sarah repeated. "*Next weekend?* That's crazy!"

"Nana insisted and that's all I can tell you," Jackie said smugly, feeling quite pleased with herself.

"Handsome just got here, and Bower will have a cow if I leave so soon after getting back," Sarah said. "And what about Laura? Isn't she still pissed at you?"

"Laura's fine with it, I swear," Jackie said. "I don't understand it either; the woman must really, really love me."

"I don't know," Sarah said. "Maybe we'll do the bachelorette after the wedding—after everything calms down and the venture capitalist mafia isn't chasing us. I hate to dampen your spirits, Jack, but I have so much going on at work, and I really need some low-key Handsome time."

"Party pooper." Jackie stuck her tongue out at the phone. "Just ask Handsome, see what he thinks. I'll wait."

"Now? You want me to ask him now?"

"Yup, I'm about to put some money down on our private party!" Jackie laughed. "Go on, just ask him. I'll wait."

Jackie continued to search for flights while some mumbling went on at the other end of the line. Several minutes later, Sarah was back.

"You're not going to believe this, but he thinks it's a brilliant idea. He has job interviews and he's going to be working our case, so he'd prefer if we were as far away as possible—less chance of our meddling. He's not thrilled that our destination is Chicago, but I promised him we'll stay far away from anything that even remotely looks like trouble."

Jackie whistled loudly. "Let's do this! I'll book your flights when I book ours. You don't need to know anything else. I'll give Handsome all the details so he'll know where we are every minute of the day. We may not be sober, but we'll at least keep our phones on."

"I'll wait a few days before I spring it on Bower," Sarah said nervously. "At least we finished all the old study paperwork and it's off to the NIH—that'll make him happy. And honestly, if he fires me, he fires me. I'm so burned out."

Jackie could hear Handsome calling for Sarah in the background. "Sounds like Prince Charming is summoning you."

"We have a dinner reservation, got to go. I'll let Nana know the plan is a go when I talk to her in the morning."

"You're not gonna regret this, Golden," Jackie said, grinning. "It's gonna be a celebration for the ages!"

• • •

Jackie was still working on securing reservations for Sarah's bachelorette party when her phone rang. She checked the screen; the call was coming from someone with a Miami area code.

"Hello," Jackie answered, "this is Jackie Larsen."

"Hi Jackie, it's Maria."

"Maria!" Jackie leaned back in her chair. "To what do I owe this pleasure?"

"I have some news . . . Sergio and I got married!"

Jackie gulped. "Married? Isn't he still in prison?"

"He is," Maria said. "We tied the knot anyway."

Jackie slapped her palm to her forehead. *What is she thinking?*

"Well—I guess congratulations are in order, then," she said hesitantly. "He's lucky to have you, Maria." She wasn't quite sure what else to say.

"Thanks." Maria sounded relieved. "I know you, Sarah, and Handsome had some reservations, but my heart belongs to him and he is the father of my son. My parents have been so supportive; they feel better now that I'm married—they're old-fashioned that way, and it meant a lot to them."

"Please give your parents and Marco my best," Jackie said, shaking her head. *Why don't you just ask a fucking axe murderer to be Marco's godfather while you're at it?*

"Thank you, I will," Maria said. "Anyway, I'm calling because Sergio wanted me to relay a message to you, Sarah, and Handsome. I don't have many details but he wanted me to tell you that Dr. Lopez and his family are out of Cuba and in a safe place."

Jackie was breathless for a moment; then she recovered her voice. "What?" she demanded.

"That's right, they are all safe—and Sergio wants to speak directly to Handsome. Can you give me his number? Sergio's able to place calls from prison."

"Sure," Jackie said. "I'll text it to you as soon as we hang up, and I'll let Handsome know he'll be hearing from him. Any idea when that will be?"

"Very soon—I guess there are some specifics that Dr. Lopez needs Handsome to know, and Sergio promised him he would convey those."

"Well I am so relieved that Dr. Lopez and his family are out of Cuba," Jackie said. "Sarah and I were really worried."

"I'm glad I could give you some good news," Maria said. "By the way, Marco is still eating the candy you filled his piñata with—he's not going to need any more candy for a long time. He had a fun time with you when you were all here. When are you coming back to visit?"

"No time soon, Maria," Jackie said honestly. "But maybe you and your folks can come out to visit San Francisco!"

"That would be lovely. You never know. Well, I need to go take Marco to his piano lesson. Take good care!"

"You too." Jackie hung up. "Wow to the fucking wow," she said out loud. She texted Handsome's contact info to Maria and then immediately called Handsome.

"Hey Jack, what's up?"

"You're not going to believe this."

Chapter 26

Victor went for a run along the Embarcadero early Monday morning. As he jogged, he plotted how he was going to take control of things and let Leland know he didn't need his help anymore. After he got back, showered, and had breakfast, he secured an early dinner reservation with Bower. Next, he called the president of the International Transplant Immunology Society.

"Hi Dr. Jasper," he greeted him when he had him on the line. "I won't take up much of your time; I just wanted to confirm that you're satisfied with all the arrangements for the cocktail party to be held the final night of the meeting in Chicago? I understand that the NIH has planned a special tribute for your colleagues who passed." Victor paced back and forth as he waited for Dr. Jasper's response.

"I think everything is in order," Dr. Jasper said. "Your assistant did an exceptional job of arranging everything—it's quite extravagant, thank you. Of course we'd love to have you come up after the tribute and briefly share a few thoughts as well."

At least Valerie handled that *before Leland gave her a vacation*, Victor thought, rolling his eyes. "Who will be introducing your NIH speaker, if I may ask?"

"We were very fortunate to get a transplant surgeon from Cuba to do the honors—which, given the turmoil between our two countries, is something of a miracle, don't you think?"

Victor got a heavy feeling in his stomach. "That *is* a miracle. Anyone I might have heard of?"

"Very possibly," Dr. Jasper said. "Dr. Lopez, he's based in Havana. He's done some great research given the restrictions he faces in Cuba. Are you familiar?"

Victor paused and noticed he was clenching his jaw. He had to concentrate to relax it. "I do know him, some of his research is quite impressive indeed."

"Seems he was in close communication with our four lost colleagues right up until their tragic accident," Dr. Jasper said. "I very much look forward to hearing his tribute to them—and his perspective on the future of tolerance. Whoops, look at the time, I need to let you go, Victor. See you soon."

"Before you go—do you happen to know where Dr. Lopez will be staying?" Victor asked quickly. "I'd love to take him to dinner when he gets to Chicago."

"I don't. My assistant confirmed his presentation through email; if you'd like to connect directly with her, go ahead. I'm running late for a meeting. See you in Chicago."

"Looking forward to it, Dr. Jasper." Victor hung up—then threw his coffee cup across the room. "FUCK! How did that asshole get out of Cuba?"

He collected himself, then searched his contacts to see if he had a number for anyone from Valerie's family. After no small amount of cursing, he finally found her sister's cell number and called her.

"Hi Alice, this is your sister's boss, Victor. Can you tell me how I can get a hold of her? It's an emergency."

"She's been pretty offline since she went on her trip," Alice said. "Wish I was on an all-expenses-paid vacation in Tahiti right now! Lucky duck. Instead I'm here in New Jersey, living through her vicariously."

Victor had to work hard to summon focus as he realized, *Another Leland hit*. "That's right, she did win that contest," he said lightly. "Do you have the name of the resort she's staying at? I forgot to make a note of it."

"Sure." Victor heard her rustling through some papers. "Here it is; they even gave her one of those fancy huts that sit over the water. Talk about lifestyles of the rich and famous."

"I need another beer—now, Alice!" a male voice bellowed in the background.

"Uh, I have to go." She hung up.

"Are you fucking kidding me!" Victor slammed his fist on the table, grabbed his briefcase, and stomped out of his suite. He'd try Valerie later.

"Victor Botsworth, is that you?"

The question came just as Victor exited the Fairmont and stepped onto the sidewalk outside. He spun around and came face to face with a tall, muscular man dressed in pressed blue jeans, a tight T-shirt, and a fitted leather jacket.

"I don't believe we've met," Victor said. "I don't mean to be rude, but I'm late for a very important meeting."

"I bet you are, my friend," the man said. "Looks like you're having a stressful day for it being so early."

"Who are you?" Victor squinted at him.

"That's none of your fucking business, asshole." With that, the man hauled off and punched him squarely in the solar plexus.

Victor dropped his briefcase and fell on the ground, gasping for air. Holding his stomach, he tried to get up.

"I think you may want to stay on the ground—unless you want another one." The man kicked him in the ribs. "Does the name Lopez mean anything to you?"

"Who the fuck *are* you—who sent you?" Victor looked up.

The man kicked him again. "I'm the one asking questions, asshole. You better fucking watch your back, 'cause I am all over you and I have a team of people who want you either dead or put in prison. Do you hear me?"

He kicked him again. Victor moaned.

The man walked away.

Victor sat up, but he waited until the man was out of sight to stand up and retrieve his briefcase from the ground. His ribs ached.

I knew it was just a matter of time before I felt the wrath of Leland for blowing off Maui, he thought as he brushed the dirt from his suit. *He must have hired someone to rough me up.*

He called Angelo; the call went to voicemail. He decided to go back to his hotel room to assess the damage, clean himself up, and regroup.

• • •

Victor placed a call to Tahiti as he pressed ice to his tender ribcage. The hotel receptionist connected him to Valerie's cabana and she picked up.

"Hello?"

"Valerie," he snapped. "What the hell happened? Where have you been?"

"Leland arranged a surprise trip for me," Valerie said, sounding surprised at his anger. "He said it was from you, for all my hard work. I can't thank you enough. I'm sorry I didn't call, but I only had a couple hours to get ready and go to the airport."

Victor put his cell on speaker, sat down, and adjusted the ice. "I didn't have anything to do with your trip. Leland is all up in my business, and he tried to get rid of me too. I need to know where you left things with Dr. Lopez and his family—every detail, it's crucial."

"Leland made it sound like it was all your idea," Valerie said, sounding concerned. "Are you okay?"

Victor could feel his skin growing numb from the ice. "Not really. I just got beat up outside my hotel by some thug—probably hired by Leland. I think I might have some cracked ribs."

Valerie gasped. "Oh my God—you should call the police, that's horrible!"

"That would only complicate things," Victor said. "Tell me about Lopez. What was the last report from Cuba? Obviously, the team we hired failed miserably from the start, because now he's in the States with his family. If he tells anyone about how I supplied him with drugs for his research, I am as good as dead in my industry." He got up and refreshed his ice.

"Last thing I did before I left for Tahiti was to confirm with the people we hired that they would make him and his family permanently go away—I paid them. I'm guessing we won't ever see that money again." She snorted.

"Did you hear from them at all afterwards," he pressed. "Anything?"

"No," she said simply. "They said the job would be done and it was best if we didn't know any details. That's usually the way we handle things, Victor: the less we know, the better. I'm not sure if there is anything we can do now." She sighed. "What a mess. I'll make a few calls and send some emails and let you know what I get. Does anyone else in the States know about our . . . 'relationship' with Dr. Lopez?"

"I don't think so—at least not yet. But Dr. Lopez is going to be standing up and speaking in front of everyone at the conference in Chicago, so who knows who he'll talk to. Obviously I'll be hunting him down before then to see if I can encourage him to keep his mouth shut. This entire thing went south so fast, Valerie. Leland brought in someone else to handle everything going forward and tried to send me to Maui, saying they want me to lie low and promising a big bonus and promotion after this thing is put to bed." Victor stretched his neck from one side to the other, eliciting a few cracks.

"That sounds like a good offer if you ask me," she said. "Can you do that?"

"Not with what's on the line—you know that. My plan for now is to make sure the new study is well on its way here, then fly to Chicago and see if I can sniff out Lopez."

"Do you want me to come home and help?"

"No, you enjoy your trip and order lots of expensive booze and food." He wanted Valerie happy and firmly on his side if shit hit the fan. "Let me know if you hear from our Cuban loser team, and you can take care of them once you get home."

"Will do—and don't you worry, I'll go top-shelf on everything." Valerie chuckled. "Call me if you need me for anything. Please be careful!"

"I will."

Victor hung up and immediately called Leland.

"How's Maui?" Leland answered.

"You know fucking well that I'm not in Maui," Victor exploded. "I can't believe you sent a thug to beat me up. Seriously, we were friends—this is totally unacceptable, Leland!" He touched his torso and winced.

"Whoa, whoa!" Leland said. "You need to take a breath. I have no idea what you're talking about. Why would I have you followed, let alone injured, if I sent you to Maui to cool things down? Where are you, anyway?"

"Where are *you*, Leland?"

"I'm in Napa at the Silverado."

Victor grunted as he shifted in his seat; his ribs were aching. "I'm back at the Fairmont, under an alias this time. If you didn't hire the guy who just used me as a punching bag, who did?"

"I honestly have no clue," Leland said. "What did this guy look like?"

"Tall guy, about six-four; dark hair, really fit; wicked right punch." Victor managed a laugh.

"Did he say anything while he was hitting you?"

"That he's watching me and there are people who want me dead. He did ask if the name Lopez meant anything to me . . . I didn't answer, obviously." Victor placed a hand over his sore ribs.

"Now we're getting somewhere," Leland said. "Who else knows about Lopez? You never told me the deal with him, anyway."

"The only two people who know anything about him, far as I know, are Sarah Golden and Jackie Larsen. When they were in Cuba, he conned them into bringing copies of his study results to Bower. Golden put a file with those results on Bower's desk, but I removed it before he saw it."

"What if Bower did get the information—do you think he'd really care?"

"I can't afford to find out," Victor said. "If he pulled that thread, it could become public that I gave Lopez the drugs under the table, and Lago would be put under pressure to explain why. We'd lose respect throughout the international transplant community—and given how consistently our stocks have been rising, I'm sure *The New York Times* would try to link it to the dead immunologists and use it to cast doubt on the collaborative study. You know when the *Times* gets their teeth in a story there's no stopping them. Just a minute, my head is killing me." Victor went to the bathroom, threw some aspirin in his mouth, chased it with water, and returned to his spot in the living room. "Okay, I'm back."

Leland wasted no time getting back to the point. "We have to nip all of this in the bud, no loose ends. Any idea at all who the guy was that beat you up? I've had someone following both the broads, and if he's with them then we'll have our man soon."

"I saw he had a gun packed under his coat when he slugged me," Victor said slowly, trying to remember. "Looked like a cop, definitely knows his way around a street fight. I felt it from his first punch. One of the research nurses from SF Transplant who I've been working for information mentioned that Golden's boyfriend is a cop . . . maybe it's him? I'll call her, she'll be able to tell me what he looks like."

"You know, Victor, this is why I wanted you out of the picture—so that if things got bad and people had to disappear, you wouldn't know anything and would have the perfect alibi." Leland sighed. "I had that sassy blonde I sent you last week waiting for you in Maui. I guess she'll just enjoy the beach and sunsets by herself."

Victor cleared his throat. "Oh, she'll have company—though I'm not sure if he's her type. I gave my fixer from Jersey the plane tickets and condo information. He's not exactly a handsome man. And it's possible he'll bring his wife."

Leland laughed. "Well, you never know. Listen, I'll see if I can find out where Lopez is staying. We need to silence him, and the broads too—one way or another."

Chapter 27

When Sarah's alarm went off at five-thirty Monday morning, the scent of coffee was coming from the kitchen. Eyes still closed, she put her hand over to find Handsome, but his side of the bed was empty.

She felt his gentle touch on her face. "Good morning, my love. I made you coffee."

Sarah sat up in bed and he handed her a cup of coffee. "You know how to wake a lady up."

Handsome sat on the edge of her bed, all showered and ready for his day. "I have a few other ideas to make sure you're wide awake."

"Hold on there, cowboy, I think we took care of that last night." She winked at him and sipped her coffee. "It's so nice to have you here."

"Here to serve, day and night." He kissed her softly. "I'm heading out—I have lots on my plate today."

Sarah looked into his rich brown eyes. "Where are you going so early?"

"I'm going to figure out who's been trailing us. I have a meeting at seven with Inspector Davidson at the SFPD;

remember, she helped us nail our killer last year? I want to let her know what's going on with us and see if she can share a few names of private investigators in case I need backup."

"Don't tell Jackie," Sarah warned. "You know her dream is to be your partner someday; she just wants you to teach her the ropes."

"This is not the kind of work Jackie should ever be doing." Handsome shook his head. "I need someone who can get physical and has a gun. I hope it doesn't go that far, but I need to have backup just in case."

Sarah's stomach clenched. "Yikes, don't like hearing the gun part. You know how I feel about those. I saw too much damage when I worked in the ER; the world would be a better place if no one carried firearms."

"They're a necessary evil," Handsome said evenly, "you just have to know when to use them. Speaking of which, I also have an interview with the San Jose PD this afternoon." He kissed her again. "You be a good girl at work today so you can get your permission slip signed to go to Chicago, okay?"

Sarah gently stroked his clean-shaven face. "Take care of yourself, okay? You don't have Campos here to watch your back. Text me—like, a lot—so I know where you are. I'm not sure what time I'll be done today, but let's catch dinner somewhere as soon as I am."

He kissed her slowly. "Sounds good on all counts, sweetheart."

As he headed for the front door, Sarah yelled after him, "It must be true love—I haven't even brushed my teeth yet."

"You know it!" he called back with laughter in his voice.

• • •

Sarah showered and got to work by six thirty—her favorite time, when no one was there and she could get prepared for her busy work day. She sipped her second coffee of the day as she scrolled through her email and confirmed her calendar.

Looks like it's going to be another nonstop day, she thought as she finished her coffee and rose from her seat. *Time to get going.*

She headed down the hall to the conference room closest to Dr. Bower's office.

Sarah opened the door and there was Dr. Bower on his phone, looking more awake than she'd seen him in a long time.

"Looks like you weren't on call last night," she said brightly. "Hey, did you ever get a chance to look at the folder from Dr. Lopez I put on your desk a week ago?"

He didn't look up. "I didn't see the folder when my assistant cleared and organized my desk, and frankly, I don't care. I'm in the middle of preparing for several abstract presentations and finishing up two articles for publication."

The Bower I know would care, Sarah thought, disappointed. *Maybe it's a bad day*. She sat down and opened her portfolio with her research notes. "Dr. McKee's study is closed and we sent everything off to NIH on Friday."

"About time," he said curtly. "Glad to hear the NIH thing is done. It's taken up way more time than it should, and I need these research nurses getting the modified study done sooner than later. All the other programs are done with their enrollment, and I don't like being last. We have three times the number of patients they do. Get it done, Sarah."

It is definitely not a good day, she thought. *He only gets this testy when something is going on at home.* Sarah recalled some of the things she'd seen the previous year when she and Jackie followed his wife in Florida as they tried to figure out who'd murdered Maria's brother. Bower's wife definitely took her wedding vows very loosely, and he knew it. He had stayed with her after her last indiscretions came out, but maybe she'd found a new boy toy.

Chris, Debbie, and Botsworth walked into the conference room together. Botsworth walked right up to Dr. Bower and shook his hand.

Is it my imagination, or is he limping a little? Sarah thought.

"Nice to see you," Victor said to Bower. "I'm glad we'll be seeing each other tonight. There's some important information I need to share with you over dinner." He sat down right next to the doctor, scrunching his face up a little as he did, like he was in pain or something.

I hope a taxi hit him—now that would be karma for you. Sarah felt better for a second; then she saw the look that passed between him and Bower, and she swallowed hard. *I wonder what that liar is going to tell him now.*

"Looking forward to it," Dr. Bower said. "So, where are we with the new study, Chris and Debbie?"

"Thanks to *all* of Victor's support"—Chris smiled and winked at Botsworth—"Debbie and I were able to get everything on the old study wrapped up and we have over 90 percent of the patients from the old study rolled over. We think we'll be able to close out enrollment by the end of this week."

Sarah quietly watched the exchange, pretended to write down notes, but she just wrote, *Fuck you, Victor!* over and over in her notes. She felt ready to throw up.

"That's great news," Dr. Bower said, the clouds clearing from his face a bit. "Victor, I can't thank you enough for stepping up to the plate. I know this work is way below your pay grade. Were you able to glean anything from the data you sent to the NIH?" He looked over at Chris.

"There were a few minor victories," she said, "but overall we weren't able to demonstrate tolerance at any level."

Sarah watched as Chris looked over at Botsworth and he nodded at her. She drew a deep breath and then let it out. "I'm not sure it's really ethical to have Mr. Botsworth here for this conversation," she blurted out, "and I have to disagree with Chris."

Dr. Bower narrowed his eyes. "Sarah, we are way beyond ethics; we need all the help we can get here, so don't look a gift horse in the mouth. I want this entire study done—over. At this point, any way we can get it done is fine with me." He looked back down at his phone. "If you have any questions about the data, take it up with Dr. Sethna; the NIH grant was given to her department, not mine."

"Oh," Sarah said quickly, "I have a meeting with her today, actually. I've carefully reviewed the data, and something is not right. We'll be discussing that—at length. Hopefully it won't influence the modified study." She glanced over at Botsworth with a smirk.

"Let me know what she thinks." Dr. Bower stood up. "I need to go to another meeting. You four can handle this."

He stood to adjourn the meeting, but Chris stopped him. "Dr. Bower, I really need to talk to you—can I walk with you to your next meeting?"

"Sure," he said, and gestured for her to precede him out of the room.

As soon as they were gone, Sarah stood up and glared at Botsworth. "I know more than you think I do, Victor."

"I have another meeting." Debbie stood up, an uncomfortable look on her face. "I'm not sure what this is all about, and I don't think I want to know." She grabbed her stuff and left the conference room.

"Don't underestimate me, Victor," Sarah warned him. "I can see the *New York Times* article now: 'International Pharmaceutical Company Goes Under Due to Extremely Unethical Practices, Putting Patient Lives in Danger to Increase Their Profit Margins.' Gee—what would that do to your lifestyle?" She smirked.

"You are not going to win this one," he said coldly. "I was so sorry to hear about your grandmother in Chicago, I hope she's okay. If I were you, I'd walk away from all of this now—just a suggestion. And by the way, how is your fiancé? I hear he's in town." Botsworth started to walk out of the room, then paused and looked over his shoulder. "It would be so sad if you became a widow before you even had the chance to get married."

Sarah felt a pounding in her ears. "Watch your back, asshole!"

He didn't even respond.

She sat back down to gain her composure for a moment, then left the conference room. She needed to talk to Jackie.

• • •

"How's it going, girl?" Jackie answered when she picked up Sarah's call.

"I'm spitting fire right now," Sarah vented. "Botsworth thinks he's got us over a barrel but he doesn't know Lopez is out of Cuba. Handsome is going to contact him today—thanks to Sergio, of all people."

"Can you believe that shit?" Jackie whistled. "Look, I want to hear everything, but I'm about to go on a surveillance run with Hank. Can I ring you back later?"

"Of course, I have another meeting now anyway."

"Okay, get going. And whatever you do, don't cancel on me for the bachelorette! I just sent the down payment for the venue and I have a few surprise guests." Jackie chuckled.

"I'm not canceling no matter what," Sarah promised. "This gives me something to look forward to. Botsworth threatened me, told me I wasn't going to win this one. Fuck him!"

"That dickwad doesn't know Handsome is on the case, with all his connections far and wide. I'll call you after Wyatt's in bed tonight, 'kay? Laura's staying in the city tonight. She has lots of autopsies to catch up on since she was out of town last week."

Sarah sighed. "Sounds good. Just have to survive the rest of this day. Love you, Jack."

"Love you too, Golden."

• • •

When Sarah arrived—late—to the monthly coordinator meeting, Chris was standing at the head of the room.

"Hi Sarah, so glad you could make it." She made a show of checking her watch. "I was just sharing with everyone how much fun we all had at the Tonga Room with Victor. I heard he had to help you back to your room after Debbie and I left—too many Mai Tais?"

Sarah looked flatly at Chris. "You shouldn't believe everything you hear. Gossip is so beneath you . . . or is it?" She looked around the room. "Let's go around and hear the updates. How are our living donor numbers?"

Each lead coordinator gave their updates; Sarah took notes, all the while wanting to jump over and strangle Chris. Botsworth must have told her his version of the story. *Big surprise.*

• • •

As Sarah moved from one meeting to the next over the next few hours, she tried to stay focused, all the time wondering how Handsome was doing. She kept checking her cell phone for a message from him, but none came.

Right before she entered Dr. Sethna's office for their scheduled meeting, she texted Handsome, *Thinking about you*, with a heart emoji. As she stepped through the doorway she put her cell in her pocket, hoping that when her meeting was over he would have replied.

Sarah smiled when she saw Dr. Sethna beaming at her.

"Good afternoon, Sarah, nice to see you. Please sit down."

"Nice to see you too, Dr. Sethna." She sat down opposite her and handed her the assessment she had done. "I'll get right to the point: I'm concerned about these data points. The biopsies were not done according to protocol at our center or the other three centers, and there are a few other inconclusive clinical outcomes."

Dr. Sethna studied Sarah's assessment for a few minutes and then looked up at her. "No wonder Dr. Bower loves you," she said. "My PhD students couldn't analyze data this well. I agree with your conclusions, but since the study was not formally completed I don't think any of it matters now—and there's nothing we can do about the other centers going off protocol. I do agree that it's interesting, however. I hope the modified study will give us more accurate information to see if we're making any headway at all. I'll keep a closer eye on this one. Are you going to the meeting in Chicago?" She handed the papers back to Sarah.

"Not planning to," Sarah said. "But you know, Chicago is my hometown; I'm due for a visit."

"It's a great city," Dr. Sethna said. "You know, one of my favorite karaoke bars in the world is on Rush Street in Chicago."

Sarah's mouth fell open. "You're into karaoke? I never would have never guessed that about you in a million years."

"Sometimes I need to let the scientist in me take a breather and go have some fun." Dr. Sethna shrugged. "I've even won some prizes in my time."

"That is seriously impressive," Sarah said. "I love karaoke. I couldn't carry a tune in a bucket, but I still give it a go sometimes." She stood up to leave. "Thanks for meeting with me, Dr. Sethna."

"You can call me Christine." She gave Sarah a big smile. "Who knows, we may see each other in Chicago—but if we don't, please do drop by every once in a while. It's always good to see you, Sarah."

"I'll be happy to keep you updated on the modified study in the coming weeks," Sarah offered.

"I've delegated it to one of my fellows and your nurse coordinator, Chris, who has already set up standing meetings with me," Dr. Sethna said. "Maybe you can join for those, your time permitting."

Sarah forced a smile. "That Chris is so organized. I'll see if I can attend the updates." She rose from her chair.

"One last thing," Dr. Sethna said. "I don't think Victor from Lago should be invited to those meetings, even though Chris practically insisted on it. That's not the way we run clinical trials in my department."

Sarah nodded. "I'll take care of that. It's not how we do things either. Thanks for letting me know."

• • •

Sarah went straight from Christine's office to Chris's, grinding her teeth the entire way. When she walked in, Victor, Chris, and Debbie were all together, laughing it up.

Sarah glared at them. "Chris, Debbie, we don't pay you to sit around and laugh. Victor, you need to leave, you know you're not supposed to be here. Please don't come back or I'll report you to our ethics committee and call your company. Have I made myself clear?"

She opened the office door and gestured for him to leave. After hesitating for a moment, he complied.

"Geez, Sarah, we were just talking about a movie." Chris looked at her with wide eyes. "You're so touchy today, do you have your period or something?"

"Inappropriate, Chris," Sarah snapped. "Consider yourself warned: I'll be writing you up for unethical behavior and insubordination, and notifying human resources. This will go in your permanent record, make no mistake about that."

With Chris and Debbie still gaping at her, Sarah spun and stalked away. As she strode to her office, she checked her phone: still nothing from Handsome. She felt acid rising in her throat.

She went through her emails, answering them as fast as she could, wrote a scathing report about Chris, and called Handsome's cell—only to be sent directly to voicemail. She texted him again: *Hey, missing you. Give me a quick thumbs-up or something so I know you're ok.*

She stared at her phone and waited . . . waited . . .

No three dots—no nothing.

Okay, now I'm starting to worry.

Chapter 28

Sitting in her cubicle at work, Jackie looked at her watch for the first time in hours. It was almost seven in the evening. She glanced at her phone: no texts or voicemails. She hoped that was a good sign.

She called Grandma, who picked right up.

"Hey Jackie, how you doing? All good here; Hal and I are about to watch *Wheel of Fortune* and Wyatt is upstairs on his PlayStation, homework done."

Jackie smiled. "Love the good news. Can you call Wyatt down so I can say good night? I have lots of paperwork to do, so if all is quiet on the home front, I think I'll stay and get it done before I head home." She glanced at the family photo she had pinned up next to her computer as Grandma hollered for Wyatt.

"Wyatt, your mama is on the phone, she wants to say good night!"

There was silence, and then Jackie heard Wyatt running down the stairs.

"Hi Mama, I can't talk long—I only get thirty more minutes till Grandma makes me get ready for bed and I'm about to beat my next level—love you!"

With that, he was gone.

Jackie laughed. *Ah—if only life were that simple for all of us.*

Grandma got back on the line. "Well, *Wheel* is starting and Hal is a fan, so if it's okay with you, I'm going to hang up now. I'll be in bed when you get home. Laura called earlier to say good night."

"Good to know," she said. "Enjoy. I'll see you tomorrow morning. And thank you!"

She called Laura next. "Hi honey, how's your day been?"

"Long!" Laura sighed. "I have four more autopsies before I can call it a night. Glad I'm staying in the city, 'cause I won't be done until after two or three this morning. Everyone is putting the pressure on."

"I'm still at the office too—this job has so much paperwork," Jackie complained.

"Every job does, honey. It's the way of the world."

"I guess you're right." Jackie spun in her chair. "Well, I'll let you go so you can get to it faster. Text me when you get to your apartment. I'm so glad they popped for that when you got promoted. Gives me peace of mind."

"Me too," Laura said. "I should be caught up to date by day after tomorrow. Text you later, love you."

"Love you too."

• • •

The next time Jackie glanced up, it was ten at night. She hadn't heard from Sarah all day, which was weird. Suddenly worried, she called her.

"I was going to call you just now," Sarah said, her voice tense. "I'm getting freaked out over here."

"What's going on?" Jackie demanded.

"I haven't heard from Handsome all day. He left my place around six thirty this morning. He was going to the SFPD and then to San Jose for an interview, but he promised he'd stay in touch—yet all day, no word. I've texted him, called and left him a message—still nothing."

Jackie's mind started to reel. "I'm in the city, I'm coming over now."

"Really?" Sarah's voice relaxed a bit. "Thanks so much, Jack. Any chance you could spend the night? Something tells me Handsome isn't coming home anytime soon, and I could use the company."

"No problem," Jackie said. "Grandma has the home front covered and Laura is staying in the city. She is way backlogged. I'll just let them both know there's been a change of plan on my end. See you soon."

• • •

As Jackie drove to Sarah's, thoughts of Handsome being killed or kidnapped went through her mind. Why hadn't he called her? He would have if he could have.

She knew Sarah was thinking the same thing.

She let herself into Sarah's apartment with her key when she got there.

"Handsome, is that you?" Sarah's voice called out as Jackie rounded the corner into the living room.

Jackie watched as Sarah's mouth went from a smile filled with hope to a crestfallen look when she saw that it was Jackie.

"Happy to see you too," Jackie joked.

"Hey." Sarah jumped up and hugged her. "I'm sorry—I just still haven't heard from him, I'm so worried. What should we do?"

"Who was he going to meet with today? Do you have any names?" Jackie walked into Sarah's kitchen, poured them each a bourbon, and then came back and sat next to her friend.

"Something's wrong, Jack, I can feel it in my gut." Sarah shook her head and sipped her whiskey. "He was meeting with Inspector Davidson at seven this morning at the SFPD."

"I remember her." Jackie lit up. "She was awesome, helped us put Kayla's killer behind bars."

"That's the one." Sarah nodded.

"Do you happened to have her number?" Jackie asked.

"I did last year, so it must be in my phone." Sarah handed Jackie her cell phone. "You look. I can't think straight. Botsworth said something today in one our meetings—that it would be too bad if I became a widow before I was even married—and it's been gnawing at me all day. That motherfucker lays *one* hand on him and I *will* kill him. Slowly. I promise."

Jackie remembered what Handsome had said about how dangerous the people they were dealing with were, and shuddered. She knew he didn't exaggerate stuff like that. "Here's her number," she said. "Calling now."

She pressed send and hit speaker phone.

"Inspector Davidson here," a brisk voice answered immediately.

Jackie hadn't expected she'd pick up so fast. "S-sorry to call so late," she stuttered. "My name is Jackie Larsen, I'm a friend of Detective Strong from Miami. I think he met with you this morning."

"Hi Jackie," Davidson said. "Of course I remember you—and Sarah too. How are you?"

"Okay, but I have to cut to the chase: did you see Detective Strong this morning?" Jackie's pulse began to race.

"Yes," Davidson said slowly. "We had coffee, and he gave me the lowdown on what was happening. I was able to do some digging and was waiting to hear back from him."

"Well, we haven't heard from him all day," Jackie said. "Sarah has texted and called multiple times—no response. And this guy does not disappear like this without a good reason. We're sitting at Sarah's apartment, freaking out. Can you help us? We know he was supposed to have an interview with the San Jose police department this afternoon . . ."

"He did tell me that," Davidson said. "I'm not going to lie, I'm concerned too. Let me make some calls and I'll call you back. Meanwhile, Strong gave me Sarah's address this morning; I'll notify our on-duty police in your area and have them stay close by. Don't answer the door or any calls unless they are from someone you know. Understand?"

"Understood."

Jackie looked over at Sarah, who was curled up in a ball on the end of the couch.

Where are you, Handsome?

Chapter 29

Jackie glanced at the clock on Sarah's kitchen wall and then over at Sarah, who was rocking back and forth on the couch. It was 11:00 p.m.

She rested her hand on Sarah's shoulder. "I know where your mind is going and I'm right there with you—but for now, try to think of good things, not bad things. We don't know what's going on, and Handsome is perfectly capable of taking care of himself." She handed Sarah her bourbon. "Take a little sip, please."

Sarah pushed the glass away. "I finally let myself love him—completely." She started to sob. "I've never loved anyone more in my life. And he really loves me—all of me, including my insane moments. I just couldn't bear it if anything happened to him, Jack, and if he got hurt today it's all my fault."

Jackie knew there was nothing she could say or do to make Sarah feel better, so she just sat next to her friend and quietly sipped her drink. The only audible sound was the ticking of the kitchen clock and Sarah's sniffles.

Five minutes later, Sarah's phone rang. Jackie glanced at it and saw Investigator Davidson's name on the caller ID.

Sarah lunged for the phone and put it on speaker as she answered, "Hello? Good news, I hope."

Davidson paused. "I wish it were, Sarah. I called the San Jose PD; he didn't show up for his interview. I tried to track his cell phone—nothing. I have no idea where he is."

Sarah slumped back into the couch, and her phone fell out of her hand.

Jackie picked it up. "This is Jackie again; Sarah's in bad shape here. Can you give us anything—anything at all?"

"I wish I could, but I don't want to give you false hope," Davidson said. "If I hear anything, I'll call you right away. Give me your cell number, will you?"

Jackie gave her the number and ended the call, then handed the phone back to Sarah. She watched as Sarah checked, for the hundredth time, to see if Handsome had texted, and then bowed her head and closed her eyes.

"You're not alone, I'm here for you." Jackie stood up and gently touched the top of Sarah's head.

Sarah tucked her head to her chest as tears flooded her cheeks and her chin trembled. "I'm going to put on my pajamas," Jackie said. "Be right back."

• • •

Jackie awoke in the dark to noises in the hallway right outside Sarah's apartment.

She had finally gotten Sarah to sleep on the couch a bit after midnight after plying her with Ativan, and had gone to bed herself not long after that. Now she sat straight up, sure that the noises she was hearing were footsteps creaking right outside the front door.

She jumped out of bed and went into the living room, her heart racing. She glanced over at Sarah, who was still sleeping, thankfully.

The doorknob started to move back and forth. Jackie darted into the kitchen, grabbed a knife, and hid behind the small wall that separated the front door and kitchen area. A man quietly walked in and closed the door without making a sound. Jackie's hand shook. *I can't believe they fucking sent someone to kill us.*

The man started to approach Sarah. She couldn't make out anything but a vague outline, it was too dark. "Stop right there, you motherfucker, or I will kill you!" she yelled, charging toward him.

The man spun around, and Jackie gasped. "Handsome! Thank God it's you!" She laid the knife down on the table and hugged him hard. "Where in the fuck have you been? I had to drug Sarah. She was so freaked out that you were dead—and honestly, so was I."

Sarah's groan interrupted them. She sat up, squinted her eyes in their direction, and then opened them wide toward Handsome. She jumped off the couch, threw herself into his arms, and started to cry.

Jackie put her hand over her heart as they embraced. "I'll make a pot of coffee. This better be a good fucking story; I thought I was going to have to commit my friend to the nut house if you didn't come home."

Handsome clasped Sarah's head against his chest. "I'm here now," he said soothingly. "Everything is going to be alright."

Sarah was sobbing, both her arms firmly wrapped around his body.

Jackie retreated to the kitchen. "Don't get started without me!" she warned as she trotted away.

• • •

Jackie set three steaming cups of coffee on the small table in the kitchen. "Okay, it's story time."

Handsome and Sarah joined her at the table and Handsome began.

"I couldn't make up what I'm about to tell you if wanted to—and the hero of this story is none other than Sergio, if you can believe that."

Sarah kept touching his face with one hand while drinking her coffee with the other. "Why didn't you at least call or text us?" she demanded. "I was out of my mind."

"Let him talk and then we'll decide how we're going to punish him." Jackie topped off everyone's coffee and they both stared at Handsome.

"They took my cell phone," he protested. "There was no way I could have contacted you."

"Who is 'they'?" Jackie threw up her hands. "It's four in the morning—you need to be way more specific."

"Sergio arranged a private Learjet to take me to Miami to see Dr. Lopez," Handsome explained. "He has friends in high places, as you'll both recall."

"Yep," Sarah said, "I definitely remember waiting for that jet to land so Amanda could get her liver transplant."

"Well, even in prison, Sergio still has solid connections outside." He took another sip of coffee. "I had to agree to give up everything I was carrying—my gun, wallet, and phone—in order to get on the jet. When I got back to SFO, they had destroyed my phone—a minor casualty, given the current situation." He shrugged. "These guys mean business. They know who we're dealing with and are going to help us. I don't know why, but I don't care so much about their motivations at this point in time."

"Maybe this is Sergio's attempt to help himself at his next parole meeting," Sarah said. "Frankly, if he can get all of us out of this mess and keep us alive—who the fuck cares."

"Agree," Jackie said.

"Anyway, Campos met me there and we got an official statement from Dr. Lopez about working with Lago, specifically Botsworth and his assistant. Everything was done by the book, so whatever direction this goes in from here, the evidence is officially on the record. Sergio also arranged a meeting with this New Jersey thug, Angelo, who looked pretty beat up by the time Campos and I interviewed him via video with our New Jersey PD partners. He was on his way to the airport to go to Maui when they picked him up. He reluctantly shared that Botsworth hired him to scare Nana and Mo—so that's part of the official record now too."

"That asshole!" Sarah hissed.

"Asshole who's hopefully in a fair bit of pain right now," Handsome said smugly.

Jackie and Sarah directed questioning looks his way.

"I paid him a little visit after my meeting with Davidson, gave him a few things to think about," Handsome said casually.

"Hell yeah," Jackie said.

"*That's* why he looked so uncomfortable at the meeting earlier," Sarah said, laughing.

"Indeed." Handsome gave her knee a squeeze. "And I followed up with the florist who sent you those flowers too." He looked at Jackie. "No trace of who sent it; it was paid with cash, and Angelo didn't know anything about that. There clearly are more players for me and Campos to chase down. I asked Detective Mars, our friend in Chicago, to be sure there's a statement from Nana and Mo on the record, so I'll need you to call Nana this morning and let her know that he'll be swinging by today; I don't want her to see a cop at her door and think she's done something wrong." He put his arm around Sarah and kissed her cheek. "Don't share any details with her, though, we don't want her to worry."

Sarah nestled into his side. "I won't."

Jackie gave them a few minutes to gaze into each other's eyes before prompting Handsome with more questions. "So when does all this go down? Are you going to arrest Botsworth today?" She smiled eagerly. "Can I watch?"

Handsome stood up and helped himself to more coffee. "Jackie, I cannot have you or Sarah near this case, it's far too dangerous—you have to understand that. Just go home and if anything weird happens, let me know right away. At this point we need Botsworth to do whatever he's doing. He's going to be our bait to catch the big fish. He can't suspect anything—anything at all."

Sarah looked up at her fiancé, who was leaning against the kitchen counter. "That man is so self-absorbed he won't notice anything. My coordinator, Chris, seems to like him a lot, so I'll keep an eye on her too." She looked up at the clock. "It's already five thirty—I'm taking a shower and getting ready for work. Want to join me?" She threw a wink at Handsome.

"Wow, Golden—don't waste any time getting right back on that horse." Jackie laughed as Handsome and Sarah moved toward the bathroom.

"You're right about that—I'm not wasting another second showing this man how much I love him," Sarah called back. "Can you make another pot of coffee?" She dragged Handsome into the bathroom, and seconds later Jackie heard the shower turn on.

"How about I make you both eggs Benedict while I'm at it," Jackie said, although she knew they couldn't hear her. She smiled to herself. *We've got the A team back on deck.*

• • •

Jackie had just finished scrolling through her email when she realized she hadn't gotten a good night text from Laura the previous evening.

That's odd, she thought, frowning, and decided to text her.

Good morning, my love, have a good one, she typed, then added a few heart and hug emojis.

She waited for a reply—nothing.

Laura usually went into the morgue early when she stayed over in the city. *Maybe she's already doing autopsies*, Jackie thought. *I'm sure she'll check in later.*

As long as everyone else was busy, she figured she might as well get on with her day. She got dressed, wrote a quick note to Sarah and Handsome—*You love birds have a good day; surveillance with Hank this morning, I'll be in touch*—and headed out the door.

Chapter 30

An hour after Sarah ejected him from Chris's office, Victor called Chris, who immediately picked up.

"Hey Victor—what's up?" she asked, sounding a bit more wary than usual.

"Sorry about earlier," he said. "Can you meet for a drink after work?"

"I wish I could but I have plans. What do you need?"

Victor hesitated. "Uh . . . I just wanted to check in with you about what you were thinking about working with us. I noticed you followed Dr. Bower after our meeting this morning, and I was wondering if you mentioned my offer to him. I'm having dinner with him tonight and I don't want to get caught off guard."

"Oh, that," Chris said. "I did let him know that I'm considering other options for myself, career-wise—but don't worry, I didn't mention I was considering a position with Lago. I also let him know that Sarah is being very harsh with me and Debbie and it has to stop. And that was before that scene in my office! He said he would take care of it."

Victor smirked. "If my boss spoke to me the way she speaks to you, I would have found another job a long time ago. Good for you for standing up for yourself."

"Thank you, appreciate it," Chris said. "I need to go, I'm late for a meeting. But I'm excited to see that offer letter, Victor."

"You'll get it soon. One more thing—I think I saw Sarah's fiancé today but didn't want to say anything since I wasn't sure it was him. What does he look like?"

"Oh, Handsome? He's a hottie for sure, I have no idea how he puts up with her bitchiness. He's tall, strong jaw, intense brown eyes, buff as hell, dark hair . . . that help?"

Yup, that was him, he thought. "Thanks, Chris—have a good one, and we'll get that letter out to you soon. Valerie is on vacation in Tahiti, but I'll have her FedEx it to your house as soon as she's back."

"Fantastic!" Chris chirped. "Talk to you soon, I hope."

"You can count on it," Victor said.

• • •

Victor arrived at Boulevard right on time, only to get a text from Dr. Bower letting him know that he was running late. He ordered a bourbon and some appetizers, then rehashed that day's events in his mind.

The thought of Lopez speaking in front of everyone in the transplant field at the Chicago meeting haunted him; he hoped Leland would take care of that situation. He recalled Sarah's threats about taking him down and loosened his collar. *I will destroy that bitch, her family, and her friends if she tries anything.* He texted Angelo to call him immediately, but got nothing back. He was staring at his phone so intensely that he didn't even notice Bower standing in front of him until the doctor spoke.

"Good evening, Victor. You okay? You look like you're ready to kill somebody."

Victor stood up and shook Bower's hand. "Oh, it's always something," he said lightly. "Nice to see you, Dr. Bower. Please sit down. I took the liberty of ordering us some hors d'oeuvres."

"That's great—and honestly, it's all I have time for." Bower sighed. "Trouble at home, I need to put out a few fires. What's on your mind?"

The waiter came and took Bower's drink order; a server followed right behind him with the hors d'oeuvres.

Victor waited for Dr. Bower to serve himself before saying, "I'm heading to Chicago the day after tomorrow—you're going to the conference, right?"

"I was planning to be there—my team has some abstract presentations—but it looks like I have to sit this one out." The waiter delivered his drink and he picked it up. "I'm going to send Chris in my stead; she met with me the other day and mentioned that she's considering a job offer away from the medical center. I don't want to lose her, so I'm throwing a few perks her way. I wish she and Sarah could get along. I don't have time for that crap." He stuffed an eggplant crostini into his mouth and washed it down with a large gulp of his cocktail.

"I need to talk to you about a Dr. Lopez from Cuba," Victor said carefully. "I understand from Sarah that you are friends?"

"More like friendly colleagues," Bower said.

"Well, you'll be happy to hear, then, that Dr. Lopez has successfully left Cuba with his family and he'll be giving a tribute to his recently lost colleagues in Chicago." Victor leaned forward slightly. "Were you aware that Dr. McKee was sharing his protocol with Lopez?"

Bower's cell rang. "Sorry, Victor, have to take this—hello? Yes, I'll be home in a half-hour." He shook his head, hung up, and finished his drink. "I had the utmost respect for Dr. McKee; if he wanted to share the protocol with the man in the moon, then he knew what he was doing," he said sharply. "Sarah has been bugging me to look at Lopez's data, and frankly, I just don't have the time. What is the big deal with Lopez?"

"I'm not really sure what the big deal is," Victor said innocently. "I just know that several folks have asked me recently about the competency of his research, and I wanted to check with you before I responded. Have you heard anything?"

"Lopez's research gets the same scrutiny we all get, and I've never heard any concerns." Bower stood up. "I'm sorry I can't be of greater help here. If there's anything else you need, just shoot me an email."

Victor stood up and shook Bower's hand again. "Thanks—will do. Say, has someone named Leland Ackerley been in touch with you? He's an old friend of mine from grad school."

Victor knew Bower well enough to see that he was measuring his response. "I did have a call with Leland," he said. "What a smart fellow; knows a lot about what's in the pharmaceutical pipeline."

Victor allowed a few seconds to pass to see if Bower offered anything else. He did not, so Victor broke the silence.

"He's definitely got his finger on the pulse of our industry," he agreed. "After a few companies went public, he gave me a heads-up—I bought my second house in Aspen thanks to him."

"We talked about quite a few things," Bower said, looking a bit nervous. "Listen, I need to head home before my wife kills me. Thanks for the drinks and food. Give me a call when you're back from Chicago, I'd love to hear the highlights."

"We'll miss you in Chicago. We've planned quite the gala. I'll be sure to call when I get back."

Bower took his leave; Victor ordered another bourbon and checked his cell to see if he had heard from Angelo—nothing.

Leland called Bower? What the fuck is that about?

He called Leland, but the asshole didn't answer.

• • •

Just as Victor walked out of Boulevard, a limousine pulled up. Victor stared as a svelte brunette in four-inch heels gracefully exited, his jaw dropping. It was Erika Mason.

She looked up and met his gaze. "Fancy running into you, Victor!" She arched an eyebrow.

"A surprise indeed," Victor said. "What brings you to the Bay Area?"

The limo driver opened the other door to let her date exit—and Leland emerged.

"Why, Victor—what a surprise to see you!" he said, smiling broadly. "Sorry to rush, but we don't want to miss our reservation." He offered his arm to Erika, and the pair moved toward the restaurant's entrance.

"So nice to see you," Erika called over her shoulder.

Victor got into a cab, boiling with anger. *What are Leland and Erika doing together in San Francisco? And why didn't she let me know she was in town when she knew I was going to be here?*

He was starting to worry.

Chapter 31

Sarah's morning was filled, as usual, with nonstop meetings and returning emails—which made it easy for her to avoid Chris's urgent messages. She was heading up to her office to eat lunch after her last meeting of the morning when she ran right into Chris, who was waiting outside her office.

"I've been trying to reach you, what's the deal?" Chris demanded. "I need you to sign off on my request so I can make my travel plans to go to Chicago for the immunology conference. Dr. Bower asked me to represent the team there last-minute."

Sarah unlocked her office door and put her food down. "This is the first I've heard of any of this. Come in, let me check the HR system so I can approve it now." She scrolled through her emails, found Chris's request, and approved it. "I know you will conduct yourself professionally in Chicago," she said, fixing Chris with a cold stare. "This is a very prestigious meeting—and, I'm sure you're aware, they will be honoring Dr. McKee, as well as the other immunologists we lost."

"Victor told me all about the tribute," Chris said, meeting Sarah's gaze. "He has been so kind; in fact, he even offered to show me around town, since this will be my first time visiting Chicago."

The hair on the back of Sarah's neck was standing up. "What a generous offer, lucky you," she said, trying to sound sincere. "I really need to get back to these emails, do you need anything else?" *I hope you're not with him when he gets arrested*, she thought.

"Nope." Chris hesitated. "I . . . sure wish there was a way we could get along better. I'm sorry about my behavior; you were right to call me out on it. I hope you'll accept my apology and we can move on."

"Apology accepted," Sarah said, remembering the admonishing email Dr. Bower had sent her that morning. "I must admit I've been under a lot of stress, and I'm sorry if I took any of it out on you. You are an excellent nurse, and we're lucky to have you on the team. Enjoy Chicago—it's a great city."

"Thanks, Sarah, I will." Chris left her office.

• • •

Sarah was about to leave her office for her first post-lunch meeting when Jackie called.

"Hi, Jack—how's your day going?"

There was silence. Then Sarah heard what sounded like gasps for breath.

"Jackie? Talk to me!"

"They tried to kill Laura," Jackie managed. "She's in surgery right now."

Sarah's heart slammed in her chest. "Where are you? I'm coming right now."

"San Francisco General, I'm on the third floor in the surgical waiting area. They shot her in the chest—missed her heart, thank god, but they were definitely aiming for it."

"Oh Jack, I'll be there as fast as I can." Sarah's eyes filled with tears. "Laura's the toughest woman I know—she'll make it."

Sarah grabbed her purse, went downstairs, and caught a cab. She texted Handsome on the way to the hospital.

Chapter 32

Jackie's Tuesday started calmly, with a meeting with Hank. He briefed her on the job—another one at the Bay Club. After he filled her in on who she was to follow and what type of photos they needed to nail the guy, she drove to the Bay Club.

She had just cased out the entry and was on the way out to her car to grab a small camera when her phone rang with an unknown number.

"Hello?"

"Is this Jackie Larsen?" a woman's voice asked.

"Yes," Jackie said brusquely, immediately on her guard.

"This is San Francisco General Hospital. Your wife was brought to the emergency room and is on her way to the operating room."

Jackie stopped in her tracks and began breathing rapidly. "What happened?" Her hands shook as she tried to find her car keys. "Is she going to be okay?"

"You'll need to speak with her surgeon when you get here," the woman said. "The police are questioning people at the medical examiner's office. She was found unconscious on the ground there, with a gunshot wound to her chest. Her staff gave us your number, as her purse was stolen."

Jackie was already driving toward the hospital, forcing herself to breathe slowly so she wouldn't crash. "I'm on my way, I'll get there as fast as I can."

• • •

Jackie was pacing in the long hallway outside the surgery waiting area when Sarah came out of the elevator. Jackie ran over to her and told her what she knew, then fell into her friend's arms and started to sob.

"First we thought we lost Handsome, and now this. Who's next, for fuck's sake?" she moaned. "They said it will be at least another hour before she gets out of surgery, maybe longer."

"Handsome should be here pretty soon," Sarah said. "He called Inspector Davidson, and she's coming too. She'll be able to give us the details about what happened; a couple of her detectives are over at the ME's office right now."

Jackie shook her head. "Our families—they are going after our families! Why? We haven't done anything. Maybe they think we're the ones who got Lopez out of Cuba?"

Sarah shrugged helplessly and held out a tissue. "I just don't know, Jack."

"There is no way this was a robbery." Jackie took the tissue and blew her nose. "It's not like Laura wore any fancy jewelry and she usually only carries a credit card, very little cash. This was no fucking robbery. They just wanted to make it look like that."

Sarah fell into step with Jackie, pacing with her and listening. She was still talking when Handsome and Davidson emerged from the elevator.

Handsome's hands were clasped loosely behind his back as his eyes met Jackie's. "Let's go outside and talk," he said. "Time for some fresh air."

• • •

They found a table in a courtyard just outside the hospital. Everyone sat down except Jackie.

"Just give it to me straight," she told Davidson. "Do you know who did this? I know this wasn't a robbery. Did you send someone to check on my family in San Rafael?"

"San Rafael PD is on it," Davidson responded. "They'll keep the rest of your family safe. And no, this wasn't a robbery; whoever shot Laura meant to kill her, and they also made sure they never got anywhere near the exterior cameras—they clearly cased out the place."

"They are doing exactly what they said they were going to if we didn't butt out—except we haven't done anything." Jackie balled up her fists. "Do you think it's Victor's gang? Are they planning on taking us all down—first Nana, now Laura, someone else next?"

"We know it's not Angelo," Handsome chimed in. "I called New Jersey PD; they have Angelo in custody, and he hasn't got any way to contact anyone. The detective there asked him point blank if he set this up before he was arrested and he swore up and down he knew nothing about this hit."

Davidson nodded in agreement. "These are professionals, and right now our best lead is the connection to Victor, who will be in Chicago soon. Detective Mars will have someone on him the minute he hits O'Hare. We know where Lopez is staying in Chicago; Mars has already met with him and put a tracer on his phone so we can hear everything when Victor gets in touch with him, which we're sure he'll do soon after getting to town."

Jackie assimilated all the information, but didn't feel satisfied. "If Victor's not the guy calling the shots, who is? Could it be his bigwig friend Leland?"

"That would make the most sense, but it'll be hard to

prove; people at Leland's level usually hire people to do their dirty work, leaving no trace behind. Hard to put these rich bastards in jail—they lawyer up big time, and without hard evidence . . ." Handsome put an arm around Jackie. "But don't worry, Jack, we're here—our team is on it. You just focus on Laura."

Jackie let out a big sigh. "Thanks—that's my plan. But I sure would like to help you catch whoever did this."

"Is there anyone else you can think of who would want Laura dead?" Davidson asked.

Jackie's neck muscles tightened. "Not that I can think of. She's never mentioned any conflict related to work the whole time she's worked at the morgue." Her cell phone rang, and she grabbed for it. "Hello—yes, this is Jackie Larsen. I'll be right there." She shoved the phone in her pocket. "Laura's out of surgery and in the recovery room. The doctor wants to see me." She grabbed Sarah's arm and started pulling her toward the hospital entrance. "Please let her be okay—please!"

Sarah picked up the pace. "She's a strong, healthy woman—she'll get through this," she said. "Let's go hear what the surgeon has to say." She glanced back at Handsome. "Keep me posted, and please be careful," she shouted. "Love you!"

• • •

Laura's surgeon was waiting from them outside the recovery area.

"First of all, your wife will be fine," she said.

Jackie almost collapsed with relief.

"She lost a lot of blood, however," the surgeon said. "We gave her several transfusions, and she'll likely need a few more once she gets up to the surgical ICU. The bullet went through the top right lobe of her lung and there was a fair amount of muscle and tissue damage in her chest area. I repaired it, but it will be a while before she'll be using her right arm. The chest tube I put in will drain the fluid from her lungs. You can go see her"—she darted a glance at Sarah—"but only *one* visitor at a time in recovery."

"Thank you so much." Jackie took several deep breaths to slow her racing heart. "I'll be out soon, Sarah."

Sarah gave her hand a squeeze. "Go get your girl, Jack."

• • •

Laura was attached to a heart monitor, several hanging IV bags were infusing fluids into her, and Jackie saw the chest tube draining bright red blood.

"Oh, my poor baby," she whispered.

Laura's nurse was taking her vitals and administering some medication through the IV. "Are you Laura's wife?" she asked.

Jackie nodded as she walked to the side of Laura's bed.

"She'll be in recovery for a couple hours and then she'll be transferred," the nurse said. "You can say a quick hello, but then I'll need you to leave. The receptionist will call you when she gets transferred to the ICU."

Jackie made her way to the head of the bed and leaned in close to Laura's ear.

"Hey honey, it's me; I'm right here," she whispered, and gently kissed Laura's cheek.

Laura slightly opened her eyes and tried to smile, then went back to sleep.

"You're going to be alright." Jackie squeezed her hand.

She's going to be alright, she thought. *Thank you God!*

• • •

"I can stay with you as long as you want," Sarah said when Jackie came back to the waiting area. "Work can wait. Why don't we go get a bite? I know a great burrito place a block away. You're going to need your energy, buddy."

"You're right," Jackie said, taking out her cell phone. "I'll call Laura's mom while we walk. She doesn't even know about any of this yet."

Grandma freaked out when Jackie gave her the news, as expected.

"Why would someone do such a thing to my daughter?" she demanded. "What kind of person does this?"

Jackie felt anger begin to replace the worry that had dominated her emotions for the last few hours. "I don't know," she said, steel in her voice. "But we're going to find out."

Chapter 33

On his flight to Chicago, Victor mentally reviewed his list of everything he had to accomplish during the conference: Find out where Lopez was staying and get him to keep his mouth closed. Hire a Chicago thug to take Lopez out, whether or not he cooperated. Close the loop with his fellow pharma CEOs, Otto and Erika.

The flight attendant interrupted his train of thought. "May I get you another drink?"

"Please, make it a double—and I'll take a cheese plate."

He took the Lopez folder out of his briefcase and studied it again to confirm what he already knew. The outcomes were horrible: Lago's new drug wasn't producing full tolerance in any of the participating patients. It wasn't doing much in the modified studies that were under way either. This was good and bad news; sure, their "miracle drug" wasn't performing, but that meant Lago would continue to make hundreds of millions on the standard anti-rejection drugs. He needed to contact Leland, so he could warn his clients; these results wouldn't make Lago stock prices plummet, but it would definitely go down when they were released.

The flight attendant arrived with his drink and food. *What was Leland doing with Erika?* he kept asking himself as he ate. He tried to shake off his anxiety. *I have to stay cool, calm, and collected. Soon this whole thing will be over—and then* I'm *fucking going to Tahiti.*

• • •

Victor's driver—he'd arranged for a car ahead of time—delivered him to The Drake without incident just before 6:00 p.m. A grand flower arrangement graced the lobby, a chandelier hung above it casting a soft hue, as Victor approached the reception desk to check in. He saw several surgeons he knew milling around in the lobby, but he wasn't quite ready to socialize; he avoided eye contact.

"Welcome to The Drake, Mr. Botsworth," the clerk said. "We've got you in our presidential suite for a week?"

"That's correct." He handed her his credit card. "Any messages?"

"Yes, in fact." She turned around and retrieved several phone messages and several sealed letters. "Here you go. Would you like one or two keys?"

"Why don't you give me two, just in case I lose one." He flashed a smile.

"My pleasure," she said, handing them over. "Your bags are on the way to your suite. May I make you a dinner reservation? There are several conventions in town, so best to be safe."

"Great idea," he said. "Why don't you book me a table for two at Gibson's for eight?"

She nodded briskly. "I'll take care of that right now and ring your room when I confirm the reservation."

Victor made his way up to his room—appreciating, as he went, how the hundred-year-old hotel exuded old-world charm, its regal blue carpeting with splashes of color and its large, fresh flower arrangements welcoming each visitor. He'd always loved the Fairmont, but after the time he'd had in San Francisco, a change of scenery was nice.

• • •

After calling Chris to invite her to dinner—she accepted, of course—Victor looked through the messages the clerk downstairs had given him. There were several from the hotel, confirming all the gala details and encouraging him to call if he had any questions. One was from Leland, who was staying in the penthouse and wanted to have an early breakfast meeting—wasn't available until then. The last one was from Dr. Lopez, who wasn't staying at the hotel but had left a number for Victor to call.

Victor called immediately, and to his delight, Dr. Lopez picked up.

"Hello?"

"Dr. Lopez? Victor Botsworth here."

"Ah, Mr. Botsworth, you got my message."

"What a surprise to hear from you," Victor said, laying the charm on thick. "Congratulations on making it out of Cuba . . . how ever did you do it?"

Dr. Lopez hesitated. "It's a long story," he finally said. "I hope we're able to have a visit before I speak at the meeting. I must say, I was very disappointed that you stopped contacting me while I was actively using your drug in my trial. I had so many questions—especially after my colleagues were killed in that horrible accident. You were the only one I could talk to. Why did you break off communication so suddenly?"

"Also a long story," Victor said delicately. "We can discuss that when we meet. But to be clear, I made it clear to you from the beginning that I was doing you a huge favor sharing those drugs; I need to tell you that I was very upset when I heard you had shared the study information with Sarah Golden." Victor poured himself a drink.

"I had no choice," Dr. Lopez said, a tinge of anger entering his tone. "You wouldn't respond to me, and I was concerned for my patients—some were experiencing awful side effects, including horrible rashes and severe shortness of breath, and as you know, we're not allowed to add any drugs that could interfere with the outcomes."

"How about we meet for lunch tomorrow so we can discuss this in detail?" Victor suggested. "Where are you staying? I can come to you."

"Actually I'm booked tomorrow," Dr. Lopez said. "I'm meeting with various program chairs about possible positions all day. Why don't we have lunch Saturday instead, at The Drake?"

Victor clenched his jaw. *Saturday? That gives him one whole day more to blab to anyone who's listening.* "Are you sure we can't squeeze something in tomorrow?"

"I'm sorry, Victor, my calendar is full," Dr. Lopez said firmly.

"Fine—but let's not meet here at The Drake, there'll be too many disruptions," Victor said quickly. He didn't want anyone seeing them together. "Meet me at The Rosebud on Taylor at noon. I'll reserve us a quiet table and we can catch up and mend some fences."

"Sounds wonderful," Dr. Lopez said.

"Perfect. And Dr. Lopez—I'd appreciate it if you wouldn't mention my sharing our drug with you; it could get me and my company in a lot of trouble, and that wouldn't be good for either of us. If this were to get out, it might shake the trust of your potential employers here in the US. I hope you appreciate that." Victor's voice was stern.

"I understand," Dr. Lopez said calmly. "I'll see you for lunch on Saturday."

"Where is your family staying while you're here?" Victor probed.

"My wife has a close friend who has offered her home to us—they are on a transatlantic cruise for two months. It's lovely, right near Lincoln Park Zoo."

"How fortunate," Victor said warmly. "Glad everything worked out for you and your family. I'll see you tomorrow."

"Good night, Victor."

Upon hanging up with Dr. Lopez, Victor immediately dialed Angelo—again, it went directly to voicemail. "Fuck!" He thought about who else could help him find someone to take Lopez out for him, but he drew a blank.

He called Leland's room to see if he was there: no response. He tried Leland's cell next: voicemail. He left a message.

"Leland, I need you to call tonight, no matter what time you get back. I need your help with something very important."

• • •

When Victor went downstairs at seven-thirty to meet Chris, the lobby was bustling with groups of people about to embark on their own Chicago adventures. He felt a hand on his back and turned around; it was the female FBI agent who had interviewed him when he was in San Francisco, he couldn't remember her name.

Oh God, why is she here?

"Hi Victor," she said. "Allison Wesley, FBI—we met in San Francisco. Nice to see you again."

Victor quickly glanced around to see if Chris was in the lobby. He didn't see her. "What on earth brings you here, Allison? This is a scientific meeting—guessing it's not your area of expertise—and I heard the FBI investigation was closed."

"Who told you that?" She cocked her head to the side. "The case is very much open, and we're going to be meeting with several close colleagues who knew the deceased immunologists."

Victor studied her face. "Anyone I know?"

"I'm not at liberty to share that—but if I were a guessing person, I would say you do know them."

Victor saw Chris approaching, wearing a very revealing top, short skirt, and high heels. *She definitely has the legs for the look*, he thought appreciatively.

"Hey Victor," she greeted him, barely glancing at Allison. "I'm ready!"

Victor smiled. "You're looking lovely tonight. Gibson's is a short walk from here." He glanced over at Allison. "Have a good evening."

As calm as he tried to be, as he and Chris exited the hotel he couldn't think about anything besides everyone who seemed to be betraying him. *Angelo told me the FBI case was closed. Who is Allison going to meet with? Is there* anyone *I can trust anymore?*

"Victor, are you okay?" Chris asked. "You haven't said a word since we left the hotel. Just to bring you back to earth, we're on Oak Street—I hope we're heading in the right direction."

Victor shook his head and tried to focus. "Sorry about that Chris, lots going on with the conference. This is the Gold Coast"—he pointed around the street—"Hermès, Prada, Dolce & Gabbana, all the designers are here."

Chris stopped to look at a bracelet in the Dolce & Gabbana window. "Only ten thousand dollars? I'll take two." She laughed.

Victor barely cracked a smile; he was too preoccupied about his conversation with the FBI agent to respond to her frivolous comments.

It's going to be a long night, he thought.

• • •

Gibson's was hopping when they got there. A large grand piano greeted them to the right of the doorway; an older man was playing and singing "Fly me to the Moon" to a group of patrons sitting around the piano enjoying their cocktails. Folks were shoulder to shoulder, and there was a buzz of excitement mixed with clinking glasses.

The hostess escorted them through the busy restaurant, waiters in white linen coats bustling around with trays of steaks, potatoes, and sides. In the middle of the dining room, Victor came to a stop. In the far left corner he saw Leland, Nixie Klein, Erika, Otto, and Dr. Sethna all sitting at the same table—a dinner he should have been invited to. *What the fuck!*

Chris turned around. "Is something wrong?"

The hostess was standing still, holding the black leather–covered menus and tapping her fingers.

"Nothing," Victor said stiffly. He followed Chris and the hostess to their table, where he made sure to take a chair that allowed him to keep an eye on Leland's table.

"I love this place," Chris exclaimed as they took their seats. "So many good-looking fellas, and the food looks amazing. Do you come here every time you're in town?"

"I do; never disappoints." Victor stood back up. "I see someone I know. Would you please excuse me, just for a moment?"

"No problem," Chris responded. "Don't stay away too long, though, or I'll eat your steak."

Victor winked at her, then laid his napkin on the table and made a beeline to Leland's table. As soon as he arrived, he glared at Leland briefly, then shifted to a smile for the rest of the guests. "So nice to see some of my favorite people all at one table. How is everyone doing tonight? Ready for the big meeting and gala reception, I hope."

Dr. Sethna nodded eagerly; Otto and Erika looked a bit uncomfortable.

Leland stood up, turned his back on his guests, and faced Victor. "Not a good idea to approach me right now," he said quietly. "I need you to keep your distance from me in public—seems the FBI is here. I think the less we are seen together, the better. Please go back to your table."

Victor felt his cheeks flush. "Call me when you get back to your room tonight," he said. "I have no idea what you're up to, but we have a situation that needs to be handled immediately." He looked past Leland and smiled again at the rest of the folks around the table. "So good to see everyone, see you bright and early at the abstract sessions."

They all nodded and smiled back at him, and then resumed their conversation.

• • •

After rejoining Chris, Victor continued to watch Leland's table for the rest of the meal. He barely paid attention to Chris, but she didn't seem to notice.

"I love chocolate, but I need your help with this pie, please." Chris pushed her dessert to the middle of the table.

"I'm not a dessert guy," he said shortly. "Just eat what you can."

"This is my first night in Chicago, ever!" she pressed on. "I heard there are some great places to dance on Rush Street. My friend told me about a place called The Hangge-Uppe, said it's open until four in the morning. Any interest?" she asked, her eyes glowing.

"I hate to be a party pooper, but I need to get back to my room to prepare for tomorrow's meetings and return some calls," Victor said. "You can walk to Rush Street from here, though, and there are lots of bars to check out; this is a convention town, no shortage of fun."

As Victor paid the bill, Chris said, "Hey—there's Dr. Sethna! I bet she'll want to go out with me!"

Before he could say anything, she rose and marched right over to Leland's table. A few seconds later, Chris waved at him, pointed at Dr. Sethna, and gave him a thumbs-up. He responded with his own thumbs-up, and made his way out of the restaurant alone.

• • •

All the way back to The Drake, Victor tried to figure out just exactly what Leland was up to—and why Nixie Klein was at dinner with his pharma colleagues. They hadn't seemed all that happy to see him—except for Dr. Sethna. Whatever was happening, she appeared to be an innocent bystander. He'd be sure to corner her tomorrow to see what the talk of their table was about.

• • •

It was close to midnight when Leland finally called. Victor was a few scotches deep by then.

"Your behavior toward me is unacceptable," Victor launched in when he answered the phone, not bothering with pleasantries. "We're supposed to be on the same team, for fuck's sake, so why are you treating me like the enemy? And thanks for the dinner invitation tonight—that was embarrassing."

"Things have gotten way out of hand," Leland snapped. "Lopez is here, and I've gotten some intelligence that he plans to share the results of his 'illegal' study after his tribute. If anyone's going down for this, it's gonna be you—just you, Victor."

"Wait, listen," Victor said. "I'm having lunch with Lopez tomorrow, at The Rosebud on Taylor. After I leave you can send someone in, make this go away. We all win that way."

“No can do,” Leland said. “With the FBI lurking around, it’s too risky.”

“If I go down, I’m taking you with me, you son of a bitch,” Victor spat. “You’re supposed to be my friend—what the fuck is wrong with you?”

“You’re taking all of this far too personally,” Leland said mildly. “If you had gone to Hawaii, everything would have been handled when you got back. Instead, you put yourself right in the middle of everything, and now there’s nothing I can do to help you. You’re on your own . . . friend.”

Leland hung up.

Chapter 34

Sarah headed back to work Tuesday afternoon after she knew Jackie was calmed down and Laura was stable. When she got back to her desk, she called Handsome and fired questions at him: "Any leads on who shot Laura? What does Davidson think? Has any new evidence surfaced?"

"Slow down, honey," he said. "The less you know, the better. "You and Jackie really have to take a backseat. There are lots of moving parts here; just know the right people are in the right places, and trust that I have things in hand."

"I do trust you, but these assholes are hurting our families," she said, tears in her eyes. "I need you to lock them up." Her computer calendar alarm went off and she glanced at the notification. "Time for liver selection, have to run. I'll see you later?"

"I'll pick you up around seven," he said. "Let's get carry-out and hit the hay early—we could both use a good night's sleep. Just go do your job and let me and my team take care of things."

"Easy for you to say, I'm freaking out here." Sarah's voice rose. "They tried to kill *Laura*."

"I know," Handsome said gently, "and you have every right to be freaked out right now. But don't give them anything to react to, that's the safest thing right now. I know it's not a fair ask, but can you do that?"

"I'll do my best," Sarah said. "That's all I can promise." She glanced at her screen again. "Yikes, I need to get going. See you soon, love you."

"Love you too."

• • •

During selection, Sarah watched as each patient was reviewed to determine if they would go on the waitlist. The usual staff—surgeons, hepatologists, nurses, social workers, and financial counselors—all weighed in on each candidate. It always came down to just a few things: were they compliant enough to take care of their new liver, did they have family support, and did they have the money to pay for the expensive transplant drugs? If all the boxes weren't checked then they were not listed, which usually meant a death sentence.

After the last patient was reviewed, everyone got up to leave.

"Sarah, I need to see you in my office," Dr. Bower said loudly.

She glanced around and saw a lot of raised eyebrows. "Sure."

She followed him out. Neither of them spoke until they stepped into his office and closed the door.

"What's up?" Sarah asked, confused by Dr. Bower's stern look. She started to pick at her fingernails.

"Did you file a report on Dr. McKee's study with the NIH?" he demanded. "I received a call today from Nixie Klein telling me as much. I couldn't believe my ears."

Sarah closed her eyes and took a deep breath. "I told you when I was wrapping up all the data that all four immunologists decreased the frequency of the kidney biopsies from weekly to monthly. I felt it only ethical to report that to the Office of Research Integrity at the NIH, as you know they track studies that are out of compliance. I thought you would want me to do that."

Bower slammed his fist on his desk. "You had no right reporting that! It should have come from a doctor who was actively involved in the study—not you. It makes everyone look suspicious, like they were falsifying data." The vein in Bower's neck was bulging; Sarah had never seen him so angry. "So now the legacies of four respected scientists who just lost their lives are in question, as is the future of their transplant programs—including ours. This could jeopardize future funding for all our institutions. Why didn't you come to me before you filed this? Did you even ask Dr. Sethna—the study was under her department, as you know, even thought they were using our patient population."

Sarah bit the inside of her cheek. "I made a mistake," she admitted. "I should have checked with Dr. Sethna. You were pushing us so hard to get everything tied up, and I had to file the report at the same time we submitted the original study data. I didn't mean to overstep, Dr. Bower. And you know how much I care about this program—I would never endanger it intentionally!"

Bower sat back and folded his arms. "I have to meet with the Dean of Medicine this afternoon and explain this. As you can imagine, I'm not looking forward to that." Glaring at her, he went on, "Because you reported this, all four centers are required to put the modified Lago study on hold until further notice. Victor doesn't even know about this yet—and after all he did to help us close out the old study and get this new one up and running." He shook his head and let out a heavy sigh. "You have jeopardized so many relationships, Sarah. I think it's best if you take a leave of absence. You haven't been thinking straight lately; you seem more interested in your relationship than this job. Maybe it's time for you to settle down and have babies, and leave the transplant world to the rest of us."

"Not only could I report you to HR for that comment, which you and I *both* know is completely inappropriate," Sarah declared, clenching her fists, "but you also know I work my ass off here, Dr. Bower. You're being disrespectful and unfair."

Dr. Bower held up his hands. "Fine, that last comment went too far. But you have to admit, Sarah, that when you have graced us with your presence lately, you've seemed to only create more chaos. Nixie Klein is going to see if she can minimize this disaster. If she hadn't called me, I would have been blindsided."

Sarah felt a lump forming in her throat. She cleared it before she said, "Dr. Bower, you have to know that I didn't intend to get anyone in trouble. The facts were the facts—the study was flawed and the results are inconclusive. Anyone who says differently is lying."

"You are naive, Sarah. Going forward, you are to have nothing to do with any research—it clearly isn't your area of expertise. In fact, I'm starting to wonder why I even hired you. I feel like I have to watch every move you make, and I'm getting lots of staff complaints about how rude you are—you're lucky I don't fire you outright." Bower walked around his desk and opened his office door.

It took everything Sarah had to hold her tears back. *I'm not letting him see me cry*, she thought. "I'm sorry to have created so much trouble for you," she said slowly. "But if I hadn't reported this, would anyone else have? I'm not so sure they would have. It's unethical, Dr. Bower. And I expect so much more from you."

Sarah didn't wait for a response; she walked out of his office, then rushed to a nearby bathroom, where she found a stall and let the tears flow. *I can't call Jackie—she's with Laura;*

or Handsome—he's in a job interview. She blew her nose. *I can't believe this is happening.*

When she finally collected herself, she went to her office, put her out-of-office message on, and grabbed some files. She'd let Handsome know there had been a change of plans on the cab ride home.

• • •

Sarah couldn't shut off her mind after she got home, so she decided to make dinner for Handsome. By the time he arrived, she had prepared baked chicken and salad and had a bottle of wine open to breathe.

"Look at you, Chef Sarah," he exclaimed. "This looks delicious." He gave her a long kiss, then sat down and took a bite of the chicken. "This is very crispy. What's your secret?"

"If you must know, it's Shake 'n Bake, one of my go-tos the five times per year I cook." Sarah winked. "Glad you like it; I know you're not marrying me for my culinary skills."

Handsome chuckled and took a sip of wine. "Any luck finding us a venue for our wedding?"

"I have calls in to several wineries I'm excited about. Anyway, tell me, how was your day? Any formal offers yet?"

"Matter of fact, SFPD wants to hire me at a rather generous salary," Handsome shared. "Davidson put in a good word for me, and I really like the department. I'm going to see what San Jose PD offers—I had a panel interview there today—but I'm leaning toward SF. Less of a commute."

Sarah got up, walked around the table, and planted a big wet kiss on Handsome's sexy lips. "I love you—thank you for being willing to leave your family and job and come out here to live with me."

"I will do whatever it takes to marry you and make you happy." He kissed her long and hard.

"Whew—I'll take more of those, please," she said, feeling her whole body tingle.

After several more long, passionate kisses, he drew Sarah over to the couch and sat her on his lap. "I'm technically still employed in Miami," he told her, "so first I need to give notice and close out whatever cases I can—Campos has been working hard on that in my absence. Then there's this Botsworth case, which I'm helping Davidson coordinate here in San Francisco, as well as in Chicago and New Jersey. The FBI has been investigating the deaths of the immunologists, and we've alerted them about Botsworth and his pal Leland Ackerley. My Miami chief said I could use my Florida license to partner with Davidson and Mars. Since we deposed Lopez in Miami, our department is involved."

He sipped his wine.

Sarah had been moving her fingers through his thick curls, but she paused mid-stroke and narrowed her eyes. "Why do I have a sneaking suspicion that you're not telling me everything?"

Handsome tilted his head to look her in the eye. "Well there are a few more details I need to share. Don't get mad, okay?"

"Hmmm. I'm not making any promises I can't keep, spill it."

"I'm going to Chicago to work with Mars. Things are heating up . . . we have plenty on Botsworth to arrest him, but we want to see if we can get hard evidence that Leland Ackerley, our venture capitalist, is connected to this whole mess. If we can do that, we will have caught us one big fish, which could lead to others that have slipped through our fingers in the past. Mars's team is protecting Lopez and his family, who are staying with friends in Chicago." Handsome paused.

Sarah studied his face. "Who will watch your back in Chicago? Campos is in Miami, and I'm guessing Mars is super busy. And after what happened to Laura, I doubt Jackie and I are going on this bachelorette trip anymore."

"First of all, you know that even if you were going to be in Chicago, I would never let you be the one to watch my back when there are killers on the loose." Handsome squeezed her. "But I hear your concern. Mars and I will be tag-teaming on a variety of things, and I trust him. I did hear from Sergio again—you're not going to like this, but full transparency here—and he said to be careful if we are going after this guy Leland. Seems Sergio has solid intel that he has made quite a few people disappear before—no trace of evidence. Leland knows how to play the game. Apparently, the FBI has been loosely keeping an eye on him ever since the suspicious disappearance of a New Jersey pharma CEO years ago, but they've never been able to get anyone to testify."

"Let me get this straight—my fiancé is walking into what could be a huge trap, without his wing woman, to confront a very wealthy, dangerous man who has the power and money to make a person disappear without a trace?" Sarah cringed.

"Technically, yes," Handsome admitted. "But babe, we have so many undercover people in Chicago right now; I feel confident they will have my back."

"Can you just walk away from this case now and have all the other players wrap this up?" Sarah slid off his lap and pulled her knees into her chest. "Does it have to be you?"

"I'm too far in now—I have to see this through." He pulled her into his chest and wrapped his arms around her. "I'll be okay honey, I promise."

Sarah let herself melt into his body. "God, I wish I had never gone to Cuba."

Chapter 35

Laura was already home recuperating by Wednesday morning—she was doing miraculously well—and her mother was taking such good care of her that there wasn't a whole lot for Jackie to do but take Wyatt to school and pick him up, since she was off work.

By Friday she was completely stir-crazy, but she didn't want to leave her family alone for a second.

When she got home from dropping off Wyatt that morning, she found Laura sitting outside in their backyard with Dusty, who hadn't left her side since she came home from the hospital.

"Hey," Laura called, smiling. "Come back here and join me."

Jackie and sat next to her. "What's up, how you feeling?"

"Getting stronger every day," Laura squeezed her thigh. "I love you but you're making me a little crazy hanging around the house all the time. I think you and Sarah should go to Chicago today, as planned, and have fun at her bachelorette party. I'm fine! Mom, Wyatt, and our trusty guard dog"—she petted Dusty who licked her hand—"are all I need."

Jackie shook her head. “I don’t think that’s such a good idea. I told Sarah we’d do her bachelorette party after the wedding—who says they have to be in order?”

Laura fixed her wife with a firm look. “I need you to go—and to have *fun*. We’re in good hands here. I even called Handsome in Chicago to ask his thoughts and he gave it the green light. I think that he likes the idea of being in the same city as Sarah, given all that’s going on. And babe, the local PD is making routine rounds in our neighborhood—we’re safe here. I never thought I’d have to beg you to go to Chicago and party, but that’s exactly what I’m doing now.”

Jackie looked at Laura. She had to admit, her overall color and energy level were improving quickly. She took her hand. “Are you sure? I couldn’t forgive myself if anything happened to you or our family and I wasn’t here.”

“My mom says Hal offered to stay here while you’re gone, just in case you’re worried.”

Jackie laughed. “Oh yeah—her sixty-five-year-old boyfriend will really stop those thugs. But that’s sweet. You’ve both been plotting this, I can tell.”

Laura’s mom stepped out on the patio. “You talking about my Hal? He’s a black belt, just so you know. I bet he could take you down, Jackie.”

“I bet he could.” Jackie threw up her hands in surrender, laughing. “So you’re both ready to kick me out of the house, is that what I’m hearing?” Jackie surveyed both of them and chuckled. “Okay, you win. I’ll call Sarah.”

• • •

Jackie and Sarah relaxed in their spacious first-class seats and sipped mimosas as the flight took off.

“First class,” Sarah marveled. “Did you win the lottery?”

“Nope—used lots of points and paid a little extra.” Jackie

grinned. "I watched *Bridesmaids* three times with Laura's mom; first class is the only way to celebrate this epic event. I did send Melissa McCarthy and Kristen Wiig an invitation, but I haven't heard back from them yet."

"You did not!" Sarah elbowed her friend. "You're ridiculous."

"Actually, I did—but who knows who monitors their email and social media? Anyway, I don't see them on the plane, but maybe they'll be at the party." Jackie smirked.

Sarah and Jackie ate, drank, and laughed their way to O'Hare Airport. In between all the food and drinks, Sarah brought Jackie up to speed on Handsome and the case.

There was a driver waiting for them when they walked through security with a name card: "Sarah-the-whore-Golden." He looked very uncomfortable.

Sarah busted out laughing while passengers stared at the sign in disgust and then over at Jackie and Sarah.

"Nice touch, Larsen," Sarah said. "I see you're really going all out."

"You know it, and this is just the beginning." Jackie had a silly grin on her face. "I only have one best friend, and you're it—so just buckle up, sister!"

• • •

The limo driver took them to Nana's neighborhood—Bridgeport, where, as Nana liked to tell everyone, Mayor Richard Daley had once lived. The car pulled up outside the American Legion, the exterior of which was decorated with tons of balloons and a huge sign declaring, "SARAH GOLDEN IS FINALLY GETTING MARRIED."

Jackie took a picture of Sarah's face as she took it all in, grinning ear to ear.

Nana ran outside and threw her arms around Sarah. "My Sarala—you're home! Have I got some surprises for you." They hugged one another while Jackie took a few pictures. "You come over here and get some of Nana's sugar too, Jackie."

Jackie melted into Nana's arms, a place she'd always felt safe during hard times at nursing school. "How's my nana?" she asked.

"So much better now that I see my girls. Come inside, young ladies." Nana escorted them through the front doors.

Inside, they were greeted by a group of Nana's Legion friends, singing "Get Me to the Church on Time" from *My Fair Lady*.

Feeling very pleased with herself, Jackie looked over at Sarah and smiled.

Once the chorus finished, Sarah and Jackie were escorted into the long bar, where all their nursing school friends screamed in unison when they saw them.

"Here's our bride-to-be!" Patty declared, and then they all swarmed around Sarah, putting a tiara on her head and sash that read, "Last night as a single woman."

"Drinks on the house!" the bartender called out.

The evening was filled with non-stop disco music, party platters from Jewel, chips and onion dip, and lots of dancing and laughter. Nana, seemingly no worse for wear from her car accident, kept up with all of it, dancing with all the older fellas who were also moving around the floor with the nursing school gals. There was one guy in particular—the bartender, Lloyd—who she seemed particularly fond of.

Gotta keep an eye on that guy, Jackie thought.

Looking around, Jackie was reminded of a scene from her favorite movie, *The Heat*, where Melissa McCarthy and Sandra Bullock danced with all the older men in a dive bar as they got drunker and drunker. She took as many photos as she could—when she wasn't busy dancing and singing at the top of her lungs with her sister nursing school pals.

It was around one in the morning when she climbed up on the bar. "Time for a square dance!" she announced.

All their nursing school friends knew exactly what to do, as Jackie had taught them how to square up when they were in nursing school. She started to sing "Oh Johnny, Oh Johnny, Oh!"—her favorite square-dance song, which she'd learned in fourth grade—and stomp on the bar. Square dancing was one of the few things she'd been good at as a child, but most people had made fun of her for it—until she got to nursing school.

They all danced until they could dance no more.

• • •

When the bachelorette crew walked outside at the end of the night, a bus was waiting to take them to Nana's house—everyone's home away from home during nursing school.

Nana had on a neon blinking vest. "Come on, you wild women," she cried out. "I have a prize for each of you."

They all bowed their heads to let Nana put a neon string of flashing lights around their necks as they boarded the bus. The bus stopped at the Wieners Circle, a hotdog stand that stayed open until four in the morning, a true Chicago icon, and everyone unloaded to order their fries and dogs with all the works, then got back on the bus and devoured them.

When the bus pulled up to Nana's house everyone was recharged and ready to keep partying. They donned their PJ's, then convened in Nana's living room, where she had laid out lots of pillows and blankets, as well as platters of homemade chocolate cookies, cognac, and water.

"I'm going to bed," Nana declared. "I'll need energy for those pancakes and bacon I'm making in the morning. Sleep tight, my special girls. I love you all."

Sarah got up and gave her a long hug. "I love you so much."

The rest of the gals lined up for their hug; Jackie was last.

"Nana," she told her, "you give the best hugs of anyone."

"Thanks for getting my girl home to celebrate with me," Nana said. "I love you too Jackie, couldn't pick a better best friend for my Sarala."

Jackie gave Nana one more squeeze, then returned to the cuddle huddle on the floor. The friends talked and laughed until the sun started to come up. Then one by one, each said her goodbyes and headed home in cabs.

• • •

Jackie was stumbling to the bathroom at nine the next morning when she saw Sarah fully dressed and about to walk out the door.

"Hey, where are you going?" she demanded. "It's seven our time in California! We were up all night!"

"You don't have to do the math for me, I know we're two hours behind Chicago—really." Sarah rolled her eyes. "I'm going to The Drake. I want to hear the tolerance abstracts and then the tribute—and it will be good to see Dr. Lopez!"

Jackie put her hands on her hips. "What did Handsome have to say about that idea?"

"He did remind me that we are under strict instructions not to engage with Victor Botsworth under any circumstances when we spoke yesterday." Sarah shrugged. "But he didn't say I had to stay away from the conference altogether!" She opened the front door. "My Uber's here."

Jackie followed Sarah outside. "I don't think this is a good idea, my friend—what if Victor provokes you? He clearly knows how to push your buttons." She shook her head. "Going in one ear and out the other, isn't it, Golden?"

Sarah hopped in her Uber and waved to Jackie.

Jackie snorted and went back inside. "No stopping that one," she said as she closed the door behind her.

"Who you talking to?" Nana asked.

Jackie turned around and saw Nana standing right behind her in sweatpants, tennis shoes, and a hoodie sweatshirt.

"Myself—I do that a lot now, it's very comforting." Jackie laughed. "Do you want a cup of coffee?" She started toward the kitchen.

"Not before my exercise class; Lloyd is picking me up in a few minutes. Where's Sarah?" Nana stood by the front window, watching for her ride.

"She went to The Drake to check out the conference, not sure when she'll be back. I may get dressed and head over there too." Jackie sipped her coffee and sighed with pleasure. "What are you up to this afternoon?"

"I cleared my dance card for you girls," Nana said. "There's a big bingo game at the Legion tonight, though; I thought it would be fun for all three of us to go. Oh, here's Lloyd—gotta run. Check with Sarah and let me know if you want to do that . . . if not, we can certainly find trouble somewhere else. Bye!" Nana headed out the door.

I hope I can move that fast at her age! Jackie marveled, smiling to herself, as Nana sped away.

• • •

Jackie got ready, caught an Uber to The Drake, and followed the signs to the conference. When she got close to the designated ballroom, there was a long line of stuffy-looking, dressed-up people waiting for coffee. She scanned the crowd to see if she could find Sarah; she figured it wouldn't be hard, since Sarah had worn a bright red sweater.

Sure enough, Jackie spotted her in seconds. She was about to walk over to her when she saw Botsworth standing up against a wall, laser focused on Sarah. Jackie backed up so he wouldn't see her and surveyed the scene.

Sarah was in a deep conversation with a short, black-haired Filipina woman. One of the hotel staff walked through the coffee area ringing a chime; the meeting was about to reconvene. Sarah and her conversation partner were turning to head into the ballroom together when Botsworth came up behind her and tapped her on the shoulder. Sarah turned around, gave him the stink-eye, and continued into the ballroom.

After most of the guests were inside, Jackie helped herself to some pastries and coffee and watched as the remaining guests outside the ballroom engaged in intense conversation. *Probably talking about a bunch of scientific shit I know nothing about*, she thought.

She glanced over her shoulder to find Botsworth standing right behind her.

"What a surprise to see you here, Jackie," he said calmly. "Didn't know you were interested in immunology. Not sure you can even spell it."

Jackie had a bitter taste in her mouth as she spun around and faced him. "Fuck you, Victor, you dickless asshole. I hope you rot in hell." She intentionally knocked into him as she stormed past him toward the hotel lobby, and was looking down when she bumped right into someone.

"Whoa, slow down there!" a familiar male voice cried out.

Both Jackie and Handsome widened their eyes as they looked at each other. He quickly led Jackie away from the busy lobby.

"What the hell are you doing here?" he asked. "I explicitly asked you and Sarah to stay away. Please don't tell me she's here too."

Jackie looked up at Handsome, her lips pursed. "She just wanted to hear the tolerance abstracts, then we're going back to Nana's. Promise."

Handsome raised his eyebrows. "I don't trust either one of you. Does Sarah even know you're here?"

Jackie looked down. "Nope. I just wanted to make sure she was okay. Um . . . full disclosure, I did bump into Botsworth just now—literally. We had words."

Jackie looked up sheepishly at Handsome, whose eyes bulged.

He took her arm firmly in his hand. "I'm putting you in a cab, *now*, and then I'm going to get Sarah and do the same thing with her."

Just as Handsome was about to walk her out the hotel doors, Jackie saw Botsworth heading out, looking furious. She tilted her head his direction. Handsome quickly looked, then turned his back and blocked Jackie from view.

Once Botsworth passed, Jackie nudged Handsome. "He's gone. How about *I* go get Sarah, since I know exactly where she is, bring her back, and we both leave together?"

Handsome gave her a tight nod. "You have five minutes. I'll be outside, to the left of the door. I need to make a quick call. Make it fast, Jackie."

Jackie briskly walked back to the ballroom, went inside—and skidded to a halt. Sarah was standing at a microphone in the middle of the main aisle, speaking.

"Sarah Golden, San Francisco Transplant Institute. I have to object to the preliminary findings of this research."

Heads turned; all eyes were on her.

"You said there was evidence of tolerance at the cellular level—as I'm sure you know, the frequency of the biopsies was modified from weekly to monthly. Given this deviation from the protocol, you can't make that assertion. And while I'm at it, there are also several other clinical discrepancies that need to be addressed."

Jackie watched Sarah walk back to her seat, her face flushed. There was a loud hum in the room, doctors whispering to each other.

The presenter at the podium cleared his throat. "I wasn't aware of that issue. Thank you for bringing that to my attention."

As the moderator announced the next abstract, Jackie walked directly over to Sarah.

"We need to go, now," she said in a low voice.

Sarah looked startled, but she didn't ask any questions; she followed Jackie out.

"Handsome is waiting for us outside," Jackie whispered to her as they pushed through the ballroom doors. "He is pissed."

"Sarah!"

They both turned around; the Filipina woman Sarah had been talking to earlier was running after them.

Sarah shook her head. "I can't talk right now, Dr. Sethna, I have to leave—"

"Just a minute!" Dr. Sethna caught up with them, a tall woman with a nametag that read "Lago" right on her heels. "I was planning on meeting with the other programs about this issue offline," she said, her face bright red. "Now you've humiliated all of us—not to mention there was a NIH coordinator in the room."

"Our CEO is going to be livid when he hears what you just did," the tall woman said.

Jackie looked over at Sarah and then at the two women. "Oh, poor Lago," she said. "Will their million-dollar stock take a dip? Tough day. Come on, Sarah, we have to go now."

"Dr. Bower is going to be furious, Sarah," Dr. Sethna said, ignoring Jackie. "I'm sorry you felt you had to air our dirty laundry in public."

"I'm sorry too—mostly that you were dragged into this, Dr. Sethna. I inherited this project when Dr. McKee died, just like you did. But I can't for the life of me understand why everyone's been so determined to ignore all the red flags surrounding it." Sarah sighed. "I guess we'll never know why these distinguished scientists went rogue on their protocol."

Jackie tugged at Sarah and they speed-walked away.

"Handsome is waiting for us outside," Jackie warned her. "Get ready for his wrath."

"Why not pile on some more pain?" Sarah groaned.

Jackie led her to where Handsome was supposed to be waiting, but he was nowhere in sight.

"Oh geez," Jackie said. "Now what?"

Chapter 36

Victor stalked into the Rosebud five minutes early for his lunch with Dr. Lopez. Photos of Frank Sinatra and the Rat Pack graced the walls of the classic Italian restaurant, whose red checkered tablecloths and dark lighting gave it a true mafia feel.

The young hostess escorted Victor to a table way in the back, as he had requested, and placed menus down. As the busboy placed a basket of warm bread and olive oil on the table, a waiter appeared. "A drink for you, sir?"

"Double vodka on the rocks." Victor unbuttoned his shirt collar and loosened his tie. *When Lopez gets here I'm going to find out exactly who he talked to and what he told them; then I'm going drug that motherfucker. He won't know what hit him.*

The waiter brought his drink. "Any appetizers?"

"Sure, bring an antipasto platter. I'll wait for my friend to get here before ordering anything else."

The waiter nodded and made himself scarce.

While Victor scrolled through emails, text messages started to blow up from his sales team who were at the meeting at The Drake, spelling out the apparent disaster that had just unfolded at the meeting. The last text was from Leland—*WTF!!!*

Heart racing, Victor caught the waiter's eye, pointed at his drink, and motioned for another. As he did, he saw Dr. Lopez walking toward him.

Victor was done being charming; he didn't bother to stand up and greet his guest with a handshake.

Dr. Lopez sat down and looked directly at Victor. "I'm sorry it has come to this," he said sadly. "It was never my intention to share this information publicly, but when you and Valerie stopped returning my emails and calls, you left me no other choice."

Victor saw that Lopez's hands were shaking. "I could call immigration on you right now, Lopez—and I will if you don't give me the names of every single person you spoke with, and exactly what you told them. I know where your family is staying, and I have no problem sending one of my friends over to make sure they are made extremely uncomfortable—do you understand?" Victor sneered.

The waiter placed the antipasto platter down. "Something to drink?"

"Your best rum on the rocks," Lopez said without taking his eyes off Victor. "A double, please."

Victor's cell rang; he dismissed the call and put his phone on silent, then folded his hands on the table and looked directly at Lopez. "I'm waiting," he said. "I don't have all day—I need to get back to the meeting, as do you."

Lopez leaned in. "As I'm sure you know, I gave my research results to Sarah Golden when she was in Cuba. I gave each study patient the prescribed amount of oral drug for two weeks, which was supposed to induce tolerance pre-transplant. By the middle of week two almost all of them were having some serious clinical symptoms—severe diarrhea, shortness of breath, we even had to intubate six patients and delay their living donor kidney transplant. I had no choice but to lower the dose and then wait until they were stable before proceeding to transplant. And even those patients who were able to tolerate your drug still needed standard anti-rejection drugs post-transplant."

The waiter brought the drinks and Lopez took a long sip. Victor was tapping his fingers on the table.

"Several of my patients who did tolerate the drug had less severe rejection episodes, but their weekly biopsies showed the same amount of rejection as the patients who were in the standard arm of the protocol."

Victor slammed his hand on the table. "Fine, the drug doesn't work like it's supposed to—but why did you have to make such a big deal and share your findings with the world? I did you a big favor letting you use it in the first place, just like the last three drugs I let you trial. You had to know that if my company found out I sent you those drugs there would be an investigation and Lago's reputation would be in question. We can't have that." Victor finished his second drink and ate a few slices of prosciutto and cheese.

"What do you expect me to do now, Victor?" Lopez turned his palms toward the ceiling. "The damage is done. It was never my intention to discredit Lago, or you, but I had patients with horrible adverse reactions and you knew that—you had to, since I know for a fact that the other immunologists were having challenges with their patients before they died as well—yet you did not share this information with your internal research team."

"Are you insinuating that I may have had something to do with their deaths? That's absurd!" Victor exclaimed. "Lago had such high hopes for this drug; none of the other pharma companies are close to creating this compound. Its success would have catapulted our company into a new marketplace, there are so many possible uses for this drug both in transplant and in other specialties. Most importantly, it would have made a difference in long-term graft survival and eventually led to the costs for transplant patients dropping substantially." Victor caught the waiter's eye and motioned for the check.

"Where do you think we should go from here, Dr. Lopez? I'm still curious how you got out of Cuba—who helped you?" As Victor reached in his pocket for his wallet, he also took out the pills he was going to add to Lopez's drink.

"It sure wasn't you—you tried to get me killed," Lopez accused.

Victor reached across the table for the bill the waiter had just dropped, and he knocked over the glass of water in front of Lopez in the process. It spilled all over the table and onto Lopez's lap.

"Shit," Victor said, "I'm so sorry."

Lopez jumped up and tried to brush all the water off his suit pants. "I don't have time to change before the meeting," he said, shaking his head. "I'm going to the men's room. I'll be right back."

The waiter and bus boy quickly cleaned the table and put fresh napkins down. As soon as they were gone, Victor—looking over his shoulder to be sure that Lopez was out of eyesight—crushed two pills, put them in Lopez's rum, and stirred it vigorously. The drug was tasteless, Lopez would never notice it—but in about twenty minutes, by which point Victor would be long gone, the chest pain would begin.

Victor paid the bill and patiently waited for Lopez to return. He turned his phone over and saw that he had five missed calls and fifteen text messages. *I'll check those on the way back to The Drake*, he thought.

Lopez came back and sat down. "Again, Victor, I am so sorry about all of this, but it's out of my hands now. I needed to be honest about my part in using your drugs illegally, no matter what the consequences. I believe honesty is the best policy—always have." He reached for his drink.

"What do you mean it's out of your hands? Whose hands is it in, exactly?" Victor demanded.

"Victor Botsworth," a man's voice came from behind him, "you are under arrest for the attempted murder in the states of Illinois and California."

Victor jolted out of his seat and swirled around to see a short, stocky man holding a badge out in front of him.

"Detective Mars, Chicago Police."

"What the fuck are you talking about, you can't arrest me—you have no proof of anything!" Victor cried.

Ignoring his protests, Detective Mars read him his Miranda rights and then cuffed him.

"Fuck you, Lopez," Victor snarled. "You will never get a job after I get done with you; you'll be looking over your shoulder the rest of your life!"

Just then, Golden's cop boyfriend, Strong, approached the table and put his hand over Lopez's drink. "Don't drink that," he warned. "He drugged it—another count of attempted murder, I'm guessing, though of course we'll have this drink tested to verify that. Add it to the list, Detective Mars."

Victor narrowed his eyes at Strong. "Oh, look who's here—pretty boy, the loser from Miami. Did you ask your girlfriend for permission to come visit?"

"Enjoy prison, you fucking asshole," Strong said. "You will never be able to dig yourself out of this ginormous hole you dug for yourself. For having an Ivy League education, you're damn stupid. Guess they don't teach you common sense, huh?" He turned his attention to Lopez. "I'm here to escort you to the conference so you can share your tribute," he told the doctor. "Would you like him to mention your whereabouts, Victor? That way they won't have to be surprised by it in *The New York Times* tomorrow?" He winked at Victor.

Victor spat in Strong's face, "Fuck you, you lowlife." He backed up when he saw the man clench his fists at his sides.

Dr. Lopez stood up. "I talked to my four immunologist friends just before the accident," he said. "I'll be sharing the details of our conversation during the tribute, but since you won't be there to hear the exciting news, Victor, here are the highlights: they weren't going to announce their breakthrough research on tolerance—there wasn't any, everyone just assumed there was. What they were going to announce was that a billionaire had offered to sponsor a non-profit pharmaceutical company with one main focus—achieving tolerance—and they were all going to be a part of it, as was I. My colleagues were going to announce the short list of transplant programs they were inviting to participate."

Victor's jaw dropped open. "That's insane."

"One last thing, Victor: When my patients were getting so sick from your company's drug but Dr. McKee's and our other colleague's patients were not having near the same level of adverse side effects, he sent me a sample of the drug he was using. It was supposed to be the same as mine, but when I had our chemists analyze his drug and compare it to the one you sent me, they found that his was 50 percent weaker. The research drug all the programs were using in the States would have never achieved complete tolerance, which means even if it had worked, everyone would have had to continue to use your current drugs in addition to this new one. Either way, Lago was going to win."

"You have no idea what you're talking about, Lopez," Victor declared.

"How much money does the pharmaceutical industry need, and at what cost? Where are the ethics?" Dr. Lopez shook his head and looked over at Strong. "I'm ready to go."

• • •

After Victor was officially booked at Cook County jail, Mars put a phone in front of him. "You get one call."

Victor called Leland's cell. For once, he actually answered.

"Leland," Victor said urgently. "Thank god. I—"

"Where the fuck are you?" Leland demanded. "You need to get to The Drake pronto and clean up this mess!"

"I'm at the Cook County jail," Victor said, "I need you to send your top lawyer over here, now."

He waited for a response, but all he heard was a click. He looked over at Mars.

"Connection dropped—I need to call him back."

"One call is one call." Mars took the phone and motioned his partner over. "Can you take him to an interrogation room? I need to make a quick call—I'll meet you there."

"Come with me." Mars's partner pulled Victor to his feet and led him away.

• • •

How am I going to get out of this? Victor thought as he waited for Mars in the small grey room the detective's partner had left him in.

No answers came to him.

After about twenty minutes, Mars came in with his partner and sat across from Victor.

"Got some real bad news for you, Victor: the chances of a lawyer showing up for you any time soon—not good. Why don't you tell us about your friend Leland Ackerley while we're waiting? He may be your only way out of this." He shrugged. "Or not! It's up to you."

Victor stared at Mars. "You don't scare me. I know there's absolutely no evidence connecting me to anything."

"Okay—if that's way you want to play this." Mars smiled. "I'll give you a little teaser to think about, though: Your friend Angelo is in a jail in New Jersey, he gave us some juicy stuff. And we had a nice long conversation with your assistant, Valerie, too." Mars opened the door and looked over at his partner. "I'll be at my desk. Let me know if our friend here decides to share anything."

Chapter 37

When they found no sign of Handsome anywhere outside The Drake, Jackie and Sarah gave up and hailed a cab back to Nana's.

"I can't believe you stood in front of that entire room and brought down Lago like that," Jackie marveled. "You are a badass!"

"I was ready to throw up," Sarah admitted. "I waited as long as I could to see if anyone was going to comment on the flaws in their study, and when no one did . . . I couldn't just sit there. Technically only doctors are supposed to speak, but oh well. I'm guessing I won't be going home to my job once Bower hears about this." Sarah turned to her pal. "And what were you doing there?"

"I wanted to make sure you were okay," Jackie said. "I had a run-in with Victor—may have shared a feeling or two with him—and then I got busted by Handsome."

Sarah laughed. "We can't get away with anything. Giving Victor some sugar, eh Jack?"

"If you consider me calling him a dickless asshole 'sugar'—then yes."

They spent the last few minutes of their ride back to Nana'a laughing hysterically.

• • •

They entered Nana's house to the aroma of freshly baked peanut butter cookies.

"Hey Nana," Sarah called, "we're home."

"I'm in the kitchen," she called back.

When they walked into the kitchen, she beamed at them. "How are my girls? Come on, give me a hug—I have to get as many as I can, since you two are leaving first thing in the morning." Sarah and Jackie pulled Nana in between them and the three enjoyed a group hug.

When they loosened their grip on her, Nana looked up at both of them. "What are we going to do on our last night together? I need to drop some of these cookies off at the Legion for bingo. Other than that, my dance card is open. We can stay for bingo, or we can do whatever else you like." She went back to take the last batch of cookies out of the oven.

"Wait, the cookies aren't for us?" Jackie's face dropped.

"I said *some*, didn't I?" Nana winked at her. "The rest are for your plane ride home, don't you worry."

"You're the best!" Jackie kissed her on the cheek.

"We are all yours tonight, Nana," Sarah offered. "Bingo sounds perfect right now." She glanced over at Jackie, who gave an affirmative nod. "What time does it start?"

"They're serving chili and cornbread at five and the bingo caller is scheduled for six sharp." She laughed. "You need to know, these people are *very* serious about their bingo."

"As they should be," Jackie said. "And how about Lloyd? Is he serious about . . . bingo?" She gave Nana a wink.

"You two sure seem to like each other," Sarah jumped in, eyes twinkling.

Nana's cheeks turned pink. "Oh hush, you two trouble-makers!" She swatted at them, laughing. "Anyway, I've been winning lately, so we may get some mean looks from Betty if we do well tonight. It's not personal, she's just a poor looser. Bakes a hell of chocolate cake, though."

"I'm going to call Handsome and pack in case the bingo party turns into a late-night rager," Sarah said, chuckling. "I'll be back, you two."

• • •

Sarah was relieved when Handsome answered her call on the second ring.

"Hello Detective, how's the round-up coming along?"

Silence. She winced.

"I know—I know—I'm in trouble," she said. "But we're at Nana's now, it's all good!"

More silence.

"Please don't be mad at me," she wheedled.

Finally, Handsome spoke up. "Things are seriously tense and potentially dangerous," he clipped out. "Not at liberty to say anything else right now. We will have words when we get back home. Give Nana my love—and as for you and Jackie, I can't even think of a proper punishment for the both of you, but I will when the dust settles on this case."

"Fair enough." Even when he was pissed at her, Sarah still felt all warm inside when she spoke with her fiancé. "You should know, after what I did today, I won't have a job when I get home, so I feel especially lucky to have you right now. I love you."

"Oh, I heard the whole story," he said. "You're just lucky someone didn't take you out, Sarah, seriously. This case is no longer about science, it's about money—big money. If I text you, respond immediately, got it? There's a good chance of things going south here."

Sarah's stomach clenched. "Got it. We'll be playing bingo with Nana at the Legion tonight, in case you need to come looking for us."

"Sounds like a wild night," Handsome said, his tone softening slightly. "I'm sure if there's any trouble those legionnaires will protect you. Love you."

"Love you too," Sarah said. "Be careful."

• • •

When Sarah got back to the kitchen, Jackie was dunking cookies in a glass of milk and chatting up Nana. There was a knock at the door. Sarah tensed, nervous after her chat with Handsome.

"I'll get it," she said. *And if it's Botsworth, I'm gonna freak!*

She was relieved, when she peeked through the window, to see Mo standing outside with flowers and a quart of Nana's favorite coffee ice cream. She hadn't seen Mo in a long time, and he was looking cute as ever. His blue eyes and short-cropped, light brown, curly hair framed his sweet face. The cast on his arm was the only thing that was different about him.

Sarah opened the door and watched as his face lit up. His beautiful smile and dimples reminded her of why she'd fallen in love with him so many years earlier.

"Mo!" she said, and gave him a big hug, careful not to squeeze his bad arm. "Nice to see you. How ever did you know I was here?"

Mo looked past her and Sarah turned around. Nana and Jackie were just behind her, watching them. "Oh—I see. You are bad, Nana."

Nana walked over, gave Mo a hug, and took the ice cream. "Let me put this in the freezer before it melts from all this heat," she said. As she headed to the kitchen, she explained, "Mo goes with me to bingo every week—tries out his new jokes on my legion friends. We're just glad you gals are joining us."

Jackie walked over and gave Mo a hug too. "Long time, my friend—good to see you. I think I'm ready to finally forgive, since my friend has found her soul mate. How's that arm?"

"Healing fast," Mo said. "And don't worry, I come in peace. Nana and I have a standing date—for real. Those seniors at the Legion are a great audience."

Jackie laughed. "Can't wait to hear the new material!"

• • •

After enjoying an early cup of coffee with Nana the next morning, Sarah and Jackie made their way to the airport. Bingo at the Legion had turned out to be a fun, light, and uninterrupted night, and they'd been home and in bed by nine thirty.

Right before they boarded their flight, Sarah texted Handsome and got a heart emoji back. She was dying to know what was happening with the case, but knowing that he was okay would have to be enough for now.

She and Jackie used the time on the plane to start planning out wedding details, aided by unlimited first-class cocktails and food.

As they rode into the city from SFO, Sarah gave Jackie's hand a squeeze. "Thanks for everything—the first-class seats, an epic bachelorette party, and making it happen amongst all this chaos. It was the best."

"Only get one chance to give your best friend a proper send-off." Jackie threw her arms around Sarah.

When the car pulled up in front of Sarah's apartment, the driver put her bag on the curb, Jackie got out, and she and Sarah gave each other another long embrace.

"Keep me posted, Golden," Jackie said as she slid back into the car.

Sarah gave her a mock salute. "Will do, Larsen."

• • •

Bower had sent Sarah multiple emails while she was away, the last of which had all but demanded that she meet with him at six Monday morning.

Typical, she thought as she headed into work at five that morning. *I wonder if he's going to actually fire me this time.*

If she was to be escorted out, she wanted to be sure she was prepared. She knew the drill: first they told you your employment had been terminated, then they asked for your phone and keys, and all the while IT was shutting down your access to your work email. Bing bang boom.

Sipping her very large coffee, Sarah scanned the walls in her office. She took down her photos, removed some private things from her desk drawer, and set her medical books on her desk. She'd find a couple boxes after she met with Bower.

If this was to be her last day at the plant, she decided she would be as positive as possible. Her wedding was only weeks away; she would focus on that. *I guess you can't have it all after all.*

She headed down to Bower's office. She was early, but she wanted to get this over sooner than later.

The outer office was dark when she entered, but she could see a light coming out from under Bower's office closed door. He was talking louder than usual.

"Excellent job on backing Victor into a corner, Leland," he said. "Rest assured, what Sarah thought she sent to the NIH never got there; it was a watered-down mishmash that they will never have the time to sort through."

Sarah began to feel nauseated. Who was this person talking? Definitely not the Bower she thought she knew.

"Turns out the head of the NIH office of research integrity went to medical school with our dean. We explained to him that

Sarah was having a nervous breakdown and had no idea what she wrote and promised to get him a revised report in a week."

Sarah felt all the muscles around her spine tighten.

"I wish you and Nixie the best," Bower went on. "Glad you were able to get out of the country; sounds like it was a close call. I'm sure your investors are pleased. And don't ever contact me again, I'll be erasing all your contact info as soon as I hang up."

Sarah dropped her head and covered her face with her hands. *You have to keep it together*, she commanded herself.

Bower walked out and clocked her presence with a start. "Good morning, Sarah; how long have you been standing there?"

"Long enough." Sarah studied his face.

He walked over to the coffee pot and poured himself a cup. "Would you like some coffee?"

"No thank you."

Bower walked back into his office and she followed him.

"You really made a mess of things in Chicago," he chided her. "Have you seen *The New York Times* this morning?" He sipped his coffee and then checked his watch. "I've got an early case." He took another gulp of his coffee and then walked out of his office and toward the elevator, clearly expecting her to follow him.

Sarah was fuming now. "You were in on this the whole time—are you fucking kidding me?"

Bower stopped and turned around. "You have no idea how this world works," he said matter-of-factly. "You play the game or you get nowhere. I thought you were smart enough to see the big picture. It appears I was wrong. So go ahead, hold on to your righteous beliefs of how the world is supposed to work. Enjoy your wedding, and don't bother coming back after your honeymoon. Make up some line of bullshit of why you're quitting—I don't care."

He kept walking and Sarah followed him, her blood boiling. "I suppose you told Sergio how to get Amanda her liver too," she spat, finally connecting all the dots.

Bower ignored her and pressed the elevator button.

"I'm reporting you to the AMA," Sarah went on. "You'll lose your license, your reputation—everything, you fucking asshole."

The elevator doors opened. Bower put a hand in to hold them, got right up in Sarah's face, and looked her dead in the eyes. "Good luck with that," he hissed. "Where's your proof?" He got in the elevator and the doors closed.

Sarah felt like punching something, kicking Bower in the nuts. But alongside her fury she felt like crying. Her boss had just broken her heart—never in a million years would she have thought he'd be capable of this.

Her phone started buzzing. She stood up and slowly made her way to the stairwell. She couldn't stop the tears.

The phone kept buzzing, but Sarah was in no shape to talk to anyone. She stumbled down the stairs, desperate for some fresh air.

Once she was outside, she took a long, deep breath. The early-morning air chilled her lungs as she silently asked herself, *Why?* over and over again.

What the hell had just happened?

• • •

True to form, a woman from HR knocked on Sarah's door minutes after she returned upstairs. Sarah surrendered her work phone and keys without protest.

"If you don't mind, I'd like to take the back elevator out," she said meekly as she picked up her boxes.

"That's fine," the HR lady agreed.

"Thank you for understanding," Sarah said, holding back tears.

The HR lady followed her out, per procedure. As soon as Sarah was outside the institute's doors, she was on her own.

Once she was in her car, she rested her head on the steering wheel and let the tears flow.

• • •

It was only after Sarah left the parking garage and was driving through Golden Gate Park that she remembered her buzzing phone. She pulled over, put the car in park, and checked her phone: ten missed calls from Handsome. *Whoa, something's up.* She called him back.

He didn't bother with any small talk. "What's wrong?" he demanded the second he answered, his voice intense. "I've been trying to get a hold of you."

"I'm not good," Sarah said. "I can't really talk right now . . . is everything okay with you?" She struggled to find some energy—it was as if all of the air had been sucked out of her spirit.

"I'm tying things up here in Chicago," he said, not seeming to register her desolate tone. "We think several suspects have fled the country, but we've got Botsworth in custody, and a solid lead on Leland."

Sarah sighed. "That's good news. I can tell you that Leland and that NIH investigator, Nixie Klein, are out of the country—not sure where, though."

"How do you know that? I asked you to lie low." Sarah could hear the irritation in his voice.

"You know what, I didn't go looking for that information," she snapped. "I was just outside Bower's office and heard him talking to Leland. Don't give me any shit right now—I can't take it. I'll call you when I get home." She ended the call.

No one—*no one*—could understand how crushed her soul was right now. She loved transplant with her whole being, had dedicated her life to it, would have done anything for

Bower because she believed in what he did—and now there was a huge void where all that passion had so recently resided.

She called Jackie.

All she managed to say was, "I need you—right now."

During their years of friendship, there had been only a few times when either one of them had called the other with that message; it needed no further explanation.

"You're at home?" Jackie asked.

"Will be in two minutes," Sarah said.

"On my way."

• • •

Jackie arrived at Sarah's ten minutes after she got home.

"I was on a stakeout but told my partner this was a 911." Jackie studied Sarah's face. "Whatever's going on, it's obviously really bad. What do you need?"

At that, Sarah started to cry uncontrollably. Jackie rushed over to her, clasped her in her arms, and patted her back. "It's going to be okay," she crooned in Sarah's ear. "Whatever it is, we'll get through it together, like always."

Sarah collapsed into Jackie's arms; there was no safer place. Once she was cried out, she shared all the details of her morning.

"Holy fuck," Jackie said when Sarah was done. "Bower knew all about this? I can't wrap my head around it."

"Tell me about it—and he's right, there's no way we can prove anything."

Sarah's phone buzzed; Handsome again.

She handed Jackie the phone. "You tell him." She went in her bathroom and washed her face with cold water. When she came out, Jackie was still on the phone.

"He wants to talk to you." Jackie handed Sarah her phone back.

"Hi," Sarah offered with all the energy she had.

"Oh, honey," he said softly, "I'm so sorry. I'm flying home tonight. Jackie is picking me up and I'm coming right to you."

"Thank goodness." Sarah crumpled down into the couch, totally sapped. "Hurry back."

She handed her phone back to Jackie, who assured Handsome she'd stay with Sarah until he was back.

The next few hours were a blur, but Jackie kept her promise: she never once left Sarah's side.

• • •

Jackie looked up from her phone. "Handsome's plane lands in ten minutes, I should head to SFO. You want to come with?"

Sarah roused herself from her stupor. "Yes."

They drove to the airport, listening to Carole King and singing all the words. Handsome was on the curb when they pulled up, and he gathered Sarah in his arms for a long embrace.

"It's going to be okay," he murmured into her hair. "I promise."

Will it? Sarah wondered.

Handsome and Jackie chitchatted all the way back to her place, but Sarah just couldn't participate.

As Jackie dropped them off, she said, "Call me tomorrow. Just let me know you're okay, alright buddy?"

"I will," Sarah said. "Thanks for today."

"I'll always be there for you—you know that, Golden." Jackie got out and gave her a bear hug before driving away.

• • •

Once they got inside Sarah's apartment, Handsome put his arms around her. "I'm so sorry about Bower," he said, shaking his head. "There's no way you could have seen that coming. You were so loyal to him; I know you really trusted and admired him."

Sarah held Handsome close. "My heart is broken," she said. "I feel so betrayed and stupid. I loved my transplant career; it was my life before you. I would have done anything for him." Her stomach aching, she let her tears flow while Handsome held her.

He didn't try to fix the problem, to her great relief; he just led her to the couch, drew her against his chest, and let her cry. Eventually, all the tears were gone, and she finally drifted off to sleep, encircled in his arms.

• • •

The next four weeks went by quickly as Sarah and Handsome finalized all their wedding and honeymoon plans. When the day arrived, Sarah felt amazing in her fitted, off-the-shoulder, white gown. She wore simple pearl earrings Nana had loaned her, and her black hair was pulled back in a classic chignon.

She kept her eyes on Handsome's face as she glided down the short aisle, accompanied by a three-piece trio playing a Tony Bennett classic—"The Way You Look Tonight." The sound from the courtyard fountain at the Kenwood Inn offered the perfect backup rhythm.

Nana was Sarah's escort, and Wyatt and his dog Dusty were the ring bearers. Jackie was, of course, her maid of honor, and Handsome's sister was his best woman. Biker Bob had gotten certified online to conduct the ceremony. He had insisted on wearing his leather chaps—a bit unusual, but Sarah couldn't have cared less. She had surrounded herself with all the people she loved and who loved her; it didn't matter what they wore.

Sarah and Handsome's vows were simple, the words "obey" and "serve" eliminated. They held each other's hands and promised to love each other through crazy times; to honor their commitment to each other and accept each other's quirks; to share their joys and fears; and to always be there for each other, no matter what happened.

Everyone clapped when Biker Bob pronounced them man and wife. Sarah planted one of her best kisses ever on Handsome's lips and the tingle only he gave her spread from her toes to the top of her head. This was her guy, her soulmate, her one; as long as her soul was tethered to his, she knew she'd be safe and loved.

Jackie walked up to her best friend and put her arm around her. "You finally did it, Golden! You let yourself fall madly in love. I'm so proud of you. It's a fucking roller coaster ride, but it's worth it." She elbowed her in the side. "Oh, hey, Laura, Wyatt, and I got you a special wedding present! I have a picture; we'll drop it off when you're back from your honeymoon." She pulled up a photo on her phone and showed it to Sarah.

Sarah stared the image—a baby pig with a pink bow on its head. "Are you kidding me—you bought us a baby pig?"

"Hey, we'll be using these pig kidneys way before they discover tolerance," Jackie said. "I thought we should get a leg up on the production line. I have a friend who said you can raise it on their farm in Marin."

"You're serious!" Sarah busted out laughing. "You're not *totally* off base here, Jack, but we haven't gotten there just yet."

"I know that—I just couldn't resist." Jackie wore a devilish grin. "You have to admit, it's a creative wedding present."

"That's why I love you," Sarah said. "Always thinking way—*way*—out of the box. I would have never made it to this moment without you . . . you know that, right? Thanks for always being there for me."

She hugged her best friend tight, and they both cried tears of joy—until the band picked up its tempo, and everyone started dancing.

Jackie darted a look toward the dance floor and held out her arm. "Shall we?"

Sarah linked her arm through her friend's, laughing. "Let's."

• • •

The next morning, a breakfast tray was waiting outside Sarah and Handsome's room with the morning paper. Handsome brought it in and placed it on their table. "Coffee?"

"Yes please." Sarah sat up in bed and studied her husband—*My husband!* she repeated to herself silently—as he carefully prepared her coffee and brought it over to her.

"I could get accustomed to this," she said, giving him a kiss.

"So could I," he said. "You planned a magical wedding and all our family and friends had a ball. Now it's time for just the two of us. Are you ready to hear about our honeymoon?"

Sarah smiled and sipped her coffee. "Ready!"

Handsome pulled a thick envelope out of his suit coat and got back into bed. "We're leaving from San Francisco early tomorrow morning on a ten-day cruise that will end in New York. I've got theater tickets and dinner reservations there, and we'll stay at the Ritz Carlton for two nights before heading home."

Sarah couldn't contain her smile. "You went all out—it sounds amazing."

She put her coffee cup down and pulled Handsome's body to hers.

"I want to hear all about this cruise," she whispered. "I just have something to take care of first."

• • •

Multiple newspapers were sitting outside of Sarah's door when she and Handsome arrived back at her apartment. She followed him inside, craning to see the headlines. She was dying to know if anything had been reported about the Lago incident in the last few days.

Handsome tried to hide the papers behind his back. "Do you really want to kill your wedding buzz?" he asked.

"I just have to see just how far of a reach these assholes have," Sarah said. "If they can keep this thing out of the papers, then we really can't trust anyone." She snatched *The New York Times* from Handsome and there on the front page was a picture of Botsworth. She scanned the piece: it covered the events surrounding his arrest and said Lago's stock was tanking. A photo of Leland was included farther down; the article said that he had left the country and was a suspect in the investigation.

Below the fold, Sarah was happy to see an article, headed by a photo of Dr. Lopez, announcing the launch of the first non-profit pharmaceutical company dedicated to transplant.

Sarah put the paper down and looked over at Handsome. "I'm guessing you knew all about this—and more. Will we ever know who killed Dr. McKee and his colleagues?"

Handsome frowned. "I hope so. There was no evidence—it was a very professional job—but we do have some leads, and we're chasing them down. Some cases take a lot longer to solve than others"—he put his hand over Sarah's—"you just have to be patient. We may never nail the likes of Leland right now, but it's only a matter of time. I'm going to take a shower . . . you good?"

"More than good, sweetheart."

Sarah went into her bedroom and had just started thinking about what to pack for the cruise when her cell rang with an unknown number.

"Hello?" she answered in a cautious tone.

"Ms. Golden, it's Dr. Lopez. I understand congratulations are in order."

"They are," she said, breaking into a smile. "How are you doing? It's so nice to hear your voice."

"I don't mean to disturb you," Dr. Lopez said. "But I'm calling with a question."

"Yes?" Sarah sat down on the edge of her bed, waiting.

"I imagine you heard about my new job?" he asked.

"I did," she said eagerly. "What an exciting project to be a part of!"

"I'm glad to hear you think so," Dr. Lopez said, "because my new company would like to offer you a job as Director of Research operations."

Sarah's eyes widened. Was this for real?

"You can stay in San Francisco," he went on, "though we would need you to travel to our main headquarters in Chicago at least four to five times a year. You don't need to give me an answer until you're back from your honeymoon," he said hastily. "But we really want you on our team. An offer letter is already in the mail. We hope you'll consider it."

Sarah was still raw from her last interaction with Bower, but she couldn't deny that the idea of joining this new organization made her heart leap a little. "I'm so honored, Dr. Lopez," she said. "I'll give it serious consideration. I'll give you a call when we're back."

"Wonderful," Dr. Lopez said. "And please give your husband my best—he's a lucky man."

"Thanks, Dr. Lopez. Take care—I'll be in touch."

• • •

When Handsome came out of the shower with a towel wrapped around his waist, bare-chested, it took all Sarah's willpower to remember that she had news to share.

"Look at you," she said, beaming. "I can never get enough."

"I love hearing that." Handsome leaned in for a kiss.

Sarah returned it enthusiastically, then shared Dr. Lopez's offer with him.

"What do you think?" she asked once she'd told him everything she knew.

"I think you need a break," Handsome said, one eyebrow arched, "but it's probably a great offer! Let's put it on the back burner until we get back from our honeymoon."

"That's what I told him. I'm still beyond pissed that most of these doctors and pharma companies will never pay for what they did." She felt an upwelling of disgust. "They'll just keep making more money! When does it stop? It just sucks."

"It's not fair at all," Handsome agreed, "but don't despair—they'll get theirs eventually." He cupped her face in his hands and kissed her. "It's our time right now; all the crooks will be here when we get back."

Sarah grinned. "You're right, it *is* our time." She took Handsome's hand and placed it on her tummy. "Guess what?"

Handsome's eyes widened. "Really? So that's why you weren't drinking at the wedding!"

"I wasn't sure if you noticed." Sarah smiled slyly. "Who knew we'd have the ultimate wedding gift?"

"I never imagined I would ever be a father until I met you, Sarah Golden." Handsome smiled from ear to ear. "And now I can't wait."

Sarah launched herself into his arms. "Neither can I . . . Daddy."

Acknowledgments

Hold was written during the time of COVID. It was an emotional time for all of us. I had one close friend, Caren Montante, die from brain cancer, and another, Sandy Ginter, die from bone cancer. It was hard to focus on a work of fiction while supporting my friends and their families during these times. I was determined to give my characters their adventure even if I was crying while I wrote. I know Caren and Sandy would have wanted me to finish *Hold* and for both of them and for my loyal readers, book three in the series found its way on to the page. With perseverance and lots of support, Hold was born. But it didn't happen in a vacuum.

First, I must thank my writing soulmate sister Betsy Graziani Fasbinder who held my hand during times of sadness, doubt and fear in creating this book. Betsy was always there for me, I'm grateful for her kindness and honesty. She is one-fourth of my valued writing tribe which we call Bella Quattro—Beautiful Four—which includes the incomparable memoir guru Linda Joy Myers, and the elegant and eloquent Christie Nelson. Twenty-three years in the making, Bella Quattro is still going strong.

Thank you to Annie Tucker for her compassion and partnership through the development process. She coached me with grace and clarity. She encouraged me to set my next book in a restaurant since I love to feed my characters a lot more than what gets on the printed page.

A big thanks to two good friends, who shall remain anonymous, for their insights into the sometimes questionable worlds of pharmaceutical research and venture capital. Thank you as well to Dr. Laura Brosch, Dr. Gwen McNatt, Michelle Cox, Kathy Beiser, Dr. Joyce Trompeta, and Cindy Ostroff for agreeing to be my Beta readers—if this crew can't keep you honest no one can.

Brooke Warner is the mastermind behind She Writes Press. She and her incomparable team have opened up a critical portal for the stories of women to find their place amongst published books throughout the world. What a force She Writes Press has become.

Thanks to my agent Kimberely Cameron for her patience as I finished this trilogy so I can write her the very best romantic comedy ever—it's coming Kimberly. I feel grateful and lucky to have her on my team.

And of course, to my beloved family, I owe huge thanks. I married Mark Schatz because I knew he'd help me to create a family full of love and fun, and that he did. Together we raised Gracie and Bennett Schatz, now two grown and happily independent adults. I couldn't be a prouder mom and I'm grateful to call these two not only my kids, but my friends.

A huge thank you to Elaine Petrocelli, co-owner of Book Passage bookstore in the San Francisco Bay Area. She and her staff facilitate one of the BEST mystery writing conferences in the country. It is at these conferences that I've gotten highly professional guidance and inspiration. What a gift she and her team provide to all readers and writers in the Bay Area. If I could rent a space to sleep over there I would. Please, please, please support your local independent bookstores—they need you and more importantly you need them.

About the Author

Amy S. Peele is the award-winning best-selling author of *Cut* and *Match*, medical mysteries with a mission and a side of humor. Originally from Chicago, she went to nursing school, fell in love with the field of transplant at University of Chicago, and then moved to San Francisco in 1985 to follow her transplant career. After thirty-five years she retired from her role as Director of Clinical Operations at UCSF, overseeing 600 solid organ transplants annually, in 2014. She studied improv at Second City Players to add levity to her intense day job. Transplantation and organ and tissue donation are in her DNA and always make their way into her mysteries. Amy loves to speak, swim, teach chair yoga, meditate, and kill the people she didn't like from work in her mysteries and use their organs—why waste the kill?

SELECTED TITLES FROM SHE WRITES PRESS

She Writes Press is an independent publishing company founded to serve women writers everywhere. Visit us at www.shewritespress.com.

Cut by Amy S. Peele. $16.95, 978-1-63152-184-3. Can you buy your way up to the top of the waiting list? In their quest to find out, transplant nurse Sarah Golden and her best friend, Jackie, end up on a sometimes fun, sometimes dangerous roller coaster ride through Miami, San Francisco, and Chicago—one from which they barely escape with their lives.

Match by Amy S. Peele. $16.95, 978-1-64742-018-5. How does a San Francisco transplant nurse who never takes drugs die of an opioid overdose in Miami? How does an eight-year-old boy avoid the ravages of dialysis and get a kidney transplant fast, and what does a high-ranking politician have to do with it? Best friends and nurses Sarah Golden and Jackie Larsen are determined to find out.

On a Quiet Street: A Dr. Pepper Hunt Mystery by J. L. Doucette. $16.95, 978- 163152-537-7. A funeral takes the place of a wedding when a woman is strangled just days before her wedding to a district attorney—and Pepper, whose former patient happens to be the brother of the victim, is soon drawn into the investigation.

Water On the Moon by Jean P. Moore. $16.95, 978-1-938314-61-2. When her home is destroyed in a freak accident, Lidia Raven, a divorced mother of two, is plunged into a mystery that involves her entire family.

In the Shadow of Lies: A Mystery Novel by M. A. Adler. $16.95, 978-1-93831-482-7. As World War II comes to a close, homicide detective Oliver Wright returns home—only to find himself caught up in the investigation of a complicated murder case rife with racial tensions.